MANCHESTER ~~~~~~ ~S

W.H. AINSWORTH

PRINTWISE PUBLICATIONS LIMITED
1992

This compilation and edition published 1992 by
PRINTWISE PUBLICATIONS LTD.
47 Bradshaw Road, Tottington,
BURY, LANCS, BL8 3PW.

Warehouse and Orders —
40-42 Willan Industrial Estate, Vere Street,
(off Eccles New Road), SALFORD, M5 2GR.
Tel: 061-745 9168 Fax: 061-737 1755

Originally published 1873
This edition taken from the 1892 version.
Published by George Routledge and Sons.

Reprint chosen and additional illustrations selected by

© *Cliff Hayes*

ISBN No. 1 872226 29 9. Limp Bound Edition
        1 872226 30 2 Hard Back Edition

Cover Illustration: *Manchester 1724*

Printed & bound by Manchester Free Press,
Paragon Mill, Jersey Street, Manchester M4 6FP.
Tel: 061-236 8822.

> *This book is reproduced from the 1892 edition of this much sought after book. I'm sure the enthralling and intriguing story far outweighs any slight blemishes on a few of the pages, which have been reproduced in the interests of authenticity.*

ABOUT THE
THE AUTHOR

Born at 21 King Street, Manchester on the 4th February 1805 Harrison Ainsworth was the eldest son of an eminent lawyer. The house is long gone but the National Westminster Bank which stands on the spot carries a proud blue plaque on its wall to denote the event.

When two years old his family moved to Beech Hall in Cheetham because the family wanted more country air. It was this house Ainsworth re-purchases in later life. Ainsworth was a literary giant of the time and his popularity even outshone Charles Dickens (who Ainsworth met in 1834 and encouraged and helped to set his first book in print).

Although pushed by his father into the family firm of Solicitors, Messrs Ainsworth Crossley and Sudlow, his love of books and history was always a strong pull and many hours were spent at Chetham's Library, not only reading but absorbing the ideas and thoughts of the great men of the time.

Ainsworth wrote 39 novels though novel does not seem the right word as the leading ones had so much real facts and real people, all woven into great stories full of romance, drama and sadness that all good Victorian novels revelled in. His first book 'Rockwood' published in 1834 has an account of Dick Turpin riding from London to York on Black Bess. The story caught the imagination of the public and many will say to this day that it was true, although a thorough search reveals it never actually happened. Rockwood was well received and following its success he was the toast of London and was found in all the best society houses.

Married twice and both unhappy, Ainsworth was a 'dandy' and fashion leader. He moved to London in 1826 and it was there he finally gave up the legal profession and moved into publishing about 1830. Many quotes at the time refer to how good looking he was, and how fair and unmarked his skin was; "the Adonis of booksellers" said one. "As thorough a gentleman as his native city of Manchester ever sent forth" was another much quoted at the time.

Success followed success, but in 1853 he left London and spent life quietly researching and writing novel after novel. He spent two years preparing his most re-printed book "The Lancashire Witches" and indeed it was Ainsworth who brought Dickens to Manchester, and Lancashire, introducing him to William and Daniel Grant who were later to appear as the Cheeryble Brothers in Nicholas Nickleby.

One measure of his popularity was a public banquet given by the City of Manchester in 1881 to honour this famous Mancunian. The Mayor in his welcome informed the distinguished guests that "in our Manchester Public Free Libraries there are 250 volumes of Mr Ainsworths works. In the last year these have been read 7,660 times, mostly by the artisan class of readers. This means that 20 books are perused in Manchester by readers of the Free Libraries every day all year through". No Small Fete.

Harrison Ainsworth died in 1882 in Reigate after being almost a recluse for his last years, but left behind a marvellous collection of literature. His Lancashire books follow one another in gathering the History of the County from "The Lancashire Witches" (1600) through to "The Manchester Rebels" and "Mervyn Clitheroe" 1800.

P.S. More details about Harrison Ainsworth may be found in "Stories of Great Lancastrians", and details of John Byrom and Jemmy Dawson are in "Stories and Tales of Old Manchester", on sale at all good bookshops at £4.95.

INTRODUCTION

This is a story of the events around the last attempt by The Stuarts in 1745 to regain the Throne of England and the importance Lancashire and Manchester had on those events, but it is also a novel, a Victorian novel written in 1873 by a master of his craft, Harrison Ainsworth, and contains all the best features in Victorian novels. The drama of the Prince's battle for the throne and the intrigue of the Jacobites and the Whigs in Manchester. The romance of the hero, Atherton Legh, his unknown background and his love for mistress Rawcliffe. The courage of Jemmy Dawson, Tom Sydall and the others of the Manchester Regiment. But most of all it is another fascinating angle of what must be one of the greatest questions ever raised in English History — what would have happened if The Pretender had carried on to London and not been persuaded to turn back.

Many of the characters concerned in the story were actual people who really were involved in the drama at the time and most of the incidents really did take place.

It really is a privilege to present, one of the best stories I have read for a very long time. I can very honestly say that it is one of the most, gripping, enthralling, saddest yet interesting books I have ever read. It has only been available as a second hand book for a very long time now and I hope you agree that bringing the book back to life and adding the maps and illustrations has been well worth the effort.

Cliff Hayes

ORIGINAL PREFACE

All my early life being spent in Manchester, where I was born, bred, and schooled, I am naturally familiar with the scenes I have attempted to depict in this Tale.

Little of the old town however, is now left. The liver of antiquity — if any such should visit Manchester — will search in vain for those picturesque black and white timber habitations, with pointed gables and latticed windows, that were common enough sixty years ago. Entire streets, embellished by such houses, have been swept away in the course of modern improvement. But I recollect them well. No great effort of imagination was therefore needed to reconstruct the old town as it existed in the middle of the last century;

When I was a boy, some elderly personages with whom I was acquainted were kind enough to describe to me events connected with Prince Charles's visit to Manchester, and the stories I then heard made a lasting impression upon me. The Jacobite feeling must have been still strong among my old friends, since they expressed much sympathy with the principal personages mentioned in the Tale — for the gallant Colonel Townley, Doctor Deacon and his unfortunate sons, Jemmy Dawson, whose hapless fate has been so tenderly sung by Shenstone, and, above all, for poor Tom Syddall. The latter, I know not why, unless it be that his head was affixed on the old Exchange, has always been a sort of hero in Manchester.

The historical materials of the story are derived from the CHEVALIER DE JOHNSTONE'S *Memoirs of the Rebellion,* and DR. HIBBERT WARE'S excellent account of Prince Charles's sojourn in the town, appended to the *History of the Manchester Foundations.* But to neither of these authorities do I owe half so much as to Beppy Byrom's delightful Journal, so fortunately discovered among her father's papers at Kersal Cell, and given by DR. PARKINSON in the *Remains of John Byrom,* published some twenty years ago, by the Cheetham Society. Apart from the vivid picture it affords of the state of Manchester at the period, of the consternation into which the inhabitants were thrown by the presence of the Rebel Army, and the striking description given in it of the young Chevalier and his staff, the Journal is exceedingly interesting, and it is impossible to read it without feeling as if one were listening to the pleasant chat of the fair writer. Pretty Beppy is before us, as sprightly and as loveable as she was in life. In no diary that I have read is the character of the writer more completely revealed than in this.

Of Beppy, the bewitching, and her admirable father, I have endeavoured to give some faint idea in these pages.

I must not omit to mention that the tragic incident I have connected with Rawcliffe Hall really occurred — though at a much more remote date than is here assigned to it — at Bewsey House, an old moated mansion, near Warrington, still, I believe, in existence.

"God Bless the King! I mean our Faith's defender;
God Bless-no harm in blessing-the Pretender!
But who Pretender is, or who is King,
God bless us all, that's quite another thing!"
John Byrom

FAITHFUL UNTO DEATH.

DEDICATION

This book is dedicated to the Rebels of Tomorrow, especially Alex, Lawrence, Chloe and Alison.

ACKNOWLEDGEMENTS

I must thank Alan Seddon of Browzers Books in Prestwich for finding a copy of the book after two years of searching and friends in the book trade who tried, and are still trying to help find out-of-print books. Also local historian Chris Makepeace for his invaluable help with the illustrations; Manchester Local Studies Unit, Central Library, Manchester for their help in tracing the original illustrations; Natalie Anglesey for all her help and support.

CONTENTS
Book 1 — Atherton Legh

CHAP		PAGE
I.	How the Infant was Stolen	13
II.	Manchester in 1745	18
III.	Introduces Dr. Deacon, Dr. Byrom, and Colonel Townley	21
IV.	Sir Richard Rawcliffe	32
V.	Introduces our Hero	36
VI.	Advice	39
VII.	Rencounter near the Old Town Cross	41
VIII.	Beppy Byrom	45
IX.	The Two Curates of St. Ann's	51
X.	Constance Rawcliffe	54
XI.	The Boroughreeve of Manchester	58
XII.	The Rescue	61
XIII.	Constance makes a Discovery	67
XIV.	St. Ann's-square	72
XV.	How Salford Bridge was saved from Destruction	78
XVI.	Tom Syddall	82
XVII.	How Tom Syddall was carried Home in Triumph	87
XVIII.	The Meeting in the Garden	92
XIX.	Mrs. Butler	95
XX.	The Jacobite Meeting in Tom Syddall's Back Room	102
XXI.	Ben Birch, the Bellman of Manchester	107

Book II — Prince Charles Edward in Manchester.

CHAP		PAGE
I.	How Manchester was taken by a Serjeant, a Drummer, and a Scottish Lassie	111
II.	The Proclamation at the Cross	116
III.	Father Jerome	120
IV.	General Sir John Macdonald	123

V.	Helen Carnegie's Story	129
VI.	Captain Lindsay	132
VII.	A Resistence is chosen for the Prince	134
VIII.	Interview between Secretary Murray and the Magistrates	138
IX.	Arrival of the First Division of the Highland Army. Lord George Murray and the Magistrates	140
X.	The Duke of Perth	143
XI.	Arrival of the Second Division	145
XII.	The Young Chevalier	148
XIII.	The Prince's Interview with Mrs. Butler and the Two Damsels	153
XIV.	The Prince's March to Head-Quarters	156
XV.	The Prince's Levee	159
XVL.	The Illuminations	167
XVII.	A Quarrel at Supper	170
XVIII.	Captain Webb	173
XIX.	Captain Webb is interrogated by the Prince	182
XX.	The Duel	185
XXI.	Castle Field	189
XXII.	Father Jerome counsels Sir Richard	196
XXIII.	The Prince attends Service at the Collegiate Church	201
XXIV.	The Prince inspects the Manchester Regiment	203
XXV.	An unsatisfactory Explanation	205
XXVI.	The Ride to Rawcliffe Hall	208
XXVII.	Rawcliffe Hall	210
XXVIII.	A startling Disclosure	213
XXIX.	The mysterious Chamber	215
XXX.	A terrible Catastophie	218
XXXI.	Sir Richard Rawcliffe's Confession	224
XXXII.	Atherton's Decision is made	230

Book III — The March to Derby, and the Retreat

I.	An Old Jacobite Dame	234
II.	Atherton's Gift to Constance	237
III.	A Retreat resolved upon	243
IV.	How the Manchester Regiment was welcomed on its return	247
V.	A fresh Subsidy demanded	250
VI.	A false Message brought to Helen	253

VII.	A Court-Martial	258
VIII.	Helen Pleads in Vain	262
IX.	Together to the Last	265
X.	Mr. James Bayley	269
XI.	The Vision	272
XII.	The Retreat from Manchester to Carlisle	277

Book IV — Carlisle.

I.	Colonel Townley appointed Commandant of the Carlisle Garrison	280
II.	Atherton taken Prisoner	282
III.	The Duke of Cumberland	287
IV.	Surrender of Carlisle to the Duke of Cumberland	289

Book V — Jemmy Dawson

CHAP		PAGE
I.	The Escape at Wigan	295
II.	The Meeting at Warrington	299
III.	Atherton takes Refuge at Rawcliffe Hall	301
IV.	An Enemy in the House	306
V.	A Point of Faith	310
VI.	A Letter from Beppy Byrom	313
VII.	Atherton questions the Priest	317
VIII.	The Search	320
IX.	Who was Found in the dismantled Rooms	323
X.	A successful Stratagem	326
XI.	Atherton meets with Dr. Deacon at Rosthern	330
XII.	A sad Communication is made to Dr. Deacon	336
XIII.	A Journey to London Proposed	339
XIV.	Jemmy Dawson's Letter	341
XV.	The Parting between Monica and her Mother	347
XVI.	The Journey	351

Book VI — Kennington Common.

I.	Monica visits Jemmy in Newgate	355
II.	Colonel Conway	358
III.	Cumberland House	361
IV.	The Trial of the Manchester Rebels	367
V.	The Night before the Executions	371
VI.	The Fatal Day	373
VII.	Five Years Later	378

THE MANCHESTER REBELS

OF

THE FATAL '45.

BOOK I.
ATHERTON LEGH.

CHAPTER I.
HOW THE INFANT HEIR WAS STOLEN.

ABOUT midnight, in the autumn of 1724, two persons cautiously approached an old moated mansion, situated in Cheshire, though close to the borders of Lancashire. The night being almost pitch-dark, very little of the ancient fabric could be distinguished; but the irregular outline of its numerous gables showed that it was of considerable size. It was, in fact, a large picturesque hall, built in the early days of Elizabeth, and was completely surrounded by an unusually broad, deep moat. The moat was crossed by a drawbridge, but this being now raised, access to the mansion could only be obtained by rousing the porter, who slept over the gateway. All the inmates of the house seemed buried in repose. Not a sound was heard. No mastiff barked to give the alarm.

A melancholy air had the old hall, even when viewed by daylight. Of late years it had been much neglected, and portions were allowed to go to decay. Several rooms were shut up. Its owner, who died rather more than a year before the date of our story, preferred a town residence, and rarely inhabited the hall. Extravagant, and fond of play, he had cut down the fine timber that ornamented his park to pay his debts. Death, however, put an end to his career before he had quite run through his fortune. He left behind him a wife and an infant son—the latter being heir to the property. As there would be a long minority, the estates, by prudent management, might be completely retrieved. On the demise of her husband, the widow quitted her town house, and took up her abode with her child at the old hall. With a greatly reduced establishment, she lived in perfect seclusion. As she was young, very beautiful, and much admired, people wondered that she could thus tear herself from the world. But her resolution remained unchanged. Her affections seemed centred in her infant son. She had few visitors, declined all invitations, and rarely strayed beyond the limits of the park.

She had got it into her head that her child would be taken from her, and would not, therefore, let him out of her sight. The infant was as carefully watched as if he had been heir to a dukedom; and at night, for fear of a surprise, the drawbridge was always raised. In the event of the young heir dying under age, the estates passed to the brother of her late husband, and of him she entertained dark suspicions that did not seem altogether unwarranted.

Having offered this brief explanation, we shall return to the mysterious pair whom we left making their way to the hall. As their design was to enter the house secretly, they did not go near the drawbridge, being provided with other means of crossing the moat. One of them carried a coracle— a light boat formed of a wicker framework covered with leather.

Though they had now reached the margin of the moat, which was fringed with reeds and bulrushes, they did not put their plan into immediate execution, but marched on in silence, till a light was observed glimmering from one of the windows. A taper had been thus placed to guide them, proving that they had a confederate in the house.

On perceiving this light, which streamed from the partly-opened casement on the dusky water beneath it, the foremost of the twain immediately halted. He was a tall man wrapped in a long black cloak, with a broad-leaved hat pulled over his brows, and was well-armed.

As soon as the 'coracle was launched, he stepped into it, and was followed by his attendant, who pushed the frail bark noiselessly across the moat.

On reaching the opposite side, the chief personage sprang ashore, leaving his follower in the boat, and made his way to a postern, which he found open, as he expected. Before entering the house, he put on a mask.

The postern communicated with a back staircase, up which the midnight visitor quickly mounted, making as little noise as possible. The staircase conducted him to a gallery, and he had not advanced far when a door was softly opened, and a young woman, who had hastily slipped on a dressing-gown, came forth, bearing a light. It was the nurse. She almost recoiled with terror on beholding the masked figure standing before her.

"What's the matter with you, Bertha? Don't you know me?" asked the mysterious personage in a low voice.

"Yes, I know you now, sir," she rejoined in the same tone. "But you look like—I won't say what."

"A truce to this folly. Where is the child?"

"In his mother's bed. I offered to take him, but she would not part with him to-night."

"She will be obliged to part with him. I must have him."

"Oh, sir! I beseech you to abandon this wicked design. I am certain it will bring destruction upon all concerned in it. Do not rob her of her child."

"These misgivings are idle, Bertha. Bring me the child without more ado, or I will snatch it from its mother's arms."

"I cannot do it. The poor soul will go distracted when she finds she has lost her darling."

"What means this sudden change, Bertha?" he said, surprised and angry. "You had no such commiseration for her when we last talked over the matter. You were willing enough to aid me then."

"You tempted me by your offer; but I now repent. I understand the enormity of the offence, and will not burden my soul with so much guilt."

"You have gone too far to retreat. Having made a bargain you must fulfil it."

"Swear to me that you will not injure the child, or I will not bring it to you."

"I have already told you I do not mean to harm it."

"But swear by all you hold sacred that you have no design upon the child's life. Do this, or I will give the alarm."

"Attempt to utter a cry and I will kill you," he said, sternly. "I have not come here to be thwarted in my purpose. Go in at once."

Terrified by the menacing tone in which the order was given, Bertha obeyed, and returned to the room from which she had issued. Perhaps she might have fastened the door if time had been allowed, but the man in the mask followed her too quickly.

It was an antechamber which she occupied as nurse. A door communicating with the inner apartment stood partly open, and in obedience to an imperious gesture from the terrible intruder, she passed through it.

She was now in a large antique bed-chamber, imperfectly lighted up by a lamp placed on a small table near the bed, in which lay one of the fairest creatures imaginable. The contour of the sleeper's countenance was exquisite, and her raven tresses, which had not been confined, flowed over her neck, contrasting strongly with its dazzling whiteness.

Close beside her, with its little head resting upon a rounded arm that might have served a sculptor as a model, slept her babe. A smile seemed to play upon the slumbering mother's lips, as if her dreams were pleasant.

The sight of this picture smote Bertha to the heart. Only a fiend, it seemed to her at that moment, could mar such happiness. Could she turn that smile to tears and misery? Could she requite the constant kindness shown her, and the trust placed in her, by the basest ingratitude and treachery? She could not do it. She would rather die. She would return to the terrible man who was waiting for her, and brave his fury.

But she found herself quite unequal to the effort, and while she remained in this state of irresolution he entered the room with his drawn sword in his hand.

He signed to her to go to the bed and take the child, but she did not obey. Half paralysed with terror, she could neither move nor utter a cry.

At once comprehending the state of the case, he determined to act alone, and stepping softly forward he extinguished the lamp that was burning on a small table beside the bed, and seizing the child enveloped it in his cloak.

The daring deed was so rapidly executed that the poor lady did not wake till she was robbed of her treasure. But becoming instantly aware that her child was gone, and hearing footsteps in the room, she raised herself, and called out in accents of alarm, "Is it you, Bertha?"

"Make no answer, but follow me quickly," whispered the terrible intruder to the nurse.

But she had now burst the spell that had hitherto bound her, and seizing him before he could reach the door held him fast.

Finding his departure effectually prevented, the remorseless villain unhesitatingly liberated himself by plunging his sword into Bertha's breast.

The wound was mortal. The unfortunate woman fell speechless, dying, just as her mistress, who had sprung from the couch, came up; while the assassin escaped with his prize.

The poor lady understood what had happened, but fright almost deprived her of her senses. She uttered scream after scream, but before any of the household came to her assistance all was silent.

When they ventured into the room a shocking spectacle greeted them. Their young mistress was lying in a state of insensibility by the side of the slaughtered nurse. The child could not be found.

How the perpetrator of this dark and daring deed entered the house remained a mystery. No one supposed that poor murdered Bertha, who had paid the penalty of her crime with life, had been his accomplice. On the contrary, it was believed that she had flown to her mistress's assistance, and had perished in the attempt to save the child.

How the murderer had crossed the moat was likewise a mystery, for the coracle was carried away when its purpose had been fulfilled. On examination, the postern-door was found to be locked and the key taken out. Nothing had been seen of the terrible visitor, the gloom of night shrouding his arrival and departure. Thus he remained wholly undiscovered.

When the poor lady recovered from the fainting fit into which she had fallen, her senses were gone. Nor did she long survive the dreadful shock she had sustained.

CHAPTER II.

MANCHESTER IN 1745.

WHEN Dr. Stukeley visited Manchester in 1724, he described the town, from personal observation, as "the largest, most rich, populous, and busy village in England." In twenty years from that date, it could no longer be called a village. Its population had doubled, and the number of houses had greatly increased. Many new streets had been completed, an Exchange built, and a fine new square laid out.

But though the town had thus grown in size and wealth, it had not yet lost its provincial air. The streets had a cheerful, bustling look, denoting that plenty of business was going on, but they were not crowded either with carts or people. The country was close at hand, and pleasant fields could be reached in a few minutes' walk from the market-place.

Seen from the ancient stone bridge spanning the Irwell, the town still presented a picturesque appearance. The view comprehended the old collegiate church (which wore a much more venerable air than it does now, inasmuch as it had not been renovated), the old houses on Hunt's Bank, Chetham Hospital crowning the red sandstone banks of the Irk, just beyond its junction with the larger river, the old water-mill, and the collection of black and white plaster habitations in the neighbourhood of the church.

This was the oldest part of the town, and its original features had not been destroyed. In all the narrow streets surrounding the collegiate church the houses bore the impress of antiquity, having served as dwelling-places for several generations. In Mill-gate, in Toad-lane, in Hanging Ditch, and Cateaton-street, scarcely a modern habitation could be descried. All the houses, with their carved gables, projecting upper stories, and bay-windows, dated back a couple of centuries. In Deansgate similar picturesque old structures predominated. Two new churches formed part of the picture— Trinity Church in Salford, and St. Ann's in the square we have already mentioned—and of course many other modern buildings were discernible, but from the point of view selected the general air of the place was ancient.

From this glance at Manchester in 1745, it will be seen that it formed an agreeable mixture of an old and new town. The rivers that washed its walls were clear, and abounded in fish. Above all, the atmosphere was pure and wholesome, unpolluted by the smoke of a thousand factory chimneys. In some respects, therefore, the old town was preferable to the mighty modern city.

The inhabitants are described by a writer of the period "as very industrious, always contriving or inventing something new to improve and set off their goods, and not much following the extravagance that prevails in other places, by which means many of them have acquired very handsome fortunes, and live thereupon in a plain, useful, and regular manner, after the custom of their forefathers."

Their manners, in fact, were somewhat primitive. The manufacturers kept early hours, and by ten o'clock at night the whole town might be said to be at rest. There were two political clubs, Whig and Tory, or Jacobite, the latter being by far the most numerous and important. The members met at their favourite taverns to drink punch, and toast King or Pretender, according to their predilections. Only four carriages were kept in the town, and these belonged to ladies. There were no lamps in the streets, lanterns being carried by all decent folks on dark nights.

In regard to the amusements of the place it may be mentioned that the annual horse-races, established at Kersal Moor in 1730, had latterly been discontinued, but they were soon afterwards revived. Under the patronage of Lady Bland—a person of great spirit—public assemblies were given at a ballroom in King-street—then, as now, the most fashionable street. A famous pack of hounds, of the old British breed, was kept near the town, and regularly hunted in the season. The leading merchants lived in a very unostentatious manner, but were exceedingly hospitable. Many of them were far more refined and much more highly educated than might have been expected; but this is easily accounted for when we state that they belonged to good county families. It had been the custom for a long period with the Lancashire and Cheshire gentry, who could not otherwise provide for their younger sons, to bring them up to mercantile pursuits, and with that object they apprenticed them to the Manchester merchants. Thenceforward a marked improvement took place in the manners and habits of the class.

CHAPTER III.

INTRODUCES DR. DEACON, DR. BYROM, AND COLONEL TOWNLEY.

DESCENDED from Cavaliers, it was certain that the Manchester merchants would embrace the political opinions of their fathers, and support the hereditary claims of the House of Stuart. They did so enthusiastically. All were staunch Jacobites, and more or less concerned in a plot which had long been forming for the restoration of James the Third to the throne. Constant meetings were held at a small inn at Didsbury, near the ferry, where the conspirators drank "The King over the Water." A secret correspondence was kept up with the exiled court, and assurances were given to the Chevalier de St. George that the whole population of the town would rise in his favour whenever the expected invasion took place.

The great spread of Jacobite opinions throughout the town could be traced to two or three influential individuals. Chief among these was Dr. Deacon—a very remarkable man, whose zeal and earnestness were calculated to extend his opinions, and make converts of those opposed to him. Dr. Deacon had been concerned in the former rebellion, and in his quality of a Nonjuring priest had assisted at the dying moments of the Reverend William Paul and Justice Hall, who were executed in 1716. The declaration delivered by them to the sheriff was written by Dr. Deacon, and produced an immense effect from its force and eloquence. Having incurred the suspicion of the Government, Dr. Deacon deemed it expedient to change his profession. Repairing to Manchester, he began to practise as a physician, and with considerable success. But this did not prevent him from carrying on his spiritual labours. He founded a Nonjuring church, of which he was regarded as the bishop. His fervour and enthusiasm gained him many disciples, and he unquestionably produced an effect upon the clergy of the collegiate church, all of whom, except the warden, Dr. Peploe, adopted his opinions, and inculcated Jacobitism from the pulpit. Though a visionary and mystic, Dr. Deacon was a man of great erudition, and a profound theologian. He had three sons, all of whom shared his political and religious opinions.

Another person quite as zealous as Dr. Deacon in promoting the cause of the Pretender, though he observed much greater caution in his proceedings, was Dr. John Byrom, whose name is still held in the greatest respect in Manchester. A native of the town, and well connected, Dr. Byrom occupied an excellent social position. He was a man of great versatility of talent—a wit, a scholar, a linguist, and a charming poet. But his witty sayings were playful, and, though smart, entirely divested of ill-nature. Clever at most things, he invented a new system of short-hand, which he taught, so long as it was necessary for him to improve his income; but on the death of his elder brother he succeeded to the family property, Kersal Cell, situated in the neighbourhood of the town. His diary and correspondence, published by the Chetham Society, give a complete insight into his truly amiable character, and not only display him in the most pleasing colours, but place him in the first rank as a letter-writer. Dr. Byrom contributed two papers to the *Spectator*, and wrote many delightful songs and humorous poems, but he will be best remembered by his admirable letters. He was fortunate in his wife, and equally fortunate in his children—a son and daughter—and it is to these members of his family, to whom he was tenderly attached, that most of his letters are addressed.

The Buildings... near Strangeways Bridge.

At the time of our story, Dr. Byrom was between fifty and sixty—a striking-looking person, tall, thin, erect. Without being handsome, his features were pleasing and benevolent in expression. His manner was singularly courteous, and his temper so even that it could scarcely be ruffled.

A third person, who made his appearance in Manchester immediately after the outbreak of the rebellion in Scotland, was Colonel Francis Townley. He belonged to an old Lancashire Roman Catholic family, the head of which, Richard Townley, of Townley Hall, took part in the rebellion of 1715, and was tried before Judge Powis, but acquitted.

Born at his father's house near Wigan, Frank Townley, at the period of our story, was just thirty-eight. Some seventeen years previously he went over to France, and being remarkably handsome, made a figure at the court of Versailles. Befriended by the Duke of Berwick, he received a commission from Louis the Fifteenth, served at the siege of Philipsburg, and was close beside the duke when the latter was killed by a cannon-shot. Subsequently he served under Marshal de Broglie in the campaign against Austria, and was present at several sieges and actions, in all of which he displayed great spirit and intrepidity, and acquired a very brilliant military reputation.

Frank Townley continued in the French service for fifteen years, and then returned to England, living for some little time in retirement. When the young Chevalier landed in Scotland, and an invasion was meditated by France, Louis sent him a colonel's commission to enable him to raise forces for the prince. With this design he came to Manchester, thinking he should have no difficulty in raising a regiment, but he was not so successful as he anticipated.

A simultaneous rising of the Jacobites in the northern counties and in some of the larger towns had been confidently looked for by the partisans of the House of Stuart, but as this did not take place, the excitement in the prince's behalf, which had been roused in Manchester, began quickly to subside. The intelligence that the victor of Preston Pans was marching southward at the head of an army of five thousand Highlanders, though it raised the hopes of some of the bolder spirits, carried consternation among the bulk of the townspeople—not only among those who were loyal, but among the disaffected. The Jacobites wished well to the Pretender, but declined to fight for him. Numbers left the town, and the shopkeepers began to remove their goods and valuables. The Presbyterians were especially alarmed, and sent away their wives and families.

News that the prince had reached Carlisle increased the excitement. The militia was quartered in the town for its defence; but the men were disbanded before the insurgent army appeared. The bridge at Warrington was destroyed to impede the march of the rebels; other bridges were blown up; and Salford Bridge was threatened, but escaped destruction.

In the midst of the general alarm and confusion now prevailing in the place, Colonel Townley found it impossible to enrol a sufficient number of men to form a regiment. All those who had been lavish in promises made excuses, or got out of the way.

By this time Carlisle had surrendered, and the prince, whose army moved in two divisions, was marching southward. Greatly disappointed by his ill success, Colonel Townley resolved to set out and meet him at Lancaster, in order to prepare him for his probable reception at Manchester.

On the night before his departure on this errand the colonel had a conference with Dr. Deacon and Dr. Byrom at the Bull's Head in the market-place—a tavern frequented mainly by the High Church Tories and Jacobites, just as the Angel Inn in Market Street Lane was resorted to by Whigs and Presbyterians.

The party met in a private room at the back of the house. A cheerful fire blazed on the hearth—it must be borne in mind that it was then in November—and a flask of claret stood on the table; but the serious looks of the three gentlemen betokened that they had not met merely for convivial purposes.

With the tall, thin figure, benevolent countenance, and courteous manner of Dr. Byrom, we have endeavoured to familiarise the reader. The doctor was attired in a murrey-coloured coat with long skirts, and wore a full-bottomed tie-wig, and a laced cravat, but had laid aside his three-cornered hat.

Dr. Deacon was somewhat advanced in years, but seemed full of vigour, both of mind and body. He had a highly intellectual physiognomy, and a look about the eyes that bespoke him an enthusiast and a visionary. He was dressed in black, but his costume was that of a physician, not a divine. Still, the Nonjuring priest could not be wholly disguised.

Colonel Townley had a very fine presence. His figure was tall, well-proportioned, and commanding. He might easily have been taken for a French officer; nor was this to be wondered at, considering his fifteen years' service in France. A grey cloth riding-dress faced with purple displayed his lofty figure to advantage. An aile-de-pigeon wig, surmounted by a small cocked hat edged with silver lace and jack-boots, completed his costume.

"Now, gentlemen," said the colonel, drawing his chair closer to them, "before I join the prince at Lancaster, I desire to have your candid opinion as to the chance of a rising in his favour in this town. Latterly I have met with nothing but disappointment. The conduct of your leading merchants fills me with rage and disgust, and how they can reconcile it with the pledges they have given his royal highness of support, I cannot conceive. Still, I hope they will act up to their professions, and maintain the honourable character they have hitherto borne. How say you, gentlemen? Can the prince calculate on a general declaration in his favour? You shake your heads. At least he may count on a thousand recruits? Five hundred? Surely five hundred Manchester men will join his standard?"

"A few weeks ago I firmly believed half the town would rise," replied Dr. Deacon. "But now I know not what to say. I will not delude the prince with any more false promises."

"'Twill be an eternal disgrace to Manchester if its inhabitants desert him at this critical juncture," cried the colonel, warmly. "Is this to be the miserable conclusion of all your plots and secret meetings? You have invited him, and now that he has complied with the invitation, and is coming hither with an army, you get out of the way, and leave him to his own resources. 'Tis infamous!"

"I still hope my fellow-townsmen may redeem their character for loyalty," said Dr. Deacon. "Perchance, when his royal highness appears, he may recall them to their duty."

"I doubt it," observed the colonel.

"I will not attempt to defend the conduct of the Manchester Jacobites," observed Dr. Byrom; "but they are not quite so culpable as they appear. They ought not to have invited the prince, unless they were resolved to support him at all hazards. But they have become alarmed, and shrink from the consequences of their own rashness. They wish him every success in his daring enterprise, but will not risk their lives and fortunes for him, as their fathers did in the ill-starred insurrection of 1715."

"In a word, they consider the prince's cause hopeless," said the colonel.

"That is so," replied Dr. Byrom. "You will do well to dissuade his royal highness from advancing beyond Preston, unless he is certain of receiving large reinforcements from France."

"Dissuade him from advancing! I will never give him such dastardly counsel. Were I indiscreet enough to do so, he would reject it. His royal highness is marching on London."

"So I conclude. But I fear the Duke of Cumberland will never allow him to get there."

"Bah! He will beat the Duke as he beat Johnnie Cope at Preston Pans. But he need not hazard a battle. He can easily elude the duke if he thinks proper."

"Not so easily, I think; but, should he do so, he will find the Elector of Hanover prepared for him. The guards and some other regiments are encamped at Finchley, as we learn by the last express, for the defence of the capital."

"You are just as timorous as the rest of your fellow-townsmen, sir. But no representations of danger will deter the heroic prince from his projected march on London. Ere long, I trust he will drive out the usurper, and cause his royal father to be proclaimed at Westminster."

"Heaven grant it may be so!" exclaimed Dr. Deacon, fervently. "'Twill be a wondrous achievement if it succeeds."

"I do not think it can succeed," said Dr. Byrom. "You think me a prophet of ill, colonel, but I am solely anxious for the prince's safety. I would not have him fall into the hands of his enemies. Even retreat is fraught with peril, for Field-Marshal Wade, with a strong force, is in his rear."

"Better go on, then, by your own showing, sir. But retreat is out of the question. I am at a loss to understand how you can reconcile your conduct with the principles you profess. The prince has need of zealous adherents, who will sacrifice their lives for him if required. Yet you and your friends, who are pledged to him, keep aloof."

"I am too old to draw the sword for the prince," said Dr. Deacon; "but I shall identify myself with his cause, and I have enjoined my three sons to enrol themselves in the Manchester Regiment."

"You have done well, sir, but only what might have been expected from you," said Colonel Townley. "Your conduct contrasts favourably with that of many of his self-styled adherents."

"I can bear the taunt, colonel," said Dr. Byrom, calmly. "Whatever opinion you may entertain to the contrary, my friends and myself are loyal to the House of Stuart, but we are also discreet. We have had our lesson, and mean to profit by it. To be plain with you, Colonel Townley, we don't like the Highlanders."

"Why not, sir? They are brave fellows, and have done no mischief. They will do none here—on that you may depend."

"Maybe not, but the people are desperately afraid of them, and think they will plunder the town."

"Mere idle fears," exclaimed Colonel Townley.

"Have you a list of recruits, colonel?" inquired Dr. Deacon.

Colonel Townley replied in the affirmative, and produced a memorandum-book.

"The list is so brief, and the names it comprises are so unimportant, that I shall feel ashamed to present it to the prince," he said. "The first person I have set down is James Dawson."

"Jemmy Dawson is a young man of very respectable family—in fact, a connexion of my own," observed Dr. Byrom. "He belongs to St. John's College, Cambridge."

"Next on the list is Mr. Peter Moss, a gentleman of this county," pursued the colonel. "Then come Mr. Thomas Morgan, a Welshman, and Mr. John Saunderson, a Northumberland gentleman. All those I have enumerated will be officers, and with them I shall couple the names of your sons, Dr. Deacon—Thomas Theodorus, Charles, and Robert."

"All three are prepared to lay down their lives in asserting the rights of their only lawful sovereign, King James the Third," said the doctor. "They have constantly prayed that Heaven may strengthen him so that he may vanquish and overcome all his enemies, that he may be brought to his kingdom, and the crown be set upon his head."

"In that prayer we all join," said the colonel. "I shall not fail to mention your sons to the prince. Then we have a young parson named Coppock, who desires to be chaplain of the regiment. From his discourse he seems to be a good specimen of the church militant."

"He will give up a good benefice if he joins you," remarked Dr. Byrom.

"He will be rewarded with a bishopric if we succeed. With a few exceptions, the rest are not persons of much rank—Andrew Blood, George Fletcher, John Berwick, Thomas Chadwick, and Thomas Syddall. The last is a member of the Nonjuring church, I believe, Dr. Deacon?"

"I am proud of him, though he is only a barber," replied the doctor. "He has never sworn allegiance to the usurper, and never will. He is the son of that Thomas Syddall who was put to an ignominious death in 1716, and his head fixed on the market-cross of this town. Thomas Syddall, the younger, inherits his father's loyalty and courage."

"He shall be an ensign," said the colonel. "Next, there is a young man, whom I have put down, though I don't feel quite sure of him. He is the handsomest young fellow I have seen in Manchester, and evidently full of spirit."

"I think I can guess whom you mean," said Dr. Byrom. "'Tis Atherton Legh."

"Right! that is the youngster's name. He was introduced to me by Theodore Deacon. Who is he? He looks as if he belonged to a good family."

"Atherton Legh is Atherton Legh—that is all I know of his family history, and I believe it is all he knows himself," replied Dr. Deacon.

"I can tell you something more about him," said Dr. Byrom. "He was brought up by a small tradesman, named Heywood, dwelling in Deansgate, educated at our grammar-school under Mr. Brooke, and afterwards apprenticed to Mr. Hibbert, a highly respectable merchant; but as to his parentage, there is a mystery. Beyond doubt, he has some wealthy relative, but he has prudently abstained from making inquiries, since it has been intimated to him that, if he does so, the present liberal allowance, which is regularly paid by some person who styles himself his guardian, will cease."

"A very good reason for remaining quiet," observed the colonel. "But I suppose Heywood is acquainted with the guardian?"

"He has not even heard his name. Atherton's allowance is paid through a banker, who is bound to secrecy. But you shall hear all I know about the matter. Some eighteen years ago, an elderly dame, who described herself as Madame Legh, having the appearance of a decayed gentlewoman, and attired in mourning, arrived in Manchester, and put up at this very inn. She had travelled by post, it appeared, from London, and brought with her a very pretty little boy, about three years old, whom she called her grandson, stating that his name was Atherton Legh. From this, it would seem, there was no disguise about the old dame, but there is every reason to believe that the names given by her were fictitious. Having made some preliminary inquiries respecting the Heywoods, and ascertained that they had no family, Madame Legh paid them a visit, taking her little grandson with her, and after some talk with Mrs. Heywood, who was a very kind-hearted woman, easily prevailed upon her to take charge of the child. All the arrangements were very satisfactorily made. Mrs. Heywood received a purse of fifty guineas, which she was told came from the boy's guardian—not his father. She was also assured that a liberal allowance would be made by the guardian for the child's maintenance and education, and the promise was most honourably fulfilled. All being settled, Madame Legh kissed her little grandson and departed, and was never seen again. The child quickly attached himself to the worthy pair, who became as fond of him as if he had been their own son. In due time, Atherton grew into a fine spirited lad, and, as I have just intimated, was sent to the grammar-school. When his education was completed, in compliance with the injunctions of his mysterious guardian, conveyed through the banker who paid the allowance, the youth was apprenticed to Mr. Hibbert—the fee being five hundred pounds, which, of course, was paid. Thenceforth, Atherton resided with Mr. Hibbert.

"Such is the young man's history, so far as it is known, and it is certainly curious. No wonder you have been struck by his appearance, colonel. He has decidedly a fine physiognomy, and his look and manner proclaim him the son of a gentleman. Whether he will venture to enrol himself in your regiment without his guardian's consent, which it is next to impossible for him to obtain, is more than I can say.

"It does not seem to me that he is bound to consult his guardian on the point," remarked Dr. Deacon. "I have told him so; but he has some scruples of conscience, which I hope to remove."

"If his guardian is a Hanoverian, he ought to have no authority over him," said the colonel. "You must win him over to the good cause, doctor. But let us have a glass of claret," he added, helping himself, and pushing the bottle towards Dr. Byrom, who was nearest him.

CHAPTER IV.

SIR RICHARD RAWCLIFFE.

"BY-THE-BYE," continued Colonel Townley, looking at his watch. "I forgot to mention that I expect Sir Richard Rawcliffe, of Rawcliffe Hall, to-night. He will be here anon. 'Tis about the hour he named. You know him, I think?"

"I knew him slightly some years ago," replied Dr. Byrom. "But I dare say he has quite forgotten me. He rarely, if ever, comes to Manchester. Indeed, he leads a very secluded life at Rawcliffe, and, as I understand, keeps no company. He has the character of being morose and gloomy, but I daresay it is undeserved, for men are generally misrepresented."

"Sir Richard Rawcliffe is certainly misrepresented, if he is so described," said Colonel Townley. "He is haughty and reserved, but not moody. When I left for France he had only just succeeded to the title and the property, and I knew little of him then, though he was an intimate friend of my uncle, Richard Townley of Townley."

"He was not, I think, engaged in the insurrection of 1715?" remarked Dr. Deacon.

"Not directly," replied the colonel. "His father, Sir Randolph, who was friendly to the Hanoverian succession, was alive then, and he did not dare to offend him."

"I thought the Rawcliffes were a Roman Catholic family?" remarked Dr. Deacon.

"Sir Randolph abjured the faith of his fathers," said Colonel Townley; "and his elder son, Oswald, was likewise a renegade. Sir Richard, of whom we are now speaking, succeeded his brother Sir Oswald on the failure of the heir."

"It has never been positively proved that the heir is dead," observed Dr. Byrom. "Sir Oswald Rawcliffe married the beautiful Henrietta Conway, and had a son by her, who was carried off while an infant in a most mysterious manner, and has never been heard of since. This happened in '24, but I cannot help thinking the true heir to Rawcliffe Hall may yet be found."

"Meantime, Sir Richard is in possession of the title and property," said Colonel Townley.

As he spoke, the door was opened by the landlord, who ushered in a tall personage, whom he announced as Sir Richard Rawcliffe.

Bowing to the company, all of whom rose on his entrance, Sir Richard sprang forward to meet Colonel Townley, and a hearty greeting passed between them.

It would have been difficult to determine the new-comer's age, but he was not fifty, though he looked much older. His features were handsome, but strongly marked, and had a sombre expression, which, however, disappeared when he was animated by converse. His eyes were dark and penetrating, and overhung by thick black brows. His pallid complexion and care-worn looks seemed to denote that he was out of health. Altogether, it was a face that could not be regarded without interest. He wore a dark riding-dress, with boots drawn above the knee. A black peruke descended over his shoulders, and a sword hung by his side.

Habitually, Sir Richard Rawcliffe's manner was haughty, but he was extremely affable towards the present company, expressing himself delighted to meet Dr. Byrom again. Towards Dr. Deacon he was almost deferential.

While they were exchanging civilities, Diggles, the landlord, re-appeared with a fresh bottle of claret and clean glasses; and bumpers being filled, Colonel Townley called out, "Here's to our master's health!"

The toast having been drunk with enthusiasm, Diggles, preparatory to his departure, inquired whether the gentlemen desired to be private.

"No," replied Colonel Townley. "I will see my *friends*. I don't think you will introduce a Hanoverian, Diggles."

"You may trust me, colonel," said the landlord. "No Whig shall enter here."

After another glass of wine, Colonel Townley said to the baronet—

"Now, Sir Richard, let us to business. I hope you bring us some recruits. We are terribly in want of them."

"I am surprised to hear that," replied Sir Richard; "and I regret that I cannot supply your need. All my tenants refuse to go out. 'Tis to explain this difficulty that I have come to Manchester. Money I can promise his royal highness, but not men."

"Well, money will be extremely useful to him. How much may I venture to tell him you will furnish?"

"A thousand pounds," replied Sir Richard. "I have brought it with me. Here 'tis," he added, giving him a pocket-book.

"By my faith, this is very handsome, Sir Richard, and I am sure the prince will be much beholden to you. I am about to join him at Lancaster, and I will place the money in the hands of his treasurer, Mr. Murray. If every Jacobite gentleman in Cheshire would contribute a like sum his royal highness would not lack funds."

Both Dr. Byrom and Dr. Deacon expressed their sense of the baronet's liberality.

"I am amazed by what you just stated about your want of recruits," said Sir Richard. "I understood that some thousands had been enrolled in Manchester."

Significant looks passed between the others, and Colonel Townley shrugged his shoulders.

"I am sorry to be obliged to undeceive you, Sir Richard," he said. "The enrolment has proceeded very badly."

"But you have the leading merchants with you. They are all pledged to the House of Stuart."

"They are indifferent to their pledges."

"Zounds!" exclaimed Sir Richard. "I was wholly unprepared for this. At all the Jacobite meetings I have attended, the boldest talkers were your Manchester merchants. How many campaigns have they fought over the bottle! But are there no young men in the town who will rally round the prince's standard?"

"Plenty, I am sure, Sir Richard," replied Dr. Deacon. "When the drum is beaten, numbers will answer to the call."

"Better they should enrol themselves beforehand, so that we might know on whom we can count. You have so much influence, Dr. Deacon, that you ought to be able to raise a regiment yourself. Your sons might lend you aid. They must have many friends."

"Theodore Deacon has already found me a fine young fellow, whom I should like to make an officer," observed Colonel Townley.

"Ah! who may that be?"

"You will be little the wiser when I mention his name, Sir Richard. 'Tis Atherton Legh."

"Atherton Legh. Is he of a Lancashire family?"

"I am unable to answer that question, Sir Richard. In fact, there is a mystery about him. But he is a gentleman born, I'm certain. 'You would say so yourself were you to see him. Ah! the opportunity offers—here he is."

As he spoke the door was opened, and the young man in question was ushered in by the landlord.

CHAPTER V.

INTRODUCES OUR HERO.

ATHERTON LEGH had a fine, open, intelligent countenance, clear grey eyes, classically moulded features, a fresh complexion, and a tall graceful figure. His manner was frank and prepossessing. His habiliments were plain, but became him well, and in lieu of a peruke, he wore his own long, flowing, brown locks. His age might be about one-and-twenty.

Such was the tall, handsome young man who stood before the company, and it may be added that he displayed no embarrassment, though he felt that a scrutinising look was fixed upon him by the baronet.

"Was I not right, Sir Richard?" whispered Colonel Townley. "Has he not the air of a gentleman?"

The baronet assented; adding in an undertone, "Tell me, in a word, who and what he is?"

"I have already stated that a mystery attaches to his birth, and so carefully is the secret kept, that, although he has a guardian who supplies him with funds, he is not even acquainted with his guardian's name."

"Strange!" exclaimed the baronet.

"Shall I present him to you, Sir Richard?"

"By all means," was the reply.

Colonel Townley then went up to the young man, shook hands with him, and after a little talk, brought him to Sir Richard, who rose on his approach, and received him very graciously.

But though the baronet's manner was exceedingly courteous, Atherton felt unaccountably repelled. Sir Richard's features seemed familiar to him, but he could not call to mind where he had seen him.

"I hope you have come to signify to Colonel Townley your adhesion to the cause of King James the Third?" remarked Sir Richard.

"Yes, yes, he means to join us," cried Colonel Townley, hastily. "I am enchanted to see him. Say that you will belong to the Manchester Regiment, Mr. Atherton Legh—say the word before these gentlemen—and I engage that you shall have a commission."

"You are too good, sir," said the young man.

"Not at all," cried the colonel. "I could not do his royal highness a greater service than to bring him such a fine young fellow."

"I shall seem but ill to repay your kindness, colonel," said Atherton, "when I decline the honourable post you offer me. I would serve in the ranks were I a free agent. You are aware that I have a guardian, whom I feel bound to obey as a father. Since you spoke to me this morning I have received a letter from him, peremptorily forbidding me to join the prince. After this interdiction, which I dare not disobey, I am compelled to withdraw the half promise I gave you."

"Were I in Colonel Townley's place I should claim fulfilment of the promise," observed Sir Richard. "As a man of honour you cannot retract."

"Nay, I must say Mr. Atherton Legh did not absolutely pledge himself," said Colonel Townley; "and he is perfectly at liberty, therefore, to withdraw if he deems proper. But I hope he will reconsider his decision. I shall be truly sorry to lose him. What is your opinion of the matter, sir?" he added, appealing to Dr. Deacon. "Is Mr. Atherton Legh bound to obey his guardian's injunctions?"

"Assuredly not," replied the doctor, emphatically. "Duty to a sovereign is paramount to every other consideration. A guardian has no right to impose such restraint upon a ward. His authority does not extend so far."

"But he may have the power to stop his ward's allowance, if his authority be set at defiance," remarked Dr. Byrom. "Therefore, I think Mr. Atherton Legh is acting very prudently."

"My opinion is not asked, but I will venture to offer it," observed Sir Richard. "Were I in Mr. Atherton Legh's place, I would run the risk of offending my guardian, and join the prince."

"I am inclined to follow your counsel, Sir Richard," cried the young man.

"No, no—you shall not, my dear fellow," interposed Colonel Townley. "Much as I desire to have you with me, you shall not be incited to take a step you may hereafter repent. Weigh the matter over. When I return to Manchester you can decide. Something may happen in the interim."

Atherton bowed, and was about to retire, when Sir Richard stopped him.

"I should like to have a little talk to you, Mr. Atherton Legh," he said, "and shall be glad if you will call upon me to-morrow at noon. I am staying at this inn."

"I will do myself the honour of waiting upon you, Sir Richard," replied the young man.

"I ought to mention that my daughter is with me, and she is an ardent Jacobite," remarked Sir Richard.

"If I have Miss Rawcliffe's assistance, I foresee what will happen," remarked Colonel Townley, with a laugh. "Her arguments are sure to prove irresistible. I consider you already enrolled. Au revoir!"

CHAPTER VI.

ADVICE.

ATHERTON LEGH had quitted the inn, and was lingering in the market-place, not altogether satisfied with himself, when Dr. Byrom came forth and joined him.

"Our road lies in the same direction," said the doctor. "Shall we walk together?"

"By all means, sir," replied the young man.

It was a beautiful night, calm and clear, and the moon shone brightly on the tower of the collegiate church, in the vicinity of which Dr. Byrom resided.

"How peaceful the town looks to-night," observed Byrom. "But in a few days all will be tumult and confusion."

"I do not think any resistance will be offered to the insurgents, sir," replied Atherton; "and luckily the militia is disbanded, though I believe a few shots would have dispersed them had they attempted to show fight."

"No, there will be no serious fighting," said Byrom. "Manchester will surrender at discretion. I don't think the prince will remain here long. He will raise as many recruits as he can, and then march on. I have no right to give you advice, young sir, but I speak to you as I would to my own son. You have promised to call upon Sir Richard Rawcliffe to-morrow, and I suppose you will be as good as your word."

"Of course."

"Then take care you are not persuaded to disobey your guardian. There is a danger you do not apprehend, and I must guard you against it. Miss Rawcliffe is exceedingly beautiful, and very captivating—at least, so I have been informed, for I have never seen her. Her father has told you she is an ardent Jacobite. As such she will deem it her duty to win you over to the good cause, and she will infallibly succeed. Very few of us are proof against the fascinations of a young and lovely woman. Though Sir Richard might not prevail, his daughter will."

"I must go prepared to resist her," replied Atherton, laughing.

"You miscalculate your strength, young man," said Byrom, gravely. "Better not expose yourself to temptation."

"Nay, I must go," said Atherton. "But I should like to know something about Sir Richard Rawcliffe. Has he a son?"

"Only one child—a daughter. Besides being very beautiful, as I have just described her, Constance Rawcliffe will be a great heiress."

"And after saying all this, you expect me to throw away the chance of meeting so charming a person. But don't imagine I am presumptuous enough to aspire to a wealthy heiress. I shall come away heart-whole, and bound by no pledges stronger than those I have already given."

"We shall see," replied Dr. Byrom, in a tone that implied considerable doubt.

They had now arrived at the door of the doctor's residence —a tolerably large, comfortable-looking house, built of red brick, in the plain, formal style of the period.

Before parting with his young companion, Dr. Byrom thought it necessary to give him a few more words of counsel.

"It may appear impertinent in me to meddle in your affairs," he said; "but believe that I am influenced by the best feelings. You are peculiarly circumstanced. You have no father—no near relative to guide you. An error now may be irretrievable. Pray consult me before you make any pledge to Sir Richard Rawcliffe, or to Dr. Deacon."

There was so much paternal kindness in his manner that Atherton could not fail to be touched by it.

"I will consult you, sir," he said, in a grateful tone; "and I thank you deeply for the interest you take in me."

"Enough," replied Dr. Byrom. "I shall hope to see you

soon again. Give me your impressions of Constance Rawcliffe."

He then bade the young man good-night, rang the door bell, and entered the house.

CHAPTER VII.

RENCOUNTER NEAR THE OLD TOWN CROSS.

A PATH led across the south side of the large churchyard surrounding the collegiate church, and on quitting Dr. Byrom, Atherton took his way along it, marching past the old gravestones, and ever and anon glancing at the venerable pile, which, being completely lighted up by the moonbeams, presented a very striking appearance. So bright was the moonlight that the crocketed pinnacles and grotesque gargoyles could have been counted. The young man was filled with admiration of the picture. On reaching the western boundary of the churchyard, he paused to gaze at the massive tower, and having contemplated its beauties for a few minutes, he proceeded towards Salford Bridge.

It has already been stated that this was the oldest and most picturesque part of the town. All the habitations were of timber and plaster, painted black and white, and those immediately adjoining the collegiate church on the west were built on a precipitous rock overlooking the Irwell.

Wherever a view could be obtained of the river, through any opening among these ancient houses—many of which were detached—a very charming scene was presented to the beholder. The river here made a wide bend, and as it swept past the high rocky bank, and flowed on towards the narrow pointed arches of the old bridge, its course was followed with delight, glittering as it then did in the moonbeams.

The old bridge itself was a singular structure, and some

of the old houses on the opposite side of the river vied in picturesque beauty with those near the church.

Atherton was enraptured with the scene. He had made his way to the very edge of the steep rocky bank, so that nothing interfered with the prospect.

Though the hour was by no means late—the old church clock had only just struck ten—the inhabitants of that quarter of the town seemed to have retired to rest. All was so tranquil that the rushing of the water through the arches of the bridge could be distinctly heard.

Soothed by the calmness which acted as a balm upon his somewhat over-excited feelings, the young man fell into a reverie, during which a very charming vision flitted before him.

The description given him of the lovely Constance Rawcliffe had powerfully affected his imagination. She seemed to be the ideal of feminine beauty which he had sought, but never found. He painted her even in brighter colours than she had been described by Dr. Byrom, and with all the romantic folly of a young man was prepared to fall madly in love with her—provided only she deigned to cast the slightest smile upon him.

Having conjured up this exquisite phantom, and invested it with charms that very likely had no existence, he was soon compelled to dismiss it, and return to actual life. It was time to go home, and good Widow Heywood, with whom he lodged, would wonder why he stopped out so late.

Heaving a sigh, with which such idle dreams as he had indulged generally end, he left the post of vantage he had occupied, and, with the design of proceeding to Deansgate, tracked a narrow alley that quickly brought him to Smithy Bank. The latter thoroughfare led to the bridge. Lower down, but not far from the point of junction with Deansgate, stood the old Town Cross.

Hitherto the young man had not seen a single individual in the streets since he left the Bull's Head, and it therefore rather surprised him to perceive a small group of persons standing near the Cross, to which allusion has just been made.

Two damsels, evidently from their attire of the higher rank, attended by a young gentleman and a man-servant—the latter being stationed at a respectful distance from the others—were talking to a well-mounted horseman, in whom Atherton had no difficulty in recognising Colonel Townley. No doubt the colonel had started on his journey to Lancaster. With him was a groom, who, like his master, was well mounted and well armed.

Even at that distance, Atherton remarked that Colonel Townley's manner was extremely deferential to the young ladies—especially towards the one with whom he was conversing. He bent low in the saddle, and appeared to be listening with deep interest and attention to what she said. Both this damsel and her fair companion were so muffled up that Atherton could not discern their features, but he persuaded himself they must be good-looking. A fine shape cannot easily be disguised, and both had symmetrical figures, while the sound of their voices was musical and pleasant.

Atherton was slowly passing on his way, which brought him somewhat nearer the group, when Colonel Townley caught sight of him, and immediately hailed him.

By no means sorry to have a nearer view of the mysterious fair ones, the young man readily responded to the summons, but if he expected an introduction to the damsels he was disappointed.

Before he came up, it was evident that the colonel had been told that this was not to be, and he carefully obeyed orders.

The young lady who had especially attracted Atherton's attention proved to be very handsome, for, though he could not obtain a full view of her face, he saw enough to satisfy him she had delicately formed features, magnificent black eyes, and black tresses.

These splendid black eyes were steadily fixed upon him for a few moments, as if she was reading his character; and after the rapid inspection, she turned to Colonel Townley, and made some remark to him in a whisper.

Without tarrying any longer, she then signed to her companions, and they all three moved off, followed by the man-servant, leaving Atherton quite bewildered. The party walked so rapidly that they were almost instantly out of sight.

"If it is not impertinent on my part, may I ask who those young ladies are?" inquired Atherton.

"I am not allowed to tell you, my dear fellow," replied the colonel, slightly laughing. "But I dare say you will meet them again."

"I must not even ask if they live in Manchester, I suppose?"

"I cannot satisfy your curiosity in any particular. I meant to present you to them, but I was forbidden. I may, however, tell you that the young lady nearest me made a flattering observation respecting you."

"That is something, from so charming a girl."

"Then you discovered that she is beautiful!"

"I never beheld such fine eyes."

Colonel Townley laughed heartily.

"Take care of yourself, my dear boy—take care of yourself," he said. "Those eyes have already done wonderful execution."

"One question more, colonel, and I have done. Are they sisters?"

"Well, I may answer that. They are not. I thought you must have known the young man who was with them."

"I fancied he was Jemmy Dawson. But I own I did not pay much attention to him."

"You were engrossed by one object. It was Jemmy Dawson. He is to be one of my officers, and I feel very proud of him, as I shall be of another gallant youth whom I count upon. But I must loiter no longer here. I shall ride to

Preston to-night, and proceed to-morrow to Lancaster. Fail not to keep your appointment with Sir Richard Rawcliffe. You will see his daughter, who will put this fair unknown out of your head."

"I scarcely think so," replied Atherton.

"Well, I shall learn all about it on my return. Adieu!"

With this, the colonel struck spurs into his horse and rode quickly across the bridge, followed by his groom, while Atherton, whose thoughts had been entirely changed within the last ten minutes, proceeded towards his lodgings in Deansgate.

CHAPTER VIII.

BEPPY BYROM.

NEXT morning, in the drawing-room of a comfortable house, situated near the collegiate church, and commanding from its windows a view of that venerable fabric, a family party, consisting of four persons—two ladies and two gentlemen—had assembled after breakfast.

Elegantly furnished in the taste of the time, the room was fitted up with japanned cabinets and numerous small brackets, on which china ware and other ornaments were placed. A crystal chandelier hung from the ceiling, and a large folding Indian screen was partly drawn round the work-table, beside which the two ladies sat. The gentlemen were standing near the fireplace.

The mistress of the house, though no longer young, as will be guessed when we mention that her daughter was turned twenty-one, while her son was some two or three years older, still retained considerable personal attractions, and had a most agreeable expression of countenance.

We may as well state at once, that this lady, who had

North View of the College.

made the best helpmate possible to the best of husbands. was the wife of our worthy friend Dr. Byrom, who had every reason to congratulate himself, as he constantly did, on the possession of such a treasure.

Very pretty, and very lively, was the younger lady— Elizabeth Byrom—Beppy as she was familiarly called. We despair of giving an idea of her features, but her eyes were bright and blue, her complexion like a damask rose, her nose slightly retroussé, and her teeth like pearls. When she laughed, her cheek displayed the prettiest dimple imaginable. Her light-brown locks were taken from the brow, and raised to a considerable height, but there were no artificial tresses among them.

Her costume suited her extremely well—her gown being of grey silk, looped round the body; and she wore a hoop petticoat—as every other girl did at the time who had any pretension to fashion.

Beppy was not a coquette—far from it—but she tried to please; nor was she vain of her figure, yet she liked to dress becomingly. Accomplished she was, undoubtedly; sang well, and played on the spinet; but she was useful as well as ornamental, and did a great many things in the house, which no girl of our own period would condescend to undertake.

With much gaiety of manner, a keen sense of the ridiculous, and a turn for satire, Beppy never said an ill-natured thing. In short, she was a very charming girl, and the wonder was, with so many agreeable qualities, that she should have remained single.

Our description would be incomplete if we omitted to state that she was an ardent Jacobite.

Her brother, Edward, resembled his father, and was gentleman-like in appearance and manner. He wore a suit of light blue, with silver buttons, and a flaxen-coloured peruke, which gave him a gay look, but in reality he was very sedate. There was nothing of the coxcomb about Edward Byrom. Nor was he of an enthusiastic temperament. Like all the members of his family, he was well inclined towards the House of Stuart, but he was not disposed to make any sacrifice, or incur any personal risk for its restoration to the throne. Edward Byrom was tall, well-made, and passably good-looking.

Mrs. Byrom was dressed in green flowered silk, which suited her: wore powder in her hair, which also suited her, and a hoop petticoat, but we will not say whether the latter suited her or not. Her husband thought it did, and he was the best judge.

"Well, papa," cried Beppy, looking up at him from her work, "what do you mean to do to-day?"

"I have a good deal to do," replied Dr. Byrom. "In the first place I shall pay a visit to Tom Syddall, the barber."

"I like Tom Syddall because he is a Jacobite, and because his father suffered for the good cause," said Beppy. "Though a barber is the least heroic of mortals, Tom Syddall always appears to me a sort of hero, with a pair of scissors and a powder-puff for weapons."

"He has thrown dust in your eyes, Beppy," said the doctor.

"He has vowed to avenge his father. Is not that creditable to him, papa?"

"Yes, he is a brave fellow, no doubt. I only hope he mayn't share his father's fate. I shall endeavour to persuade him to keep quiet."

"Is it quite certain the prince will come to Manchester?" asked Mrs. Byrom, anxiously.

"He will be here in two or three days at the latest with his army. But don't alarm yourself, my love."

"Oh, dear!" she exclaimed. "I think we had better leave the town."

"You are needlessly afraid, mamma," cried Beppy. "I am not frightened in the least. It may be prudent in some people to get out of the way; but depend upon it *we* shan't be molested. Papa's opinions are too well known. I wouldn't for the world miss seeing the prince. I dare say we shall all be presented to him."

"You talk of the prince as if he had already arrived, Beppy," observed Edward Byrom, gravely. "After all, he may never reach Manchester."

"You hope he won't come," cried his sister. "You are a Hanoverian, Teddy, and don't belong to us."

"'Tis because I wish the prince well that I hope he mayn't come," said Teddy. "The wisest thing he could do would be to retreat."

"I disown you, sir," cried the young lady. "The prince will never retreat, unless compelled, and success has hitherto attended him."

"Are you aware that the townspeople of Liverpool have raised a regiment seven hundred strong?"

"For the prince?"

"For King George. Chester, also, has been put into a state of defence against the insurgents, though there are many Roman Catholic families in the city."

"I won't be discouraged," said Beppy. "I am certain the right will triumph. What do you think, papa?"

Dr. Byrom made no response to this appeal.

"Your papa has great misgivings, my dear," observed Mrs. Byrom; "and so have I. I should most heartily rejoice if the danger that threatens us could be averted. Rebellion is a dreadful thing. We must take no part in this contest. How miserable I should have been if your brother had joined the insurgents!"

"Happily, Teddy has more discretion," said Dr. Byrom, casting an approving look at his son. "Some of our friends, I fear, will rue the consequences of their folly. Jemmy Dawson has joined the Manchester Regiment, and of course Dr. Deacon's three sons are to be enrolled in it."

"Were I a man I would join likewise," cried Beppy.

"My dear!" exclaimed her mother, half reproachfully.

"Forgive me if I have hurt your feelings, dearest mamma,"

said Beppy, getting up and kissing her. "You know I would do nothing to displease you."

"Jemmy Dawson will incur his father's anger by the step he has taken," remarked Edward Byrom. "But powerful influence has been brought to bear upon him. A young lady, quite as enthusiastic a Jacobite as you are, Beppy, to whom he is attached, has done the mischief."

"Indeed! I should like to know who she is?" said his sister.

"Nay, you must not question me. You will learn the secret in due time, I make no doubt."

"I have guessed it already," said Beppy. "'Tis Monica Butler. I have seen Jemmy with her. She is just the girl who could induce him to join the insurrection, for she is heart and soul in the cause."

"You are right. Monica Butler is Jemmy's fair enslaver. His assent was to be the price of her hand. I believe they are affianced."

"I hope the engagement will end well, but it does not commence auspiciously," said Dr. Byrom. "Their creeds are different. Monica is a Roman Catholic—at least, I conclude so, since her mother belongs to that religion."

"Mrs. Butler is a widow, I believe?" remarked Mrs. Byrom.

"She is widow of Captain Butler, and sister of Sir Richard Rawcliffe. Consequently, Monica is cousin to the beautiful Constance Rawcliffe. Though so well connected, Mrs. Butler is far from rich, and lives in great privacy, as you know, in Salford. She is very proud of her ancient descent, and I almost wonder she consented to Monica's engagement to young Dawson. By-the-bye, Sir Richard Rawcliffe and his daughter are now in Manchester, and are staying at the Bull's Head. I met Sir Richard last night. He is very anxious to obtain recruits for the prince, and tried hard to enlist Atherton Legh. The young man resisted, but he will have to go through a different ordeal to-day, for he will be exposed to the fascinations of the fair Constance. I shall be curious to learn the result."

"So shall I," said Beppy, with some vivacity.

"Do you take any interest in the young man?" asked her father.

"I think him very handsome," she replied, blushing. "And I think he would be a very great acquisition to the prince. But it would certainly be a pity——"

"That so handsome a young fellow should be executed as a rebel," supplied the father. "I quite agree with you, Beppy, and I therefore hope he will remain firm."

CHAPTER IX.

THE TWO CURATES OF ST. ANN'S.

JUST then a female servant ushered in two young divines, both of them assistant curates of St. Ann's—the Rev. Thomas Lewthwaite and the Rev. Benjamin Nichols. Mr. Hoole, the rector of St. Ann's, was inclined to Nonjuring principles, which he had imbibed from Dr. Deacon, and was very popular with the High Church party, but his curates were Whigs, and belonged to the Low Church, and had both preached against rebellion. Mr. Lewthwaite was a suitor to Beppy, but she did not give him much encouragement, and, indeed, rather laughed at him.

Both the reverend gentlemen looked rather grave, and gave a description of the state of the town that brought back all Mrs. Byrom's alarms.

"An express has just come in," said Mr. Lewthwaite, "bringing word that the rebels have reached Lancaster, and that Marshal Wade has turned back to Newcastle. The rebel force is estimated at seven thousand men, but other accounts affirm that it now amounts to thirty thousand and upwards."

"I hope the latter accounts are correct," observed Beppy.

"We shall certainly have the Pretender here in a couple of days," pursued the curate.

"Pray don't call him the Pretender, sir," cried Beppy. "Speak of him with proper respect as Prince Charles Edward."

"I can't do that," said Mr. Lewthwaite, "being a loyal subject of King George."

"Whom some people regard as a usurper," muttered Beppy.

"The news has thrown the whole town into consternation," said Mr. Nichols. "Everybody is preparing for flight. Almost all the warehouses are closed. Half the shops are shut, and as Mr. Lewthwaite and myself passed through the square just now, we didn't see half a dozen persons. Before night the place will be empty."

"Well, we shan't go," said Beppy.

"The Earl of Warrington has sent away all his plate," pursued Mr. Nichols.

"I have very little plate to send away," observed Dr. Byrom. "Besides, I am not afraid of being plundered."

"You may not feel quite so secure, sir, when I tell you that the magistrates have thrown open the doors of the House of Correction," said Mr. Nichols.

"Very considerate of them, indeed," said Dr. Byrom. "The townspeople will appreciate their attention. Have you any more agreeable intelligence?"

"Yes; the postmaster has started for London this morning to stop any further remittances from the bankers, lest the money should fall into the hands of the rebels."

"That looks as if the authorities were becoming really alarmed," observed Edward Byrom.

"They are rather late in bestirring themselves," said Mr. Nichols. "The boroughreeve and constables have learnt that a good deal of unlawful recruiting for the Pretender has been going on under their very noses, and are determined to put an end to it. Colonel Townley would have been arrested last night if he had not saved himself by a hasty departure. But I understand that an important arrest will be made this morning."

"An arrest!—of whom?" inquired Dr. Byrom, uneasily.

"I can't tell you precisely, sir," replied Mr. Nichols. "But the person is a Jacobite gentleman of some consequence, who has only just arrived in Manchester."

"It must be Sir Richard Rawcliffe," mentally ejaculated Dr. Byrom. "I must warn him of his danger without delay. Excuse me, gentlemen," he said, "I have just recollected an appointment. I fear I shall be rather late."

And he was hurrying out of the room, but before he could reach the door, it was opened by the servant, and Atherton Legh came in.

Under the circumstances the interruption was vexatious, but quickly recovering from the confusion into which he was thrown, the doctor exclaimed, "You are the person I wanted to see."

Seizing the young man's arm, he led him to a small adjoining room that served as a study.

"You will think my conduct strange," he said, "but there is no time for explanation. Will you take a message from me to Sir Richard Rawcliffe?"

"Willingly," replied Atherton, "I was going to him after I had said a few words to you."

"Our conference must be postponed," said the doctor.

He then sat down and tracing a few hasty lines on a sheet of paper, directed and sealed the note, and gave it to Atherton.

"Take this to Sir Richard, without loss of time," he said. "You will render him an important service."

"I shall be very glad to serve him," replied the young man. "But may I not know the nature of my mission?"

"Be satisfied that it is important," said the doctor. "I

shall see you again later on. Perhaps Sir Richard may have a message to send to me."

Dr. Byrom then conducted the young man to the hall-door, and let him out himself; after which he returned to the study, not caring to go back to the drawing-room.

Great was Beppy's disappointment that Atherton was carried off so suddenly by her father; but she had some suspicion of the truth. As to the two curates, they thought the doctor's conduct rather singular, but forebore to make any remarks.

CHAPTER X.

CONSTANCE RAWCLIFFE.

On quitting Dr. Byrom's house, Atherton proceeded quickly along Old Mill Gate towards the market-place.

This street, one of the oldest and busiest in the town, presented a very unwonted appearance—several of the shops being shut, while carts half-filled with goods were standing at the doors, showing that the owners were removing their property.

Very little business seemed to be going on, and there were some symptoms of a disturbance, for a band of rough-looking fellows, armed with bludgeons, was marching along the street, and pushing decent people from the narrow footway.

In the market-place several groups were collected, eagerly discussing the news; and at the doors of the Exchange, then newly erected, a few merchants were assembled, but they all had an anxious look, and did not seem to be engaged on business.

Except the Exchange, to which we have just adverted, there was not a modern building near the market-place. All the habitations were old, and constructed of timber and plaster. In the midst of these, on the left, stood the Bull's Head. The old inn ran back to a considerable distance, and possessed a court-yard large enough to hold three or four post-chaises and an occasional stage-coach.

Entering the court-yard, Atherton sought out Diggles, the landlord, and inquired for Sir Richard Rawcliffe, but, to his great disappointment, learnt that the baronet had just gone out.

"That is unlucky," cried the young man. "I have an important communication for him."

"He will be back presently," said the landlord. "But perhaps Miss Rawcliffe will see you. She is within. Her cousin, Miss Butler, is with her."

Atherton assented to this proposition, and was conducted by the host to a room on the first floor, and evidently situated in the front part of the house.

Tapping at the door Diggles went in, and almost immediately returned to say that Miss Rawcliffe would be happy to receive Mr. Atherton Legh.

Atherton was then ushered into the presence of two young ladies—one of whom rose on his appearance and received him very courteously.

Could he believe his eyes? Yes! it must be the fair creature he had seen on the previous night, who had made such a powerful impression upon him. But if he had thought her beautiful then, how much more exquisite did she appear now that her charming features could be fully distinguished.

While bowing to the other young lady, whose name he had learnt from the landlord, he felt equally sure that she had been Miss Rawcliffe's companion on the previous night.

Monica Butler offered a strong contrast to her cousin—the one being a brunette and the other a blonde. But each was charming in her way—each set off the other. Constance's eyes were dark as night, and her tresses of corresponding hue; while Monica's eyes were tender and blue as a summer sky, and her locks fleecy as a summer cloud.

"I see you recognise us, Mr. Atherton Legh," said Miss Rawcliffe, smiling. "It would be useless, therefore, to attempt any disguise. My cousin, Monica Butler, and myself were talking to Colonel Townley when you came up last night. He would fain have presented you to us, but I would not allow him, for I did not think it quite proper that an introduction should take place under such peculiar circumstances. As you may naturally wonder why two young damsels should be abroad so late, I will explain. Wishing to have Monica's company during my stay at this inn, I went to fetch her, escorted by your friend Jemmy Dawson. As we were coming back, we accidentally encountered Colonel Townley near the Cross. All the rest you know."

"I am very agreeably surprised," said Atherton. "I have been dying to know who you both were, for Colonel Townley refused to gratify my curiosity."

"I am glad to find he obeyed my orders," observed Miss Rawcliffe, smiling. "At that time I did not imagine I should ever see you again. But this morning papa told me he had made an appointment with you at noon. I ought to apologise for his absence—but you are rather before your time."

"'Tis I who ought to apologise," said Atherton. "But I am the bearer of a note to Sir Richard," he added, handing it to her. "'Tis from Dr. Byrom, and I believe it contains matter of urgent importance. At all events, Dr. Byrom requested me to deliver it without delay."

"I hope it contains good news," said Constance. "Pray take a seat. You must please to await papa's return. He much wishes to see you; and I may tell you he hopes to induce you to join the prince's army. We are all ardent Jacobites, as you know, and anxious to obtain recruits. If I had any influence with you I would urge you to enrol yourself in Colonel Townley's regiment. Jemmy Dawson has just joined. Why not follow his example?"

"I have already explained to Colonel Townley why it is impossible for me to comply with his request."

"Your reasons have been mentioned to me, but I confess I do not see their force. Jemmy Dawson has not been swayed by such feelings, but has risked his father's displeasure to serve the prince. He did not hesitate when told that a young lady's hand would be the reward of his compliance with her request."

"Till this moment I did not know why Jemmy had joined, having heard him express indifference to the cause. May I venture to ask the name of the fair temptress?"

"Excuse me. You will learn the secret in due time."

"He shall learn it now," interposed Monica. "I do not blush to own that I am the temptress. I am proud of my Jemmy's devotion—proud, also, of having gained the prince so important a recruit."

"You may well be proud of Jemmy, Monica," said Constance. "He has many noble qualities and cannot fail to distinguish himself."

"He is as brave as he is gentle," said Monica—"a veritable preux et hardi chevalier, and will live or die like a hero."

"You are an enthusiastic girl," said Constance.

"In my place you would be just as enthusiastic, Constance," rejoined the other.

Atherton listened with a beating heart to this discourse, which was well calculated to stir his feelings.

Just then, however, an interruption was offered by the entrance of Sir Richard Rawcliffe.

"Very glad to see you, sir," cried the baronet, shaking hands with Atherton. "I perceive you have already made the acquaintance of my daughter and her cousin, Miss Butler, so I needn't introduce you. Are you aware that my neice is engaged to your friend, Jemmy Dawson?"

"Yes, Mr. Atherton Legh knows all about it, papa," said Constance. "He has brought you a letter from Dr. Byrom," she added, giving it to him.

"Excuse me," said Sir Richard, opening the note.

As he hastily scanned its contents, his countenance fell.

"Has something gone wrong, papa?" cried Constance, uneasily.

"I am threatened with arrest for treasonable practices," replied Sir Richard. "Dr. Byrom counsels immediate flight, or concealment. But where am I to fly?—where conceal myself?" he added, looking quite bewildered.

"You had better leave the inn at once, papa," said Constance, who, though greatly alarmed, had not lost her presence of mind.

At this moment, a noise was heard outside that increased the uneasiness of the party.

CHAPTER XI.

THE BOROUGHREEVE OF MANCHESTER.

SITUATED in the front of the house, the room commanded the market-place. Atherton rushed to the window to ascertain what was taking place, and was followed by the baronet.

"Do not show yourself, Sir Richard," cried the young man, motioning him to keep back. "The chief magistrates are outside—Mr. Fielden, the boroughreeve, and Mr. Walley and Mr. Fowden, the constables. They have a posse of peace-officers with them."

"They are come to arrest me!" exclaimed Sir Richard.

"Save yourself, papa!—save yourself!" cried Constance. "Not a moment is to be lost."

Her exhortations were seconded by Monica and Atherton, but Sir Richard did not move, and looked quite stupefied.

"'Tis too late!" cried Atherton. "I hear them on the stairs."

As he spoke the door burst open, and Diggles rushed in— his looks betokening great alarm.

"The magistrates are here, Sir Richard, and their purpose is to arrest you. Flight is impossible. Every exit from the house is guarded. I could not warn you before."

"If you have any letters or papers that might compromise you, papa, give them to me," said Constance.

Sir Richard hesitated for a moment, and then produced a packet, saying, as he gave it to her, "I confide this to you. Take every care of it."

She had just concealed the packet when the magistrates entered the room. The officers who followed them stationed themselves outside the door.

Mr. John Fielden, the boroughreeve, who preceded the two constables, was a man of very gentleman-like appearance and deportment. After saluting the baronet, who advanced a few steps to meet him, he said, in accents that were not devoid of sympathy—

"I have a very unpleasant duty to discharge, Sir Richard, but I must fulfil it. In the king's name I arrest you for treasonable practices."

"Of what treasonable practices am I accused, sir?" demanded the baronet, who had now gained his composure.

"You are charged with wickedly and traitorously conspiring to change and subvert the rule and government of this kingdom; with seeking to depose our sovereign lord the king of his title, honour, and royal state; and with seeking to raise and exalt the person pretending to be, and taking upon himself the style and title of King of England, by the name of James the Third, to the imperial rule and government of this kingdom."

"What more, sir?" said Sir Richard.

"You are charged with falsely and traitorously inciting certain of his Majesty's faithful subjects to rebellion; and with striving to raise recruits for the son of the Popish Pretender to the throne, who is now waging war against his Majesty King George the Second."

"I deny the charges," rejoined the baronet, sternly.

"I trust you can disprove them, Sir Richard," said the boroughreeve. "To-morrow your examination will take place, and, in the meantime, you will be lodged in the Old Bailey."

" Lodged in a prison !" exclaimed Constance, indignantly.

" It must be," said the boroughreeve. " I have no option. But I promise you Sir Richard shall undergo no hardship. His imprisonment, I hope, may be brief."

" I thank you for your consideration, sir," said the baronet. " May I be allowed a few minutes to prepare ?"

" I am sorry I cannot grant the request, Sir Richard."

" Then farewell, my dear child !—farewell, Monica !" cried the baronet, tenderly embracing them. "My captivity will not be long," he added, in a low voice to his daughter. " I shall be set at liberty on the prince's arrival—if not before."

Constance maintained a show of firmness which she did not feel, but Monica was much moved, and could not repress her tears.

After bidding adieu to Atherton, Sir Richard signified to the boroughreeve that he was ready to attend him, and passed out.

As he did so, the officers took charge of him, and the door was shut.

Constance's courage then entirely forsook her, and uttering a cry, she sank into a chair. Monica strove to comfort her —but in vain.

"I shall go distracted," she cried. "I cannot bear the thought that papa should be imprisoned."

"Make yourself easy on that score, Miss Rawcliffe," said Atherton. "Imprisoned he shall not be. I will undertake to rescue him."

"You !" she exclaimed, gazing at him through her streaming eyes. "If you could save him this indignity, I should be for ever beholden to you. But no !—you must not attempt it. The risk is too great."

"I care not for the risk," cried Atherton. "I will do it. You shall soon learn that your father is free."

And he rushed out of the room.

"A brave young man," cried Monica. "He has all my Jemmy's spirit. I feel sure he will accomplish what he has undertaken."

"I hope no harm will befall him," said Constance.

Shortly afterwards a great disturbance was heard in the market-place, and flying to the windows, they witnessed a very exciting scene.

CHAPTER XII.

THE RESCUE.

THE visit of the boroughreeve and constables to the Bull's Head attracted a considerable crowd to the market-place—it being rumoured that the magistrates were about to arrest an important Jacobite gentleman.

A political arrest at this juncture, when the town was in such an inflamed state, seemed to most persons, whatever their opinions might be, an exceedingly ill-advised step, and the magistrates were much blamed for taking it.

Murmurs were heard, and some manifestations of sympathy with the luckless Jacobite would undoubtedly have been made by the assemblage had they not been kept in awe by the strong body of constables drawn up in front of the inn.

As might be expected, the lower orders predominated in the concourse, but there were some persons of a superior class present, who had been brought thither by curiosity. The crowd momently increased, until the market-place, which was not very spacious, was more than half full, while the disposition to tumult became more apparent as the numbers grew.

At length a large old-fashioned coach was seen to issue from the entrance of the court-yard, and it was at once conjectured that the prisoner was inside the vehicle, from the fact that a constable was seated on the box beside the coachman, while half a dozen officers marched in front, to clear a passage through the throng.

But this could not be accomplished without the liberal use of staves, and the progress of the coach was necessarily slow. Groans, hootings, and angry exclamations arose from the crowd, but these were directed against the constables and not at the prisoner, who could be seen through the windows of the coach. Sir Richard was recognised by some of the nearest spectators, and his name being called out to those further off, it speedily became known to the whole assemblage, and the noise increased.

At this moment Atherton Legh rushed from the door of the inn and shouted in a loud voice, "A rescue!—a rescue!"

The cry thus raised was echoed by a hundred voices, and in another minute all was confusion.

"A rescue!—a rescue!" resounded on all sides. The coachman tried to extricate himself from the throng, but the heads of the horses being seized, he could not move on.

The constables endeavoured to get near the coach, as well to guard the prisoner as to protect the magistrates, who were inside the roomy vehicle with him.

But Atherton, who was remarkably athletic, snatched a truncheon from one of them, and laying about him vigorously with this weapon, and being supported by the crowd, soon forced his way to the door, and was about to pull it open, when the boroughreeve thrust his head through the window, and called out to him to forbear.

"Beware how you violate the law, young man," cried Mr. Fielden, in a firm and authoritative voice, that showed he was not daunted. "You must be aware that in constituting yourself the leader of a riotous mob, and attempting to rescue a prisoner, you are committing a very grave offence. Desist, while there is yet time. You are known to me and my brother magistrates."

"We do not intend you any personal injury, Mr. Fielden —nor do we mean to injure your brother magistrates," rejoined Atherton, resolutely. "But we are determined to liberate Sir Richard Rawcliffe. Set him free, and there will be an end to the disturbance. You must plainly perceive, sir, that resistance would be useless."

While this was going on, the band of desperadoes, already alluded to, had hurried back to the market-place, and now came up flourishing their bludgeons, and shouting, "Down with the Presbyterians!" "Down with the Hanoverians!" And some of them even went so far as to add "Down with King George!"

These shouts were echoed by the greater part of the concourse, which had now become very turbulent and excited.

Mr. Fielden called to the constables to keep back the mob, and move on, but the officers were utterly powerless to obey him. If a riot commenced, there was no saying where it would end; so, addressing a final remonstrance to Atherton, which proved as ineffectual as all he had said before, the boroughreeve withdrew from the window.

Atherton then opened the coach door, and told Sir Richard, who had been anxiously watching the course of events, that he was free.

On this the baronet arose, and bade a polite adieu to the magistrates, who made no attempt to prevent his departure.

As Sir Richard came forth and stood for a short space on the step of the carriage, so that he could be seen by all the assemblage, a deafening and triumphant shout arose.

"I thank you, my good friends, for delivering me," vociferated the baronet. "I have been illegally arrested. I am guilty of no crime. God bless the king!"

"Which king?" cried several voices, amid loud laughter and applause.

"Choose for yourselves!" responded Sir Richard. "You

64   THE MANCHESTER REBELS

CONSTANCE RAWCLIFFE GAINS A RECRUIT.

have rendered me a great service; but if you would serve me still more, and also serve the good cause which I represent, you will retire quietly. Bide your time. 'Twill soon come."

This short harangue was greeted by a loud cheer, amid which the baronet descended, and shook hands heartily with Atherton, who was standing near him.

"I owe my deliverance to you," he said; "and be sure I shall ever feel grateful."

Just then a rush was made towards them by the constables, who were, however, kept back by the crowd.

"Meddle not with us, and we won't meddle with you," cried Atherton.

Prudently acting upon the advice, the constables kept quiet.

Every facility for escape was afforded Sir Richard by the concourse. A narrow lane was opened for him, through which he passed, accompanied by Atherton.

Without pausing to consider whither they were going, they hurried on, till they reached Smithy Doer—a narrow street, so designated, and leading from the bottom of the market-place, in the direction of Salford Bridge.

Feeling secure, they then stopped to hold a brief consultation.

"It won't do for me to return to the inn," observed Sir Richard. "Nor is it necessary I should return thither. My daughter and her cousin are in no danger, and I shall easily find some means of communicating with them. They will know I am safe."

"Were I able to do so, I would gladly take a message from you to Miss Rawcliffe, Sir Richard," said Atherton. "But I am now in as much danger as yourself. I am known to the magistrates, and they will certainly send the officers in search of me."

"You shall run no more risk on my account," said Sir Richard. "My daughter is so courageous that she will feel no alarm when she learns I have escaped. You must find a hiding-place till the prince arrives in Manchester, and then all will be right. If I could procure a horse, I would ride on to Preston. I have a couple of hunters in the stables at the Bull's Head, but they are useless to me now."

As he spoke, a young man was seen approaching them, mounted on a strong roadster. Both recognised the horseman, who was no other than Jemmy Dawson, of whom mention has already been made.

A very handsome young fellow was Jemmy Dawson—tall, rather slightly built, but extremely well made, and looking to advantage in the saddle.

On this occasion Jemmy wore a green cloth riding-dress, made in the fashion of the time, with immense cuffs and ample skirts; the coat being laced with silver, and having silver buttons. His cocked hat surmounted a light bob peruke. He had a sword by his side, and carried a riding-whip in his hand.

On descrying Sir Richard, he instantly accelerated his pace, and no sooner learnt how the baronet was circumstanced than he jumped down, and offered him his horse.

Sir Richard unhesitatingly sprang into the saddle which the other had just quitted.

"Here is the whip," said Jemmy, handing it to him. "But the horse needs neither whip nor spur, as you will find, Sir Richard. He will soon take you to Preston."

"I hope to bring him back safe and sound, Jemmy," said the baronet. "But if aught happens, you shall have my favourite hunter in exchange. As soon as the crowd in the market-place has dispersed, go to the Bull's Head, and let the girls know how well you have mounted me, and whither I am gone."

Addressing a few parting words to Atherton, he then dashed off, clattering over the stones as he shaped his course towards Salford Bridge.

"I envy you your good fortune, Atherton," said Jemmy, as they were left together. "The part you have played belonged of right to me, but I should not have performed it half so well. I wish you could go back with me to receive Constance Rawcliffe's thanks for the service you have rendered her father; but that must not be. Where shall I find you?"

"I know not, for I cannot return to my lodgings. You will hear of me at Tom Syddall's. He will help me to a hiding-place."

"Ay, that he will. Our Jacobite barber is the trustiest fellow in Manchester. You will be perfectly safe with him. But take care how you enter his shop. 'Tis not unlikely you may be watched. We must not have another arrest."

They then separated—Atherton proceeding quickly towards the bridge, not far from which the barber's shop was situated, while Jemmy Dawson mingled with the crowd in the market-place. The magistrates were gone, but the constables blocked up the approaches to the Bull's Head. However, they readily allowed him to enter the inn.

CHAPTER XIII.

CONSTANCE MAKES A DISCOVERY.

FROM the deep bay-windows of the old inn Constance and Monica witnessed all that had occurred, and were both filled with admiration at the gallantry and spirit displayed by Atherton.

Miss Rawcliffe especially was struck by the young man's courageous deportment as he confronted the boroughreeve, and without reflecting that he was violating the law, saw in him only her father's deliverer.

"Look, Monica!" she cried. "Has he not a noble expression of countenance? He is taller than any of those around him, and seems able to cope with half a dozen such varlets as have beset him."

"He has certainly shown himself more than a match for the constables, if you mean to describe them as 'varlets,'" rejoined Monica.

"They did not dare to lay hands upon him," cried Constance. "But see, papa is coming out of the coach, and is about to address the assemblage. Let us open the window to hear what he says."

This was done, and they both waved their handkerchiefs to Sir Richard when he concluded his harangue.

"Atherton looked up at the moment, and received a similar greeting. Constance's eloquent glances and approving smiles more than repaid him for what he had done.

From their position the two damsels could discern all that subsequently took place. They beheld Sir Richard and the gallant youth who had rescued him pass safely through the crowd, and disappear at the lower end of the market-place.

Then feeling satisfied that the fugitives were safe, they retired from the window, nor did they look out again, though the shouting and tumult still continued, till Jemmy Dawson made his appearance. Both were delighted to see him.

"Oh, I am so glad you are come, Jemmy!" cried Monica. "What is going on? I hope there won't be a riot?"

"Have you seen papa and Mr. Atherton Legh?" asked Constance.

"Yes, I have seen them both; and I am happy to be able to relieve your anxiety respecting Sir Richard. He is out of all danger. By this time I trust he is a mile or two on the road to Preston. I have provided him with a horse."

"Heaven be thanked!" she exclaimed. "But what of young Atherton Legh? I hope there is no chance of his falling into the hands of the enemy. I should never forgive myself if anything were to happen to him, for I feel that I incited him to this hazardous attempt."

"No doubt you did, Constance," observed Monica.

"You need not make yourself uneasy about him," said Jemmy. "He will easily find a secure retreat till the prince appears."

There was a moment's pause, during which the lovers exchanged tender glances, and Constance appeared preoccupied.

"Who is Atherton Legh?" she inquired, at length. "I begin to feel interested about him."

"I would rather you didn't ask me the question," replied Jemmy. "I can't answer it very readily. However, I will tell you all I know about him."

And he proceeded to relate such particulars of the young man's history as the reader is already acquainted with.

Constance listened with great interest.

"It appears, then, from what you say, that he is dependent upon a guardian whom he has never seen, and of whose very name he is ignorant."

"That is so," replied Jemmy. "But I am convinced he is a gentleman born."

"The mystery attaching to his birth does not lessen my interest in him," said Constance.

"I should be surprised if it did," observed Monica. "You can give him any rank you please. I am sorry to disturb your romantic ideas respecting him, but you must recollect he has been an apprentice to a Manchester merchant, and has only just served his time."

"His career now may be wholly changed, and he may never embark in trade," said Constance. "But if he were to do so I cannot see that he would be degraded, any more than he is degraded by having been an apprentice."

"Cadets of our best Lancashire and Cheshire families are constantly apprenticed, so there is nothing in that," remarked Jemmy. "I repeat my conviction that Atherton is a gentleman born. Dr. Byrom is of the same opinion."

"Dr. Byrom may be influenced by partiality. I fancy he would like the young man as a son-in-law," said Monica.

"Beppy Byrom certainly would not object to the arrangement," she added, with a significant smile that conveyed a good deal.

"Is Beppy Byrom pretty?" asked Constance.

"Decidedly so—one of the prettiest girls in Manchester," rejoi ed Monica.

"And is Mr. Atherton Legh insensible to her attractions?" inquired Constance, as carelessly as she could.

"That I can't pretend to say," returned her cousin. "But I should scarcely think he can be so."

"At all events, he pays her very little attention," remarked Jemmy.

Constance cast down her magnificent eyes, and her countenance assumed a thoughtful expression that seemed to heighten its beauty.

While she remained thus preoccupied, Monica and her lover moved towards the window and looked out, or appeared to be looking out, for it is highly probable they only saw each other.

Presently Constance arose, and saying she desired to be alone for a few minutes, left them together.

Proceeding to her own chamber, she sat down and began to review as calmly as she could the strange and hurried events of the morning, in which Atherton Legh had played a conspicuous part, and though the rest of the picture presented to her mental gaze appeared somewhat confused, his image rose distinctly before her.

The young man's singular story, as related by Jemmy Dawson, had greatly stimulated her curiosity, and she indulged in many idle fancies respecting him—such as will flash through a young girl's brain—sometimes endeavouring to account for the mystery of his birth in one way, sometimes in another, but always feeling sure he was well-born.

"If any one ever proclaimed himself a gentleman by look and manner, it is Atherton Legh," she thought. "And as to his courage it is indisputable. But I have   thinking only of this young man all the time," she reflected, with a feeling of self-reproach, " when I ought to have been thinking of papa. I ought to have locked up the packet of important papers that he confided to me before his arrest. I will repair my neglect at once."

With this resolve she arose, and taking out the packet was about to place it in her writing-case, when a letter fell to the ground.

The letter was partly open, and a name caught her eye that made her start.

The impulse to glance at the contents of the letter was irresistible, and she found, to her infinite surprise, that the communication related to Atherton Legh, and was addressed by a Manchester banker to Sir Richard Rawcliffe, leaving no doubt whatever on her mind that her father was the young man's mysterious guardian.

In fact, Mr. Marriott, the banker in question, stated that, in compliance with Sir Richard's order, he had paid a certain sum to Mr. Atherton Legh, and had also delivered the letter enclosed by the baronet to the young man.

Astonishment at the discovery almost took away her breath, and she remained gazing at the letter as if doubting whether she had read it aright, till it dropped from her hands.

" My father Atherton's guardian!" she exclaimed. " How comes it he has never made the slightest allusion to his ward? Why have I been kept so completely in the dark? Till I came to Manchester last night I had never heard there was such a person as Atherton Legh. Chance seems to have revealed the secret to me. Yet it must have been something more than chance. Otherwise, the letter could never have fallen into my hands at this particular juncture. But what have I discovered? Only that my father is Atherton's mysterious guardian—nothing respecting the young man's parentage. That is the real secret which I fear will never be cleared up by my father—even if I venture to question him. Let me reflect. The reason why this young man has been brought up thus must be that he belongs to some old Jacobite family, the chief members of which have been banished. That would account for all. My father corresponds with several important persons who were engaged in the last rebellion, and are now abroad. I need not seek further for an explanation—yet I am not altogether satisfied. I must not breathe a word to Monica of the singular discovery I have made, for the secret, I feel, would not be safe with her. But methinks my father might have trusted me. Till I see him again, my lips shall be sealed—even to Atherton, should I happen to meet him. Doubtless these letters," she continued, taking up the packet, and examining it, "would afford me full information respecting the young man, but, though strongly tempted, I will read nothing more, without my father's sanction."

She then replaced the letter she had dropped with the others, and had just locked up the packet in a small valise, when her cousin came in quest of her.

CHAPTER XIV.

ST. ANN'S SQUARE.

"THE crowd in the market-place has dispersed, and all seems quiet," said Monica. "Shall we take an airing in St. Ann's Square? Jemmy will escort us. 'Tis a fine day—as fine a day, at least, as one can expect in November."

Constance assented, and they forthwith prepared for a walk—each arraying herself in a black hood and scarf, and each taking a large fan with her, though the necessity for such an article at that late season of the year did not seem very obvious. But at the period of which we treat, a woman, with any pretension to mode, had always a fan dangling from her wrist.

Attended by Jemmy Dawson, who was looked upon as one of the beaux of the town, they sallied forth, and passing the Exchange, where a couple of porters standing in the doorway were the only persons to be seen, they took their way through a narrow alley, called Acres Court, filled with small shops, and leading from the back of the Exchange to the square.

Usually, Acres Court was crowded, but no one was to be seen there now, and the shops were shut.

Not many years previous to the date of our history, St. Ann's Square was an open field—Acres Field being its designation.

The area was tolerably spacious—the houses surrounding it being some three or four stories high, plain and formal in appearance, with small windows, large doorways, and heavy wooden balustrades, meant to be ornamental, at the top. Most of them were private residences.

On either side of the square was a row of young plane trees. At the further end stood the church, of the architectural beauty of which we cannot say much; but it had its admirers in those days, and perhaps may have admirers in our own, for it still stands where it did. In fact, the square retains a good deal of its original appearance.

Here the beau monde of the town was wont to congregate in the middle of the last century—the ladies in their hoop petticoats, balloon-like sacques, and high-heeled shoes, with powder in their locks, and patches on their cheeks; and the gentlemen in laced coats of divers colours, cocked hats, and periwigs, ruffles at the wrist, and solitaires round the throat, sword by the side, and clouded cane in hand. Here they met to criticise each other and talk scandal, in imitation of the fine folks to be seen on the Mall at St. James's.

But none of these triflers appeared in St. Ann's Square when Miss Rawcliffe and her companions entered it. Only one young lady, attended by a couple of clergymen, could be descried pacing to and fro on the broad pavement.

In this damsel Monica at once recognised Beppy Byrom,

but she made no remark on the subject to Constance, and stopped Jemmy, who was about to blab.

Presently, Beppy turned and advanced towards them, and then Constance could not fail to be struck by her good looks, and inquired who she was?

"Can't you guess?" cried Monica.

"Is it Beppy Byrom?" said Constance, colouring.

Monica nodded. "What do you think of her?"

Before a reply could be made, Beppy came up, and an introduction took place. Beppy and Constance scrutinised each other with a rapid glance. But no fault could be detected on either side.

"Allow me to congratulate you on Sir Richard's escape, Miss Rawcliffe," said Beppy. "Papa sent a warning letter to him, as no doubt you know, but Sir Richard did not receive it in time to avoid the arrest. How courageously Mr. Atherton Legh seens to have behaved on the occasion."

"Yes, papa owes his deliverance entirely to Mr. Legh," rejoined Constance. "We have good reason to feel grateful to him."

"'Tis perhaps a superfluous offer," said Beppy. "But since Sir Richard has been compelled to fly, can we be of any service to you? Our house is roomy, and we can accommodate you without the slightest inconvenience."

"You are extremely kind," said Constance. "I shall probably remain at the inn; but if I do move, it will be to my Aunt Butler's."

"Yes, mamma would be hurt if my Cousin Constance did not come to her," interposed Monica. "We are going to her presently. She is out of the way of these disturbances, and has probably never heard of them."

"Your mamma, I believe, is a great invalid, Miss Butler?" remarked Beppy. "I have heard Dr. Deacon speak of her."

"Yes, she rarely leaves the house. But she has a most capital nurse—so that I can leave her without the slightest apprehension."

"That is fortunate," said Beppy. "I hope you will soon have good tidings of Sir Richard, Miss Rawcliffe?"

"I don't expect to hear anything of him till he re-appears with the prince," replied Constance, in a low tone. "I am under no alarm about him."

"Well, perhaps, the person in greatest jeopardy is Atherton Legh," said Beppy. "I should like to feel quite sure he is safe."

"Then take the assurance from me, Miss Byrom," observed Jemmy.

"Do tell me where he is?" she asked.

"He has taken refuge with Tom Syddall," was the reply, in an undertone.

"She takes a deep interest in him," thought Constance.

The two clergymen, who were no other than Mr. Nichols and Mr. Lewthwaite, and who had stood aside during this discourse, now came forward, and were presented to Miss Rawcliffe.

The conversation then became general, and was proceeding pleasantly enough, when a very alarming sound put a sudden stop to it.

It was a fire-bell. And the clangour evidently came from the tower of the collegiate church.

The conversation instantly ceased, as we have said, and those who had been engaged in it glanced at each other uneasily.

"Heaven preserve us!" ejaculated Mr. Lewthwaite. "With how many plagues is this unfortunate town to be visited? Are we to have a conflagration in addition to the other calamities by which we are menaced?"

Meantime, the clangour increased in violence, and shouts of "Fire! fire!" resounded in all directions.

But the alarm of the party was considerably heightened when another fire-bell began to ring—this time close to them.

From the tower of St. Ann's Church the warning sounds now came—stunning and terrifying those who listened to them; and bringing forth many of the occupants of the houses in the square.

"It must be a great fire!—perhaps the work of an incendiary!" cried Mr. Nichols. "I will not attribute the mischief to Jacobite plotters, but I fear it will turn out that they are the instigators of it."

"It looks suspicious, I must own," remarked Mr. Lewthwaite.

"You have no warrant for these observations, gentlemen," said Jemmy, indignantly.

Still the fire-bells rang on with undiminished fury, and numbers of people were seen running across the square—shouting loudly as they hurried along.

"Where is the fire?" cried Beppy.

"It must be in the neighbourhood of the collegiate church," replied Mr. Lewthwaite. "All the houses are old in that quarter, and built of timber. Half the town will be consumed. That will be lamentable, but it will not be surprising, since the inhabitants have assuredly called down a judgment upon their heads from their propensity to rebellion."

Jemmy Dawson, who had great difficulty in controlling his anger, was about to make a sharp rejoinder to this speech, when a look from Monica checked him.

Just then several men ran past, and he hailed one of them, who stopped.

"Can you tell me where the fire is?" he asked.

"There be no fire, sir," replied the man, with a grin.

"No fire!" exclaimed Jemmy, astounded. "Why, then, the fire-bells being rung thus loudly?"

"To collect a mob, if yo mun know," rejoined the man.

"For what purpose?" demanded Jemmy.

"Rebellion! rebellion! Can you doubt it?" said Mr. Lewthwaite.

"Ay, yo may ca' it rebellion an yo like, but this be the plain truth," said the man. "T' magistrates ha' just gi'en orders that Salford Bridge shan be blowed up to hinder t'

Pretender, as yo ca' him, or t' prince, as we ca' him, fro' comin' into t' town, wi' his army. Now we Jacobites won't let the bridge be meddled with, so we han had the fire-bells rung to rouse the townsfolk."

"And you mean to resist the authorities?" cried Mr. Lewthwaite.

"Ay, that we do," rejoined the man, defiantly. "They shan't move a stone of the bridge."

"Beware what you do! You are rebelling against your lawful sovereign as represented by the magistrates. Forget not that rebellion provokes the Lord's anger, and will bring down his vengeance upon you."

"I canna bide to listen to a sarmon just now," rejoined the man, hurrying off.

"Can't we obtain a sight of what is going on at the bridge from the banks of the river?" said Constance.

"Yes, I will take you to a spot that commands a complete view of the bridge," rejoined Jemmy; "where you can see all that is to be seen, and yet not run the slightest risk."

"Shall we go, Monica?" said Constance.

"By all means," cried the other.

"I should like to make one of the party," said Beppy, who had just recollected that Tom Syddall's shop, where she knew Atherton had taken refuge, adjoined the bridge, and she thought it almost certain the young man would take part in this new disturbance.

"I advise you not to go, Miss Byrom," said Mr. Lewthwaite. "Neither Mr. Nichols nor myself can sanction such a lawless proceeding by our presence."

"As you please," said Beppy.

"Pray come with us, Miss Byrom," cried Jemmy. "I will engage that no harm shall befall you."

So they set off, leaving the two curates behind, both looking very much disconcerted.

CHAPTER XV.

HOW SALFORD BRIDGE WAS SAVED FROM DESTRUCTION.

By this time the fire-bells had ceased to ring, but the effect had been produced, and a great crowd, much more excited than that which had previously assembled in the marketplace, was collected in the immediate neighbourhood of the bridge.

Salford Bridge, which must have been a couple of centuries old at the least, was strongly built of stone, and had several narrow-pointed arches, strengthened by enormous piers. These arches almost choked up the course of the river. Only a single carriage could cross the bridge at a time, but there were deep angular recesses in which foot-passengers could take refuge. It will be seen at once that such a structure could be stoutly defended against a force approaching from Salford, though it was commanded by the precipitous banks on the Manchester side. Moreover, the Irwell was here of considerable depth.

Before commencing operations, the magistrates, who were not without apprehension of a tumult, stopped all traffic across the bridge, and placed a strong guard at either extremity, to protect the workmen and engineers from any hindrance on the part of the populace.

A couple of large caissons, containing, it was supposed, a sufficient quantity of powder to overthrow the solid pier, had been sunk under the central arch of the bridge. Above the spot, in a boat, sat two engineers ready to fire the powder-chests when the signal should be given.

But the preparations had been watched by two daring individuals, who were determined to prevent them. One of these persons, who was no other than Tom Syddall, the Jacobite barber—a very active, resolute little fellow—ran up to the collegiate church, which was at no great distance from his shop, and soon found the man of whom he was in search—Isaac Clegg, the beadle.

Now Isaac being a Jacobite, like himself, was easily persuaded to ring the fire-bell; and the alarm being thus given, a mob was quickly raised. But no effectual opposition could be offered—the approach to the bridge from Smithy Bank being strongly barricaded. Behind the barricades stood the constables, who laughed at the mob, and set them at defiance.

"The boroughreeve will blow up the bridge in spite of you," they cried.

"If he does, he'll repent it," answered several angry voices from the crowd, which rapidly increased in number, and presented a very formidable appearance.

Already it had been joined by the desperadoes armed with bludgeons, who had figured in the previous disturbance in the market-place, and were quite ready for more mischief.

The usual Jacobite cries were heard, but these were now varied by "Down with the boroughreeve!" "Down with the constables!"

Mr. Fielden himself was on the bridge, with his brother magistrates, superintending the operations, and irritated by the insolent shouts of the mob, he came forward to address them.

For a few minutes they would not listen to him, but at last he obtained a hearing.

"Go home quietly," he cried, in a loud voice. "Go home like loyal and peaceful subjects of the king. We mean to destroy the bridge to prevent the entrance of the rebels."

On this there was a terrific shout, accompanied by groans, yells, and hootings.

"Down with Fielden!—down with Fielden!" cried a hundred voices. "He shan't do it!"

"Mark my words," vociferated the boroughreeve, who remained perfectly unmoved amid the storm, "in five minutes from this time the central arch will be blown up."

"We will prevent it," roared the mob, shaking their hands at him.

"You can't prevent it," rejoined the boroughreeve, contemptuously. "Two large boxes filled with gunpowder are sunk beneath the arch, and on a signal from me will be fired."

Surprise kept the mob quiet for a moment, and before another outburst could take place, the boroughreeve had turned on his heel, and marched off.

Meantime, the three young damsels, under the careful guidance of Jemmy Dawson, had made their way, without experiencing any annoyance, to the precipitous rock on which Atherton Legh had stood, while contemplating the same scene on the previous night.

From this lofty position, as the reader is aware, the bridge was completely commanded. Another person was on the rock when they reached it. This was Isaac Clegg, the beadle, who was well known to Beppy. He instantly made way for her and her friends, and proved useful in giving them some necessary information.

He told them exactly what was going on on the bridge—explained how the angry mob was kept back by the barricade—pointed out the boroughreeve—and finally drew their attention to the engineers in the boat beneath the arch ready to fire the caissons.

As will readily be supposed, it was this part of the singular scene that excited the greatest interest among the spectators asembled on the rock. But, shortly afterwards, their interest was intensified to the highest degree.

A boat was suddenly seen on the river, about a bow-shot above the bridge. It must have been concealed somewhere, for its appearance took all the beholders by surprise. The boat was rowed by two men, who seemed to have disguised themselves, for they were strangely muffled up. Plying their oars vigorously, they came down the stream with great swiftness.

From the course taken it would almost seem as if they

were making for the central arch, beneath which the engineers were posted. Evidently the engineers thought so, for they stood up in their boat and shouted lustily to the others to keep off. But the two oarsmen held on their course, and even increased their speed.

Though the two men had disguised themselves, they did not altogether escape detection, for as they dashed past the rock on which Constance and the others were stationed, the foremost oarsman momentarily turned his head in that direction, and disclosed the features of Atherton Legh; while Isaac Clegg declared his conviction that the second oarsman was no other than Tom Syddall.

"'Tis Tom, I be sartin," said Isaac. "He has put on a different sort of wig from that he usually wears, and has tied a handkerchief over his keven-huller, but I'd swear to his nose. What can have induced him to make this mad attempt?"

It was a moment of breathless suspense, for the purpose of the daring oarsmen could no longer be doubted. Not only were they anxiously watched by the spectators on the rock, but the gaze of hundreds was fixed upon them.

Mingled and contradictory shouts were raised—"Keep off!" "Go on!" But the latter predominated.

The engineers prepared to receive the shock they could not avert. In another instant, the boat propelled by all the force the rowers could exert, dashed into them, and staved in the side of their bark.

No longer any question of blowing up the arch. The engineers were both precipitated into the river by the collision, and had to swim ashore.

Leaving them, however, to shift for themselves, the two daring oarsmen continued their rapid course down the stream, amid the deafening shouts of the crowd on Smithy Bank.

Such excitement was caused by this bold exploit that the mob could no longer be kept back.

Breaking through the barricade, and driving off the guard,

after a short struggle, they took possession of the bridge—declaring their fixed determination not to allow it to be damaged. Compelled to beat a hasty retreat into Salford, the magistrates were glad to escape without injury.

CHAPTER XVI.

TOM SYDDALL.

FOR some time the two oarsmen rowed on as swiftly as they could, fancying they should be pursued, but finding this was not the case, they began to relax their efforts, and liberated themselves from their disguises.

When divested of the handkerchief tied round his head, and of some other coverings concealing the lower part of his visage, Tom Syddall was fully revealed.

'Twas a physiognomy not easily to be mistaken, owing to the size of the nose, which, besides being enormous, was sin-singularly formed. Moreover, Tom's face was hatchet-shaped.

He had a great soul in a small body. Though a little fellow, he was extremely active, and full of spirit—capable, in his own opinion, of great things. A slight boaster, perhaps, but good-tempered, rarely taking offence if laughed at. Tom despised his vocation, and declared he was cut out for a soldier, but he also declared he would never serve King George—so a barber he remained.

Though there was something ludicrous in his assumption, no one who knew him doubted that he would fight—and fight manfully, too—for the Stuarts, should the opportunity ever be offered him.

Ordinarily, Tom Syddall's manner was comic, but he put on a sombre and tragic expression, when alluding to his father, who was executed for taking part in the rebellion of 1715—his head being fixed upon a spike in the market-place

Chetham's from Hunts Bank.

Tom had vowed to avenge his father, and frequently referred to the oath. Such was Tom Syddall, whose personal appearance and peculiarities rendered him a noticeable character in Manchester at the time.

His companion, it is scarcely necessary to say, was Atherton Legh.

As they rested for a moment upon their oars they both laughed heartily.

"We may be proud of the exploit we have performed," cried Tom. "We have served the prince, and saved the bridge. Three minutes later and the arch would have been blown up. The scheme was well-designed, and well-executed."

"You deserve entire credit both for plan and execution, Tom," rejoined Atherton.

"Nay, sir," said Syddall with affected modesty. "'Twas a bold and well-conceived scheme I admit, but I could not have carried it out without your aid. I trust we may always be successful in our joint undertakings. With you for a leader I would not shrink from any enterprise, however hazardous it might appear. I was struck with your coolness. 'Tis a good sign in a young man."

"Well, I think we are both taking it easily enough, Tom," said Atherton. "We are loitering here as calmly as if nothing had happened. However, I don't think any pursuit need be apprehended. The boroughreeve will have enough to do to look after the mob."

"Ay, that he will," said Syddall. "He has but a very short tenure of office left. The prince will soon be here, and then all will be changed. Did you notice those ladies on the rock near the bridge? They seemed greatly excited, and cheered us."

"Yes, I saw them, and I am glad they saw us, Tom One of them was Sir Richard Rawcliffe's daughter. I felt my arm strengthened when I found she was watching us. I think I could have done twice as much as I did."

"You did quite enough, sir," observed Syddall, smiling. "But shall we land, or drop quietly down the river for a mile or two, and then return by some roundabout road?"

"Let us go on," said Atherton. "I don't think it will be safe to return just yet."

By this time, though they had not left the bridge much more than half-a-mile behind, they were completely in the country. On the right the banks were still high and rocky, narrowing the stream, and shutting out the view.

But though the modern part of the town extended in this direction, two or three fields intervened between the houses and the river. On the left, the banks being low, the eye could range over pleasant meadows around which the Irwell meandered, forming a charming prospect from the heights overlooking the wide valley through which it pursued its winding course.

So nearly complete was the circle described by the river, that the upper part of the stream was here not very far distant from the lower.

But our object in depicting this locality is to show how wonderfully it is changed. The meadows just alluded to, intersected by hedgerows, and with only two or three farmhouses to be seen amidst them, are now covered with buildings of all kinds—warehouses, mills, and other vast structures. Bridges now span the river; innumerable houses are reared upon its banks; and scarce a foot of ground remains unoccupied.

In a word, an immense and populous town has sprung up, covering the whole area encircled by the Irwell, and the pleasing country scene we have endeavoured to describe has for ever vanished. Few persons would imagine that the polluted river was once bright and clear, and its banks picturesque, and fringed with trees. Yet such was the case little more than a century ago.

Salford at that time was comprised within very narrow limits, and only possessed a single street, which communicated with the old bridge. In Manchester, between the upper part of Deansgate and the river, there were fields entirely unbuilt upon, and a lane bordered by hedges ran down through these fields to the quay.

The quay itself was very small, and consisted of a wharf with a house and warehouse attached to it.

It seems astonishing that a town so important as was Manchester in 1745, should not have had a larger storehouse for goods, but apparently the merchants were content with it. Barges were then towed up the river as far as the quay, but not beyond.

As Atherton and his companion rowed slowly down the river, they did not encounter a single boat till they came in sight of the wharf, where a barge and a few small craft were moored. They now debated with themselves whether to land here or go lower down: and at length decided upon halting, thinking there could be no danger. But they were mistaken. As they drew near the wharf, three men armed with muskets suddenly appeared on the deck of the barge, and commanded them to stop.

"You are prisoners," cried one of these persons. "We have just received information by a mounted messenger of the occurrence at Salford Bridge, and we know you to be the men who ran down the engineers. You are prisoners, I repeat. Attempt to move off and we will fire upon you."

As the muskets were levelled at their heads from so short a distance, Atherton and his companion felt that resistance would be useless, so they surrendered at discretion, and prepared to disembark. Some other men, who were standing by, took charge of them as they stepped ashore.

CHAPTER XVII.

HOW TOM SYDDALL WAS CARRIED HOME IN TRIUMPH.

In another minute the person who had addressed them from the barge came up, and Tom Syddall, who now recognised him as Matthew Sharrocks, the wharf-master, inquired what he meant to do with them.

"Detain you till I learn the magistrates' intentions respecting you," replied Sharrocks. "The boroughreeve will be forthwith acquainted with the capture. The messenger is waiting. Do you deny the offence?"

"No, I glory in the deed," rejoined Syddall. "Tis an action of which we may be justly proud. We have saved the bridge from destruction at the risk of our own lives."

"You will be clapped into prison and punished for what you have done," said Sharrocks.

"If we should be imprisoned, Sharrocks, which I doubt," rejoined Syddall, confidently, "the people will deliver us. Know you who I am?"

"Well enough; you are Tom Syddall, the barber," said the other.

"I am the son of that Tom Syddall who approved his devotion to the royal House of Stuart with his blood."

"Ay, I recollect seeing your father's head stuck up in the market-place," said Sharrocks. "Take care your own is not set up in the same spot."

He then marched off to despatch the messenger to the boroughreeve, and on his return caused the prisoners to be taken to the great storehouse, from an upper window of which was suspended a flag, emblazoned with the royal arms.

"I tell you what, Sharrocks," said Syddall, "before two days that flag will be hauled down."

"I rather think not," rejoined the wharf-master dryly.

Atherton Legh took no part in this discourse, but maintained a dignified silence.

The prisoners were then shut up in a small room near the entrance of the storehouse, and a porter armed with a loaded musket was placed as a sentinel at the door.

However, except for the restraint, they had no reason to complain of their treatment. A pint of wine was brought them, with which they regaled themselves, and after drinking a couple of glasses, Tom, who had become rather downcast, felt his spirits considerably revive.

Knocking at the door, he called out to the porter, " I say, friend, if not against rules, I should very much like a pipe."

The porter being a good-natured fellow said he would see about it, and presently returned with a pipe and a paper of tobacco. His wants being thus supplied, Tom sat down and smoked away very comfortably.

Atherton paid very little attention to him. Truth to say, he was thinking of Constance Rawcliffe.

Rather more than an hour had elapsed, and Mr. Sharrocks was expecting an answer from the boroughreeve, when he heard a tumultuous sound in the lane, already described as leading from the top of Deansgate to the quay.

Alarmed by this noise, he hurried to the great gate, which he had previously ordered to be closed, and looking out, perceived a mob, consisting of some three or four hundred persons, hurrying towards the spot.

If he had any doubt as to their intentions it would have been dispelled by hearing that their cry was " Tom Syddall ! " Evidently they were coming to liberate the brave barber.

Hastily shutting and barring the gate, and ordering the porters to guard it, he flew to the room in which Tom and his companion were confined, and found the one tranquilly smoking his pipe, as we have related, and the other seated in a chair opposite him, and plunged in a reverie.

" Well, Sharrocks," said Tom, blowing a whiff from his mouth, and looking up quietly at him, " have you come to say that the boroughreeve has ordered us to be clapped in prison? ha!"

"I have come to set you free, gentlemen," said the wharf-master, blandly. "You are quite at liberty to depart."

"Ho! ho!" cried Tom. "You have altered your tone, methinks, Sharrocks."

"I am in no hurry," said Atherton. "I am quite comfortable here."

"But you *must* and *shall* go," cried Sharrocks.

"Must! and shall!!" echoed Atherton. "Suppose we refuse to stir!—what then?"

"Yes, what then, Sharrocks?" said Tom, replacing the pipe in his mouth.

The wharf-master was about to make an angry rejoinder, when a loud noise outside convinced him that the porters had yielded to the mob, and thrown open the gates.

"Zounds! they have got into the yard!" he exclaimed.

"Who have got in?" cried Atherton, springing to his feet.

"Your friends, the mob," replied Sharrocks.

"Hurrah!" exclaimed Syddall, jumping up likewise, and waving his pipe over his head. "I knew the people would come to release us. Hurrah! hurrah!"

Almost frantic with delight, he ran out into the yard, followed by Atherton—Sharrocks bringing up the rear.

Already the yard was half-full of people, most of whom were gathered thickly in front of the storehouse, and the moment they perceived Tom Syddall and Atherton, they set up a tremendous shout.

But Tom was their especial favourite. Those nearest placed him on the top of an empty cask, so that he could be seen by the whole assemblage, and in reply to their prolonged cheers, he thanked them heartily for coming to deliver him and his companion, telling them they would soon see the prince in Manchester, and bidding them, in conclusion, shout for King James the Third and Charles, Prince Regent—setting them the example himself.

While the yard was ringing with treasonable shouts and outcries, Tom quitted his post, but he soon reappeared. He had made his way to the upper room of the building, from the window of which the obnoxious flag was displayed. Hauling it down, he tore off the silken banner in sight of the crowd, and replacing it with a white handkerchief, brought down the rebel flag he had thus improvised, and gave it to one of the spectators, who carried it about in triumph.

Hitherto the mob had behaved peaceably enough, but they now grew rather disorderly, and some of them declared they would not go away empty-handed.

Fearing they might plunder the store-house, which was full of goods of various kinds, Sharrocks came up to Tom Syddall and besought him to use his influence with them to depart peaceably.

"I'll try what I can do, Sharrocks," replied Tom. "Though you made some uncalled-for observations upon me just now, I don't bear any malice."

"I'm very sorry for what I said, Mr. Syddall," rejoined the wharf-master, apologetically—"very sorry, indeed."

"Enough. I can afford to be magnanimous, Sharrocks. I forgive the remarks. But you will find you were wrong, sir—you will find that I *shall* avenge my father."

"I have no doubt of it, Mr. Syddall," rejoined Sharrocks. "But in the meantime, save the storehouse from plunder, and you shall have my good word with the boroughreeve."

"I don't want your good word, Sharrocks," said Tom, disdainfully.

With Atherton's assistance he then once more mounted the cask, and the crowd seeing he was about to address them became silent.

"I have a few words to say to you, my friends," he cried, in a voice that all could hear. "Don't spoil the good work you have done by committing any excesses. Don't let the

Hanoverians and Presbyterians have the power of casting reproach upon us. Don't disgrace the good cause. Our royal prince shoots every Highlander who pillages. He won't shoot any of you, but he'll think better of you if you abstain from plunder."

The commencement of this address was received with some murmurs, but these ceased as the speaker went on, and at the close he was loudly cheered, and it was evident from their altered demeanour that the crowd intended to follow his advice.

" I am glad to find you mean to behave like good Jacobites and honest men. Now let us go home quietly, and unless we're assaulted we won't break the peace."

"We'll carry you home safely," shouted several of the bystanders. " A chair! a chair! Give us a chair!"

These demands were promptly complied with by Sharrocks, who brought out a large arm-chair, in which Tom being installed, was immediately hoisted aloft by four sturdy individuals.

Thus placed, he bowed right and left, in acknowledgement of the cheers of the assemblage.

Not wishing to take a prominent part in these proceedings, Atherton had kept aloof, but he now came up to Syddall, and shaking hands with him, told him in a whisper that he might expect to see him at night.

The brave little Jacobite barber was then borne off in triumph, surrounded by his friends—a tall man marching before him carrying the white flag.

The procession took its way up the lane to Deansgate, along which thoroughfare it slowly moved, its numbers continually increasing as it went on, while the windows of the houses were thronged with spectators.

Thus triumphantly was Tom conveyed to his dwelling. Throughout the whole route no molestation was offered him —the magistrates prudently abstaining from further interference.

Before quitting him, the crowd promised to come to his succour should any attempt be made to arrest him.

Atherton did not join the procession, but took a totally different route.

Leaving the boat with the wharf-master, who volunteered to take care of it, he caused himself to be ferried across the river, and soon afterwards entered a path leading across the fields in the direction of Salford.

He walked along very slowly, being anxious to hold a little self-communion; and stopped now and then to give free scope to his reflections.

CHAPTER XVIII.

THE MEETING IN THE GARDEN.

FROM these fields, the town, which was scarcely a mile distant, could be seen in its full extent. In saying "town," we include Salford, for no break in the continuity of the houses was distinguishable. The buildings on either side of the Irwell seemed massed together; and the bridge was entirely hidden.

It was not a very bright day—we must recollect it was November—but the lights chanced to be favourable, and brought out certain objects in a striking manner. For instance, the collegiate church, which formed almost the central part of the picture, stood out in bold relief, with its massive tower against a clear sky. A gleam of sunshine fell upon St. Ann's Church and upon the modern buildings near it, and Trinity Church in Salford was equally favoured. Other charming effects were produced, which excited the young man's admiration, and he remained gazing for some time at the prospect. He then accelerated his pace, and soon reached the outskirts of Salford.

At the entrance of the main street stood Trinity Church, to which we have just alluded—a modern pile of no great beauty, but possessing a lofty tower ornamented with pinnacles, and surmounted by a short spire. The row of houses on the right side of the street formed pleasant residences, for they had extensive gardens running down to the banks of the river.

Opposite the church, but withdrawn from the street, stood an old-fashioned mansion with a garden in front, surrounded by high walls. The place had a neglected air. Large gates of wrought iron, fashioned in various devices, opened upon the garden. Recollecting to have heard that this old mansion was occupied by ˙Mrs. Butler—Monica's mother and Constance's aunt—Atherton stopped to look at it, and while peering through the iron gates, he beheld Miss Rawcliffe herself in the garden.

She was alone, and the impulse that prompted him to say a few words to her being too strong to be resisted, he opened the gates and went in. She had disappeared, but he found her seated in an arbour.

On beholding him she uttered a cry of surprise, and started up. For a moment the colour deserted her cheek, but the next instant a blush succeeded.

"I am glad to see you, Mr. Atherton Legh," she said. "But how did you learn I was here?"

"Accident has brought me hither," he replied. "While passing the garden gates I chanced to see you, and ventured in. If I have been too bold, I will retire at once."

"Oh, no—pray stay! I am delighted to see you. But you are very incautious to venture forth. You ought to keep in some place of concealment. However, let me offer you my meed of admiration. I was wonderstruck by your last gallant exploit."

"You helped me to accomplish it."

"*I* helped you—how? I was merely a spectator."

"That was quite sufficient. I felt your eyes were upon me. I fancied I had your approval."

"I most heartily wished you success," she rejoined, again blushing deeply. "But I think you are excessively rash. Suppose the caissons had been fired, you would have been destroyed by the explosion."

"In that case I might have had your sympathy."

"Yes, but my sympathy would have been worth very little. It would not have brought you to life."

"It would have made death easy."

"With such exalted sentiments, 'tis a pity you did not live in the days of chivalry."

"If I had I would have maintained the peerless beauty of the dame I worshipped against all comers."

"Now you are beginning to talk high-flown nonsense, so I must stop you."

But she did not look offended.

Presently she added, "Do you desire to win distinction? Do you wish to please me?"

"I desire to please you more than any one on earth, Miss Rawcliffe," he rejoined, earnestly. "I will do whatever you ask me."

"Then join the prince. But no! I ought not to extort this pledge from you. Reflect! reflect!"

"No need of reflection. My decision is made. I will join the Manchester Regiment."

"Then I will place the sash on your shoulder, and gird on your sword," she said.

A fire seemed kindled in the young man's breast by these words. Casting an impassioned glance at the fair maiden, he prostrated himself at her feet, and taking her hand, which she did not withhold, pressed it to his lips.

"I devote myself to you," he said, in a fervent tone.

"And to the good cause?" she cried.

"To the good cause," he rejoined. "But chiefly to you."

Before he could rise from his kneeling posture, Monica and

Jemmy Dawson, who had come forth from the house, approached the arbour, but seeing how matters stood, they would have retired; but Constance, who did not exhibit the slightest embarrassment, advanced to meet them.

"I have gained another recruit for the prince," she said.

"So I see," replied Monica. "His royal highness could not have a better officer."

"I am sure not," said Jemmy Dawson.

And embracing his friend, he cried, "I longed for you as a companion-in-arms, and my desire is gratified. We shall serve together—conquer together—or die together. Whatever it may be, apparently our destiny will be the same."

"You are certain of a rich reward," said Atherton. "But I——"

"Live in hope," murmured Constance.

"Not till I have discovered the secret of my birth will I presume to ask your hand," said the young man.

Constance thought of the packet confided to her by her father—of the letter she had read—and felt certain the mystery would be soon unravelled.

Just then Monica interposed.

"Pray come into the house, Mr. Atherton Legh," she said. "Mamma will be much pleased to see you. We have been extolling you to the skies. She is a great invalid, and rarely leaves her room, but to-day, for a wonder, she is downstairs."

Atherton did not require a second bidding, but went with them into the house.

CHAPTER XIX.

MRS. BUTLER.

IN a large, gloomy-looking, plainly-furnished room might be seen a middle-aged dame, who looked like the superior of a religious house—inasmuch as she wore a conventual robe of dark stuff, with a close hood that fell over her shoulders, and a frontlet beneath it that concealed her locks—blanched by sorrow more than age. From her girdle hung a rosary. Her figure was thin almost to emaciation, but it was hidden by her dress; her cheeks were pallid; her eyes deep sunk in their sockets; but her profile still retained its delicacy and regularity of outline, and showed she must once have possessed rare beauty. Her countenance wore a sweet, sad, resigned expression.

Mrs. Butler—for she it was—suffered from great debility, brought on, not merely by ill-health, but by frequent vigils and fasting. So feeble was she that she seldom moved beyond a small room, adjoining her bed-chamber, which she used as an oratory; but on that day she had been induced by her daughter to come down-stairs.

She was seated in a strong, oaken chair, destitute of a cushion, and propped up by a pillow, which she deemed too great an indulgence, but which was absolutely requisite for her support. Her small feet—of which she had once been vain—rested on a fauteuil. On a little table beside her lay a book of devotion.

On the opposite side of the fireplace sat a thin, dark-complexioned man, in age between fifty and sixty, whose black habiliments and full powdered wig did not indicate that he was a Romish priest. Such, however, was the case. He was Sir Richard Rawcliffe's confessor, Father Jerome. At the time when we discover them, the priest was addressing words of ghostly counsel to the lady, who was listening attentively to his exhortations.

They were interrupted by the entrance of the party.

As Atherton was conducted towards her, Mrs. Butler essayed to rise, but being unequal to the effort, would have immediately sunk back if her daughter had not supported her.

She seemed very much struck by the young man, and could not remove her gaze from him.

"Who is this, Monica?" she murmured.

"He is the young gentleman, mamma, of whose courage Constance has been speaking to you in such glowing terms—who so gallantly liberated Sir Richard from arrest this morning, and subsequently preserved Salford Bridge from destruction. It is Mr. Atherton Legh. I felt sure you would like to see him."

"You judged quite right, my dear," Mrs. Butler replied, in her soft, sweet accents. "I am very glad to see you, sir. Pardon my gazing at you so fixedly. You bear a strong resemblance to one long since dead—a near relation of my own. Do you not remark the likeness, father?" she added to the priest.

"Indeed, madam, I am much struck by it," replied Father Jerome.

"I am sure you mean my uncle, Sir Oswald," observed Constance.

"True. But as Mr. Legh has probably never heard of him, I did not mention his name."

"I think you have a miniature of my uncle?" said Constance.

"I had one," returned Mrs. Butler. "But I know not what has become of it."

"Strange! I never saw a portrait of him," remarked Constance. "There is not one at Rawcliffe. Nor is there a portrait of his beautiful wife, who did not long survive him."

"There you are mistaken, Miss Rawcliffe," observed Father Jerome. "Portraits of both are in existence, for I myself have seen them. But they are locked up in a closet."

"Why should they be locked up?" cried Monica.

"Probably Sir Richard does not care to see them," said her mother, sighing deeply. "But let us change the subject We are talking on family matters that can have no interest to Mr. Atherton Legh."

Atherton would have been pleased if more had been said on the subject, but he made no remark. Constance was lost in reflection. Many strange thoughts crossed her mind.

At this juncture Jemmy Dawson interposed.

"You will be glad to learn, madam," he said to Mrs. Butler, "that my friend Atherton Legh has decided on joining the Manchester Regiment. Constance has the credit of gaining him as a recruit."

"That a young man of so much spirit as your friend should support the cause of the Stuarts cannot fail to be highly satisfactory to me, in common with every zealous Jacobite," said Mrs. Butler. "May success attend you both! But it is for you, father, to bless them—not for me."

Thus enjoined, the two young men bent reverently before the priest, who, extending his hands over them, ejaculated fervently:

"May the Lord of Hosts be with you on the day of battle, and grant you victory! May you both return in safety and claim your reward!"

To this Mrs. Butler added, with great earnestness and emotion:

"Should Heaven permit them to be vanquished—should they be taken captive—may they be spared the cruel fate that befel so many, who, in by-gone days, fought in the same righteous cause, and suffered death for their loyalty and devotion."

This supplication, uttered in sorrowful tones, produced a powerful impression upon all the hearers.

"Why have you drawn this sad picture, mamma?" said Monica, half reproachfully.

"I could not repress my feelings, my child. A terrible scene perpetually rises before me, and I feel it will haunt me to the last."

"Have you witnessed such a scene, mamma?" cried her daughter, trembling. "You have never spoken of it to me?"

"I have often wished to do so, but I felt the description

would give you pain. Are you equal to it now, do yo think?"

"Yes," she replied, with attempted firmness, but quivering lip.

"And you, Constance?" said Mrs. Butler.

"I can listen to you, aunt," rejoined Constance, in tones that did not falter.

Before commencing, Mrs. Butler consulted Father Jerome by a glance, and his counsel to her was conveyed in these words, "Better relieve your mind, madam."

"I was very young," she said, "younger than you, Monica, when the greatest sorrow of my life occurred. At the time of the former rising in 1715, my faith was plighted to one who held a command in the insurgent army. I will not breathe his name, but he belonged to a noble family that had made great sacrifices for King James the Second, and was prepared to make equal sacrifices for the Chevalier de St. George. The brave and noble youth to whom I was betrothed was sanguine of success, and I had no misgivings. I was with him at Preston during the battle, and when the capitulation took place, he confided me to a friend whom he loved as a brother, saying to him, 'Should my life be taken by our bloodthirsty foes, as I have reason to fear it will, be to her what I would have been. Regard her as my widow—wed her.' His friend gave the promise he required, and he kept his word."

Here she paused for a short time, while Monica and Constance—neither of whom had ever heard of this singular promise, or of the betrothal that preceded it—looked at each other.

Meanwhile, a change came over Mrs. Butler's countenance —the expression being that of horror.

Her lips were slightly opened, her large dark eyes dilated, and though they were fixed on vacancy, it was easy to perceive that a fearful vision was rising before her.

"Ay, there it is," she cried, in tones and with a look that

froze the blood of her hearers—" there is the scaffold!" stretching out her hand, as if pointing to some object. "'Tis there, as I beheld it on that fatal morn on Tower Hill. 'Tis draped in black. The block is there, the axe, the coffin, the executioner. A vast concourse is assembled—and what an expression is in their faces! But where is he? I see him not. Ah! now he steps upon the scaffold. How young, how handsome he looks! How undaunted is his bearing! Every eye is fixed upon him, and a murmur of pity bursts from the multitude. He looks calmly round. He has discovered me. He smiles, and encourages me by his looks. Some ceremonies have to be performed, but these are quickly over. He examines the block—the coffin—with unshaken firmness—and feels the edge of the axe. Then he prays with the priest who attends him. All his preparations made, he bows an eternal farewell to me, and turns——Ha! I can see no more —'tis gone!"

And she sank back half fainting in the chair, while her daughter and niece sought to revive her.

So vivid had been the effect produced, that those present almost fancied they had witnessed the terrible scene described.

For a brief space not a word was spoken. At the end of that time, Mrs. Butler opened her eyes, and fixing them upon the young men, exclaimed:

"Again, I pray Heaven to avert such a fate from you both!"

Monica burst into tears. Her lover flew towards her, and as she seemed about to swoon, he caught her in his arms.

"Ah! Jemmy," she exclaimed, looking up at him tenderly, "how could I live if I lost you! You must not join this perilous expedition."

"Nay, I cannot honourably withdraw," he replied. "My promise is given to the prince. Were I to retire now I should be termed a coward. And all my love for you would not enable me to bear that dreadful reproach."

"'Tis I who induced you to join," she cried. "If you

perish, I shall be guilty of your death. You must not—shall not go."

"How is this?" he cried. "I cannot believe you are the brave Jacobite girl who urged me to take arms for the good cause."

"My love, I find, is stronger than my loyalty," she replied. "Do not leave me, Jemmy. A sad presentiment has come over me, and I dread lest you should perish by the hand of the executioner."

"This idle foreboding of ill is solely caused by your mother's fancied vision. Shake it off, and be yourself."

"Ay, be yourself, Monica," said Constance, stepping towards them. "This weakness is unworthy of you. 'Tis quite impossible for Jemmy to retreat with honour from his plighted word. Those who have embarked in this hazardous enterprise must go through it at whatever risk."

And she glanced at Atherton, who maintained a firm countenance.

But Monica fixed a supplicating look on her lover, and sought to move him.

Fearing he might yield to her entreaties, Constance seized his hand.

"For your sake I am bound to interpose, Jemmy," she said. "You will for ever repent it, if you make a false step now. What is life without honour?"

"Heed her not!" exclaimed Monica. "Listen to me! Till now I never knew how dear you are to me. I cannot—will not part with you."

Both Mrs. Butler and Father Jerome heard what was passing, but did not deem it necessary to interfere—leaving the task to Constance.

"Take him hence!" said Constance, in a low tone to Atherton. "She may shake his determination. Ere long she will recover her energies, and think quite differently."

After bidding adieu to Mrs. Butler and the priest, Atherton tried to lead Jemmy gently away. But Monica still clung to him.

"Come with me," said Atherton. "I want to say a few words to you in private."

"Say what you have to tell him here," observed Monica.

"This is mere childishness, Monica," observed Constance. "Let him go with his friend."

Monica offered no further resistance, and the two young men quitted the room together.

No sooner were they gone than Monica flew towards Mrs. Butler, and throwing herself at her feet, exclaimed:

"Oh, mother! let us pray that Jemmy may not share the tragical fate of him you have mourned so long. Let us pray that he may not die the death of a traitor!"

"A traitor!" exclaimed Mrs. Butler. "He whom I mourn was no traitor."

"Listen to me, daughter," said Father Jerome, in a tone of solemn rebuke. "Should he to whom you are betrothed fall a sacrifice to tyranny, oppression, and usurpation—should he suffer in the cause of truth and justice—should he lay down his life in asserting the right of his only lawful sovereign, King James the Third—then be assured that he will not die a traitor, but a martyr."

Monica bore this reproof well. Looking up at her mother and the priest, she said, in penitential tones:

"Forgive me. I see my error. I will no longer try to dissuade him, but will pray that he may have grace to fulfil the task he has undertaken."

CHAPTER XX.

THE JACOBITE MEETING IN TOM SYDDALL'S BACK ROOM.

TOM SYDDALL's shop was situated on Smithy Bank, in the immediate neighbourhood both of the Cross and of Salford Bridge.

The house was a diminutive specimen of the numerous timber and plaster habitations, chequered black and white, that abounded on the spot; but it was quite large enough for Tom. The gables were terminated by grotesquely-carved faces, that seemed perpetually grinning and thrusting out their tongues at the passers-by; and a bay-window projected over the porch, the latter being ornamented with a large barber's pole and a brass basin, as indications of Tom's calling, though his shop was sufficiently well-known without them.

The door usually stood invitingly open, even at an early hour in the morning, and the barber himself could be seen in the low-roofed room, covering some broad-visaged customer's cheeks with lather, or plying the keen razor over his chin, while half-a-dozen others could be descried seated on benches patiently waiting their turn.

At a somewhat later hour the more important business of wig-dressing began, and then Tom retired to a back room, where the highest mysteries of his art were screened from the vulgar gaze—and from which sacred retreat, when a customer emerged, he appeared in all the dignity of a well-powdered peruke, a full-bottomed tie-wig, a bob, a bob-major, or an apothecary's bust, as the case might be.

Tom did a great deal of business, and dressed some of the best "heads" in Manchester—not only ladies' heads, but gentlemen's—but, of course, he attended the ladies at their own houses.

But Tom Syddall, as we have seen, was not only a perruquier, but an ardent politician. Frequent Jacobite meetings were held in his back room, and plots were frequently hatched when it was thought that perukes alone were being dressed.

Perfectly loyal and trustworthy was Tom. Many secrets were confided to him, but none were ever betrayed. Every opportunity was afforded him for playing the spy, had he been so minded, but he would have scorned the office.

However, he had his special objects of dislike, and would neither dress the wig of a Whig, nor shave a Presbyterian if he knew it. Equally decided was Tom on his religious opinions, being a zealous member of Dr. Deacon's True British Catholic Church.

After his great exploit at the bridge, and his subsequent deliverance by the mob, several Jacobites came in the evening —when his shop was closed—to offer him their congratulations, and were introduced—as they arrived singly, or two or three at a time—to the back room, of which we have just made mention.

By-and-by a tolerably large party assembled, all of whom being very decided Jacobites, a good deal of treason was naturally talked.

As there were not chairs for all, several of the company sat where they could, and a droll effect was produced in consequence of their being mixed up with the wig-blocks, one of which, from its elevated position, seemed to preside over the assemblage, and caused much laughter.

Among the persons present were Dr. Byrom and Dr. Deacon, the latter of them having with him his three sons, all of whom were fine-looking young men.

Besides these there was the Rev. Thomas Coppock, who, it may be remembered, had been promised the appointment of chaplain to the Manchester Regiment by Colonel Townley. Though the young Jacobite divine wore his cassock and bands, he looked as if martial accoutrements would have suited him better. His big looks and blustering manner did not harmonise with his clerical habit. Vain and ambitious, Parson Coppock fully believed—if the expedition proved successful—he should be created Bishop of Chester, or, at least, be made warden of the collegiate church.

With those we have particularised were four other young men who had been promised commissions—Thomas Chadwick, John Berwick, George Fletcher, and Samuel Maddocks.

When we have added the names of Jemmy Dawson and Atherton Legh, the list of the party will be complete.

An important communication had been made to the

meeting by Dr. Deacon, who had just received an express informing him that the prince had arrived at Preston with the first division of his army, so that Lord Pitsligo's regiment of horse might be expected to reach Manchester on the morrow.

"Of this information, gentlemen," pursued Dr. Deacon, "you alone are in possession, for precautions have been taken to prevent any other express from being sent from Preston to the authorities of Manchester. The magistrates, therefore, will be in complete ignorance of the prince's approach till he is close at hand. It will now be apparent to you how great has been the service rendered by Mr. Atherton Legh and our brave Tom Syddall. Had Salford Bridge been destroyed—according to the boroughreeve's plan—the prince could not have entered Manchester, without making a lengthened and troublesome détour, that might have exposed him to some unforeseen attack, whereas he will now march into the town at the head of his army without encountering any obstacle."

Expressions of approval were heard on all sides, and Syddall appeared quite elated by the commendations bestowed upon him.

"Since the prince will be here so soon it behoves us to prepare for him," he said. "Care must be taken that he does not want food for his men and forage for his horses. As you are all no doubt aware, a great quantity of provisions has been sent out of the town. This must be stopped."

"You are right, Tom," cried Dr. Byrom. "But how stop it?"

"Very easily," replied Syddall. "We must engage Ben Birch, the bellman, to go round to-night, and warn the townsfolk not to remove any more provisions."

"A good plan," cried Dr. Byrom. "But will Ben Birch obey the order?"

"If he won't I'll seize his bell and go round myself," rejoined Syddall. "But never fear, doctor; Ben will do it if he's well paid."

Part of Market Place, Manchester.

"But where is he to be found?" cried Dr. Byrom. "'Tis getting late."

"I know where to find him," replied Tom. "Before going home to bed he always takes his pot of ale and smokes his pipe at the Half Moon in Hanging Ditch. He's there now I'll warrant you."

Everybody agreed that the plan was excellent, and ought to be carried out without delay, and Syddall, who undertook the entire management of the affair, was just preparing to set off to Hanging Ditch, which was at no great distance from his dwelling, when a knock was heard at the outer door.

The company looked at each other. So many strange things occurred at this juncture that they could not help feeling some little uneasiness.

"Don't be alarmed, gentlemen," said Tom. "I'll go and reconnoitre."

So saying, he hurried up a staircase that quickly brought him to an upper room overlooking the street.

CHAPTER XXI.

BEN BIRCH, THE BELLMAN OF MANCHESTER.

It was a fine moonlight night, almost as bright as day, and when Tom looked out he saw that the person who had just knocked was no other than Ben Birch.

Now the bellman was a very important functionary at the time, and it seemed as if the town could not get on without him. Whenever anything was to be done the bellman was sent round. The magistrates constantly employed him, and he paced about the streets ringing his bell, and giving public notices of one kind or other, all day long.

Tall and stout, with a very red face, Ben Birch looked like a beadle, for he wore a laced cocked hat and a laced great-coat.

Fully aware of the importance of his office, he was consequential in manner, and his voice, when he chose to exert it, was perfectly stentorian. Ben Birch, we ought to add, was suspected of being a Jacobite.

"Why, Ben, is that you?" cried Tom, looking at him from the window.

"Ay, Mester Syddall, it's me, sure enough," replied the bellman. "I've got summat to tell you. Some mischievous chaps has been making free with your pow, and what dun yo think they've stuck on it?"

"I can't tell, Ben."

"Why, your feyther's skull. Yo can see it if yo look down. I noticed it as I were passing, and thought I'd stop and tell you."

"I should like to hang the rascal, whoever he may be, that has dared to profane that precious relic," cried Tom, furiously. "It must have been stolen, for I kept it carefully in a box."

"Well, it's a woundy bad joke, to say the least of it," rejoined Ben, with difficulty repressing a laugh. "Luckily, there's no harm done."

So saying, he took the pole and handed up the skull to the barber, who received it very reverently.

"Much obliged to you, Ben," he said, in a voice husky with emotion. "If I can only find out the rascal who has played me this trick he shall bitterly repent it."

"A Presbyterian, no doubt," cried the bellman.

"Ay, those prick-eared curs are all my enemies," said Syddall. "But we shall soon have a change. Wait a moment, Ben, I've got a job for you."

He then restored the relic to the box from which it had been abstracted, and went down-stairs.

On returning to the room where the company was assembled, he explained to them that the bellman was without, but said nothing about the indignity he himself had undergone.

"Shall I settle matters with him, or bring him in?" he asked.

"Bring him in," cried the assemblage.

In another moment Ben was introduced. Greatly surprised to find the room thus crowded, he stared at the party.

"What is your pleasure, gentlemen?" he said, removing his cocked hat and bowing.

"We have heard with great concern, Ben," said Mr. Coppock, gravely, "that provisions are beginning to run short in the town. We, therefore, desire that you will go round this very night, and give notice to the inhabitants that no victuals or stores of any kind must be removed on any pretext whatsoever."

"I am very willing to obey you, gentlemen, particularly as such a notice can do no harm," said Ben; "but I ought to have an order from the magistrates."

"This will do as well, I fancy," said Coppock, giving him a guinea.

"I'll do the job," rejoined the bellman, pocketing the fee. "I shan't fail to end my proclamation with 'God save the king!' but I shall leave those who hear me to guess *which* king I mean."

Wishing the company good-night he then went out, and shortly afterwards the loud ringing of his bell was heard in the street.

His first proclamation was made at the corner of Deansgate, and by this time—though the street had previously appeared quite empty—he had got a small crowd round him, while several persons appeared at the doors and windows.

"No more provisions to be taken away!" cried one of the bystanders; "that means the town is about to be besieged."

"That's not it," cried another. "It means that the young Pretender and his army will soon be here."

"Whatever it means you must obey the order," said the bellman. "And so, God save the king!"

"God save King James the Third!" "Down with the Elector of Hanover!" shouted several persons.

And as these were violently opposed by the supporters of the reigning monarch, and a fight seemed likely to ensue, the bellman marched off to repeat his proclamation elsewhere.

Meanwhile, the party assembled in Tom Syddall's back room had separated, but not before they had agreed upon another meeting at an early hour on the morrow.

Miniature of Bonnie Prince Charlie.

BOOK II.

PRINCE CHARLES EDWARD IN MANCHESTER.

CHAPTER I.

HOW MANCHESTER WAS TAKEN BY A SERGEANT, A DRUMMER, AND A SCOTTISH LASSIE.

MANCHESTER arose next day in a state of great ferment. No one exactly knew what was about to occur, but everybody felt something was at hand.

The proclamation made overnight by the bellman, and the studiously guarded answers given by that discreet functionary to the questions put to him, had caused considerable anxiety. No news had been received from Preston—except the secret express sent to the heads of the Jacobite party—but a notion prevailed that the prince would make his appearance in the course of the day.

Any real defence of the town was out of the question, since the militia was disbanded, but some staunch Whigs and zealous Presbyterians declared they would certainly make a stand. This, however, was looked upon as mere idle bravado. Most of those who had delayed their departure to the last moment now took flight. At an early hour on that very morning all the justices and lawyers had quitted the town. The boroughreeve had gone, but the constables remained at their post. As on the previous day, no business whatever was transacted, and the majority of the shops continued closed.

As the day went on the total want of news increased the public anxiety, for the few who were in possession of authentic information took care to keep it to themselves. The excitement, therefore, was increased by a variety of contradictory rumours, none of which had any foundation in truth, the Hanoverians doggedly maintaining that the young Pretender had turned back at Preston, and was now in full retreat to Scotland; while the Jacobites declared with equal warmth that the prince was within half a day's march of Manchester, and would soon present himself before the town.

Whatever might be the feelings of others, it is quite certain that all the prettiest damsels were impatiently expecting the handsome prince, and would have been sadly disappointed if he had turned back.

As the weather chanced to be fine, and no business was going on, a great many persons were in the streets, and the town had quite a holiday air.

Towards the afternoon, the crowds that had been rambling about during the morning had returned to their mid-day meal, when a cry arose from Salford that the advanced guard of the rebel army was in sight.

The report proved incorrect; yet it was not entirely without foundation. Three persons in Highland dresses, and no doubt belonging to the insurgent army, had actually entered the town by the Preston road, and were riding slowly along, looking about them in a very easy and unconcerned manner. All the beholders stared in astonishment, but nobody meddled with them, for it was naturally concluded that the regiment t ey belonged to must be close behind.

From its singularity, the little party was sufficient in it elf to attract general attention. It consisted of a sergeant, a drummer, and an exceedingly pretty Scottish lassie. All t iree were well mounted, though the state of their horses showed they had ridden many miles. Both the men were in full Highland dress, wore plumed caps, and were armed with claymore, dirk, and target. Moreover, the sergeant had a blunderbuss at his saddle-bow, but his comrade was content with the drum.

Sergeant Erick Dickson, a young Highlander, and bold as a lion, was handsome, well-proportioned, and possessed of great strength and activity. Sandy Rollo, the drummer, was likewise a very daring young fellow.

Helen Carnegie, the Scottish damsel, deserves a few more words. Her beauty and virtue were constant themes of praise among officers and men in the Highland army. Having given her heart to Erick Dickson, Helen Carnegie had accompanied him in the march from Edinburgh, after the victory at Preston Pans—or Gladsmuir, as the Highlanders called it—but her character was without reproach. Any man who had breathed a word against her fair fame would have had a quick reckoning with Erick.

Helen Carnegie was not yet nineteen, and perhaps her charms were not fully developed, but she was very beautiful notwithstanding. Her golden locks had first set the sergeant's heart on fire, and her bright blue eyes had kept up the flame ever since. Yet, after all, her exquisite figure was her greatest beauty. No nymph was ever more gracefully proportioned than Helen, and no costume could have suited her better than the one she adopted—the kilt being as long as a petticoat, while a plaid shawl was thrown over her knee when she was on horseback. The blue bonnet that crowned her golden locks was adorned with a white cockade.

Such was the little party that had entered Salford, and they all seemed much amused by the curiosity they excited.

Leaving them on their way to the bridge, it may now be proper to inquire what had brought them thither.

At Preston, on the previous evening, Sergeant Dickson came up to the Chevalier de Johnstone, his commanding officer, and aide-de-camp to Lord George Murray, lieutenant-general of the Highland army, and saluting him, said:

"May I have a word with you, colonel? I have been beating about Preston for recruits all day without getting one, and I am the more vexed, because the other sergeants have been very lucky."

"You ought to have taken Helen Carnegie with you, Erick," said Colonel Johnstone, laughing.

"That's exactly what I propose to do, colonel," said Dickson. "I've come to ask your honour's permission to set out an hour before dawn to-morrow for Manchester, and so get a day's march ahead of the army. I shall then be able to secure some recruits."

"I cannot grant your request," rejoined Colonel Johnstone. "What would you do alone in a strange town? You will be instantly taken prisoner—if you are not killed."

"Your honour needn't alarm yourself about me," replied Erick, in a wheedling voice, which, however, did not produce the desired effect. "I know how to take care of myself. If I get leave to go I'll take Helen Carnegie with me, and Rollo, the drummer."

Again the colonel shook his head.

"No, no, you mustn't think of it, Erick," he cried. "Go to your quarters, and don't stir out again to-night."

Sergeant Dickson retired, resolved to disobey orders, feeling certain the offence would be overlooked if he proved successful.

He therefore set out from Preston in good time next morning, accompanied by Helen and Rollo.

We left them riding towards Salford Bridge, and when they were within fifty yards of it, they came to a halt, and Rollo began to beat the drum vigorously. The din soon brought a great number of persons round them, who began to shout lustily, when the sergeant, judging the fitting moment had arrived to commence operations, silenced the drum, and doffing his plumed cap—his example being followed by his companions—called out in a loud voice, "God save King James the Third!"

Some cheers followed, but they were overpowered by angry outcries, and several voices exclaimed, "Down with the rebels!"

Judging from these menacing expressions that he was likely to be assailed, Erick, whose masculine visage had begun to assume a very formidable expression, placed himself in front of Helen so as to shield her from attack, and then hastily putting on his target, and getting his blunderbuss ready for immediate use, he glared fiercely round at the assemblage, roaring out:

"Keep off!—if ye wadna ha' the contents of this among ye."

Alarmed by his looks and gestures, the concourse held back; but only for a few moments. Some of them tried to lay hands on Helen, but they were baffled by the rapidity with which the sergeant wheeled round, dashing them back, and upsetting half-a-dozen of them.

But he had instantly to defend himself from another attack, and this he did with equal vigour and address, receiving all blows aimed at him on his target, and pointing the blunderbuss at those who attempted to seize him. However, he was careful not to fire, and shortly afterwards gave the blunderbuss to Helen and drew his claymore.

Meantime, Rollo, who was a very courageous fellow, though he had not the sergeant's activity, rendered what aid he could; but he was now beginning to be sorely pressed on all sides.

The conflict had lasted two or three minutes without any disadvantage to the sergeant, when several persons called upon him to yield. To this summons he answered disdainfully that he had never yet yielded, and never would, while his hand could grasp a sword.

"I have come to raise recruits for the yellow-haired laddie," he cried. "Will none of you join me? Will none of you serve the prince?"

Some voices answered in the affirmative, but those who called out were at a distance.

"Here, friends, here!" shouted Dickson, waving his claymore to them. "I want recruits for the yellow-haired laddie. Ye ken weel whom I mean."

"Ay, ay. We'll join!—we'll join!" cried twenty voices.

And the speakers tried to force their way toward Erick, but were prevented by the Presbyterians in the crowd.

The tumult that ensued operated in the sergeant's favour, and enabled him to keep his assailants at bay till assistance really arrived in the shape of a band of some fifty or sixty Jacobites, mustered on the instant, and headed by Tom Syddall.

It was now a scene of triumph and rejoicing. Since his opponents had taken to flight, and he was so numerously supported, Sergeant Dickson declared he would take possession of the town in the name of his sovereign, King James the Third, and the proposition was received with loud shouts. These shouts, with the continuous beating of the drum by Rollo, soon brought large additions to the numbers friendly to the Jacobite cause; and Dickson, with Helen by his side, and attended by Syddall on foot, crossed the bridge at the head of a victorious host, who made the air ring with their acclamations.

CHAPTER II.

THE PROCLAMATION AT THE CROSS.

ON reaching the Cross, the sergeant placed himself in front of it, and waiting for a few minutes till the concourse had gathered round him, in a loud voice he proclaimed King James the Third. A tremendous shout followed, accompanied by the waving of hats.

Among the spectators of this singular scene were Dr. Byrom and Beppy. Being stationed at an open window, they were free from any annoyance from the crowd.

Both were much struck by the sergeant's fine athletic figure and manly features, but they were chiefly interested by Helen, whom Beppy thought the prettiest creature she had ever beheld.

"Do look at her lovely golden locks, papa!" she said. "Don't you think they would be completely spoiled by powder? And then her eyes!—how bright they are! And her teeth!—how brilliantly white! I declare I never saw an English beauty to compare with her."

"She certainly is exceedingly pretty," replied Dr. Byrom. "And there is an air of freshness and innocence about her scarcely to be expected in a girl circumstanced as she is, that heightens her beauty."

"She is as good as she is pretty, I am quite sure," said Beppy.

"I hope so," returned Dr. Byrom, rather gravely. "I will make some inquiries about her."

"Never will I place faith in a physiognomy again, if hers proves deceptive," cried Beppy.

Beppy, however, was not the only person bewitched by Helen.

When beheld at the Cross the fair Scottish lassie electrified the crowd, and many a youth lost his heart to her.

As soon as the proclamation had been made, Sergeant Dickson addressed himself to the business on which he had come. Causing the drum to be beaten, he made a brief speech, in which he urged all brave young men who heard him to take up arms for their lawful sovereign, and help to restore him to the throne.

"All who have a mind to serve his royal highness, Prince Charles, are invited to come forward," he cried. "Five guineas in advance."

Many young men promptly responded to the call, and

pressed towards the sergeant, who still remained on horseback near the Cross, with Helen beside him. Rollo, likewise, was close at hand, and kept constantly drubbing away at the drum.

Helen gained as many recruits as the sergeant himself—perhaps more. Her smile proved irresistible. When an applicant hesitated, a few words from her decided him. Each name was entered in a book by the sergeant, but the payment of the five guineas was necessarily deferred until the arrival of Mr. Murray, the prince's secretary.

Altogether, a great deal of enthusiasm prevailed, and the sergeant had good reason to be satisfied with the result of his advance-march from Preston. He remained nearly half an hour at the Cross, and then proceeded to the market-place, accompanied by all the new recruits, and followed by an immense crowd.

As they passed the house at the windows of which Beppy Byrom and her father were stationed, a momentary halt took place, during which Beppy came forward, and waved her handkerchief to the Scottish damsel. Helen bowed in acknowledgment with a grace peculiarly her own, and taking off her bonnet, pointed significantly to the white cockade that decked it.

"Will ye wear this, my bonnie young leddy, an I gie it ye?" she cried.

"Ay, that I will," replied Beppy.

Helen immediately rode up to the window, which she saw was quite within reach, and detaching the ribbon from her bonnet gave it to her admirer, who received it with every expression of delight, and instantly proceeded to fix it upon her own breast.

"Ye are now bound to find a recruit for Prince Charlie, my bonnie young leddy," said Helen, as she moved away amid the laughter and cheers of the beholders.

Previously to this little occurrence, Dr. Byrom and his daughter had been made acquainted with Helen's history by

Tom Syddall, and had learnt that her character was irreproachable.

"I hope I shall see her again," said Beppy. "I should like so much to converse with her."

"Well, I make no doubt your wish can be gratified," said her father. "I'll speak to Syddall, and he will bid her call upon you. But why do you take so much interest in her?"

"I can't exactly tell," replied Beppy. "She seems to me to possess a great many good qualities, and, at all events, I admire her romantic attachment to her lover. Still, I don't think I should have been so very much charmed with her if she hadn't been so exceedingly pretty. And now you have the truth, papa."

"Good looks evidently go a long way with you, Beppy," said her father, laughing.

"Indeed they do, papa. But now that the street has become clear, let us go and speak to Tom Syddall."

The room from which they had viewed the proceedings at the Cross formed the upper part of a draper's shop. Thanking the owner, they now took their departure, and sought out Tom Syddall, whom they found at his door. He readily undertook to send Helen Carnegie to Miss Byrom as soon as the recruiting was over.

But the sergeant had a great deal to do, and did not care to part with either of his companions.

He continued to parade the town for some hours, enlisting all who offered themselves; and the number of the recruits soon exceeded a hundred.

The authorities did not interfere with him—probably deeming it useless to do so. Had they really surrendered the town they could not have proved more submissive.

CHAPTER III.

FATHER JEROME.

NOTHING had been heard of Sir Richard Rawcliffe since his sudden flight, but Constance had no fears for his safety, for all danger was over as soon as he got fairly out of Manchester.

But she looked forward to his return with an uneasiness such as she had never before experienced. Her father loved her dearly—better than any one else—for she was his only child. But he was of a violent temper—easily offended, and by no means easily appeased, as she herself had found, for she had more than once incurred his displeasure, though for matters of very trifling import. From her knowledge of his character, she could not doubt he would be exceedingly angry that she had read the letter relating to Atherton Legh, and though it would be easy to say nothing about it, she could not reconcile herself to such a disingenuous course.

After some reflection, she determined to consult Father Jerome, and be guided by his advice. Accordingly she sought a private conference with him, and told him all that had occurred.

The priest listened to her recital with great attention, and then said:

"I am glad you have spoken to me, daughter. If the matter is mentioned to Sir Richard it must be by me—not by you. It would trouble him exceedingly to think you are acquainted with this secret. He would blame himself for committing the papers to your care, and he would blame you for reading them."

"I have only read a single letter, father, as I have explained to you."

"That I quite understand; but I fear Sir Richard will suspect you have indulged your curiosity to a greater extent."

"My father will believe what I tell him," said Constance, proudly.

" 'Tis better not to give him so much annoyance if it can be helped," rejoined the priest; "and though frankness is generally desirable, there are occasions when reticence is necessary. This is one of them. Have you the packet with you?"

"Yes, 'tis here," she replied, producing it.

"Give it me," he cried, taking it from her. "I will restore it to Sir Richard. He will then say nothing more to you. But mark me!" he added, gravely, "the secret you have thus accidentally obtained must be strictly kept. Breathe it to no one. And now I must not neglect to caution you on another point. Yesterday I saw this young man—this Atherton Legh—of whom we have just been speaking. He is very handsome, and well calculated to inspire regard in the female breast. I trust you have no such feeling for him."

"Father," she replied, blushing deeply, "I will hide nothing from you. I love him."

"I grieve to hear the avowal," he said. "But you must conquer the passion—'twill be easy to do so in the commencement. Sir Richard would never consent to your union with an obscure adventurer. I therefore forbid you in your father's name to think further of the young man. Any hopes you may have indulged must be crushed at once."

"But I cannot—will not treat him in this way, father."

"I charge you to dismiss him. Recollect you are the daughter and heiress of Sir Richard Rawcliffe. You have committed a great imprudence: but the error must be at once repaired. Disobedience to my injunctions would be as culpable as disobedience to your father, whom I represent. Again I say the young man must be dismissed."

Before she could make any answer, the door opened, and the very person in question entered, accompanied by Monica.

"He has come to receive his sentence," said the priest, in a low, unpitying tone.

"Not now," she cried, with a supplicating look.

"Yes, now," he rejoined, coldly.

On this he went up to Monica, and telling her he had something to say, led her out of the room, leaving Atherton and Constance alone together.

"I fear I have come at a most inopportune moment," said the young man, who could not fail to be struck by her embarrassment.

"You have come at the close of a very severe lecture which I have just received from Father Jerome," she replied. "He blames me for the encouragement I have given you, and forbids me, in my father's name, to see you again."

"But you do not mean to obey him?" cried Atherton. "Surely you will not allow him to exercise this control over you? He is acting without authority."

"Not entirely without authority, for my father is guided by his advice in many things. This must be our last interview."

"Oh! say not so. You drive me to despair. Give me some hope—however slight. May I speak to Sir Richard?"

"'Twould be useless," she replied, sadly. "Father Jerome has convinced me that he never would consent to our union. No, we must part—part for ever!"

"You have pronounced my doom, and I must submit. Oh! Constance—for I will venture to call you so for one moment—I did not think you could have so quickly changed!"

"My feelings towards you are unaltered," she rejoined. "But I am obliged to put a constraint upon them. We must forget what has passed."

"The attempt would be vain on my part," cried Atherton, bitterly. "Oh! Constance, if you knew the anguish I now endure you would pity me. But I will not seek to move your compassion—neither will I reproach you—though you have raised up my hopes only to crush them. Farewell!"

"Stay—one moment!" she cried. "I may never have an explanation with you——"

"I do not want an explanation," he rejoined. "I can easily understand why Father Jerome has given you this counsel. So long as a mystery attaches to my birth, he holds that I have no right to pretend to your hand. That is his opinion. That would be Sir Richard's opinion."

"No, it could not be my father's opinion," she cried.

"Why do you think so?" he exclaimed, eagerly.

She was hesitating as to the answer she should give him, when the priest reappeared. He was alone.

"You are impatient for my departure, sir," said Atherton. "But you need not be uneasy. Miss Rawcliffe has followed your advice. All is at an end between us."

With a farewell look at Constance, he then passed out.

CHAPTER IV.

GENERAL SIR JOHN MACDONALD.

TOWARDS evening, on the same day, Lord Pitsligo's regiment of horse, commanded by General Sir John MacDonald—Lord Pitsligo, owing to his age and infirmities, being compelled to occupy the prince's carriage—entered the town.

The two divisions of the Highland army were left respectively at Wigan and Leigh. Lord Pitsligo's regiment, though its numbers were small, scarcely exceeding a hundred and fifty, made a very good show, being composed chiefly of gentlemen—all wearing their national costume, and all being tolerably well mounted.

General MacDonald had ordered the official authorities to meet him at the Cross, and he found the two constables waiting for him there; but an excuse was made for the borough-reeve. The general demanded quarters for ten thousand men to be ready on the morrow, when the prince would arrive with the army, and immediate accommodation for himself, his officers, and men; intimating that his followers must not be treated like common troopers.

Declaring that they acted on compulsion, the constables, who were very much awed by Sir John's manner, promised compliance with his injunctions. They recommended him to take up his quarters for the night at the Bull's Head, and undertook that the Highland gentlemen composing the troop should be well lodged.

Satisfied with this promise, General MacDonald rode on to the market-place, attended by his officers, while the troopers were billeted without delay under the direction of the constables and their deputies.

It may be thought that the arrival of this regiment—one of the best in the Highland army—would have created a much greater sensation than the trivial affair of the morning. But such was not the case. Sergeant Dickson, being first in the field, gained all the glory. The popular excitement was over. No shouting crowds followed General MacDonald to the Black Bull, and the streets were almost empty, as the troopers were billeted.

Later on, the all-important bellman was sent round to give notice that quarters for ten thousand men would be required next day. At the same time a fresh prohibition was issued against the removal of provisions.

Among the few whose curiosity took them to the neighbourhood of the Cross to witness the new arrival, were Beppy and her father. They were joined by Atherton Legh, who had been wandering about in a very disconsolate state ever since his parting with Constance.

Remarking that he looked very much dejected, Beppy inquired the cause, and easily ascertained the truth; and as she regarded Constance in the light of a rival, she was not sorry that a misunderstanding had occurred between them. Naturally, she did her best to cheer the young man, and though she could not entirely cure his wounded feelings, she partially succeeded.

From the Cross the little party proceeded to the marketplace, and as they drew near the Bull's Head they were surprised to see Sir Richard Rawcliffe, who had evidently just alighted, and was conversing with General MacDonald at the entrance to the inn. No sooner did the baronet descry Dr. Byrom than he called to him, and presented him to the general, who shook hands with him very cordially.

But Sir Richard's conduct towards Atherton was marked by great rudeness, and he returned the young man's salutation in a very distant and haughty fashion, and as if he scarcely recognised him.

"Apparently Sir Richard has quite forgotten the important service you rendered him," remarked Beppy, who could not help noticing the slight.

Deeply mortified, Atherton would have turned away, but she induced him to remain, and shortly afterwards he was brought forward unexpectedly.

General MacDonald being much struck by his appearance, inquired his name, and on hearing it exclaimed:

"Why this is the young man who delivered you from arrest, Sir Richard. Have you nothing to say to him?"

"I have already thanked him," replied the baronet, coldly. "And he shall not find me ungrateful."

"Zounds! you have a strange way of showing your gratitude."

Atherton could not help hearing these observations, and he immediately stepped up and said with great haughtiness:

"I have asked no favour from you, Sir Richard, and will accept none."

The baronet was so confounded that he could make no reply. Bowing to General MacDonald, Atherton was about to retire, but the other stopped him.

"There is one thing you will accept from Sir Richard, I am sure," he said, "and that is an apology, and I hope he will make you a handsome one for the rudeness with which he has treated you."

"I cannot discuss private matters in public, Sir John," said Rawcliffe. "But from what I have heard since my return—and I have called at my sister's house and seen Father Jerome—I think I have good reason to complain of Mr. Atherton Legh's conduct."

"I must bear what you have said in silence, Sir Richard, and with such patience as I can," rejoined Atherton. "But you have no reason to complain of my conduct."

"I am certainly of that opinion, and I happen to know something of the matter," observed Dr. Byrom. "I think Mr. Atherton Legh has behaved remarkably well."

"Cannot the matter be adjusted?" asked General MacDonald.

"Impossible," replied Sir Richard. "And I am sure you will agree with me, Sir John, when I give you an explanation in private."

"But you are bound to state, Sir Richard," said Dr. Byrom, "that Mr. Atherton Legh's conduct has been in no respect unbecoming a gentleman."

"That I am quite willing to admit," rejoined the baronet.

"And with that admission I am satisfied," observed Atherton.

"'Tis a thousand pities the difference, whatever it may be, cannot be amicably arranged," said the general; "but since that appears impracticable, 'twill be best to let the matter drop."

Then turning to Dr. Byrom, he added, "Am I wrong, doctor, in supposing that the young lady standing near us is your daughter. If so, pray present me to her."

Dr. Byrom readily complied, and Sir John seemed delighted by the zeal which the fair damsel displayed in the Jacobite cause.

"I see you already wear the white rose," he said, glancing at the favour which she had pinned on her breast.

"It was given me by Helen Carnegie," replied Beppy.

"And you needn't scruple to wear it, for she is as honest and true-hearted a lassie as ever breathed," said Sir John. "I know all about her. Though she has been exposed to many temptations, her character is quite irreproachable."

"You hear what General MacDonald says, papa?" cried Beppy. "It confirms the good opinion I had formed of her. She seems to me to possess a great many good qualities, and at all events I admire her romantic attachment to her lover. Still, I don't think I should have been so very much charmed with her if she hadn't been so exceedingly pretty."

"Ay, there's her danger," cried Sir John. "But I trust she will come to no harm. I hear Sergeant Dickson has brought her with him in his advance-march. 'Tis a bold step."

"But it has proved successful," said Beppy. "They have gained more than a hundred recruits."

At this moment the beating of a drum was heard, followed by a shout that seemed to proceed from the direction of Market Street Lane, a thoroughfare which turned out of the market-place on the left near the Exchange.

Immediately afterwards Sergeant Dickson and his companions made their appearance, followed by a great number of young men, all of whom turned out to be volunteers.

As soon as Dickson became aware of the arrival of Sir John MacDonald, he led his large company of recruits towards the inn, and drawing them up in front of the house, dismounted and presented himself to the general.

Helen alighted at the same time, but did not come forward.

While this movement took place, all the officers had issued from the court-yard, and collected near their leader.

"Well, Dickson," cried MacDonald, glancing at the band of young men drawn up before him. "Are these your recruits?"

"They are, general," replied the sergeant, proudly.

"And I trust Colonel Johnstone will be satisfied with me."

"You have done well, that's certain," said Sir John. "But, to speak truth, how many of these fine young fellows do you owe to Helen?"

"I can't tell, general. 'Tis enough for me that they've agreed to serve King James."

"Nay, then, I must question her."

At a sign from the sergeant, Helen left her horse with Rollo, and stepping forward, made Sir John a military salute.

She had now thrown off the plaid shawl which she had worn while on horseback, so that the exquisite symmetry of her lower limbs, set off by the tartan hose, was revealed. Her tiny feet were almost hidden by the buckles in her shoes.

Beppy gazed at her with admiration, and thought she looked even better than she had done on horseback. But she had other and more ardent admirers than Miss Byrom. Among the officers was a Captain Lindsay, a very handsome young man, who had long been desperately enamoured of her, but had managed to constrain his passion. He now kept his eyes constantly fixed upon her, and strove—though vainly— to attract her attention. Whenever Helen met his ardent glances, she turned aside her gaze.

"Aweel, Helen," cried MacDonald; "I have been congratulating the sergeant on his success. But I think he mainly owes it to you, lassie. A blink o' your bonnie blue een has done more than all his fair speeches."

"You are mista'en, general," replied Helen. "I may have gained a dizen, but not mair."

"You do yourself an injustice, lassie. Half those brave lads belong to you."

"I could tell you how many she enlisted at the Cross, for I was present at the time," remarked Beppy.

"Then you must needs tell the general that I enlisted

yerself, fair leddy, and that ye promised to find me a recruit," said Helen.

"And so I will," said Beppy. "Can I do aught more for you?"

"Give me a few yards of blue and white ribbon to make cockades, and I will thank you heartily," rejoined Helen.

"Come home with me, and you shall have as much ribbon as you require, and I will help you to make the cockades," said Beppy.

"You cannot refuse that offer, Helen," remarked General MacDonald.

"I am na like to refuse it," was the rejoinder. "The young leddy is ower gude."

Helen then consulted the sergeant, who signified his assent, upon which she told Beppy she was ready to go with her. Excusing herself to the general, Beppy then took her father's arm, and they set off for the doctor's residence, accompanied by the Scottish damsel.

CHAPTER V.

HELEN CARNEGIE'S STORY.

AFTER Helen Carnegie had partaken of some refreshment, and drunk a glass of mead, with which she was mightily pleased, she went with Beppy to the young lady's boudoir, where a basket full of blue and white ribbons was found upon the work-table, and they sat down together to make cockades—chatting merrily as ther proceeded with their task.

By this time the frank Scottish lassie had become quite confidential with her new friend, and had told her simple story—explaining that she was merely a husbandman's daughter, and had passed eighteen summers and winters among the hills near Ruthven. She had first seen Sergeant

Erick Dickson at Perth, when the Highland army came there. He had wooed her and won her heart, but she refused to wed him till the fighting was over. She afterwards saw him at Edinburgh, after the battle of Gladsmuir, and he pressed her so strongly to accompany him on the march to England that she consented. She had suffered far less than might have been expected from the fatigues of the long march, and thought she was now quite as strong and as able to endure hardship as Erick himself.

"You may blame me for the bold step I have taken, dear young leddy," she said, "and I ken fu' weel it was imprudent, but as yet I have had no cause to repent it. I loo'd Erick dearly, an' didna like to pairt wi' him. Sae I ha' ridden by his side a' the way frae Edinburgh to this toon, and shall gae on wi' him to Lunnon, if the prince should gang sae far, as Heaven grant he may! To a young leddy like yersel, siccan a life as I hae led wadna be possible, but to a mountain lassie there's nae hardship in it, but great enjoyment. Everywhere on the march, sin we crossed the Border, the Southrons hae shown me kindness. 'Twas only to ask and have. Never have I wanted a night's lodging. As to Erick, you will readily guess how carefully he has tented me. But he has never neglected his duty, and I have helped him to discharge it as far as I could. Our love has been tried, and has stood the test, and is now stronger than ever. Loosome as ye are, young leddy, ye must needs hae a lover, and I trust he may prove as fond and faithful as Erick. Then you'll never regret your choice."

"I thank you for the good wish, Helen," said Beppy, smiling. "But I have no lover."

"I canna believe it. I'm much mista'en if I didna see a weel-faur'd callant cast lovin' een upon ye in the market-place just now. He wasna far off when the general spoke to me."

"Mr. Atherton Legh, I suppose you mean?" observed Beppy, blushing.

"Ay, that's his name. I heard the general ca' him sae."

"And so you have no fault to find with your lover?" said Beppy, anxious to change the subject.

"Fawt!—nane!" exclaimed Helen. "Erick hasna a fawt."

"Is he never jealous?"

"Aweel, I canna deny that he is a wee bit jealous, if ye ca' that a fawt; but his jealousy only proves his love. I should be jealous mysel if he talked to the lasses."

"But do you talk to the lads, Helen?"

"My certie, na! but ther win talk to me, and that makes Erick angry sometimes. But I soon laugh it off."

"Well, if it's nothing more serious than that it doesn't signify," said Beppy. "You can't prevent the young men from paying you compliments, you know."

"And I maun be ceevil to them in return. But there's one person that troubles me, and troubles Erick too—Captain Lindsay. He's an officer in Lord Pitsligo's regiment. Maybe you noticed him?—a fine-looking young man, taller than the rest; but weelfaur'd as he is, he's not to compare with Erick."

"You always keep Captain Lindsay at a distance, I hope, Helen?"

"I do my best. I never listen to his saft nonsense. I never accept any of the trinkets he offers me—but he winna be said."

"Continue to treat him coldly, and his assiduities will soon cease," observed Beppy.

"I'm not so sure of that. If he persists I fear there'll be mischief, for he drives Erick furious."

"I hope it mayn't come to that, Helen," said Beppy, rather gravely. "But much will depend on your discretion."

They then went on with their task in silence.

By this time they had made two or three dozen cockades, and when nearly as many more were finished, Helen expressed surprise that Erick had not come to fetch her.

"He promised to come for me in an hour," she said, "and it's now gettin' late."

"Don't make yourself uneasy," replied Beppy. "He'll be here soon. Where do you lodge to-night?"

"At the Angel in Market Street Lane. Why, there's a clock has just struck nine. I must go. You'll please to excuse me, miss. I'll come betimes to-morrow and help you to finish the cockades."

"Well, if you won't stay any longer, I'll send some one with you to the Angel."

Helen declined the offer, saying she was not afraid to walk there by herself.

"But are you sure you can find the way?"

"Quite sure," replied Helen.

And thanking the young lady for her kindness, she bade her good-night, and took her departure.

CHAPTER VI.

CAPTAIN LINDSAY.

THE moon shone brightly as Helen was crossing the churchyard, but she had not gone far when she heard quick footsteps behind her, and thinking it must be Erick she stopped.

It was not her lover, but a tall Highland officer, whom she instantly recognised.

Surprised and alarmed at the sight, she would have fled, but Captain Lindsay, for it was he, sprang forward, and seized her arm.

"Let me go, I insist, sir," she cried indignantly.

"Not till I have had a few words with you, Helen," replied the captain. "I have been waiting an hour for you here. I found out that Miss Byrom had taken you home with her, so I kept watch near the door of the house for your coming forth. Erick, I knew, couldn't interrupt us, for I had contrived to get him out of the way."

"He shall hear of your base design, sir," she cried, looking round for help. But she could see no one in the churchyard.

"Listen to me, Helen," said Captain Lindsay. "I am so passionately in love that I would make any sacrifice for you. You must and shall be mine!"

"Never!" she cried, struggling vainly to get free. "I am plighted to Erick, as ye ken fu' weel, and think you I wad break my vow to him? and for you, whom I hate!"

"Hate me or not, you shall be mine!" he cried. "Listen to reason, you foolish girl. Erick cannot love you as I love you."

"He loves me far better—but I dinna mind that."

"If you wed him, you will only be a poor soldier's wife. With me you will have wealth and luxury."

"Ye are merely wastin' yer breath, sir," she cried. "A' your arguments have no effect on me. Were you to fill my lap with gowd, I wad fling it from me wi' scorn. I care na for wealth and luxury—I care only for Erick."

"To the devil with him!" cried Captain Lindsay, fiercely. "You are enough to drive one mad. If you won't yield to persuasion, you shall yield to force. Mine you shall be, whether you will or not."

And he would have clasped her in his arms, but she seized the dirk which hung from his girdle and held it to his breast.

"Release me instantly, or I will plunge this to your heart," she cried.

The energy with which she spoke left no doubt that she would execute her threat, and the baffled captain set her free.

At this moment assistance came. Erick could be seen hurrying towards them from the further side of the churchyard.

As soon as Helen perceived him she flung the dirk at Captain Lindsay's feet, and flew to meet her lover.

"What's the matter, lass?" cried the sergeant. "Has the villain insulted you? If he has, he shall pay for it wi' his life."

"Na! na!" cried Helen, stopping him. "Ye shall na gae near him. There'll be mischief. You should ha' come sooner, Erick, and then this wadna ha' happened."

"I could na come afore, lassie," replied the sergeant. "I now see the trick that has been played me by this cunning villain; but he shall rue it."

"Ye shall na stay anither minute in this unchancy kirk-yard," cried Helen, forcing him away with her.

Just as they went out at the gate, Helen cast a look back at Captain Lindsay, and saw him still standing, as if stupefied, on the spot where she had left him. He had not even picked up the dirk, for she could distinguish it glittering in the moonlight at his feet.

CHAPTER VII.

A RESIDENCE IS CHOSEN FOR THE PRINCE.

AT an early hour on the following morning, a carriage drawn by four strong horses, and attended by a mounted guard, entered the town.

It contained four persons, all of a certain importance. Chief among them was Lord Pitsligo, than whom no one in the Highland army was more beloved and respected. The venerable Scottish nobleman was in full military costume, and would have ridden at the head of his regiment, had not his infirm state of health prevented him.

The next person whom we shall mention was Mr. John Murray of Broughton, a gentleman of great ability, who acted as the prince's secretary and treasurer, and managed all his royal highness's affairs extremely well. Mr. Murray had a sharp intelligent countenance, and wore a suit of brown velvet with a tie-wig.

Opposite to him sat the prince's tutor and adviser, Sir Thomas Sheridan, one of the numerous Irish gentlemen who had attached themselves to the cause of the Stuarts. Sir Thomas, who was a strict Roman Catholic, exercised almost as much influence over the prince as Father Petre once did over the prince's grandsire, James the Second.

Next to Sir Thomas sat a very brilliant personage, wearing a rich suit of sky-blue cloth trimmed with silver, laced ruffles, a laced cravat, and a three-cornered hat, likewise laced with silver. This was the Marquis d'Eguilles, an envoy from Louis the Fifteenth, who had brought over a large sum of money and nearly three thousand stand of arms from his royal master. The marquis had the refined and graceful manner of a French courtier of the period, and carried a diamond snuff-box, which was always at the service of his companions.

As the persons we have described crossed the bridge, they looked with some interest at the town they were just entering, and bowed in return for the shouts of the crowd, who had rushed out to greet them.

Seeing such a large and handsome equipage attended by an escort, the townspeople naturally supposed it must be the prince himself, and when they found out their mistake, they did not shout quite so loudly.

The carriage drove to the market-place, where Lord Pitsligo and the others descended at the Bull's Head. A substantial repast had been prepared for them by order of Sir John MacDonald, to which they at once sat down.

Before breakfast was over, Colonel Townley arrived, and at once joined the party. Several Jacobites likewise repaired to the inn and volunteered their services to Mr. Secretary

Murray, who received them very affably, and introduced them to Lord Pitsligo.

Amongst the new-comers were Dr. Deacon and Dr. Byrom. Mr. Murray's first business was to find a suitable residence for the prince during his stay in the town, and after consulting the two gentlemen we have named, he went out attended by Colonel Townley, the Marquis d'Eguilles, Sir Thomas Sheridan, and Dr. Byrom, to inspect the principal mansions in the place. Half a dozen soldiers went with them to keep back the crowd.

They first proceeded to Deansgate, where they examined a large house belonging to Mr. Touchet, one of the chief merchants of the place; but this was deemed unsuitable, being partly used as a warehouse, and was therefore assigned to Lord Elcho.

Mr. Floyd's house, near St. Ann's Square, was next visited; a handsome mansion, ornamented with pilasters, having a Belvidere on the summit, and approached by a noble flight of steps, but it did not entirely satisfy Mr. Murray, so he allotted it to Lord Pitsligo and Lord George Murray.

The next mansion inspected was Mr. Croxton's, in King Street, a large building converted at a later period into the town-hall. Here quarters were found for Lord Balmerino, Lord Kilmarnock, and Lord Strathallan.

Mr. Marriott's house, in Brown-street, was assigned to the Earl of Kelly and Lord Ogilvy; Mr. Gartside's mansion was appropriated to the Duke of Perth; and a fine house in Market Street Lane, occupied by Mr. Marsden, was allotted to the Marquis of Tullibardine and Lord Nairne.

Good quarters having thus been provided for all the principal personages in the Highland army there remained only the prince; and at length Mr. Dickenson's house, in Market Street Lane, was fixed upon as affording fitting head-quarters for his royal highness.

The mansion, one of the best in the town, was built of red brick, in the formal taste of the period. Still, it was

ERICK, WITH HELEN AND ROLLO, PROCLAIM KING JAMES AT MANCHESTER

large and commodious, and contained some handsome apartments. Standing back from the street, it had a paved court in front surrounded by iron railings, and a lofty flight of steps led to the doorway. A glance at the internal arrangements decided Mr. Murray in his choice, and he gave orders that the house should be immediately prepared for the prince.

Some of the houses selected for the Jacobite leaders, we believe, are still in existence, but Mr. Dickenson's mansion has been pulled down. After its occupation by the prince at the memorable period in question, it was always known as "The Palace."

Perfectly satisfied with the arrangements he had made, Mr. Murray left his companions behind, and took his way down Market Street Lane, then a narrow, but extremely picturesque thoroughfare, and abounding in ancient habitations.

CHAPTER VIII.

INTERVIEW BETWEEN SECRETARY MURRAY AND THE MAGISTRATES.

In front of the Angel Inn, over the doorway of which hung a flag, a number of young men were assembled, each being distinguished by a white cockade. On horseback in the midst of these recruits were Sergeant Dickson, Helen Carnegie, and Rollo.

Halting for a moment to give some instructions to the sergeant and congratulate him on his success, Mr. Murray passed on to the market-place, where a large concourse was collected. Cheers greeted the party, and attended them to the Bull's Head, at the door of which two sentries were now stationed.

On entering the inn, Mr. Murray was informed by Diggles that the magistrates were waiting to see him; and he was then conducted to a room on the ground floor, in which he found Mr. Walley and Mr. Fowden.

Courteously saluting them, he begged them to be seated at a table placed in the centre of the room, furnished them with a list of the houses he had selected, and, after they had examined it, he proceeded to give them some further directions as to the arrangements necessary to be made for the prince.

"His royal highness will not dine till a late hour," he said. "Only the Duke of Perth, Lord George Murray, the Marquis of Tullibardine, Lord Pitsligo, the Marquis d'Eguilles, Sir Thomas Sheridan, and myself will have the honour of dining with him. The repast must be served in private."

The magistrates bowed.

"Another sumptuous repast, with the choicest wines you can procure, must be prepared at seven o'clock for forty of the principal officers."

Again the magistrates bowed.

"We will do our best to content the prince," said Mr. Fowden. "As regards the houses mentioned in this list, those for whom they have been chosen will find them ready for their reception. For how many men, may we ask, will quarters be required?"

"For five thousand; and rations for the like number. But the commanding officer, on his arrival, will give you precise orders, in obedience to which you will furnish the quarter-masters and adjutants with the necessary warrants. Another important matter must be attended to. As the prince's treasurer, I require that all persons connected with the excise, and all innkeepers, shall forthwith bring me the full amount of their imposts, and all moneys in their hands belonging to the Government—on pain of military execution."

"Public notice to that effect shall immediately be given," said Mr. Fowden; "but should the innkeepers or any others prove remiss we must not be blamed for their negligence."

"All defaulters will be shot to-morrow. Make that

known," said Mr. Murray. "I trust, gentlemen," he added, rising, "that due honour will be done to the prince on his arrival."

"It would be inconsistent with the office we hold, and might expose us to serious consequences, were we to give orders for public rejoicings," said Mr. Fowden; "but we will take care the town shall be illuminated and bonfires lighted."

"That is all I could require from you, gentlemen. On the arrival of the prince, if you will attend at head-quarters, I shall have the honour of presenting you to his royal highness."

"We are fully sensible of the great honour intended us," said the magistrates, hesitating; "but——"

"I see, gentlemen. You are afraid of compromising yourselves," remarked Mr. Murray, smiling. "Make yourselves quite easy. I have a device that will obviate all difficulty. A silk curtain shall be hung across the audience-chamber. Of course you won't know who may be behind the curtain—though you may guess."

"An excellent plan," cried the magistrates.

Bowing ceremoniously to the secretary, they then withdrew.

CHAPTER IX.

ARRIVAL OF THE FIRST DIVISION OF THE HIGHLAND ARMY.
LORD GEORGE MURRAY.

SHORTLY after the departure of the magistrates, the bells of all the churches in the town began to ring joyously, and were soon answered by loud and merry peals from the only church on the other side of the Irwell.

Summoned by this exhilarating clamour, multitudes

flocked into the streets, decked in holiday attire, and most of them crossed the bridge into Salford in expectation of witnessing the entrance of the Highland army.

The weather was most propitious. Never was finer day seen in November, and the bright sunshine diffused general gaiety and good-humour among the concourse.

Good-looking damsels predominated in the crowd—Manchester has always been noted for female beauty—and they were all exceedingly curious to behold the handsome young prince and the Scottish chiefs.

There was a great deal of talk about the Insurrection of '15, but this was chiefly among the older people, for as the first rising took place before the young folks were born, they could not be expected to feel much interest in it.

It may seem strange that the approach of the much-dreaded Highlanders should not have caused alarm, but by this time the inhabitants generally had got over their fears, and were disposed to welcome the insurgents as friends, and not treat them as enemies.

Among the fair sex, as we have said, the youth, courage, romantic character, and good looks of the prince excited the greatest interest and sympathy. Whatever the men might be, the women were all Jacobites.

Meanwhile, the bells continued to peal joyfully, and multitudes crossed into Salford, and stationed themselves on either side of the main street, through which it was expected the prince and the army would pass.

Everything looked bright and gay, and everybody—except a few moody Presbyterians—appeared happy.

On the summit of the lofty tower of the collegiate church floated a large standard fashioned of white, red, and blue silk. This broad banner, which attracted great attention from the concourse, had been placed in its present conspicuous position by the management of Tom Syddall.

The patience of the large crowd assembled in Salford was somewhat sorely tried. Those who had secured good places for the spectacle did not like to leave them, and they had nothing to do but talk and jest with each other; but at length the shrill notes of the bagpipes proclaimed that the Highlanders were at hand, and the trampling of horse was heard.

First to appear was a troop of horse commanded by Lord Strathallan. This was quickly followed by a regiment of Highlanders, with their pipers marching in front.

The sight of these fine, stalwart men, in their picturesque garb, each armed with firelock, claymore, and dirk, and bearing a target on his shoulder, caused the greatest excitement among the beholders, who cheered them lustily as they marched on.

The regiment was commanded by Lord George Murray, one of the most distinguished and important persons in the prince's service, who had been created a lieutenant-general of the Highland army. He was a younger brother of the Marquis of Tullibardine. Lord George was not young, as will be understood, when it is mentioned that he was concerned in the outbreak of 1715; but he was still in the prime of life, undoubtedly the boldest and ablest leader in the rebel forces and the one best able to direct the movements of the present campaign; but though he was a prominent member of the council, his advice was rarely taken, owing to the bluntness of his manner, which was highly displeasing to the prince, as well as to several of his royal highness's advisers.

In this respect Lord George offered a marked contrast to his rival the courtly Duke of Perth, of whom we shall have occasion to speak anon.

Lord George Murray was tall, powerfully built, and possessed great personal strength. A thorough soldier, of undaunted courage, and capable of undergoing any amount of fatigue, he was unpopular from his rough and somewhat contemptuous manner. His character could be easily read in his haughty demeanour and strongly marked countenance. Lord George was attended by his aide-de-camp, the Chevalier de

Johnstone. As he rode along and eyed the crowd on either side, his stern glance struck terror into many a breast.

CHAPTER X.

THE DUKE OF PERTH.

NAIRNE'S Athole men came next, and were followed by other fine Highland regiments, respectively commanded by General Gordon of Glenbucket, Lord Ogilvy of Strathmore, and Roy Stuart. Each regiment had two captains, two lieutenants, and two ensigns.

Next came a troop of light cavalry, under the command of Lord Balmerino; and then followed Lord Kilmarnock's hussars with the baggage and artillery.

The train of artillery consisted of sixteen field-pieces, two waggons laden with powder, and a great number of sumpter-horses.

This division of the Highland army was commanded by the Duke of Perth, whose presence excited general admiration.

Both the Duke and his aide-de-camp, who rode beside him, were remarkably well mounted, and both perfect horsemen.

Among the many Scottish nobles who had determined to share the fortunes of Prince Charles Edward, none could compare in personal appearance and deportment with James Lord Drummond, third titular Duke of Perth. The duke's courtesy, refined manners, and unfailing good temper, rendered him popular with all. Though not so thorough a soldier as Lord George Murray, he was equally brave, and in brilliant qualities far surpassed him.

Between these two distinguished personages a great rivalry existed. No member of the council possessed so much influence with the prince as the Duke of Perth, and the favour shown his rival often caused great umbrage to Lord George Murray, who did not care to conceal his resentment.

The duke had warm friends in Secretary Murray and Sir Thomas Sheridan, so that his position as first favourite was unassailable, certainly by Lord George.

The duke, who was in the very prime of manhood, being only just turned thirty, was grandson of the Earl of Perth, created duke by James the Second on his retirement to France.

Nothing could be more striking than the effect produced by these clan regiments as they marched through Salford on that morning, the different hues of the plaids worn by each corps giving variety and colour to the picture, while the sinewy frames, fierce countenances, and active movements of the men inspired a certain feeling akin to fear among the beholders, which the war-like notes of the bagpipe did not tend to diminish.

The front ranks of each regiment were composed of gentlemen, whose arms and equipments were superior to those of the others, causing them to look like officers; but they had no rank. All the men were in good spirits, and seemed as if victory lay before them.

Regiment after regiment marched over the bridge, with the sun shining brightly on their picturesque dresses, and glittering on their firelocks and arms—with their colours and pipes playing—bells pealing, and spectators shouting loudly, producing a most extraordinarily animating effect.

Scarcely less striking was it as the Highlanders marched through the town and drew up in St. Ann's Square.

Completely filled by these clan regiments, the large area presented a picture such as it has never since exhibited.

But a scene of a very different kind was being enacted at the same time. While these armed men were gathering in front of the church, a sad ceremonial took place in the churchyard.

A grave had been opened to receive the remains of a respected inhabitant of the town, and the last rites were then being performed by Mr. Lewthwaite, who proceeded as calmly as circumstances would permit.

But other mourners than those expected gathered round the grave as the coffin was lowered into it—Highland officers bare-headed, and noticeable for their respectful demeanour.

The Highland regiments did not remain long in St. Ann's Square. Having received their billets, the men were taken to their lodgings by the quarter-masters. The artillery and baggage-waggons proceeded to Castle Field, where a park was formed, and strongly guarded.

CHAPTER XI.

ARRIVAL OF THE SECOND DIVISION.

MULTITUDES of people still remained in Salford, patiently awaiting the arrival of the prince with the second division of the Highland army.

All the inmates of Mrs. Butler's dwelling, which, it will be remembered, was situated at the upper end of the main street, had witnessed the march past of the first division. Even the invalid lady herself, who had not quitted the house for a lengthened period, and could not do so now without considerable risk, came forth to see the young prince.

Not being able to walk so far, she was carried out into the garden, and placed near the gate, which was thrown open. From this position she commanded the road, and could see all that was to be seen.

Near her stood Monica and Constance, both of whom were attired in white dresses, with blue scarves, while in close attendance upon her were her brother, Sir Richard Rawcliffe, Father Jerome, and Jemmy Dawson.

Notwithstanding the excitement of the occasion, Constance looked pensive and absent—her thoughts being occupied with Atherton Legh. Very little conversation had taken place between her and her father, since Sir Richard's return from Preston, and then only in the presence of Father Jerome. All allusion to the young man had been studiously avoided.

By this time Monica had quite shaken off her fears, and when the stirring spectacle commenced, and the clan regiments marched past the gate, her breast glowed with enthusiasm, and all her former ardour returned. She thought no more of her lover's danger, but of the glory he would win; and if he had held back, she would now have urged him on.

But Jemmy required no spurring; he was eager to be an actor in such a scene, and was anxiously expecting his promised commission.

As to Mrs. Butler, she looked on with mingled feelings. What memories were awakened by the sight of those Highland regiments! The men looked the same, wore the same garb, and bore the same arms as those she had seen in former days. Yet the chiefs who had fought in the civil war of 1715, and their faithful clansmen, were all swept away. Were those who had now taken their places destined to victory or defeat? She trembled as she asked herself the question.

Many a glance was thrown at the fair damsels in the garden as the young officers marched past, and frequent salutes were offered to Sir Richard by those in command of the regiment, but no one halted except the Duke of Perth, who paused to say a few words to him, and was presented to the ladies—delighting them with his courteous manner.

Before the duke rode off, he told them that more than an hour would elapse before the second division came up, and so it turned out.

During this interval, Mrs. Butler remained in the garden, and of course the others did not leave her. Some slight refreshments, with wine, were brought her by a man-servant

OF THE FATAL '45.

from the house, and of these she partook in order to support her strength, which she feared might fail her. She listened anxiously for any sounds that might announce the prince's approach, but it was long before he came.

At length the loud notes of the bagpipes were heard in the distance, and soon afterwards a regiment of cavalry came up, commanded by Lord Elcho, who carried his sword in his hand, as did the men. These were the life-guards. Blue coats with red facings formed the uniform of the troop. And the men wore gold-laced hats with white cockades in them. Indeed, we may remark that all the officers and soldiers of the Highland army wore white cockades in hat or bonnet.

The life-guards were soon gone, and then **a personage appeared,** upon whom all eyes were fixed.

John Byrom

Byrom's House.

CHAPTER XII.

THE YOUNG CHEVALIER.

ATTENDED by a dozen or more nobles and officers of high rank, all dressed in blue coats faced with red, and wearing gold-laced hats, marched with a light elastic step, that showed he was not in the slightest degree fatigued, a tall, well-proportioned, fair-complexioned, handsome young man, of some five-and-twenty, dressed in a Highland garb, armed with a broadsword, and carrying a target on his shoulder. He wore no star upon his breast—no ornament of any kind—merely a white rose in his bonnet, and a blue silk scarf, yet his dignified and graceful deportment proclaimed at once that it was Prince Charles Edward.

The prince's frame was slight, but full of vigour. His features were regular and delicately moulded, his complexion fair, and his eyes bright and blue. His natural blonde locks would no doubt have become him better than the flaxen-coloured peruke which he wore, though that suited him. His expression was extremely amiable and engaging, and his youth, grace, and good looks produced a most favourable impression upon the beholders.

Charles Edward was preceded by a hundred Highland pipers, and as all were playing vigorously, the din caused by them was astounding.

This handsome young prince, who, at the period of his introduction to the reader, was full of romantic ardour and courage, and confident of recovering the throne of his ancestors, was the eldest son of James Stuart, known as the Chevalier de Saint George, and the Princess Maria Sobieski. Perfect in all manly exercises, Prince Charles Edward possessed powers of endurance that admirably fitted him for the enterprize he had undertaken. His early years had been passed in obscurity in Rome, but he had always cherished the thought of invading England, and at last the opportunity presented itself.

Great efforts had been made by the Jacobite party in Paris to induce the French monarch to aid in the restoration of the Stuart dynasty, but without effect. However, when the celebrated Cardinal de Tencin became first minister of state, he judged that a civil war in England would be highly beneficial to France, and therefore invited Charles Edward to repair to Paris.

Preparations, meanwhile, had been made to land an army of fifteen thousand men in England under Field-Marshal Saxe, and it was arranged that the prince should accompany the expedition as commander-in-chief.

The fleet set sail, but being dispersed by a violent tempest, suffered so much loss that the project was abandoned.

But the hopes of the young prince were encouraged by the cardinal minister, who said to him, " The king is averse to another expedition after the disastrous result of the first. But why should you not go alone, or with a few attendants, and land on the North of Scotland? Your presence alone would revive your party, and create an army."

This advice was too much in accordance with the aspirations of the brave and adventurous young prince not to be eagerly adopted.

Provided with money and arms by the cardinal, he set sail from Dunquerque in July, 1745, in the *Dentelle* sloop of war, and after some hazardous escapes, landed on the northwest coast of Scotland, where he was met by Mr. Murray, who became his secretary and treasurer. His standard having been reared, he was speedily joined by the MacDonalds, the Camerons, and other Highland chiefs, the Duke of Perth, the Marquis of Tullibardine, Lord Elcho, and Lord George Murray.

Having mustered an army of four thousand men, he marched on Perth, and arrived there on the 3rd of September.

After a short stay at Perth, he proceeded at the head of his army to Edinburgh, and the Scottish capital opened its gates to the grandson of James the Second. Here he took possession of the palace of his ancestors; caused his father to be proclaimed at the Cross by the title of King James the Eighth of Scotland, and himself as Regent; and after the ceremonial gave a splendid ball at Holyrood. At Edinburgh he was joined by Lord Nairne with a thousand men.

On the 21st of September occurred the battle of Preston Pans, in which Sir John Cope was completely routed. The news of the young Chevalier's unlooked-for and decisive victory animated the Jacobites in every quarter, greatly alarmed the English Government, and brought back George the Second from Hanover.

Having received considerable reinforcements, the prince gave a troop of horse to Lord Balmerino, and another to Lord Kilmarnock. Money and arms also arrived most opportunely from France, and in one of the vessels that brought these supplies came the Marquis d'Eguilles. The court continued to be held at Holyrood, and the receptions were now most brilliantly attended, especially by the fair sex.

Meanwhile, Marshal Wade having assembled an army at Newcastle, the prince determined to cross the Border and give him battle.

Several of his council, among whom was Lord George Murray, sought to dissuade him from his design, urging him to await the arrival of the expected reinforcements from France; but no representations either of difficulty or danger could induce the chivalrous prince to give up his scheme, or even defer it.

He told his councillors that he saw they were determined to stay in Scotland, and defend their own country; but he added, in a tone that showed his resolution was taken, "I am not less determined to try my fate in England, even though I should go alone."

On the last day of October he marched out of Edinburgh at the head of an army of five thousand five hundred men. His first object was to attack Carlisle, and as Marshal Wade had not advanced from Newcastle, he did not anticipate an engagement with him.

Carlisle surrendered to the Duke of Perth, and on the 17th November, Charles Edward made a triumphal entry into the city. At a council held there, the prince, flushed by success, proposed to continue his march to the metropolis, expressing a firm conviction that he should be joined by a large party in Lancashire and Cheshire, while the Marquis d'Eguilles felt equally confident that reinforcements would arrive from France.

Some opposition to the plan was offered by Lord George Murray, who affirmed that the Duke of Cumberland had assembled an army nearly doubling in number that of his royal highness, which must be encountered, and that Marshal Wade had made a demonstration for the relief of Carlisle, but the advice was overruled.

Resuming his march, the prince passed through Lancaster,

and arrived with his whole army at Preston on the 26th. From Preston the Highland army marched to Manchester, in two divisions, as related.

Rash as the young Chevalier's enterprise may appear, it is more than probable that it would have been accomplished if he had received the support he expected.

Before quitting Scotland he had received invitations and promises of aid from many important Jacobite families in the northern counties; and he had been led to believe that a general rising in his favour would be made in Lancashire, Cheshire, and North Wales.

But he soon found these promises fallacious. Very few persons of importance joined his standard, and no risings took place. He had expected powerful reinforcements from France, but none arrived. Yet he had advanced boldly and successfully, and though unaided, it appeared not unlikely that he would achieve the daring project he had conceived.

Hopes were still entertained by some of his counsellors that a large number of volunteers would join at Manchester, and the warm reception given him by the inhabitants as he approached the town, seemed to warrant these expectations.

As the prince marched a few paces in front of his attendants, he was at once distinguishable; but even if he had been mixed up with them, his dignified deportment would have rendered him conspicuous.

Amongst the nobles and Highland chiefs who attended him were the Marquis of Tullibardine, Glengarry, Ardshiel, Colonel Ker of Gradon, and Colonel O'Sullivan.

Behind them came a body-guard of Highlanders.

The second division of the army consisted of regiments belonging to the chiefs previously mentioned, but these regiments were now left to the command of the officers, their leaders preferring to march on foot with the prince. A troop of hussars under the command of Lord Balmerino brought up the rear.

CHAPTER XIII.

THE PRINCE'S INTERVIEW WITH MRS. BUTLER AND THE TWO DAMSELS.

As the young Chevalier approached Mrs. Butler's residence, he chanced to cast his eye into the garden—the gate of which, as we have said, was standing wide open—and the charming group formed by the two beautiful girls and the invalid lady attracted his attention.

Standing close beside them, he perceived Sir Richard Rawcliffe, whom he had seen at Preston the day before.

On beholding the young Chevalier, Mrs. Butler rose from her chair, and stepping forward, made him a profound obeisance.

Something in the earnest look fixed upon him by the invalid lady interested the prince, and he could not resist the impulse that prompted him to speak to her.

Accordingly he signified his intention to the Marquis of Tullibardine; a halt was immediately called, the pipers ceased playing, while the prince stepped out of the line, followed by that nobleman, and entered the garden.

Nothing could exceed the surprise and delight caused by this gracious act, not only to the object of it, but to the two fair damsels who stood beside her. It may be thought that these lovely girls would have attracted the prince to the garden rather than an elderly dame, but he seemed scarcely aware of their presence till he was close beside them.

Instantly divining the prince's intention, Sir Richard Rawcliffe presented his sister. Charles could not prevent her from kneeling, but he immediately raised her, and remarking that she looked very faint, conducted her, with much solicitude, to a seat.

He then turned to the two fair damsels, who were likewise presented to him by Sir Richard, and received them with much grace and dignity.

Not till this moment did he become aware of Constance's surpassing beauty, and he then remarked to her father:

"I was told that you had a lovely daughter, Sir Richard, but I did not imagine she was so beautiful as I find her."

"Such praise coming from your royal highness will make her vain," said the baronet.

"Nay, I meant not to call blushes to her cheek, though they do not spoil it," said Charles. "But Miss Rawcliffe has another great merit in my eyes besides her personal attractions. If I am not misinformed, she is devoted to the royal cause."

"Heart and soul!" cried Constance, enthusiastically. "Your royal highness has not a more zealous adherent than myself."

"I cannot doubt it. But I hoped you have proved your zeal by bringing me a hundred swords."

"I have brought you one," she replied—"but it is worth a hundred."

"Ah! to whom does it belong?" inquired the prince, smiling.

"To a brave young man, whose name must be utterly unknown to your royal highness—Mr. Atherton Legh."

"There you are mistaken. His name has been mentioned to me by Colonel Townley, who described him—I have no doubt quite correctly—as the finest young man in Manchester. Mr. Atherton Legh shall have a commission on your recommendation, Miss Rawcliffe. You will present him to me, Sir Richard."

"It will be better, perhaps, that Colonel Townley should present him to your royal highness," said Sir Richard.

The reluctance displayed by the baronet did not escape the prince, whose perceptions were very acute, but a glance at Constance served partly to explain matters to him, and he remarked with apparent indifference:

"Be it so;" adding significantly, "I shall not forget that I am indebted to you, Miss Rawcliffe, for this brave young recruit."

It was now Jemmy Dawson's turn to be presented, and he had no cause to complain of his reception. The few words said to him by the prince were calculated to rouse his zeal, while they highly gratified Monica.

"I can claim as much credit as my cousin Constance," she said. "Each of us has brought a recruit; and we both feel equally sure your royal highness will be well served."

By this time Mrs. Butler had recovered from her faintness, and perceiving that her gaze was anxiously fixed upon him, the prince went to speak to her.

"You have something to say to me, madam, methinks?" he observed.

"I only desire to tell you, prince, that I have prayed daily for the restoration of your royal house. You will therefore understand what my feelings must be when I behold you at the head of an army determined to wrest the crown of this kingdom from the usurper who now wears it. May Heaven strengthen your arm, and fight for you, so that you may regain your own, and the rights and liberties of your faithful subjects may be preserved, and the old religion be restored!"

"I have come to win a kingdom for my royal father, or to perish in the attempt," said Charles Edward, energetically.

"Victory awaits you, prince," she cried. "I feel assured of it. The tidings of your triumph will efface my sad recollections of the former ill-starred attempt, and I shall die content."

"My sister lost one who was very dear to her, in the fatal affair of '15," remarked Sir Richard.

"I cannot wonder then that she should have sad memories connected with that unfortunate struggle," said the prince, in a tone of profound sympathy. "Farewell, madam.

I hope you will have no more to mourn—but many to greet as victors."

He then addressed the two fair damsels, expressing a hope that he might see them again during his brief stay in Manchester; after which, with a graceful inclination of his person towards the party, he stepped back, and resumed his place in the line of march.

Before, however, the troops could be put in motion, another slight interruption occurred. It was caused by the Rev. Mr. Clayton, the chaplain of the collegiate church.

Mr. Clayton, as will be conjectured from what we are about to narrate, was a Jacobite and a Nonjuror.

Taking advantage of the halt, he threw himself at the prince's feet, and in most fervent tones implored the Divine blessing on his head—praying that the enterprise on which he was engaged might prove successful.

As the chaplain was in full canonicals the incident caused a great sensation, and was particularly gratifying to the prince.

When the benediction was concluded, and Mr. Clayton had retired, the word was given, the pipers began to play as loudly as before, and the march was resumed.

Shortly afterwards, Prince Charles Edward crossed the bridge, and, amid loud acclamations, entered Manchester.

CHAPTER XIV.

THE PRINCE'S MARCH TO HEAD-QUARTERS.

No sooner did the vast assemblage collected near the approaches to the bridge distinguish the tall graceful figure of the young Chevalier amid the throng of Scottish nobles and chiefs, than all heads were instantly uncovered, and a loud cry arose of "Long live King James the Third, and prince Charles Edward!"

At the same time a band of musicians, stationed at Tom Syddall's door, and directed by the Jacobite barber in person, struck up the old air of "The king shall have his own again." But this could scarcely be heard amid the din caused by the pipers.

Most of the open windows on either side of the street were adorned by damsels dressed in white, and these fair adherents to the royal House of Stuart now leaned forward and waved their handkerchiefs to the prince.

Such a demonstration could not be otherwise than highly gratifying to the young Chevalier, and he bowed and smiled in acknowledgment of the salutations offered him, the grace of his manner eliciting fresh cheers.

So greatly was the crowd excited, that it was with difficulty the foremost ranks could be prevented from pressing on the prince, who, however, would not allow his body-guard of Highlanders to interfere.

No untoward circumstance marred the general satisfaction. Bells were pealing blithely, drums beating, pipes playing, colours flying, men shouting, kerchiefs waving all the way from the bridge to the market-place, where a brief halt was made.

Having been joined by his secretary, Mr. Murray, who explained where his head-quarters were situated, the prince resumed his march, still preceded by the pipers, and attended by his body-guard of Highlanders. On reaching the house designed for him, he entered it with his suite, and disappeared from the view of the shouting crowd who had followed him. The pipers and the Highland guard drew up in the courtyard.

A sumptuous repast had been prepared in the dining room, and to this Charles and his attendants at once sat down.

Little repose, however, was allowed the indefatigable prince. The chief magistrates, Mr. Fowden and Mr. Walley, were waiting to confer with him in the audience-chamber, across which, in accordance with Mr. Murray's suggestion, a green silk curtain had been drawn—the stuff, however, being slight in texture, the persons on either side the hanging could be easily distinguished.

The magistrates, therefore, seeing the prince enter the room, attended by Mr. Murray and Sir Thomas Sheridan, bowed profoundly, and their obeisances were graciously returned.

Charles Edward then seated himself, and the conference was opened by his secretary.

"His royal highness thanks you, gentlemen," said Mr. Murray, "for the excellent arrangements made for him, and desires to express his gratification at the enthusiastic reception given him on his entrance into your loyal town. He will now have to put the zeal and devotion of your fellow-townsmen to the test."

"In what way, sir?" demanded Mr. Walley, uneasily. "We have given orders that the whole of the prince's forces shall be billeted, and have directed the excise-money to be sent to you as treasurer. What further proof can we give of our desire to serve his royal highness?"

"I will explain, gentlemen, in a word," replied the secretary. "The prince requires a subsidy from the town of five thousand pounds. War cannot be carried on without money, and our coffers are well-nigh emptied."

"I fear it will be impossible to raise that amount," said Mr. Fowden.

"We should grieve to have to levy the money by force, but we must have it. Consult together, gentlemen, and give us your answer."

After a moment's deliberation with his brother magistrate, Mr. Fowden asked if half the amount would not suffice; whereupon Charles remarked, in a loud peremptory tone, "Bid them furnish three thousand pounds—not less."

"You hear, gentlemen. Three thousand pounds must be

furnished to the treasury without delay. You know the penalty of neglect."

"We will do our best," said Mr. Fowden. "But pray give us till to-morrow."

"Be it so," replied the secretary.

The magistrates then asked if the prince had any further commands.

"His Majesty King James the Third will be proclaimed at the Cross," said Mr. Murray; "and it is necessary that both of you should be present at the ceremony. It is also necessary that one of you should repeat the proclamation."

The magistrates tried to excuse themselves, but the secretary cut them short, saying, "You have nothing to fear, gentlemen. We will make it appear you are acting on compulsion. But take care that the prince's manifesto and declaration, copies of which will be delivered to you, are distributed to the crowd. And now, gentlemen, we will not detain you longer. His royal highness expects to see you to-morrow—with the money."

The audience then terminated, and the magistrates, who were full of perplexity, quitted the chamber. The prince and his companions laughed very heartily when they were gone.

Several other persons were admitted to a private interview, after which the prince adjourned to a much larger room which had been prepared for his receptions.

CHAPTER XV.

THE PRINCE'S LEVEE.

THE room had a very brilliant appearance, being crowded with officers of high rank. In the antechamber all who desired the honour of a presentation were assembled.

On the entrance of the prince, who proceeded towards the upper end of the room, and took up a station there, all the nobles and heads of clans formed a semicircle around him—those nearest his royal highness, on the right and left, being the Duke of Perth, the Marquis of Tullibardine, the Marquis d'Eguilles, Lords George Murray, Pitsligo, Nairne, Kilmarnock, and Balmerino.

The first persons to approach the prince were Colonel Townley and the Chevalier de Johnstone, the latter of whom, as already stated, being aide-de-camp to Lord George Gordon.

Colonel Townley, who was in full uniform, wore a plaid waistcoat, and a plaid sash lined with white silk. He came to inform the prince that the Manchester Regiment was now embodied, and would be paraded on the morrow.

"The deficiency in men, of which I complained to your royal highness, has been made good by Colonel Johnstone, who has delivered over to me all the recruits raised for him in this town by Sergeant Dickson."

"You have done well, colonel," remarked the prince, approvingly, to Johnstone. "How many men has Sergeant Dickson enlisted?"

"Nearly two hundred," was the reply. "They are all fine fellows, and will make excellent soldiers."

"I esteem myself singularly fortunate in obtaining them," observed Colonel Townley. "I was almost in despair, not being able to find fifty volunteers myself."

"Sergeant Dickson deserves promotion," said the prince. "I am told that he entered the town, attended only by Helen Carnegie and a drummer."

"It is perfectly true," replied Johnstone. "I would not detract from the brave fellow's merit; but without Helen he would have done nothing."

"Between them they have raised the Manchester Regiment," remarked Colonel Townley, "and saved me a vast deal of trouble."

"Have all the officers joined?" asked the prince.

"All," replied Townley. "Two of them are in the ante-chamber. Captains James Dawson and Atherton Legh. May I have the honour of presenting them to your royal highness?"

Charles Edward having graciously signified his assent, Colonel Townley bowed and retired, reappearing in another moment with the two young officers in question.

They now wore the uniform of the regiment—red faced with white—and looked so well that Colonel Townley felt very proud of them as he led them towards the prince, by whom they were received with the utmost condescension.

Atherton Legh's appearance seemed particularly to please him, and at the close of the brief interview, he desired him to remain in the house, as he had some orders to give him.

Much gratified by the command, Atherton bowed and retired with his friend.

Several other presentations then took place, which need not be recorded, the two persons chiefly distinguished by the prince's notice being Dr. Deacon and Dr. Byrom.

To the latter he said many flattering things well calculated to gratify him; towards the other he adopted a more serious tone, and thanked him earnestly for the zealous attachment he had always shown to the royal cause.

"You have proved your devotion in many ways, doctor," he said, "but never more than in causing your three sons to enrol themselves in the Manchester Regiment. I thank you in the king my father's name, and in my own."

"Heaven grant that my sons may serve your royal father well, most gracious prince!" said Dr. Deacon. "I can only aid you with my prayers."

Overcome by his emotion, he then bowed deeply and retired.

At this juncture the doors of the ante-chamber were thrown open, and a bevy of ladies, all attired in white, and wearing plaid sashes, came forth, imparting a much more lively character to the scene.

Most of these fair Jacobites were young, and many of them being exceedingly pretty, it is not wonderful that their appearance should produce an effect upon the excitable Highlanders, who did not care to conceal their admiration of the Southron beauties. Their assiduities, however, did not seem disagreeable to the Manchester damsels.

Meantime the ladies were conducted in succession to the prince, and each had the honour of kissing his hand. Some of them received a pretty compliment into the bargain. So well turned were these compliments, and so captivating the smiles that accompanied them, that the younger damsels were quite bewitched, and declared that so charming a prince had never been seen.

By far the prettiest of those presented was Beppy Byrom, who was quite as much influenced as any of the others by the witchery of the prince's manner.

As she drew near, she scarcely dared to raise her eyes towards him, but a few pleasant words soon set her at her ease, and the smile that lighted up her fair features so improved their expression that Charles was as much charmed with her as she was with him.

After their presentation the ladies were taken to an adjoining parlour. It fell to Atherton's lot to conduct Beppy to this room, which was crowded with fair damsels and Highland officers, laughing, chattering, and quaffing champagne. Large glasses of the same wine were offered them on their entrance, and having drunk the appointed toast with enthusiasm, they seated themselves on a sofa.

Whether the excitement of the occasion gave unwonted lustre to Beppy's eyes, we know not, but it is certain that Atherton felt their force more than he had ever done before.

"I wonder whether you will return to Manchester when the campaign is over, Captain Legh?" she inquired, looking rather languishingly at him as she spoke.

"Does Miss Byrom care to see me again?" he asked. "If so, I shall make a point of coming back, supposing I am able to do so."

"You pay me a great compliment," she remarked. "But surely, I am not the only person you desire to see again? You must have many dear friends?"

"I have none," he replied, rather gloomily. "You know I am quite alone in the world. If I fall in this expedition, not a tear will be shed for me."

"There you are mistaken," she rejoined, in a sympathetic tone. "But you speak rather bitterly. I fear you have been badly treated."

"No, I have no right to complain. I am only paying the penalty of my folly. I have been deluded by false hopes; but I shall try to act more sensibly in future."

"An excellent resolution, and I trust you will keep to it. Never fall in love again—if you can help it. That's my advice."

"But you don't expect me to follow it?"

"I have no influence over you, and cannot therefore expect you to be guided by my counsels. But I repeat—don't fall in love again."

"The warning comes too late," he said. "I must make a desperate effort, or I shall be caught in fresh toils."

"Well, the effort can be easily made, since you are going away."

"But I shall carry the remembrance with me. I shall not forget our present conversation, and if I return I will remind you of it."

"I have very little faith in the promise. By that time you will probably have changed your mind."

"You must entertain a very poor opinion of me, Miss Byrom, if you really think so."

"I don't imagine you differ from the rest of your sex. Men are proverbially inconstant. 'Out of sight, out of mind,'

"On my return you will find me unchanged," he said.

So engrossed was Atherton by the young lady near him, that he had not noticed the entrance of Constance, with Jemmy Dawson and Monica. But chancing to look up at the moment, he perceived her standing at a little distance, with her large eyes fixed upon him. The expression of her countenance showed that she had overheard what had passed between him and Miss Byrom. With a disdainful glance, she moved away with her father.

Atherton was quite confounded, and for a moment could not speak, but at length he stammered:

"Do you see who is in the room?"

"Miss Rawcliffe you mean," replied Beppy. "Yes, I saw her come in. I did not tell you, because I fancied you had no longer any interest in her. But I begin to think you have not so completely shaken off your fetters as you imagined. If all is at an end, why should her presence trouble you?"

"I am not quite master of my feelings," he rejoined.

"So I perceive," said Beppy. She then added, in a good-natured tone: "Well, we have stayed here long enough. Let us go."

Much relieved by the proposal, the young man instantly arose, and offering her his arm, prepared to quit the room.

But, in making their way through the crowd, they were soon brought to a stand-still, and found themselves face to face with Constance.

By this time Atherton had recovered his self-possession, and bowed coldly, and his salutation was as distantly returned. Beppy, however, who had some little malice in her composition, rather enjoyed the situation, and not feeling inclined to put an end to it, immediately engaged Miss Rawcliffe in conversation, and left Atherton to Monica and Jemmy Dawson.

Fain would he have escaped, but he could not leave Beppy, who, indeed, did not relinquish her hold of his arm. Luckily, champagne was brought by the attendants, and everybody took a glass, as in duty bound.

Again the prince's health was drunk, and with as much enthusiasm as before, though Beppy only placed the glass to her lips.

"You have not done justice to the toast, Miss Byrom," cried a voice near her.

And turning, she perceived Colonel Townley, who had just entered the room with her father.

"I have already drunk it," she replied. "But I have wine enough left to drink 'Success to the Manchester Regiment,' and I do so."

And she again raised the glass to her lips.

Colonel Townley bowed, and expressed his thanks.

"More champagne," he cried to the attendants. "Gentlemen," he added, to his officers, "let us drink to Miss Rawcliffe and the ladies who have helped to raise the regiment."

Due honour was done to the toast. As Atherton bowed to Constance, she regarded him coldly, and scarcely acknowledged the attention.

"Something is wrong," thought Colonel Townley. "I must endeavour to set it right. You will be pleased to hear, Miss Rawcliffe," he said, "that his royal highness fully appreciates the service you have rendered him. I took care to tell him the Manchester Regiment owed Captain Legh to you."

"The circumstance was scarcely worth mentioning," she rejoined, with affected indifference.

"The prince thought otherwise," remarked Colonel Townley "I will not repeat the flattering things he said——"

"Oh, pray do not!" she interrupted. "I would rather not hear them."

"But they relate chiefly to Captain Legh."

"Then keep them for his private ear," she rejoined.

The colonel shrugged his shoulders and said no more.

Just then the pipers stationed in the court began to play, and as the hall-door stood open, the lively strains resounded through the house, and made the Highland officers eager for a dance.

They began to talk about Scotch reels and other national dances, of which the young ladies had never heard, but they did not venture to propose any such agreeable exercise, as it would have been contrary to etiquette.

The pipers, in fact, had been ordered to play as an intimation to the assemblage that the prince's levée was over, and as soon as this was understood the company began to depart.

Colonel Townley offered his arm to Constance, and conducted her to the entrance-hall, where they found Sir Richard Rawcliffe, Dr. Byrom, and several other gentlemen who were waiting for their wives and daughters.

As soon as the young ladies had been consigned to their natural protectors, Colonel Townley turned to Atherton, and said:

"You will return at eight o'clock to-night, Captain Legh. You are bidden to the supper by the prince. I was specially commanded to bring you. His royal highness seems to have taken a fancy to you. But tell me!—what is the cause of the misunderstanding between you and Miss Rawcliffe?"

"I know not," replied Atherton. "But she looks coldly upon me—and her father has treated me with great rudeness."

"Indeed!" exclaimed Colonel Townley. "I will have an explanation from him. Remember that the regiment will be paraded in St. Ann's Square at ten o'clock to-morrow."

They then separated, and Atherton quitted the house.

The court was filled by the Highland body-guard and the pipers. The latter, drawn up in two lines, through which the company passed, were making a prodigious din, greatly to the delight of the crowd collected in the street.

CHAPTER XVI.

THE ILLUMINATIONS.

The town now presented a most extraordinary appearance, and looked as if occupied by a hostile army—the streets being filled with Highland soldiers, who were wandering about, staring at the houses and shops, and besieging the taverns.

The townspeople seemed on very good terms with their visitors, and the occupants of the houses at which the soldiers were billeted received them as well as could be expected.

By this time all the principal personages connected with the Highland army had taken possession of the quarters assigned them, and sentries were placed at the doorways or at the gates.

Large bonfires were lighted in various parts of the town— in the market-place, in Spring Fields, on Shude Hill, on Hunt's Bank, and at the foot of the bridge, and preparations were made for a general illumination at night.

Nothing was neglected by the magistrates. In obedience to the injunctions they had received from Mr. Murray, they attended at the Town Cross to assist at the proclamation of his Majesty King James the Third. A large concourse assembled to witness the ceremony, and shouted lustily at its conclusion.

As yet, no disturbance whatever had occurred—for the Whigs and Presbyterians consulted their own safety by remaining quiet, well knowing if they made a demonstration they would be quickly overpowered. Consequently, the town continued tranquil.

As soon as it became dusk, the illuminations commenced. They were general, for no one dared to disobey the order, and the obnoxious Whigs and Presbyterians burnt more candles than their Jacobite neighbours. But the display did not save their windows. A large mob armed with bludgeons went about the town shouting, "Long live King James the Third, and Charles, Prince Regent!" and when they came to a house the owner of which was offensive to them, a great smashing of glass took place.

No efforts were made to check these lawless proceedings. Every license was allowed the mob, so long as they confined their playful attentions to the opposite party. For the sufferers there was no redress, since the streets swarmed with Highland soldiers who enjoyed the sport.

Additional excitement was given by the pipers, who marched about playing loudly upon their shrill instruments. What with the bonfires, the illuminations, the uproarious crowd, the Highlanders, and the pipers, the ordinary aspect of the town seemed entirely changed.

The spectacle was so novel and curious, that many of the gentler sex came forth to witness it, and it must be said, to the credit of the crowd, that the ladies experienced no sort of annoyance.

Luckily the night was fine, though sufficiently dark to give full effect to the illuminations.

Beppy and her father, accompanied by Atherton, walked about for nearly two hours, and Miss Byrom declared it was the prettiest sight she ever beheld. She had seen an illumination before, but never on so grand a scale, while the strange accompaniments greatly amused her.

Oddly enough, the illuminations in the old parts of the town were more effective than in the modern streets. With their lattice windows lighted up, the ancient habitations looked exceedingly picturesque.

But by far the most striking object in the town was the collegiate church. Partly buried in gloom—partly revealed by the bonfires kindled in its vicinity, the flames of which were reflected upon its massive tower, battlements, and buttresses—the venerable pile was seen to the greatest advantage. Very few, however, except the persons we have mentioned, cared to gaze at it. Those who crossed the churchyard made the best of their way to the streets, to see the illuminations and mingle with the crowd.

After bidding good-night to his friends, Atherton repaired to the only house in Manchester which was not illuminated.

But though the prince's residence was not lighted up, abundant evidence was furnished that a grand entertainment was about to take place inside it. The Highland guard was drawn up in two lines, extending from the gate to the doorway, and through this avenue all the nobles, chiefs of clans, and officers who were invited to sup with the prince, made their way into the house.

Some of them arrived in sedan-chairs, but the majority came on foot, since no coaches could be procured. But however they came, their appearance was greeted with cheers by the concourse collected in front of the mansion, and many an eye followed them as the door was flung open to give them admittance.

Naturally, Atherton felt elated on finding himself among so important an assemblage; but a great distinction was reserved for him.

It chanced that the prince was in the hall as he entered, and on seeing him, his royal highness addressed him with the most gracious familiarity, and taking him apart, said:

"Captain Legh, I am going round the town after supper, and I mean to take you with me."

Atherton bowed.

"I am told the illuminations are very good, and I want to see them. But I do not desire to be recognised, and I shall therefore take no other attendant except yourself."

Again Atherton bowed deeply—his looks expressing his gratification.

"Do not mention my purpose," continued the prince, "as I would not have it known. Some of my immediate attendants would insist on accompanying me, and I would rather be without them. In a word, I wish to be incognito, like the Caliph Haroun Al Raschid."

"Your royal highness may rely on my discretion," said Atherton.

"After supper," pursued the prince, "when the company has begun to disperse, come to this hall, and wait till I appear."

Atherton bowed profoundly, and the prince passed on

CHAPTER XVII.

A QUARREL AT SUPPER.

SHORTLY afterwards, supper was served in the dining-room. The repast was profuse, but no great ceremony was observed, for the prince supped in private with the Duke of Perth, the Marquis of Tullibardine, Lord George Murray, and some other nobles.

Atherton sat next to Colonel Townley, who took the opportunity of giving him some instructions as to the duties he would have to discharge.

"The men will be drilled previous to the muster to-morrow," said the colonel, "and I hope we shall get through it tolerably well. Every allowance will be made for raw recruits. In a few days they will have learnt their duties, and all will be right."

On the opposite side of the table sat Sir Richard Rawcliffe, and Atherton remarked that the baronet's eye was often fixed suspiciously upon him. Colonel Townley also made the same remark.

"Sir Richard is far from pleased to see you here," he observed. "From some cause or other he seems to have taken a strong aversion to you."

"You are acquainted with my history, I know, colonel," said Atherton. "I cannot help thinking that Sir Richard, if he chose, could clear up the mystery that hangs over my birth."

This observation, which was not made in a very low tone, reached the quick ears of the baronet, who darted an angry look at the speaker.

"Colonel Townley," he said, "pray tell your neighbour that I am totally ignorant of his parentage."

"That does not satisfy me," cried Atherton, addressing the baronet. "I am determined to have an explanation."

Sir Richard laughed contemptuously, but made no reply.

"This discussion cannot be prolonged," said Colonel Townley, who perceived that the attention of those near them was attracted to what was passing. "But some explanation must be given."

No more was said at the time, but when supper was over, and the company had risen from the table, Colonel Townley followed the baronet, and taking him apart, said to him, in a grave tone:

"You have publicly insulted Captain Legh, Sir Richard. He demands an apology."

"I have none to make," rejoined the baronet, haughtily.

"In that case, Captain Legh will require satisfaction, and an early meeting must be appointed."

"I decline to meet Captain Legh," said the baronet.

"On what ground?" demanded Colonel Townley.

"I do not consider myself bound to give any reason for my refusal. Enough that I will not meet him."

"Your pardon, Sir Richard. 'Tis not enough for me. Since you decline to apologise to Captain Legh, or to give him satisfaction, you will have to fight me."

"If you think proper to espouse his quarrel, I will not balk you. The Chevalier de Johnstone, I am sure, will act for me, and your second can make all necessary arrangements with him."

"The affair must not be delayed. Will an early hour to-morrow morning suit you?"

"Perfectly," replied Sir Richard. "As early as you please."

"Swords, of course?" said the colonel.

"Swords, by all means."

Bowing stiffly towards each other, they then separated, and Colonel Townley repaired to the entrance-hall, where he expected to find Atherton.

As he was looking round, he noticed the Chevalier de Johnstone, and going up to him, inquired if he had seen Captain Legh.

"Yes," replied Johnstone; "he was here not a minute or two ago. But he has gone upon a nocturnal ramble with the prince. You look incredulous—but 'tis even so. His royal highness has just gone forth to see the illuminations, or in quest of some adventure, and has taken Captain Legh with him. As he passed quickly through this hall the prince did not stop to speak to any one, but signed to Captain Legh, who instantly followed him. This is all I have to relate; but it proves that the young man is in high favour. His royal highness was muffled in a plaid shawl, different from the one he usually wears, and otherwise disguised; but I knew him."

"'Tis strange he did not take his aide-de-camp, Colonel Ker, with him, in preference to Captain Legh," remarked Colonel Townley. "But I have something to say to you in reference to an affair in which this highly-favoured young man is concerned. Sir Richard Rawcliffe refuses to offer satisfaction to Legh for the rudeness he offered him at supper. I have taken up the quarrel, for I will not allow an officer in my regiment to be insulted. You won't refuse, I presume, to act as Rawcliffe's second?"

"Certainly not," replied Johnstone. "But I wish the duel could be prevented. It seems a very trifling matter to fight about."

"I think Sir Richard has behaved very badly to the young man, and I will have an apology from him."

"Well, since it must be so, there is no help. Send your second to me."

"Colonel Ker will be my second. I will send him to you as soon as he makes his appearance."

"Meantime, I will consult Sir Richard—though I don't fancy he will apologise."

He then went in quest of the baronet, whom he soon found, while Colonel Townley seated himself in the hall with the intention of awaiting Atherton's return.

CHAPTER XVIII.

CAPTAIN WEIR.

MUFFLED in a plaid shawl, and otherwise disguised, as we have said, the prince passed unrecognised through the guard, and taking his way down Market Street Lane, proceeded to a short distance, and then halted to allow Atherton to overtake him.

In uncovering the lower part of his face to speak to the young man, Charles betrayed himself to an individual who had seen him come forth from the mansion, and suspecting his condition, had followed him cautiously.

This person, whose name was Weir, and who acted as a spy to the Duke of Cumberland, had conceived the daring idea of capturing the prince, and sending him prisoner to the duke, whose head-quarters were at Lichfield. He had been stimulated by the hope of a large reward to undertake this desperate project. A price of thirty thousand pounds had been set upon Charles Edward's head, and though Weir shrank from assassination, he had no scruples as to capturing the prince, neither was he deterred by the extraordinary danger of the attempt. All he wanted was an opportunity to execute his design.

Captain Weir, as he was styled, though he had no real military rank, usually acted alone, but on this occasion he had three subordinate officers with him, on whose courage and fidelity he could perfectly rely. They were now close at hand, watching his movements, and waiting for orders. Like himself, they were all well armed.

Signing to these personages to follow him, Captain Weir continued to track the prince's course down Market Street Lane.

Meanwhile, the young Chevalier was marching along quietly, with Atherton by his side, never for a moment imagining he was in danger, or even that his disguise had been detected.

Scores of Highland soldiers were in the street, but none of them knew their commander-in-chief. Had they done so, they would have formed a guard round his person. But this was precisely what Charles objected to. Wherever there was a crowd he strove to avoid it; but the obstructions were frequent. He was rejoiced, however, to perceive that the white cockade everywhere prevailed, while such observations as reached him indicated that the populace was decidedly favourable to his cause.

It was such honest expressions of opinion as these that he desired to hear, and where a group of persons were talking loudly, he stopped to listen to their discourse.

As may well be supposed, he cared little for the illuminations except as evidencing the goodwill of the townsfolk, but he was struck by the picturesque appearance of the old houses when thus lighted up. After several halts from one cause or other, he and Atherton at last reached the market-place.

Here, in the centre of the area, was a large bonfire, with a great crowd collected round it. Moreover, a barrel of ale, provided by the magistrates, had just been broached, enabling the crowd to drink the prince's health, coupled with that of his august sire, James the Third, in flowing cups.

Much amused by the scene, Charles stopped to look at it, as well as to examine the curious picture presented by the illuminated market-place.

While he was thus occupied, a sudden movement in the throng separated him from his attendant, and he was endeavouring to free himself from the press when a strong grasp was laid upon his arm.

The person who had thus seized him was no other than Sergeant Dickson.

"Unmuffle, and show your face, if you be not ashamed of it," cried the sergeant. "I suspect you are a Hanoverian spy. I have heard there are some in the town, and you don't look like a Highland officer."

"Hands off, fellow," said the prince, authoritatively. "Help me out of the crowd."

"Help you to escape! not I!" cried Dickson. "Unmuffle, I say, and let us see your face."

Several of the bystanders now called out, "A spy! a spy!" and Charles would have been unpleasantly circumstanced, if Helen Carnegie, who was near the sergeant, had not interposed.

"You are wrong, Erick," she cried. "This is no spy. Release him."

But the sergeant was not inclined to part with his prisoner, and was only prevented from plucking the covering from his face by Atherton, who by this time had forced his way up.

A word breathed in the ear of the sergeant instantly changed the complexion of affairs, and he was now just as anxious to get the prince off as he had before been to detain him.

"All right," he shouted. "His royal highness has not a better friend than this noble gentleman. I'll answer for him. Stand back! stand back! my masters, and let the gentleman pass."

Vigorously seconding these injunctions with his strong arm, he cleared a way for the prince, who was soon out of the crowd; and this being accomplished, the sergeant humbly besought pardon for his maladroit proceeding.

"You ought to have known me under any disguise, sergeant," was the prince's good-natured reply. "You are not half so sharp-witted as Helen. She knew me at once."

"I canna take upon mysel to declare that, your highness," replied the Scottish lassie, who had followed in their wake; "but I ken'd fu' weel ye were na a fawse spy, but a leal gentleman."

"Well, sergeant, I am willing to overlook your fault for Helen's sake," said Charles.

"I shall na sae readily forgive mysel," replied the sergeant. "But in truth my thoughts were runnin' on spies. May I be permitted to attend your highness?"

"No, I forbid you to follow me," said Charles.

So saying, he marched off with Atherton, leaving the sergeant greatly chagrined by the interdiction.

"This'll be a gude lesson t' ye, Erick," observed Helen. "In future, ye'll ken the prince when you see him, whether he be muffled in a shawl or na."

"Come wi' me, lassie. I'm resolved to follow his highness at a respectful distance. The night's not ower yet, and something tells me I may be useful to him."

"Ye ought na to disobey orders, Erick; but sin ye win gang yer ain gate, I'll e'en gae wi' ye."

With this they followed in the direction taken by Charles and his companion, but before reaching the bottom of Old Mill Gate, they lost sight of them. The sergeant questioned a person whom he saw standing at the corner of the street, and was told that two officers had gone towards the bridge. The information was not altogether correct, but the person who gave it was Captain Weir.

Scarcely was the sergeant gone, when a man on a powerful steed came up, and dismounting, delivered the horse to Weir, who was evidently waiting for him.

Accompanied by this man, who marched by his side, Weir rode along Hanging Ditch, and soon overtook his two myrmidons, who were following the prince. They pointed out their intended captive about fifty yards in advance.

"I need not repeat my instructions," said Weir, bending down as he addressed them, and speaking in a low voice. "But I again enjoin you to use the utmost despatch. Success mainly depends upon the celerity with which the work is done. If I can secure him, I will answer for the rest. Now go on, and draw a little nearer to him."

"With this, he dropped slightly behind, got ready a belt, which he meant to use, and examined the holsters to see that the pistols within them were all right.

Had Charles Edward been playing into their hands he could not have taken a course more favourable to the designs of these desperate men. His intention had been to return by the collegiate church; but he was deterred by the uproarious crowds collected round the two large bonfires burning at the back of the venerable fabric, and proceeded up Withy Grove, by the advice of Atherton, who being well acquainted with the locality, explained to him that he could easily and expeditiously regain his head-quarters by crossing an open field on the right at the top of this thoroughfare.

When Weir and his accomplices found that the prince had elected this course they felt sure he was delivered into their hands.

At the rear of the small and scattered tenements, then constituting Withy Grove, were extensive gardens, and beyond these, as already stated, there were two or three fields, as yet entirely unbuilt upon.

Into these fields the prince and his attendant now turned, but the place looked so gloomy, from its contrast with the lights blazing in the distance, that Atherton thought it would be prudent to turn back. Charles, however, having no fear, determined to go on.

Shortly afterwards, a real alarm occurred. A horseman, accompanied by three men on foot, suddenly entered the field. At first, neither the prince nor Atherton imagined that their design was hostile, but they were quickly undeceived. Before he could offer any effectual resistance,

Charles was seized by two strong men, who bound his arms behind his back, and twisting the shawl over his mouth, prevented him from uttering an outcry.

At the same time, the horseman dealt a blow at Atherton with a hanger, which the young man avoided, but he had next to defend himself against the attack of the third ruffian on foot, so that he could render no immediate assistance to the prince.

While he was thus engaged, the two desperadoes who had seized Charles lifted him from the ground, and despite his struggles, set him on the horse behind their leader, with his face towards the crupper, while Weir passed a broad leather belt round his waist, so as to secure him, and was in the act of buckling it in front, when the bridle was seized by Atherton, who, by a lucky thrust, had delivered himself from his assailant.

Just in time. In another minute rescue would have been impossible. Hitherto, not a shot had been fired; but Weir now drew a pistol, and levelling it at Atherton, bade him instantly retire on peril of his life.

The gallant young man, however, still held on, but was unable to use his sword, owing to the rearing of the steed.

Weir then fired, but missed his mark, the shot taking effect in his horse's head. With a cry of pain the mortally-wounded animal broke away, but almost instantly sank to the ground and rolled over.

Unbuckling the belt, Weir disengaged himself as quickly as he could from the prostrate steed, and full of rage that his attempt should be thus foiled, the miscreant might have raised his hand against the defenceless prince, if loud shouts had not warned him that assistance was at hand. He then sought safety in flight, and was speeding towards the back of the field, followed by his men, two of whom had been severely wounded by Atherton.

The shout that had alarmed Weir proceeded from Sergeant Dickson and Tom Syddall.

Between the College Church and the river were small houses and twisting streets.

When he was on his way to the bridge, the sergeant encountered the barber, and the latter satisfied him that the prince had not gone in that direction.

His suspicions being excited, Dickson turned back instantly, and Syddall accompanied him—Helen, of course, continuing with her lover.

Some information picked up caused them to turn into Withy Grove, and they had just tracked that thoroughfare, and were debating whether they should go on to Shude Hill, when the noise of a conflict was heard in the field on the right.

"My forebodings have come true," cried the sergeant, "some villains are attacking the prince."

As the words were uttered, the report of a pistol increased their alarm.

Shouting lustily, Erick drew his claymore, and dashed into the field, followed by Helen and Syddall.

Though too late to render assistance, the sergeant was in time to help Atherton to liberate the prince. By their united efforts Charles was soon on his feet, and freed from his bonds.

"I trust in Heaven that your highness has sustained no harm?" cried Atherton, anxiously.

"No, I am entirely uninjured," said Charles, in a cheerful voice. "I have to thank you most heartily, Captain Legh, for freeing me from villains whose design was evidently to carry me off as a prisoner to the Duke of Cumberland."

"I think I have sufficiently punished two of the villains," said Atherton, "but it enrages me that their leader, and doubtless the contriver of this atrocious scheme, has escaped."

"He may yet be captured," cried the sergeant. "Tom Syddall was with me when I entered the field, and has gone in pursuit. He will give the alarm."

"Then I must hasten to head-quarters, and show myself," said the prince, moving on.

But after walking quickly for some forty or fifty yards, he was compelled to halt.

"I am more shaken than I thought," he said. "Give me your arm, Helen, I must have some support."

Proceeding in this manner, he had nearly reached the limits of the field, and was approaching an unfinished street that communicated with Market Street Lane, when a sudden light revealed a picket of Highland soldiers. At the head of the party, several of whom carried torches, was Colonel Ker, accompanied by Colonel Townley and the Chevalier de Johnstone.

In another moment, a wild and joyful shout announced that the Highlanders had discovered their beloved prince. They rushed forward in a body, and the foremost flung themselves at his feet, while those behind gave vent to their delight in another ringing shout.

Colonel Ker did not choose to interrupt this demonstration; but, as soon as it was over, he advanced with the two distinguished officers just mentioned, and all three offered their congratulations to his royal highness on his escape.

After warmly thanking them, Charles called Atherton forward, and told them that he owed his deliverance entirely to the young man's gallant conduct, explaining what had been done, and concluding emphatically with these words, "But for Captain Legh, I should at this moment be a prisoner."

Naturally, the young man was much gratified by these observations, as well as by the praises bestowed on him by Colonel Ker and the others, but he received their commendations with great modesty.

The prince then asked Colonel Townley how he had heard of the attack made upon him, and learnt that the alarming news had been brought by Tom Syddall.

"Syddall came to me," said Colonel Townley, "and I immediately took him to Colonel Ker, as his statement might not have been credited."

"Where is he?" demanded Charles. "I must thank him for what he has done."

"After explaining where your highness would be found, Syddall begged to be allowed to go in quest of the villains who had assailed you," said Colonel Ker, "being fully persuaded that he could accomplish the capture of their daring leader, and as Colonel Townley knew the spot where your royal highness would be found, I did not refuse the request."

"If the villain should be captured to-night," said Charles, which I think scarce likely, let him be brought before me at once. I will interrogate him myself."

"Your commands shall be obeyed," rejoined Ker. "Shall we now return to head-quarters?"

"By all means," replied Charles. "But march slowly."

Colonel Ker was about to give orders, when another party of soldiers, having a prisoner in their midst, was seen advancing along the unfinished street. The party was guided by Tom Syddall, who carried a torch.

CHAPTER XIX.

CAPTAIN WEIR IS INTERROGATED BY THE PRINCE.

As soon as the prince was descried, the advancing party halted, and Syddall giving the torch to one of the men, pressed forward towards Charles, and making a profound obeisance, said:

"The villain who attacked your royal highness has been captured. He had taken refuge in a stable at the back of the Angel Inn. He is here, if you desire to question him."

In obedience to the prince's command the prisoner then stepped forward between two soldiers. He did not appear intimidated by the position in which he was placed, but bore himself very boldly.

Charles looked at him for a few moments, and calling to Atherton, asked him if he recognised the man.

"I recognise him as the leader of the attack," was the reply.

"Such is my own opinion," observed the prince. "How say you?" he added to the prisoner. "Do you deny the charge?"

"No," replied the prisoner. "I am the man."

"You avow your guilt," said Charles, surprised by his boldness. "How are you named?"

"I am known as Captain Weir," replied the other.

"Have you aught to allege why you should not be delivered to the provost-marshal for immediate execution?" observed Charles, sternly.

"My life is justly forfeited," replied the prisoner, "yet your royal highness will do well to spare me."

"Wherefore?" demanded the prince, whose curiosity was excited.

"My reasons are only for your private ear," replied the prisoner.

After a moment's reflection, during which he kept his eye fixed on Weir, Charles ordered the guard to retire.

"Leave the prisoner with me," he said. "But if he attempts to fly—shoot him."

As soon as the command was obeyed, he said:

"You can speak freely now. Why should I spare your life?"

"Firstly, because it will prove to the world that you are a magnanimous prince, and in that respect superior to your enemies, who are notorious for their severity," replied Weir. "Next, because I can tell much that it behoves your royal highness to know, as will be evident when I declare that I am employed by the Duke of Cumberland as a spy, and am, therefore, necessarily in his royal highness's confidence. If my life be spared, and I am allowed to go back to Lichfield, where the duke is quartered, I can mislead him by erroneous information, while I shall be able to acquaint you with his plans—exact knowledge of which I need not say will be eminently serviceable."

"There is much in what you say, I must own," replied the prince. "But what guarantee have I that you will not prove a double traitor?"

"My gratitude," replied Weir. "I could never prove faithless to a prince so generous."

"I can make no promise," replied Charles; but in a tone that held out some encouragement to the prisoner.

At a sign from the prince the guard then advanced, and again took charge of Weir. Shortly afterwards, the prisoner was removed, it being understood that his execution was deferred—much to the disappointment of the Highland guard, who would willingly have shot him.

Charles then addressed a few kindly observations to Syddall, who had been mainly instrumental in the capture of the spy, telling him that the service should not pass unrequited. Nor did the prince neglect to offer his renewed thanks to Sergeant Dickson and Helen for the zeal and devotion they had both displayed. For Atherton a signal manifestation of favour was reserved.

During the march back to head-quarters, which were not far distant, the prince kept the young man near him, and occasionally took his arm. When the party arrived at the mansion in Market Street Lane they found it completely invested by an anxious crowd, who shouted joyfully on beholding the prince.

But this was nothing to the scene that took place when his royal highness entered the house. Almost all the nobles and Highland chiefs were assembled in the hall, and as Charles entered they pressed around him to offer their warmest congratulations on his escape.

After thanking them in accents that bespoke the deepest emotion, the prince presented Atherton to them, saying, "It is to Captain Legh that I owe my preservation."

The young man was quite overwhelmed by the plaudits that followed this gracious speech.

Thus ended the most important day that had hitherto occurred in Atherton's career. It found him an unknown, and undistinguished; but it left him apparently on the road to honour and preferment.

CHAPTER XX.

THE DUEL.

Next morning, at an early hour, Colonel Townley and Colonel Ker issued from the prince's head-quarters, and, rather to the surprise of the guard drawn up in the court-yard, proceeded at a quick pace along the road leading to Stockport.

In a very few minutes they had left the town behind, for beyond Market Street Lane it was then open country. Not many persons were on the road, and these were chiefly country folk bringing poultry, butter, and milk to market.

Some hundred yards in advance, however, were an officer of rank in the Highland army, and a tall middle-aged gentleman wrapped in a cloak. These persons were evidently bent on the same errand as themselves, and marched on quickly for about a quarter of a mile, when they stopped at the gate of a large meadow. The ground appeared suitable to their purpose, inasmuch as it sank at the further end, and formed a hollow which was screened from view.

Sir Richard Rawcliffe and the Chevalier de Johnstone, for they were the individuals who had thus halted, punctiliously saluted the others when they came up, and Johnstone asked Colonel Ker if he thought the ground would suit.

After consulting his principal, Ker replied in the affirmative, upon which they all passed through the gate, and made their way to the hollow.

Before the preliminaries of the duel were entered upon an ineffectual effort was made by the seconds to adjust the difference. Nothing less than an apology would satisfy Colonel Townley, but this Sir Richard haughtily refused.

Finding their efforts fruitless, the seconds then retired—swords were drawn—hats taken off—and instantly after the salute, the combatants engaged—the attack being made by a thrust in carte delivered by Sir Richard, which was well warded by his adversary.

Several passes were then exchanged, and it was evident to the lookers-on that Colonel Townley meant to disarm his antagonist, and he soon succeeded in the design by skilfully parrying another thrust, seizing the shell of Sir Richard's sword, and compelling him to surrender the weapon.

The seconds then interfered to prevent a renewal of the conflict, but the baronet, who had received his sword from his adversary, insisted on going on, when the clatter of horses' hoofs was heard rapidly approaching the spot, and the next moment the prince appeared, mounted on a splendid bay charger, and attended by an orderly.

Without waiting a moment, Charles rode down into the hollow, and pushing between the combatants, ordered them to sheathe their swords. Of course the command was instantly obeyed.

"A word with you, gentlemen," said the prince, sternly. "You must have been aware that a hostile meeting between persons of your rank would be highly displeasing to me, as well as prejudicial to our cause, and I ought to [mark my disapproval of your conduct by something more than a reprimand, but I am willing to overlook it, provided a reconciliation takes place between you."

Both bowed, and Colonel Townley signified his assent, but the baronet maintained a sullen silence.

"I am aware of the grounds of your quarrel," pursued the prince, "and I hold that you, Sir Richard Rawcliffe, are in the wrong. I trust you will offer a sufficient apology—

not merely to Colonel Townley, but to Captain Legh, whom you have insulted."

"Your royal highness's injunctions must needs be obeyed," rejoined the baronet, haughtily. "To Colonel Townley I am quite willing to apologise; but to Captain Legh——"

"I will accept no apology from you, Sir Richard, in which my friend is not included," interrupted Colonel Townley. "I have now a right to demand the cause of the insolent treatment Captain Legh has received, and an explanation of your reason for refusing him the satisfaction to which he was entitled."

"Come with me for a moment, Sir Richard," said Charles, taking him aside. Then bending down towards him, and lowering his voice, he added, "Certain circumstances have just come to my knowledge, showing that you must have some knowledge of Atherton Legh's history, and accounting in some measure for your otherwise incomprehensible conduct towards him."

Sir Richard endeavoured to hide the confusion into which he was thrown, but could not conceal it from the searching glance fixed upon him by the prince.

"Answer me one question?" pursued Charles. "Answer it explicitly? Are you not Atherton Legh's mysterious guardian?"

The baronet's confusion perceptibly increased. Charles seemed to read his thoughts.

"I am wholly at a loss to conceive whence your royal highness has obtained this information respecting me," he said at length.

"No matter how it has been obtained," remarked Charles, sternly. "Is it true?"

"It is correct in the main," replied the baronet. "Although I would gladly be excused from giving any further explanation, I shall be willing to do so at some more convenient opportunity."

"The explanation cannot be deferred," said the prince,

authoritatively. "After the levée this morning you shall have a private audience."

"I will not fail to attend upon your royal highness," replied Sir Richard, evidently much relieved.

But his brow again clouded, when the prince said:

"You will be pleased to bring your daughter with you."

"My daughter!" exclaimed the baronet. "She has nothing whatever to do with the explanation I have to offer."

"You have heard my injunction, Sir Richard. Both Miss Rawcliffe and Captain Legh must be present at the audience."

"I make no objection," replied the baronet; "but it pains me to find that I am viewed with suspicion by your royal highness, to whom I have given unquestionable proofs of my zeal and devotion."

"Justice must be done, Sir Richard," rejoined the prince, sternly. "If there has been a wrong it must be righted. The mystery attaching to this young man's birth must be cleared up, and since you are able to give the information required, you are bound to furnish it. I shall expect you and Miss Rawcliffe after the levée."

Then turning to Colonel Townley, he added: "All obstacles to a perfect reconciliation between you and Sir Richard are now removed. I hope, therefore, to have the pleasure of seeing you shake hands, and trust you will become as good friends as ever."

The injunction having been complied with, the prince prepared to take his departure, saying:

"After a morning duel in France, all those engaged in it—if the principals are fortunately unhurt, or but slightly wounded—make a point of breakfasting together, and I don't see why the custom should not be adopted in this country."

"Nor I," cried Colonel Townley. "I have gained an excellent appetite."

"Then I shall expect you all at breakfast an hour hence," said the prince. "I have much to do to-day. Among other important matters I have to attend the muster of your Manchester Regiment," he added to Colonel Townley.

"I was afraid your royal highness might be prevented," said the colonel. "And that would have been a great disappointment to us. I trust you do not feel any ill effects from the rough shake you got last night."

"A little stiffness—that is all," replied Charles.

"Have you come to any determination in regard to Weir?" inquired Colonel Ker. "Is he to be shot?"

"No," replied the prince. "I shall send him to the Duke of Cumberland. Now for a ride round the town. I shall be back in time for breakfast. Au revoir!"

With this he bounded up the side of the hollow and rode off in the direction of the town, followed by the orderly.

CHAPTER XXI.

CASTLE FIELD.

IT was a fine November morning, and as the surrounding hills were clearly distinguishable, the prince enjoyed the prospect as he cantered along.

The atmosphere being free from smoke as well as fog, the town had a bright, clean, and cheerful look, which it seldom wears now-a-days. What would Charles have thought if he could have conjured up in imagination the smoky factories and huge warehouses now covering the pleasant orchards and gardens near which he rode?

Manchester in '45, as we have already stated, resembled a country town, and on no side was the resemblance more complete than on this, since not more than half a dozen scattered habitations could be descried, the upper end of Market Street being then really a lane.

But though the outskirts of the town were quiet enough,

it was evident from the tumultuous sounds that reached the ear, not only that the inhabitants generally were astir, but that the numerous companies billeted upon them were likewise moving about.

The call of the bugle resounded from various quarters, and the beating of the drum was heard in almost every street. Charles listened delightedly to sounds that proclaimed the presence of his army. He thought of the advance he had already made—how another week's march would bring him to London; his breast beat high with hope and ardour; and he fully believed at that moment that his romantic expedition would be crowned with success.

Just then the bells of all the churches began to ring, and their joyful peals heightened his enthusiasm.

Not wishing to enter the town, he commanded the orderly to guide him to Castle Field; upon which the man rode on in front, and describing a wide circuit then entirely unbuilt upon, but now converted into densely-populated districts and large streets, brought him at last to a large open piece of ground, almost encircled by the river Medlock, and partly surrounded by the crumbling walls of an old Roman-British castle, in the centre of which the artillery was parked.

Not far from the field-pieces were the powder carriages; while a large portion of the area was occupied by baggage-waggons; the remainder of the space being filled by artillery-men and their horses.

No better place in the town or neighbourhood could have been found for the purpose. Castle Field would have accommodated double the number of cannon, and thrice the men, it now held.

It was a very pleasant spot, and a favourite resort of the townsfolk. Sports of various kinds took place within the ring, and an annual fair was held there. But it had never looked more picturesque than it did now, filled as it was with cannon, ammunition, baggage-waggons, sumpter-horses, and men.

Early as was the hour, there were numerous spectators on the spot—women as well as men, for the artillery was a great attraction—and some dozens had climbed the old walls, and planted themselves on the top, to obtain a better view of the novel scene.

As soon as the crowd collected on Castle Field became aware of the prince's arrival, they gathered around him, cheering and expressing heartfelt satisfaction that he had escaped the treacherous attack made upon him overnight.

There could be no doubt from the enthusiasm displayed that the prince's escape had greatly increased his popularity, all those who got near him declaring they were ready to defend him to the death.

Warmly thanking them for their zeal, Charles extricated himself from the press, and was joined by the Duke of Perth, and some officers of artillery, with whom he rode over the field, examining different matters as he went along.

While making this inspection he encountered many ladies, from all of whom he received congratulations, and to whom he had something agreeable to say.

Amongst others, whose curiosity had induced them to pay an early visit to Castle Field, was Beppy. She had come thither, attended by Helen Carnegie.

Charles stopped to speak to the young lady, and noticing that she was decked in white, and wore a St. Andrew's cross, he said, "You have not forgotten, I perceive, Miss Byrom, that this is the fête-day of our Scottish patron saint."

"I was reminded of it by Helen Carnegie, your highness," replied Beppy. "She came to tell me of your most fortunate escape, for which I cannot be sufficiently grateful, and offered to make me a cross."

"No one has done me a like good turn," laughed Charles.

"Here is a braw St. Andrew's cross, if your royal highness will deign to wear it," cried Helen, offering him one.

Charles smiled his thanks, and fastened the cross to his jacket.

"Are you staying with Miss Byrom, Helen?" he inquired.

"'Deed I am, your royal highness," she replied.

"She will have a lodging at my father's house so long as the army remains in the town," added Beppy.

"I am glad to hear it," replied the prince. "I am certain she will be well cared for."

He then bowed graciously to the young lady, and bestowing a parting smile on Helen, rode on.

But he soon came to another halt.

A little further off he discovered Constance Rawcliffe and Monica. They were attended by Father Jerome. Graciously saluting the two damsels, and bowing to the priest, he said to Miss Rawcliffe:

"You are the very person I desired to see. I have some news for you—but it is for your private ear."

On this intimation Monica and the priest drew back.

Charles then continued in a low voice: "You will be surprised to learn that your father has just fought a duel." Seeing her change colour, he hastened to add: "You need have no sort of uneasiness. He is unhurt. I left the ground only a short time ago, and can therefore speak positively."

"With whom was the duel fought?" inquired Constance, unable to repress her emotion. "Not with——"

"Not with Atherton Legh," supplied the prince, "though the quarrel was on his account. Sir Richard's adversary was Colonel Townley. Luckily, your father was disarmed, and so the affair was brought to an end. The duel appears to have been unavoidable, since Sir Richard refused to apologise to Captain Legh for rudeness offered him, and would not even give him satisfaction. Colonel Townley, therefore, took up the quarrel, and you know the result."

"Is the affair ended?" she asked, eagerly.

"Not quite. A full explanation seems to me to be due from Sir Richard Rawcliffe to Captain Legh; and to insure it, I have laid my commands upon Sir Richard to meet

Captain Legh in my presence after the levée, in order that he may answer certain questions which I shall then put to him. I fear this will not be agreeable to your father; but he might have avoided it. A few words would set all right, but these he refuses to utter. I had, therefore, no alternative but to compel him to speak out."

"It is right that Captain Legh should know the truth," remarked Constance.

"I felt sure you would think so, and I therefore enjoined Sir Richard to bring you with him; but if you see any objections, I will excuse your attendance."

"Perhaps my presence may be necessary," she rejoined. "I will come."

"That is well," said the prince. "I owe Captain Legh a large debt of gratitude, and am anxious to pay it. I shall begin by setting him right. That done, I shall use all my influence to effect a reconciliation between—— You understand my meaning, I am quite sure."

"No more on that subject, I implore your highness," she rejoined, blushing deeply.

"I hope I have said enough to prove how much interested I am in the young man, and how anxious I am to promote his happiness," he said. "Why, here he is!" he exclaimed, as Atherton was seen riding towards the spot. "If I had summoned him, he could not have appeared more à propos. I hope Miss Rawcliffe will not continue to look coldly upon him."

"I am bound to obey," she rejoined, demurely.

"I wonder what message he brings me?" remarked the prince.

"I dare say your royal highness could give a shrewd guess," she rejoined, with an almost imperceptible smile.

At this moment Atherton came up, and, removing his hat, delivered a letter to the prince.

"From Lord George Murray," he said, still remaining uncovered.

"'Tis not very important," observed Charles, opening it, and glancing at its contents. "But I am glad you have brought it, since it gives me the opportunity of placing you in attendance upon Miss Rawcliffe, who may want an escort when she quits the ground."

"I shall be charmed with the office," rejoined Atherton; "but I am not sure that Miss Rawcliffe will be equally well pleased."

"Have no misgiving," replied Charles, with a significant look, which implied that all was arranged. "I have some further orders to give you, but it will be time enough when you return to head-quarters. Meanwhile, I charge you to take especial care of these young ladies."

With this he rode off, and almost immediately afterwards quitted the ground, accompanied by the Duke of Perth.

How much surprised Monica and Father Jerome had been by the earnest discourse that took place between the prince and Constance, we need scarcely state; but they were still more surprised when Atherton came up, and was placed in attendance upon the young lady.

It was quite clear to the lookers-on that the prince had generously taken Atherton's cause in hand, and meant to carry it through to a successful issue. Monica, who had been much pained at the misunderstanding between the lovers, was rejoiced; but the priest felt differently.

Meantime, Atherton, by no means certain that he was welcome, endeavoured to excuse himself to Constance.

"I trust Miss Rawcliffe will not blame me for this intrusion," he said. "She can dismiss me as soon as she thinks proper."

"That would be impossible, since you have been left with me by the prince," she rejoined. "But I have no desire to dismiss you. On the contrary, I am glad to have an opportunity of congratulating you on your good fortune. You have gained the prince's favour, and are therefore on the high road to distinction."

"If I am restored to your good opinion I shall be satisfied," he rejoined.

"My good opinion is worth little," she said.

"'Tis everything to me," he cried.

She made no direct reply, but after a moment's pause remarked:

"To-day may prove as eventful to you as yesterday. Has not the prince acquainted you with his intentions?"

"He has told me nothing. I am ordered to attend him after the levée—that is all."

"'Tis to meet my father, who, by his highness's command, will disclose certain matters to you. But pray ask me no more questions. I ought not to have told you so much. You will learn all in good time. And now I must relieve you from this irksome attendance."

"You know very well it is not irksome," he replied, with a look of reproach.

"At all events, you must have other duties to attend to. You have to prepare for the muster of your regiment. Jemmy Dawson is fully occupied, or he would be here with Monica. I really must set you at liberty."

"Pray let me see you safely from the ground?" entreated Atherton.

"Well, I cannot object to that."

Then turning to Monica, she said:

"Are you ready to depart?"

"Quite," replied the other.

Atherton cleared the way, and having brought them to the long unfinished street that led from Castle Field to the centre of the town, he bowed, and rode off, fondly persuading himself he should soon meet Constance again.

CHAPTER XXII.

FATHER JEROME COUNSELS SIR RICHARD.

"You must see your father without delay, Miss Rawcliffe," said the priest in an authoritative tone to Constance, as soon as Atherton was gone. "We are almost certain to find Sir Richard at the Bull's Head, and if he should not be within, he will have left a message for you, or a letter."

Constance quite agreed that it would be proper to call at the Bull's Head, though she felt quite sure her father would make all needful arrangements for the meeting appointed by the prince, and they accordingly proceeded to the inn.

So crowded was the market-place with troops, that they had considerable difficulty in crossing, and when at length they reached their destination, Sir Richard was absent.

"He had gone out at a very early hour," said Diggles, "and had not yet returned."

"He cannot be long," observed Father Jerome. "We must wait for him."

"I vote that we order breakfast," said Monica. "I am frightfully hungry."

As Constance and the priest both sympathised with her, breakfast was ordered, and it was lucky the precaution was taken, for nearly an hour elapsed before Sir Richard made his appearance.

Long ere this, they had finished their meal, and when the baronet entered the room, were watching the troops from the windows that commanded the market-place, and listening to the shrill notes of the pipes.

Sir Richard did not seem surprised, and perhaps expected to find them there. Constance sprang forward to meet him, and bidding him good morrow, said eagerly:

"I know all about the arrangements, papa. I have seen the prince at Castle Field."

"I am aware of it," he said, sternly. "I have just left his royal highness."

"Of course you will attend the meeting he has appointed?" she said, alarmed by his manner.

He made no reply, and scarcely noticing Monica, signed to the priest, who understood the gesture, and followed him into the adjoining room.

"What does this mean?" said Monica, uneasily.

"I cannot tell," replied Constance. "But I hope papa will not disobey the prince."

"Surely he will not," cried the other.

"All will depend upon the counsel given him," said Constance. "Unluckily, Father Jerome is no friend to Atherton Legh."

"But your influence will prevail."

"You are quite mistaken, Monica. Papa won't listen to me. You saw how sternly he regarded me just now. He is displeased with me, as if I were to blame, because things have gone contrary to his wishes."

"I cannot conceive why he dislikes Atherton so much," said Monica, "but I am sure his aversion is most unreasonable."

"I hoped it might be overcome," sighed Constance, "but I now begin to despair. Even the prince, I fear, will not be successful."

"Do you think Sir Richard has an ill-adviser?" remarked Monica, significantly.

"I hope not," rejoined Constance.

Let us now see what passed between Sir Richard and the priest when they were closeted together.

For a few moments the baronet seemed indisposed to commence the conversation; but as Father Jerome remained silent, he forced himself to speak.

"I am placed in a very awkward dilemma, as you are doubtless aware," he said, "and scarcely know how to act. Having consented to meet Atherton Legh in the prince's presence I am unable to retreat with honour, and yet I cannot answer certain questions that will inevitably be put to me."

"Can you not brave it out?" rejoined Father Jerome. "The prince cannot be acquainted with any secret matters connected with this young man."

"He knows more than is desirable," rejoined the baronet. "Some one has evidently informed him that I have acted as the young man's guardian."

"Mr. Marriott cannot have betrayed your confidence?" remarked Father Jerome.

"I do not think so," rejoined the other.

"Who else can have given the information?" observed the priest. "Have you no suspicion?"

"Ha! a light flashes upon me. Should it be so!—though I would fain hope not—the meeting would be doubly dangerous—for she is to be present."

"I can set your mind at rest. She knows nothing more than this one fact."

"But that may lead to a discovery of all the rest," cried Sir Richard.

"Not since you are prepared. 'Tis a pity the packet was left with her?"

"'Twas a great error, I admit. But I will not commit another imprudent act. I will not be interrogated by the prince."

"Again I say you had better brave it out than fly—and fly you must if you neglect to obey the prince's commands. Your disappearance will give rise to unpleasant suspicions."

"But some excuse may be framed. You can help me. You have a ready wit."

"Well, the invention must be plausible, or it won't pass. Suppose you go to Rawcliffe Hall to fetch some documents, which are necessary to a full explanation of this matter. You intend to come back to-morrow—but are unavoidably detained—and do not return till the prince has left Manchester."

"That will do admirably!" cried Sir Richard eagerly. "You have saved me. You must take my excuse to the prince. He will then believe it."

"But to give a colour to the excuse you must really go to Rawcliffe Hall."

"I require no urging," rejoined Sir Richard. "I am most anxious to get away, and heartily regret that I ever joined the insurrection. I wish I could make terms with the Government."

"Perhaps you may be able to do so—but of that hereafter," rejoined the priest. "First effect a secure retreat. I will do all I can to cover it."

"I will set off at once," said Sir Richard. "But I must take leave of my daughter."

"Better not," said the priest. "I will bid her adieu for you."

Sir Richard suffered himself to be persuaded, and presently left the room. Ordering his horse, on the pretext of attending the muster of the Manchester Regiment, he rode out of the town.

Not till some quarter of an hour after the baronet's departure did Father Jerome present himself to the two damsels, who were alarmed at seeing him appear alone.

"Where is papa?" exclaimed Constance eagerly.

"He has started for Rawcliffe," replied the priest.

"Gone!—without a word to me! Impossible!" she cried.

"'Tis nevertheless true," replied Father Jerome, gravely. "He wished to avoid any discussion. He has gone to fetch certain documents, without which he declines to appear before the prince."

"His highness will regard it as an act of disobedience, and will be justly offended," cried Constance.

"I do not think so, when I have explained matters to him," rejoined the priest.

"I am not to be duped," said Constance, bitterly. "Atherton will learn nothing more."

S.W. View of the Collegiate Church Tower Manchester.

CHAPTER XXIII.

THE PRINCE ATTENDS SERVICE AT THE COLLEGIATE CHURCH.

THIS being the festival of St. Andrew, as already intimated, the Scottish nobles and chiefs desired that a special morning service should be performed for them at the collegiate church, and arrangements were accordingly made for compliance with their request.

Prayers were to be read by the Rev. William Shrigley, one of the chaplains, and an avowed Nonjuror, and the sermon was to be preached by the Rev. Mr. Coppock, chaplain to the Manchester Regiment, who was chosen for the occasion by the prince.

A certain number of men from each regiment being permitted to attend the service, the whole of the nave, except the mid aisle, which was reserved for the officers, was entirely filled by Highland soldiers; and as the men were in their full accoutrements, and armed with targets, claymores, and firelocks, the effect was exceedingly striking.

Yet more imposing was the scene when the long central aisle was crowded with officers—when the side aisles were thronged with the townspeople, and the transepts were full of ladies. Those present on that memorable occasion, and whose gaze ranged over the picturesque crowd of armed mountaineers, could not fail to be struck by the tall, graceful pillars on either side the nave, with their beautiful pointed arches, above which rose the clerestory windows—with the exquisitely moulded roof enriched with sculptures and other appropriate ornaments—with the chantries—and with the splendidly carved screen separating the choir from the nave.

The choir itself, with its fine panelled roof and its thirty elaborately carved stalls—fifteen on each side—was reserved for the prince, and the nobles and chiefs with him.

These stalls, with their florid tabernacle work, gloriously

carved canopies, and pendent pinnacles of extraordinary richness and beauty, were admirably adapted to the occasion. In front of the sedilia were book-desks, encircled with armorial bearings, cognisances, and monograms.

Around the chancel were several exquisite chantries, most of them possessing screens of rare workmanship; and in these chapels many important personages connected with the town, or belonging to the Jacobite party, were now assembled.

In the Lady chapel were some of the fellows of the church, who did not care to make themselves too conspicuous.

In the Jesus chantry were Dr. Byrom and his family, with Mr. Walley and Mr. Fowden; and in St. John's chapel were Dr. Deacon, Mr. Cattell, Mr. Clayton, and several others.

But not merely was the interior of the sacred fabric thronged, hundreds of persons who had failed to obtain admittance were collected outside.

Precisely at eleven o'clock, Prince Charles Edward, mounted on a richly caparisoned charger, preceded by a guard of honour, and attended by all the nobles and chieftains belonging to his army, rode up to the gates of the churchyard, where he alighted. A lane was formed for him by the spectators, through which he passed, and on entering the church by the south porch, he was ceremoniously conducted to the choir, where he took his seat in the warden's stall.

Next to him sat the Duke of Perth, and on the same side were ranged the Duke of Athole, Lord George Murray, Lord Kilmarnock, Lord Elcho, Lord Ogilvie, Lord Balmerino, and the Marquis d'Eguilles. In the opposite stalls were Lord Pitsligo, Lord Nairne, Lord Strathallan, General Gordon of Glenbucket, Colonel Ker, Secretary Murray, and Sir Thomas Sheridan.

From the stall occupied by the prince, which was the first on the right of the choir, and commanded the whole interior of the edifice, the coup-d'œil of the nave, with its compact mass of Highlanders, was splendid, and as Charles gazed at it, he was filled with stirring thoughts, that were softened down, however, by the solemn sounds of the organ pealing along the roof.

Of course the Protestant form of worship was adopted; but strict Romanist as he was, Charles allowed no symptom of disapproval to escape him, but listened devoutly to Mr. Shrigley, who performed the service admirably, being excited by the presence of the prince.

The reverend gentleman prayed for the king, but without naming the sovereign. All his hearers, however, knew that James the Third was meant.

Mr. Coppock was not so guarded. He prayed for James the Third, for Charles Prince of Wales, Regent of England, and for the Duke of York.

Taking for his text the words "*Render unto Cæsar the things that are Cæsar's*," he preached a most fiery sermon, in which he announced the speedy restoration of the Stuart dynasty, and the downfall of the House of Hanover.

Whatever might have been thought of this treasonable discourse by a certain portion of the congregation, no voice was raised against it. That it pleased the prince and his attendants was sufficient for the ambitious young divine.

CHAPTER XXIV.

THE PRINCE INSPECTS THE MANCHESTER REGIMENT.

On coming forth from the church, Charles and his attendants found the newly-formed Manchester Regiment drawn up in the churchyard.

The corps numbered about three hundred men; most of them being fine stalwart young fellows, averaging six feet in height. Till that morning none of them had donned their uniforms, or even shouldered a musket, but by the exertions of Colonel Townley, the Chevalier de Johnstone, and Sergeant Dickson, they had been got into something like order, and now presented a very creditable appearance.

The officers looked exceedingly well in their handsome uniforms—red faced with blue. On this occasion each wore a plaid waistcoat with laced loops, a plaid sash lined with white silk, and had a white cockade in his hat. In addition to the broadsword by his side, each officer had a brace of pistols attached to his girdle.

Though all, from the colonel downwards, were fine, handsome men, unquestionably the handsomest young man in the corps was Captain Legh.

The flag of the regiment was borne by Ensign Syddall. On one side was the motto LIBERTY AND PROPERTY; on the other CHURCH AND COUNTRY.

The standard-bearer looked proud of his office. Nothing now of the barber about Ensign Syddall. So changed was his aspect, so upright his thin figure, that he could scarcely be recognised. To look at him, no one would believe that he could ever smile. He seemed to have grown two or three inches taller. His deportment might be somewhat too stiff, but he had a true military air; and his acquaintances, of whom there were many in the crowd, regarded him with wonder and admiration.

The ensign, however, took no notice of any familiar observations addressed to him, having become suddenly haughty and distant.

With the regiment were four field-pieces.

Their chargers having been brought round, Charles and his suite rode slowly past the front of the line—the prince halting occasionally to make a commendatory remark to the men, who responded to these gratifying observations by enthusiastic shouts.

"I am glad the flag of the regiment has been entrusted to you, Syddall," said Charles to the new ensign. "No one, I am sure, could take better care of it."

"I will defend it with my life," replied Syddall, earnestly.

This hasty inspection finished, Charles quitted the churchyard with his suite, and rode back to his head-quarters.

The Manchester Regiment soon followed. Elated by the commendations of the prince, which they flattered themselves were merited, the men marched through the market-place, and past the Exchange to St. Ann's-square, in tolerably good order, and in high good humour, which was not diminished by the cheers of the spectators. Colonel Townley then gave them some necessary orders, after which they dispersed, and repaired to their various quarters.

CHAPTER XXV.

AN UNSATISFACTORY EXPLANATION.

HAVING partaken of a slight repast, the prince again mounted his charger and rode out of the town in a different direction from any he had previously taken, being desirous to see the country.

He was only attended by Colonel Ker and the Chevalier de Johnstone, having dismissed his guard of honour.

At that time the environs of Manchester were exceedingly pretty, and the prospects spread out before him had a wild character of which little can now be discerned. Smedley Hall formed the limit of his ride, and having gazed at this picturesque old structure, which was situated in a valley, with a clear stream flowing past it, and a range of bleak-looking hills in the distance, he turned off on the left, and made his way through a heathy and uncultivated district to Kersal Moor.

From these uplands he obtained a charming view of the valley of the Irwell, bounded by the collegiate church, and the old buildings around it, and after contemplating the prospect for a short time, he descended from the heights and returned to the town.

Not being expected at the time, he passed very quietly through the streets, and reached his head-quarters without hindrance, having greatly enjoyed his ride.

Immediately after his return a levée was held, which being more numerously attended than that on the preceding day, occupied nearly two hours.

After this he had a conference with the magistrates in the audience chamber, and he then repaired to his private cabinet, where he expected to find Sir Richard Rawcliffe and the others, whose attendance he had commanded.

Constance was there and Atherton, but in place of the baronet appeared Father Jerome. Repressing his displeasure, Charles graciously saluted the party, and then addressing Constance said:

"Why is not Sir Richard here, Miss Rawcliffe?"

"Father Jerome will explain the cause of his absence," she replied. "I had no conversation with him before his departure."

"Then he is gone!" cried Charles, frowning. "I trust your explanation of his strange conduct may prove satisfactory," he added to the priest.

"The step I own appears strange," replied Father Jerome in a deprecatory tone; "but I trust it may be excused. Sir Richard has gone to Rawcliffe Hall to procure certain documents which he desires to lay before your royal highness."

"But why did he not ask my permission before setting out?" observed Charles, sternly.

"Unquestionably, that would have been the proper course," rejoined the priest. "But I presume he hoped to be back in time."

"He could not have thought so," cried Charles, sharply "The distance is too great. He shrinks from the interrogations which he knows would be addressed to him. But I will not be trifled with. I will learn the truth. If he does not come I will send a guard for him. I will not detain you longer now, Miss Rawcliffe, he added to Constance. "Possibly, I may require your attendance again, and yours, also, father."

On this intimation Constance made a profound obeisance and retired with the priest.

As soon as they were gone, the prince's countenance assumed a very singular expression, and he said to Atherton, "What think you of all this?"

"My opinion is that Sir Richard Rawcliffe does not mean to return, and has sent Father Jerome to make these excuses for him," replied Atherton.

"I have come to the same conclusion," replied Charles. "He has set my authority at defiance, but he shall find that I can reach him. You must set out at once for Rawcliffe Hall, and bring him hither."

"I am ready to obey your highness's orders," replied Atherton. "I have never seen Sir Richard's residence; but I know it is situated near Warrington, about eighteen miles from Manchester. I can get there in a couple of hours—perhaps in less."

"Provided you bring back the unruly baronet before night I shall be satisfied," said Charles.

He then sat down at the table, on which writing materials were placed, wrote a few lines on a sheet of paper, and, after attaching the sign manual to the order, gave it to Atherton.

"Sir Richard will not dare to resist that mandate," he said. "I do not think a guard will be necessary. But you shall take Sergeant Dickson with you. You will find him with the Chevalier de Johnstone at Lord George Murray's quarters. Show this order to Colonel Johnstone, and he will provide you with a good horse, and give all necessary directions to the sergeant. He will also explain the cause of your absence to Colonel Townley. Understand that you are to bring back Sir Richard with you at all hazards."

"I will not fail," replied Atherton.

Bowing deeply, he then quitted the prince's presence, and proceeded at once to Lord George Murray's quarters in Deansgate, where he found the Chevalier de Johnstone and Sergeant Dickson.

The Chevalier de Johnstone understood the matter at once, and immediately ordered the sergeant to provide two strong horses for Captain Legh and himself, bidding him go well armed.

Although the sergeant was told by his colonel to lose no time, he easily prevailed upon Atherton to let him bid adieu to Helen, who, as the reader is aware, had found a lodging with Beppy Byrom.

Very little delay, however, occurred, for as the sergeant rode up to the doctor's dwelling, Helen, who seemed to be on the watch, rushed out to greet him, and learnt his errand, receiving a kiss at the same time.

CHAPTER XXVI.

THE RIDE TO RAWCLIFFE HALL.

CROSSING the bridge, and passing through Salford, Atherton and his attendant proceeded at a rapid pace towards the pretty little village of Pendleton. Skirting the wide green, in the midst of which stood the renowned May-pole, they hastened on through a pleasant country to Eccles—proceeding thence, without drawing bridle, to Barton-on-Irwell.

The road they were now pursuing formed a sort of causeway, bounded on the left by the deeply-flowing river, and on the right by the dark and dreary waste which could be seen stretching out for miles, almost as far as the town towards which they were speeding. This dangerous morass was then wholly impassable, except by those familiar with it; and, as Atherton's eye wandered over its treacherous surface, he pointed out to his attendant a distant spot on the extreme verge of the marsh, observing, with a singular smile:

" Yonder is Warrington."

" Indeed!" exclaimed Dickson. " Then we might shorten our distance materially by crossing the morass."

" No doubt, if we *could* cross it," rejoined Atherton. " But we should be swallowed up, horse and man, before we had proceeded far. Many an incautious traveller has met his death in Chat Moss."

" It looks an unchancy place, I must say," observed the sergeant, shuddering, as he gazed at it.

Beyond Boysnape the causeway narrowed, bringing them in dangerous proximity both with the river and the morass; but they rode on past Irlam, until they reached the point of junction between the Irwell and the Mersey—the last-named river dividing Cheshire from Lancashire. They had now ridden full ten miles; but, as their steeds showed no signs of fatigue, they went without slackening their pace to Glazebrook and Rixton. Chat Moss had been left behind, and for the last two miles they had been passing through a well-wooded district, and had now reached another dangerous morass, called Risley Moss, which compelled them to keep close to the Mersey. Little, however, could be seen of the river, its banks being thickly fringed with willows and other trees. Passing Martinscroft and Woolston, they held on till they came within half-a-mile of Warrington, even then a considerable town. Though the bridge at Warrington had been destroyed, a ford was pointed out to them, and they were soon on the other side of the Mersey, and in Cheshire.

From inquiries which they now made at a small roadside inn, where they halted for a few minutes to refresh themselves and their horses, they ascertained they were within a mile of Rawcliffe Park, and after a short colloquy with the host, who was very curious to learn what was doing at Manchester, and who told them he had seen Sir Richard Rawcliffe ride past some three or four hours ago, they resumed their journey, and soon arrived at the gates of the park.

CHAPTER XXVII.

RAWCLIFFE HALL.

THE domain was extensive, but had a neglected appearance, and did not possess any old timber, all the well-grown trees having been cut down in the time of the former proprietor, Sir Oswald Rawcliffe. Neither was the park picturesque, being flat, and in some places marshy. On one side it was bounded by the Mersey, and its melancholy look impressed Atherton as he gazed around.

Still he felt a singular interest in the place for which he could not account, unless it were that Constance was connected with it.

At length, they came in sight of the old mansion, near which grew some of the finest trees they had yet seen. The house had a gloomy look that harmonised with the melancholy appearance of the park.

Atherton had never beheld the place before, yet he seemed somehow familiar with it. The wide moat by which it was surrounded, the drawbridge, the gate-tower, the numerous gables, the bay-windows, all seemed like an imperfectly recollected picture.

So struck was he with the notion that he drew in the rein for a few minutes, and gazed stedfastly at the antique mansion, endeavouring to recall the circumstances under which he could have beheld it, but it vanished like a dream.

Before riding up to the house, he held a brief consultation with the sergeant, as to how it would be best to proceed.

Hitherto they had seen no one in the park, which, as

already stated, had a thoroughly neglected air; nor, as far as they could judge, had their approach been remarked by any of the inmates of the house.

Gloom seemed to brood over the place. So silent was it that it might have been uninhabited.

"If I had not been assured that Sir Richard is at home, I should not have thought so," remarked Atherton. "The house has not a very cheerful or hospitable air."

"Luckily, the drawbridge is down, or we might have been kept on the wrong side of the moat," remarked the sergeant. "My advice is that we enter the fort before we are discovered, or we may never get in at all."

Acting upon the counsel, Atherton put spurs to his horse and rode up to the house, which did not look a whit more cheerful as he approached it, and without halting to ring the bell, dashed across the drawbridge, passed through the open gateway and entered the court-yard, which to the young man's great surprise did not look so neglected as the exterior of the mansion had led him to anticipate.

The noise they made on entering the court-yard seemed to have roused the inmates from the sleep into which they had apparently been plunged. An old butler, followed by a couple of footmen, came out of the house, and with evident alarm depicted in his countenance, requested to know their business.

"Our business is with Sir Richard Rawcliffe," replied Atherton. "We must see him immediately."

"I do not think Sir Richard will see you, gentlemen," replied the butler. "He is much fatigued. I will deliver any message to him with which you may charge me."

"We must see him," cried the sergeant, authoritatively. "We come from the prince."

The butler no longer hesitated, but assuming a deferential air, said he would at once conduct the gentlemen to his master.

As they had already dismounted, he bade one of the servants take their horses to the stable, and ushered the unwelcome visitors into a large entrance-hall, in which a wood fire was burning.

Remarking that the butler stared at him very hard, Atherton said:

"You look at me as if you had seen me before. Is it so? I have no recollection of you."

"I don't think I have seen you before, sir," replied the man, gravely. "But I have seen some one very like you. Whom shall I announce to Sir Richard?"

"I am Captain Legh," said Atherton. "But there is no necessity to announce me. Conduct me to your master at once."

The butler, though evidently uneasy, did not venture to disobey, but led him to a room that opened out of the hall. The sergeant followed close behind Atherton.

They had been ushered into the library. Sir Richard was writing at a table, but raising his eyes on their entrance, he started up, and exclaimed in an angry voice:

"Why have you brought these persons here, Markland. I told you I would not be disturbed."

"Your servant is not to blame, Sir Richard," interposed Atherton. "I insisted upon seeing you. I am sent to bring you to the prince."

"It is my intention to return to Manchester to-night," replied the baronet, haughtily. "But I have some affairs to arrange."

"I shall be sorry to inconvenience you, Sir Richard," observed Atherton. "But my orders are precise. You must present yourself at the prince's head-quarters before midnight."

"I engage to do so," replied the baronet.

"But you must be content to accompany me, Sir Richard. Such are my orders from his royal highness."

"And mine," added Sergeant Dickson.

Controlling his anger by a powerful effort, Sir Richard said with forced calmness:

"Since such are the prince's orders I shall not dispute them. I will return with you to Manchester. We will set out in two hours' time. In the interim I shall be able to arrange some papers which I came for, and which I desire to take with me. By that time you will have rested, and your horses will be ready for the journey."

Then turning to Markland, he added:

"Conduct Captain Legh and Sergeant Dickson to the dining-room, and set some refreshment before them without delay."

"Take me to the servants' hall, Mr. Markland," said Dickson. "I cannot sit down with my officer."

Just as Atherton was about to leave the room, Sir Richard stepped up to him and said in a low tone:

"Before we start, I should like to have a little conversation with you in private, Captain Legh."

"I am quite at your service now, Sir Richard," replied the young man.

He then glanced significantly at Dickson, who went out with the butler, leaving him alone with the baronet.

CHAPTER XXVIII.

A STARTLING DISCLOSURE.

WHEN the door was closed, Sir Richard's manner somewhat changed towards the young man, and with less haughtiness than he had hitherto manifested, he said to him:

"Pray be seated. I have much to say to you."

Atherton complied, but for some minutes Sir Richard continued to pace rapidly to and fro within the room, as if unwilling to commence the conversation he had proposed.

At last, he seated himself opposite the young man, who had watched him with surprise.

"Are you acquainted with the history of my family?" he inquired, looking steadfastly at his auditor.

"I have some slight acquaintance with it," replied Atherton.

"You are aware, I presume, that the Rawcliffes have occupied this old mansion for upwards of two centuries?"

Atherton bowed, but made no remark. Sir Richard went on:

"My ancestors have all been high and honourable men, and have handed a proud name from one generation to another. Would it not be grievous if a stain were affixed on a name, hitherto unsullied, like ours? Yet if this inquiry which the prince has instituted be pursued, such must infallibly be the case. A dark secret connected with our family may be brought to light. Now listen to me, and you shall judge:

"Some twenty years ago, Sir Oswald Rawcliffe, my elder brother, died, leaving a widow and an infant son. Lady Rawcliffe came to reside here with her child—do you note what I say?"

"I think I have heard that the child was stolen under mysterious circumstances," said Atherton, "and that the lady subsequently died of grief."

"You have heard the truth," said Sir Richard, with a strange look. "As the child could not be found, I succeeded to the title and the estates."

A pause ensued, during which such fearful suspicions crossed Atherton that he averted his gaze from the baronet.

Suddenly, Sir Richard rose in his chair, leaned forward, and gazing fixedly at Atherton, exclaimed:

"What will you say if I tell you that the child who was carried off, and supposed to be dead, is still living? What will you say if I tell you that you are Conway Rawcliffe, the son of Sir Oswald, and rightful heir to the property?"

"Amazement!" cried the listener.

"For many years I have deprived you of your inheritance

and your title—have appropriated your estates, and have dwelt in your house. But I have been haunted by remorse, and have known no happiness. Sleep has been scared from my eyelids by the pale lady who died of grief in this very house, and I have known no rest. But I shall sleep soundly soon," he added, with terrible significance. "I will make reparation for the wrongs I have done. I will restore all I have taken from you—house, lands, name, title."

Again there was a pause. The young man was struck dumb by astonishment, and it was Sir Richard who broke silence.

"What think you I was engaged on when you entered this room? I will tell you. I was writing out a full confession of the crime I have committed, in the hope of atoning for my guilt. Already I have narrated part of the dark story. I have told how you were carried off and whither you were conveyed; but I have yet to relate how you were brought up in Manchester in complete ignorance of the secret of your birth, and how I acted as your guardian. Full details shall be given so that your identity can easily be established. When my confession is finished, I will deliver it to you, and you can show it to the prince."

"However you may have acted previously, you are acting well now," remarked Atherton. "But I will no longer interrupt you in your task."

"Stay!" cried the baronet. "I will show you a room which I myself have not seen for years. I have not dared to enter it, but I can enter it now. Follow me!"

CHAPTER XXIX.

THE MYSTERIOUS CHAMBER.

OPENING a movable shelf in the bookcase, he disclosed a narrow passage, along which they proceeded till they came to a small back staircase, evidently communicating by a small outlet with the moat.

Mounting this staircase, Sir Richard unfastened a door, which admitted them to a dark corridor. From its appearance it was evident that this part of the mansion was shut up.

A stifling sensation, caused by the close, oppressive atmosphere, affected Atherton, and vague terrors assailed him. Two doors faced them. Sir Richard opened one of the doors, and led his companion into an antechamber, the furniture of which was mouldering and covered with dust.

A door communicating with an inner room stood ajar. After a moment's hesitation Sir Richard passed through it, and was followed by Atherton.

The chamber was buried in gloom, but on a window-shutter being opened a strange scene was disclosed. At the further end of the apartment stood an old bedstead, which seemed fully prepared for some occupant, though it could not have been slept in for many years. Quilt and pillow were mildewed and mouldering, and the sheets yellow with age. The hangings were covered with dust. Altogether, the room had a ghostly look.

For some moments Atherton could not remove his gaze from that old bed, which seemed to exercise a sort of fascination, but when he looked at Sir Richard, he was appalled by the terrible change that had come over him.

He looked the picture of horror and despair. His pallid countenance was writhen with anguish, and his limbs shook. A deep groan burst from his labouring breast.

"The hour is near at hand," he muttered, in tones scarcely human. "But I am not yet ready. Spare me till my task is finished!"

With a ghastly look he then added to Atherton: "The whole scene rises before me as it occurred on that dreadful night. The room is hushed and quiet, and within that bed a child is peacefully slumbering on his mother's breast. A masked intruder comes in—admitted by the nurse, who has betrayed her mistress. Unmoved by a picture of innocence that might have touched any heart less savage than his own, he snatches up the child, and is bearing it off when the mother awakes. Her piercing shriek still rings through my ears. I cannot describe what follows—but 'tis soon over—and when the worse than robber departs with his prize, he leaves the wretched mother lying senseless on the floor, and the nurse dead—slain by his ruthless hand!"

"Horror!" exclaimed Atherton, unable to control his feelings.

"Let us hence, or I shall become mad," cried Sir Richard, hurrying him away.

So bewildered was Atherton, that he could scarcely tell how he regained the library, but when he got there, he sank into a chair, and covered his eyes with his hands, as if to exclude the terrible vision by which he had been beset.

On rousing himself from the stupor into which he had fallen, he perceived Sir Richard seated at the table, writing his confession, and feeling that his presence might disturb him, he rose to depart.

Sir Richard rose likewise, and while conducting him to the door, said:

"I will send for you when I have done. I shall be best alone for a short time. But let me give you a word of counsel, and do not distrust it because it comes from me. 'Tis my wish, as you know, to repair the wrong I have done. I would not have you forfeit the lofty position you have just obtained."

"I hope I shall not forfeit it," said Atherton, proudly.

"You will not long hold it," rejoined Sir Richard, in a solemn tone, "unless you withdraw from this ill-fated expedition. It will end in your destruction. Attend to my warning!"

"I cannot honourably retreat," said Atherton.

"You must," cried Sir Richard, sternly. "Why throw away your life from a fancied sense of honour, when such fair prospects are opening upon you? 'Twill be madness to persist."

Atherton made no reply, and Sir Richard said no more.

But as he opened the door he gave the young man a look so full of strange significance that he almost guessed its import.

Sir Richard paused for a moment as he went back to the table.

"What is the use of this?" he exclaimed aloud. "No remonstrance will deter him. He will go on to destruction. The estates will pass away from us. Perchance a few words, written at the last moment, may change him! Heaven grant it. I will try. But now to complete my task. All will soon be over!"

With this he sat down at the table, and with a strange composure resumed his writing.

CHAPTER XXX.

A TERRIBLE CATASTROPHE.

ON returning to the entrance-hall Atherton found Markland, the butler. The old man looked at him very wistfully, and said:

"Excuse me, sir, if I venture to say a few words to you. Has an important communication been made to you by Sir Richard?"

"A very important communication, indeed," replied Atherton. "And when I tell you what it is, I think I shall surprise you?"

"No, you won't surprise me in the least, sir," replied Markland. "The moment I set eyes upon you I felt certain that you were the rightful heir of this property. You are the very image of my former master, Sir Oswald. I hope

Sir Richard intends to do you justice and acknowledge you?"

"Be satisfied, my good friend, he does," replied Atherton.

"I am truly glad to hear it," said Markland. "This will take off a weight that has lain on his breast for years, and make him a happy man once more. Strange! I always felt sure the infant heir would turn up. I never believed he was dead. But I didn't expect to behold so fine a young gentleman. I hope you are not going to leave us again now you have come back."

"I must leave you for a time, Markland, however inclined I may be to stay. I have joined the prince's army, and am a captain in the Manchester Regiment."

"So I heard from the gallant Highlander who came with you. But things have changed now. Since you have become Sir Conway Rawcliffe——"

"What mean you, Markland?"

"Conway was the name of the infant heir who was stolen —he was so called after his mother, the beautiful Henrietta Conway."

"For the present I must remain Captain Legh," interrupted the young man. "Nor would I have a word breathed on the subject to your fellow-servants till I have spoken with Sir Richard. You understand?"

"Perfectly," replied the old butler. "You may rely on my discretion."

But though Markland was forbidden to give the young baronet his proper title, he could not be prevented from showing him the profoundest respect, and it was with great reverence that he conducted him to the dining-room, where they found Sergeant Dickson seated at a table with a cold sirloin of beef before him, flanked by a tankard of strong ale.

Atherton—as we shall still continue to call our hero— desired the sergeant not to disturb himself, but declined to follow his example, though urged by Markland to try a little cold beef.

DEATH OF SIR RICHARD RAWCLIFFE.

The butler, however, would not be denied, but disappearing for a minute or two returned with a cobwebbed flask, which he uncorked, and then filling a big glass to the brim, handed it to the young gentleman with these words:

"This madeira was bottled some five-and-twenty years ago in the time of the former owner of this mansion, Sir Oswald Rawcliffe. I pray you taste it, Sir——I beg pardon," he added, hastily correcting himself—"I mean Captain Legh."

As Atherton placed the goblet to his lips, but did not half empty it, the butler whispered in his ear, while handing him a biscuit, "'Tis your father's wine."

Atherton gave him a look and emptied the glass.

Another bumper was then filled for Sergeant Dickson, who smacked his lips, but declared that for his part he preferred usquebaugh.

"Usquebaugh!" exclaimed Markland, contemptuously. "Good wine is thrown away upon you, I perceive, sergeant. Nothing better was ever drunk than this madeira. Let me prevail upon you to try it again, Sir—Captain, I mean."

But as Atherton declined, he set down the bottle beside him, and left the room.

Full half an hour elapsed before he reappeared, and then his looks so alarmed those who beheld him, that they both started to their feet.

"What is the matter?" cried Atherton, struck by a foreboding of ill. "Nothing, I trust, has happened to Sir Richard?"

"I don't know—I hope not," cried the terrified butler. "I went into the library just now to see if his honour wanted anything. To my surprise he was not there, though I had been in the entrance-hall, and hadn't seem him go out. On the writing-table was a packet, that somehow attracted my attention, and I stepped forward to look at it. It was sealed with black wax, and addressed to Sir Conway Rawcliffe, Baronet."

Atherton uttered an exclamation of astonishment, and his forebodings of ill grew stronger.

"The sight of this mysterious packet filled me with uneasiness," pursued the butler. "I laid it down, and was considering what had become of Sir Richard, when I remarked that a secret door in one of the bookcases, of which I was previously ignorant, was standing open. Impelled by a feeling stronger than curiosity, I passed through it, and had reached the foot of a small staircase, when I heard the report of a pistol, almost immediately succeeded by a heavy fall. I guessed what had happened; but not liking to go up-stairs alone, I hurried back as fast as I could, and came to you."

"However disinclined you may feel, you must go with me, Markland," said Atherton. "I know where we shall find Sir Richard. You must also come with us, sergeant. Not a moment must be lost."

Full of the direst apprehensions they set off. As they entered the library Atherton perceived the packet, which he knew contained the unhappy man's confession, lying on the writing-table, but he did not stop to take it up.

Dashing through the secret door he threaded the passage, and ascended the narrow staircase, three steps at a time, followed by the others.

The door of the antechamber was shut, and he feared it might be locked, but it yielded instantly to his touch.

The room was empty; but it was evident that the dreadful catastrophe he anticipated had taken place in the inner room, since a dark stream of blood could be seen trickling beneath the door, which was standing ajar.

Atherton endeavoured to push it open, but encountering some resistance, was obliged to use a slight degree of force to accomplish his object, and he then went in, closely followed by the others.

A dreadful spectacle met their gaze. Stretched upon the floor amid a pool of blood, with a pistol grasped in his hand, showing how the deed had been done, lay Sir Richard.

He had shot himself through the heart, so that his death must have been almost instantaneous.

The sight would have been ghastly enough under any circumstances; but beheld in that chamber, so full of fearful associations, it acquired additional horror. The group gathered round the body—the young baronet in his military attire—the Highlander in his accoutrements—and the old butler—formed a striking picture. That the guilty man should die there seemed like the work of retribution.

As the nephew he had so deeply injured, and deprived of his inheritance, looked down upon his dark and stern visage, now stilled in death, he could not but pity him.

"May Heaven forgive him, as I forgive him!" he ejaculated.

"If he has sinned deeply his penitence has been sincere," said Markland, sorrowfully. "Half his time has been spent in fasting and prayer. Heaven have mercy on his sinful soul!"

"It seems to me as if he had something clutched in his left hand," remarked the sergeant.

"I think so, too," said Atherton. "See what it is."

Thereupon, Erick knelt down beside the body, and opening the fingers, which were not yet stiffened, took from them a small slip of paper, and gave it to Atherton.

It had been crushed in the death gripe, but on being unfolded, these warning words appeared:

"'Tis given to those on the point of death to see into the future, and I read danger and destruction in the expedition you have joined. Be warned by your unhappy uncle, and abandon it."

"Whatever may be the consequence, I cannot abandon the expedition," thought Atherton.

While forming this resolution, he gazed at his lifeless monitor, and it seemed to him as if a frown passed over the dead man's countenance.

CHAPTER XXXI.

SIR RICHARD RAWCLIFFE'S CONFESSION.

AFTER considering what ought to be done under circumstances so painful and extraordinary, Atherton left Sergeant Dickson with the body, and then descending with Markland to the hall, ordered him to assemble the whole house without delay, and acquaint them with the dreadful catastrophe that had occurred.

Thereupon, Markland rang the alarm bell, and the summons was immediately answered by all the male part of the household, and several women, who hurried to the entrance-hall to see what was the matter.

In reply to their anxious inquiries, the butler told them what had happened, and the appalling intelligence was received with expressions of horror by the men, and by shrieks from the women—some of the latter seeming ready to faint.

Bidding all follow him who chose, Markland then led three or four stout-hearted men to the room where the dire event had occurred.

They found Sergeant Dickson watching beside the body, and, after regarding it for a few moments with fearful curiosity, they raised it from the floor, and placed it upon the bed.

This done, they all quitted the chamber of death, and the door was locked.

Markland, however, deemed it necessary to leave a man in the ante-room, and, having taken this precaution, he descended with the others to the lower part of the house.

The sergeant then proceeded to the library to ascertain whether Captain Legh had made any change in his plans.

"No," replied Atherton, "I must return to Manchester to-night, in order to explain matters to the prince. If his royal highness can dispense with my services, I shall retire from the Manchester Regiment. If not, I must go on. That is my fixed determination."

"'Tis the resolve of a man of honour," replied the sergeant.

"I have to read through this paper, and besides, I have some directions to give," said Atherton. "But I shall start in an hour."

"Good," replied Erick. "I shall be quite ready."

And fancying Captain Legh desired to be alone, he left the room.

Shortly afterwards Markland appeared with lights, which he placed on the writing-table.

"I am very sorry to find you are resolved to go, sir," he remarked.

"If the prince can spare me I shall return at once."

"Our chance of seeing you again is but slight, sir," rejoined the butler, shaking his head. "The prince is not likely to part with you. Shall Sir Richard's groom, Holden, attend you? Should you have any message to send to me, he will bring it back."

"Yes, I will take him with me," replied Atherton. "Perhaps Miss Rawcliffe may require him."

"You have eaten nothing, sir."

"I have no appetite. But let a slight repast be prepared for me in half an hour."

The butler bowed and left the room.

As yet Atherton had only read certain portions of his unhappy uncle's confession; but he now unfolded the manuscript with the intention of carefully perusing it.

The narration, written in a firm, bold hand, ran as follows.

In the name of the Almighty Power whom I have so deeply offended, and before whose throne I shall presently appear to answer for my manifold offences, I hereby solemnly declare that the young man now known as Atherton Legh is no other than my nephew Conway, only son of my brother

Sir Oswald Rawcliffe, whom I have wickedly kept out of his inheritance for twenty years, by carrying him off when an infant, as I shall proceed to relate.

All possible reparation for the great wrong done him shall be made to my nephew. I hereby restore him all the estates and property of which he has so long been deprived, and I implore his forgiveness.

Let it not be imagined that the possession of the property and title has brought me happiness! Since I have committed this terrible crime, peace has been a stranger to my breast My slumbers have been disturbed by fearful dreams, and when sleep has fled from my pillow my brother's angry shade has appeared before me, menacing me with eternal bale for the wrong done to his son.

Sometimes another phantom has appeared—the shade of the sweet lady who died of grief for the loss of her infant.

Though I was thus wretched, and life had become a burden to me, my heart was hardened, and I still clung tenaciously to the lands and title I had so wickedly acquired. Though they brought me nothing but misery I could not give them up. I recoiled with terror from the scaffold that awaited me if I avowed myself a robber and a murderer, for my hands were red with the blood of Bertha, the wretched nurse.

But my conduct was not altogether ill, and I trust that the little good I have done may tell in my favour. I had consigned my nephew to the care of strangers, but I watched over him. I supplied all his wants—educated him as a gentleman—and made him a liberal allowance.

It was my intention to have greatly increased the allowance, so as in part to restore my ill-gotten gains. But this was not to be. Heaven had other designs, and mine were thwarted.

For reasons that seemed good to me, though interested in the cause I forbade my nephew to join the rising in favour of the House of Stuart; but he heeded not my counsel.

Suddenly, when I least expected it, discovery of my crime seemed imminent. From some information he had privily received, the prince's suspicions were awakened, and he commanded me to appear before him, and answer certain questions he meant to put to me in the presence of my nephew and my daughter.

From such a terrible ordeal as this I naturally shrank. Death appeared preferable. But before putting an end to an existence that had long been a burden to me, I resolved to make all the atonement in my power for my evil deeds. With that intent have I come here.

In the ebony cabinet standing in the library, which contains all my private papers and letters, will be found incontestable evidences that my nephew is entitled to the estates, and that he is, in fact, the long-lost Conway Rawcliffe.

'Tis meet I should die at Rawcliffe, and in the very room where the crime was committed.

That I should thus rush unbidden into the presence of my Maker may seem to be adding to the weight of my offences, and to preclude all hope of salvation, but I trust in His mercy and forgiveness. He will judge me rightfully. He knows the torments I endure, and that they drive me to madness and despair. I must end them. Whether there will be rest in the grave for my perturbed spirit remains to be seen. Of the world I have already taken leave.

To the sole being to whom my heart clings with affection —to my daughter—I must now bid an eternal farewell! I cannot write to her, and she will understand why I cannot. I implore her prayers. When I am gone she will have no protector, and I trust that her cousin, Conway, will watch over her. My private property will be hers. Though small in comparison with Rawcliffe, 'twill be enough.

I have still much to say, for thick-coming thoughts press upon me; but I must not give them way. Were I to delay longer, my resolution might waver. Adieu, Conway! Adieu, Constance! Forgive me!—pray for me!

RICHARD RAWCLIFFE.

Enclosed within the packet was the key of the cabinet.

There was likewise another manuscript written by the unhappy baronet and signed by him, giving full particulars of the terrible occurrence alluded to; but since the reader is already acquainted with the details it is not necessary to reproduce them.

Atherton was profoundly moved by the perusal of this letter, and remained for some time buried in reflection.

Rousing himself at length from the reverie into which he had fallen, he looked round for the ebony cabinet, and easily discovered it. Unlocking it, he found that it contained a large bundle of letters and papers labelled in the late baronet's hand, "Documents relating to Conway Rawcliffe, with proofs of his title to the Rawcliffe estate."

He searched no further. He did not even untie the bundle, feeling certain it contained all the necessary evidences; but having carefully secured Sir Richard's last letter and confession, he locked the cabinet, and put the key in his pocket.

He then rang the bell, and when Markland made his appearance, he said to him:

"Before my departure from Manchester, Markland, it is necessary that I should give you some instructions, in case I should not be able to return, for the prince may be unwilling to release me from my engagements. I am sure you have faithfully served your late unfortunate master, and I am equally sure of your attachment to his daughter, and I have therefore every confidence in you. My great anxiety is respecting Miss Rawcliffe," he continued, in accents that bespoke the deepest feeling. "Intelligence of this dreadful event will be communicated to her to-morrow. How she will bear it I know not."

"If I may venture to give an opinion, sir," and I have known the dear young lady from childhood, and am therefore well acquainted with her temperament and disposition—"when the first shock is over, she will bear the bereavement with resignation and firmness. She was familiar with Sir Richard's wayward moods, and has often feared that something dreadful would happen to him. No doubt the shock will be a terrible one to her, and I can only hope she will be equal to it."

"All precautions shall be taken to break the sad tidings to her," said Atherton. "When she comes here it is my wish that she should be treated precisely as heretofore—you understand, Markland."

The butler bowed.

"I hope she will bring her cousin—*my* cousin, Miss Butler, with her. Mrs. Butler, I fear, may not be equal to the journey, but you will prepare for her, and for Father Jerome."

"Your orders shall be strictly attended to, sir," said the butler.

"And now with regard to my unfortunate uncle," paused the young baronet. "In case I am unable to return, I must leave the care of everything to you. Certain formalities of justice, rendered necessary by the case, must be observed, and you will take care that nothing is neglected. On all other points Miss Rawcliffe must be consulted."

"I will not fail to consult her, sir. But I am sure she would desire that her father's remains should be laid in the vault beneath the chapel where his ancestors repose, and that the funeral rites should be performed with the utmost privacy."

This conference ended, Atherton proceeded to the dining-room, and partook of a slight repast, after which he prepared for his departure.

The horses had already been brought round by Holden, the groom, and the night being extremely dark, the courtyard was illumined by torches, their yellow glare revealing the picturesque architecture of the old mansion.

Before mounting his steed, Atherton gave his hand to Markland, who pressed it respectfully, earnestly assuring the young gentleman that all his directions should be followed out.

The old butler then took leave of the sergeant, who had been in readiness for some minutes.

In consequence of the darkness, it was deemed advisable that Holden should lead the way. Accordingly, he was the first to cross the drawbridge, but the others kept close behind him.

CHAPTER XXXII.

ATHERTON'S DECISION IS MADE.

IT was with strange sensations that Atherton looked back at the darkling outline of the old mansion, and when it became undistinguishable in the gloom, he felt as if he had been indulging in an idle dream.

But no! the broad domains that spread around him on either side were his own. All he could discern belonged to him.

His meditations were not disturbed by either of his attendants, for the sergeant was a short distance behind him, and the groom about twenty or thirty yards in advance. As they trotted on quickly they were soon out of the park, and were now making their way somewhat more slowly along the road leading to Warrington. Presently they turned off on the right, in order to reach the ford, and were skirting the banks of the Mersey, when Holden came back and said that he perceived some men armed with muskets guarding the ford.

A brief consultation was then held. As the groom declared that the river was only fordable at this point, Atherton resolved to go on at all hazards.

As they drew near the ford they found it guarded—as

Holden had stated—by half a dozen armed militia-men, who were evidently determined to dispute their passage.

"Stand! in the king's name!" cried the leader of the party in an authoritative voice. "We can discern that one of you is a Highlander, and we believe you are all rebels and traitors. Stand! I say!"

"Rebels and traitors yourselves!" thundered the sergeant in reply. "We own no sovereign but King James the Third."

"Out of our way, fellows!" cried Atherton. "We mean to pass the ford!"

Drawing his sword as he spoke, he struck spurs into his steed, and dashed down the bank, followed closely by the sergeant and Holden—the former having likewise drawn his claymore.

The militia-men drew back, but fired at them as they were crossing the river, though without doing them any harm.

Having escaped this danger, they proceeded at the same rapid pace as before, and in the same order, the groom riding about twenty yards in advance. The few travellers they met with got out of their way.

By the time they reached Chat Moss the moon had risen, and her beams illumined the dreary swamp.

The scene looked far more striking than it did by daylight, but Atherton gazed at it with a different eye. Other thoughts now occupied his breast, and he seemed changed even to himself. When he tracked that road, a few hours ago, he was a mere adventurer—without name—without fortune—now he had a title and large estates. Reflections on this sudden and extraordinary change in his position now completely engrossed him, and he fell into a reverie which lasted till he reached Pendleton, and then waking up, as if from a dream, he was astonished to find he had got so far.

From this elevation the town of Manchester could be descried, and as the houses were again illuminated, and bonfires were lighted in different quarters, it presented a very striking appearance.

Just as Atherton crossed Salford Bridge, the clock of the collegiate church told forth eleven; and so crowded were the streets, owing to the illuminations, that nearly another quarter of an hour was required to reach the prince's headquarters.

Atherton was attended only by the groom, the sergeant having gone to report himself on his return to the Chevalier de Johnstone.

Dismounting at the gate, he entered the mansion, and orders having been given to that effect he was at once admitted to the prince, who was alone in his private cabinet.

Charles instantly inquired if he had brought Sir Richard Rawcliffe with him.

"He is unable to obey your royal highness's summons," replied the other.

"How?" exclaimed the prince, frowning.

"He is lying dead at Rawcliffe, having perished by his own hand. But he has left a written confession, wherein he acknowledges that he has wrongfully deprived me of my inheritance."

"This is strange indeed!" exclaimed the prince. "His extraordinary conduct to you is now explained, and the mystery that hung over your birth is solved. You are the lost son of the former baronet. I suspected as much, and meant to force the truth from Sir Richard. However, he has spared me the trouble. Pray let me know all that has occurred?"

Atherton then commenced his relation, to which the prince listened with the greatest interest, and when the story was brought to a conclusion he said:

"I will not affect to pity your unhappy uncle. He has escaped earthly punishment, and perhaps the deep remorse he appears to have felt may obtain him mercy on High. Let us hope so—since he has striven at the last to make some amends for his heavy offences. But to turn to yourself. Your position is now materially changed. You entered my service as an unknown adventurer, and not as a wealthy baronet. Considering this, and feeling, also, that I am under great personal obligation to you, I will not wait for any solicitation on your part, but at once release you from your engagement to me."

Atherton was much moved.

"Your royal highness overwhelms me by your kindness," he said. "But though Rawcliffe Hall and its domains may be mine by right, I do not intend to deprive Constance of the property. Furthermore, I shall not assume my real name and title till the close of the campaign. For the present I shall remain Atherton Legh. I trust your highness will approve of the course I intend to pursue?"

"I do approve of it," replied Charles, earnestly. "The resolution you have taken does you honour. Since you are determined to join me, it shall not be as a mere officer in the Manchester Regiment, but as one of my aides-de-camp. All needful explanation shall be given to Colonel Townley. I shall march at an early hour in the morning. But no matter. You can follow. You must see Constance before you leave, and if you are detained by any unforeseen cause, I will excuse you. Nay, no thanks. Good-night."

End of the Second Book.

BOOK III.

THE MARCH TO DERBY, AND THE RETREAT.

CHAPTER I.

AN OLD JACOBITE DAME.

NEXT morning the prince quitted Manchester, marching on foot at the head of two regiments of infantry which formed the advanced guard. The main body of the army, with the cavalry and artillery, was to follow at a later hour.

As the two regiments in question, which were composed of remarkably fine men, marched up Market Street Lane, preceded by a dozen pipers, they were accompanied by a vast concourse of people, who came to witness the prince's departure, and shouted lustily as he came forth from his headquarters, attended by Sir Thomas Sheridan and Colonel Ker.

Designing to make Macclesfield the limit of his first day's march, Charles took the road to Cheadle, and several hundred persons walked, or rather ran, by the side of the Highlanders for a mile or two, when they dropped off and returned, being unable to keep up with the active mountaineers.

Parties of men had been sent on previously to make a temporary bridge across the Mersey by felling trees; but the bridge not being completed on his arrival, the prince forded the river at the head of his troops.

On the opposite bank of the Mersey, several Cheshire

gentlemen of good family were waiting to greet him, and wish him success in his enterprise.

Among them was an aged dame, Mrs. Skyring, who, being very infirm, was led forward by a Roman Catholic priest. Kneeling before the prince, she pressed his hand to her lips.

Much impressed by her venerable looks, Charles immediately raised her, and on learning her name, told her he had often heard of her as a devoted adherent of his house.

"Give ear to me for a few moments, I pray you, most gracious prince," she said, in faltering accents. "Eighty-five years ago, when an infant, I was lifted up in my mother's arms to see the happy landing at Dover of your great uncle, King Charles the Second. My father was a staunch Cavalier, served in the Civil Wars, and fought at Worcester. My mother was equally attached to the House of Stuart. I inherited their loyalty and devotion. When your grandsire, King James the Second, was driven from the throne, I prayed daily for his restoration."

"You did more than pray, madam," said the prince. "I am quite aware that you remitted half your income to our family; and this you have done for more than fifty years. I thank you in my grandsire's name—in my father's name— and in my own."

Sobs checked the old lady's utterance for a moment, but at length she went on:

"When I learnt that you were marching on England at the head of an army, determined to drive out the Hanoverian usurper, and regain your crown, I was filled with despair that I could not assist you; but I sold my plate, my jewels, and every trinket I possessed. They did not produce much —not half so much as I hoped—but all they produced is in this purse. I pray your royal highness to accept it as an earnest of my devotion."

While uttering these words, which greatly touched

Charles, she again bent before him, and placed the purse in his hands.

"Pain me not by a refusal, I implore you, most gracious prince," she said. "And think not you are depriving me of aught. I cannot live long, and I have no children. 'Tis the last assistance I shall be able to render your royal house—for which I have lived, and for which I would die."

"I accept the gift, madam," replied Charles, with unaffected emotion, "with as much gratitude as if you had placed a large sum at my disposal. You are, indeed, a noble dame; and our family may well be proud of a servant so loyal! If I succeed in my enterprise, I will recompense you a hundred fold."

"I am fully recompensed by these gracious words, prince," she rejoined.

"Nay, madam," he cried, pressing her hand to his lips; "mere thanks are not enough. You have not confined yourself to words."

"My eyes are very dim, prince," said the old dame; "and what you say to me will not make me see more clearly. Yet let me look upon your face, and I will tell you what I think of you. I am too old to flatter."

"You will not offend me by plain speaking," said Charles, smiling.

"You are a true Stuart," she continued, trying to peruse his features. "But there are some lines in your comely countenance that bode——"

"Not misfortune, I trust?" said Charles, finding she hesitated.

She regarded him anxiously, and made an effort to reply, but could not.

"What ails you, madam?" cried the prince, greatly alarmed by the deathly hue that overspread her features.

Her strength was gone, and she would have fallen, if he had not caught her in his arms.

Her friends, who were standing near, rushed forward to her assistance.

"Alas, all is over!" exclaimed Charles, mournfully, as he consigned her inanimate frame to them.

"She is scarcely to be pitied, prince," said the Romish priest. "'Tis thus she desired to die. May the angels receive her soul, and present it before the Lord!"

"The sum she has bestowed upon me shall buy masses for the repose of her soul," said Charles.

"Nay, prince," rejoined the priest. "Her soul is already at rest. Employ the money, I beseech you, as she requested."

Much affected by this incident, Charles continued his march through a fine champaign country, well-timbered and richly cultivated, containing numerous homesteads, and here and there an old hall of the true Cheshire type, and comprehending views of Bowden Downs and Dunham Park on the left, with Norbury and Lyme Park on the right.

At Headforth Hall he halted with his body-guard, and claimed the hospitality of its owner; while his troops marched on to Wilmslow, and forced the inhabitants of that pretty little village to supply their wants.

From Wilmslow the prince's march was continued to Macclesfield, where he fixed his quarters at an old mansion near the Chester Gate.

CHAPTER II.

ATHERTON'S GIFT TO CONSTANCE.

THE prince's departure from Manchester took place on Sunday, December the 1st; but as the main body of the army did not leave till the middle of the day, and great confusion prevailed in the town, no service took place in the churches.

The cavalry was drawn up in St. Ann's Square; the

different regiments of infantry collected at various points in the town; and the Manchester Regiment assembled in the collegiate churchyard.

While the troops were thus getting into order, preparatory to setting out for Macclesfield, a great number of the inhabitants of the town came forth to look at them—very much increasing the tumult and confusion.

The Manchester Regiment got into marching order about noon, and was one of the first to quit the town. Officers and men were in high spirits, and looked very well.

As the regiment passed up Market Street Lane, with Colonel Townley riding at its head, the colours borne by Ensign Syddall, and the band playing, it was loudly cheered.

The regularity of the march was considerably interfered with by the number of persons who accompanied their friends as far as Didsbury, and supplied them rather too liberally with usquebaugh, ratifia, and other spirituous drinks.

The courage of the men being raised to a high pitch by these stimulants, they expressed a strong anxiety for an early engagement with the Duke of Cumberland's forces, feeling sure they should beat them.

After a short halt at Didsbury, their friends left them, and their courage was somewhat cooled by fording the river below Stockport. They were likewise obliged to wade through the little river Bollin, before reaching Wilmslow, where they halted for the night.

Atherton had not yet left Manchester. He had some business to transact which obliged him to employ a lawyer, and he was engaged with this gentleman for two or three hours in the morning. He had previously written to Constance to say that it was necessary he should see her before his departure, and as soon as his affairs were arranged he rode to Mrs. Butler's house in Salford.

Leaving his horse with Holden, by whom he was attended, he entered the garden, and was crossing the lawn, when he encountered Jemmy Dawson, who, having just parted with Monica, looked greatly depressed.

In reply to his anxious inquiries, Jemmy informed him that Constance had borne the shock better than might have been expected, and had passed the night in prayer. "I have not seen her," he said, "but Monica tells me she is now perfectly composed, and however much she may suffer, she represses all outward manifestation of grief. In this respect she is very different from Monica herself, who, poor girl! has not her emotions under control, and I left her in a state almost of distraction."

Without a word more he hurried away, while Atherton entered the house, and was shown into a parlour on the ground floor. No one was in the room at the time, and his first step was to lay a packet on the table.

Presently Constance made her appearance. Her features were excessively pale, and bore evident traces of grief, but she was perfectly composed, and Atherton thought he had never seen her look so beautiful.

She saluted him gravely, but more distantly than before.

"I cannot condole with you on the terrible event that has occurred," he said; "but I can offer you my profound sympathy. And let me say at once that I freely and fully forgive your unfortunate father for all the wrong he has done me."

"I thank you for the assurance," she rejoined. "'Tis an infinite relief to me, and proves the goodness of your heart."

"Do not dwell upon this, Constance," he said. "Hereafter we will talk over the matter—not now. Should you feel equal to the journey, I hope you will immediately return to Rawcliffe."

"I will return thither, with your kind permission, to see my poor father laid in the family vault. That sad duty performed, I shall quit the house for ever."

"No, Constance—that must not be," he rejoined. "My object in coming hither this morning is to tell you that I do not design to dispossess you of the house and property. On the contrary, you will be as much the mistress of Rawcliffe Hall as ever—more so, perhaps. Nay, do not interrupt me—I have not finished. Many things may happen. I may meet a soldier's fate. The hazardous enterprise I am bent upon may fail—I may be captured—may die as a rebel on the scaffold. If I should not return, the house and all within it—all the domains attached to it—are yours. By that deed I have made them over to you."

And he pointed to the packet which he had laid upon the table.

Constance was greatly moved. Tears rushed to her eyes, and for a few minutes she was so overpowered that she could not speak.

Atherton took her hand, which she did not attempt to withdraw.

"I am profoundly touched by your generosity," she said. "But I cannot accept your gift."

"Nay you must accept it, dearest Constance," he said. "You well know you have my heart's love, and I think you will not refuse to be mine."

"'Twould be too great happiness to be yours," she rejoined. "But no—no—I ought not to consent."

By way of reply, he pressed her to his heart, and kissed her passionately.

"Now will you refuse?" he cried.

"How can I, since you have wrested my consent from me?" she rejoined. "But how am I to address you?"

"You must still call me Atherton Legh," he replied.

"Well, then, dearest Atherton, my heart misgives me. In urging you to join this expedition I fear I have done wrong. Should any misfortune happen to you I shall deem myself the cause of it. I tremble to think of the consequences of my folly. Must you go?" she added, looking imploringly at him.

"Yes," he replied. "Not even you, dearest Constance, can turn me from my purpose. The prince has relieved me from my engagement, but I cannot honourably retire. Come what may, I shall go on."

"I will not attempt to dissuade you from your purpose," she rejoined. "But I find it doubly hard to part now. And your danger seems greater."

"Mere fancy," he said. "You love me better than you did—that is the cause of your increased apprehension."

For some moments they remained gazing at each other in silence.

At last Atherton spoke.

"'Tis with difficulty that I can tear myself away from you, dearest Constance. But I hope soon to behold you again. Meantime, you will remain at Rawcliffe Hall as I have suggested."

"I will do whatever you desire," she rejoined.

"I hope you will induce Mrs. Butler and Monica to stay with you, and that I shall find them at Rawcliffe on my return. I would not anticipate disaster—but 'tis desirable to be prepared for the worst. Should ill success attend our enterprise, and I should be compelled to seek safety in flight, I might find a hiding-place in Rawcliffe Hall."

"No doubt," she rejoined. "You could easily be concealed there—even should strict search be made. All necessary preparations shall be taken. Whenever you arrive at Rawcliffe you will find all ready for you. I will go there to-morrow, and I trust Mrs. Butler and Monica will be able to follow immediately. Will you not see them?"

"Not now," he replied. "Bid them farewell for me. If I stay longer, my resolution might give way. Remember what I have said to you. In any event you are mistress of Rawcliffe. Adieu!"

Pressing her again to his breast, he rushed out of the room.

View of Macclesfield.

CHAPTER III.

A RETREAT RESOLVED UPON.

Mounting his horse, which he had left at the gate of Mrs. Butler's residence, and followed by Holden, Atherton rode towards the bridge—being obliged to pass through the town in order to gain the Stockport road.

The place was still in a state of great confusion—none of the cavalry having as yet departed; but he contrived to make his way through the crowded thoroughfares, and was soon in the open country.

At Didsbury he overtook the Manchester Regiment and had a long conversation with Colonel Townley, who explained to him that he meant to pass the night at Wilmslow.

Atherton then pursued his journey, crossed the Mersey at Cheadle, and came up with the prince and the advanced guard about four miles from Macclesfield. He was then sent on to make preparations for his royal highness, and executed his task very satisfactorily.

On the following day, while the prince, with the infantry, continued his march to Leek, Lord George Gordon, with his regiment of horse, proceeded to Congleton, and Captain Legh received orders from his royal highness to accompany him.

At Congleton information being obtained that the Duke of Cumberland was posted at Newcastle-under-Lyne, with ten thousand men, Lord George went thither to reconnoitre, and found that the duke, on hearing of the onward march of the insurgent forces, had retired with his army on Lichfield.

With marvellous despatch Atherton rode across the country and brought the intelligence to Charles, who had arrived at Leek.

No change, however, was made in the prince's plans. He did not desire an engagement with the duke, but rather to elude him.

Accordingly, he pressed on, and on the fourth day after leaving Manchester, arrived with his entire forces at Derby.

Charles was still full of confidence, and as he was now a day's march nearer London than the enemy, he persuaded himself that he should be able to reach the capital without hazarding a battle. Though he had been coldly received at all places since he left Manchester, and had not obtained any more recruits, he was not discouraged.

He fixed his head-quarters at a large mansion in Full Street, which has since been demolished,

On the morning after his arrival at Derby, he rode round the town, attended only by Colonel Ker and Captain Legh, and was very coldly received by the inhabitants—no cheers attending his progress through the streets, and many of the houses being shut up.

Much dispirited by this unfavourable reception, he returned to his head-quarters, where a council of war was held, which was attended by all the leaders of his army.

The general aspect of the assemblage was gloomy, and far from calculated to raise his spirits. Sir Thomas Sheridan alone seemed to retain his former confidence.

Graciously saluting them all, Charles said:

"I have summoned you, my lords and gentlemen, simply to inform you that after halting for another day in Derby to refresh my troops, I shall proceed with all possible despatch, and without another halt, if I can avoid it—to London—there to give battle to the usurper. From the feeling evinced towards me, I doubt not I shall obtain many recruits during the hurried march, and perhaps some important reinforcements—but be this as it may, I shall persevere in my design."

He then looked round, but as he encountered only gloomy looks, and all continued silent, he exclaimed sharply:

"How is this? Do you hesitate to follow me further?"

"Since your royal highness puts the question to us," replied Lord George Gordon, gravely, "I am bound to answer it distinctly. We think we have already done enough to prove our devotion. Feeling certain we have no chance whatever of success, we decline to throw away our lives. We have now reached the very heart of England, and our march has been unopposed, but we have obtained none of the large reinforcements promised us, and only a single regiment at Manchester. Scarcely any person of distinction has joined us—and very few have sent us funds. Since we left Manchester we have been everywhere coldly received—and here, at Derby, we are regarded with unmistakable aversion. The populace are only held in check by our numbers. Further south, the disposition would probably be still more unfavourable, and retreat would be out of the question. If your royal highness can show us letters from any persons of distinction promising aid, or can assure us that a descent upon the English shores will be made from France, we are willing to go on. If not, we must consult our own safety."

"What do I hear?" cried the prince, who had listened in the utmost consternation. "Would you abandon me—now that we have advanced so far—now that victory is assured?"

"Our position is critical," replied Lord George. "If we advance further, our retreat will be cut off by Marshal Wade, who is close in our rear, and by the Duke of Cumberland, who has an army doubling our own in number, only a few leagues from us. If we hazard a battle, and obtain a victory, the losses we should necessarily sustain would so weaken our forces, that without reinforcements, we could not hope to vanquish the large army which we know is encamped at Finchley to secure the capital. Retreat is, therefore, unavoidable."

"Is this the unanimous opinion?" demanded Charles, looking anxiously round at the assemblage.

With the exception of Mr. Murray, the secretary, Sir Thomas Sheridan, and the Marquis d'Eguilles, every voice answered:

"It is."

"Then leave me," cried the prince, fiercely and scornfully. "Leave me to my fate. I will go on alone."

"If your royal highness will view the matter calmly, you will perceive that we are not wanting in fidelity and attachment to your person in making this proposition," said Lord Kilmarnock. "The cause here is hopeless. Let us return to Scotland, where we shall find reinforcements and obtain aid and supplies from France."

"No; I will not return to Scotland ingloriously," cried Charles.

"Listen to me, prince," said the Duke of Perth. "There is every inducement to return to Scotland, where a large force awaits you. I have just received intelligence that my brother, Lord John Drummond, has landed at Montrose with his regiment newly raised in France. With the Highlanders whom we left behind, this will make a large force—probably three thousand men."

"And no doubt there will be large additions," said Sir Thomas Sheridan. "By this time the Irish Brigade must have embarked from France, with the promised French regiments."

"There is nothing for it but a retreat to Scotland," said Lord Pitsligo. "It would be madness to face an army of thirty thousand men."

"You are a traitor like the rest, Pitsligo," cried the prince, fiercely.

The old Scottish noble flushed deeply, and with difficulty mastered his indignation.

"I never thought to hear that opprobrious term applied to me by one of your royal house, prince," he said. "But since you have stigmatised all these loyal gentlemen in the same manner, I must bear the reproach as best I can."

"Forgive me, my dear old friend," cried Charles, seizing his hand, and pressing it warmly. "I meant not what I said. No one could possess stauncher friends than I do—no one could appreciate their devotion more profoundly than myself.

But my heart is crushed by this bitter and unexpected disappointment. It has come upon me like a clap of thunder—at the very moment when I anticipated success. Since it must be so, we will retreat, though it will half kill me to give the word. Leave me now, I pray of you. I will strive to reconcile myself to the alternative."

Thus enjoined, they all quitted the chamber, and Charles was left alone.

Flinging himself into a chair he remained for some time with his face buried in his hands.

When he raised his eyes, he saw Atherton standing beside him.

"I knew not you were here," said the prince.

"I came to learn your royal highness's commands," replied the other. "Something, I fear, has greatly disturbed you."

"Disturbed me! ay!" cried Charles. "I am forced to retreat."

"By the enemy?" exclaimed Atherton.

"By my generals," replied Charles. "We shall advance no further. You may prepare to return to Manchester."

CHAPTER IV.

HOW THE MANCHESTER REGIMENT WAS WELCOMED ON ITS RETURN.

CHARLES could not shake off the bitter disappointment he experienced at this sudden and unlooked-for extinction of his hopes. He had made up his mind to march on London, and he thought his Highland army would follow him. But he now discovered his mistake.

He did not go forth again during the day, but shut himself up in his room, and left Lord George Gordon and the Duke of Perth to make all arrangements necessary for the retreat.

They decided to pass through Manchester on the way to

Carlisle. The men were kept in profound ignorance of the change of plan, but when they discovered that they were retreating their rage and disappointment found vent in the wildest lamentations. "Had they been beaten," says the Chevalier de Johnstone, "their grief could not have been greater." It was almost feared they would mutiny.

On the Manchester Regiment the retreat had a most dispiriting effect. Officers and men had joined on the understanding that they were to march to London, and they were deeply mortified when they found they were to retreat to Scotland.

The men looked sullen and downcast, and so many desertions took place that the ranks were perceptibly thinned. It was certain that two or three of the officers only waited a favourable opportunity to escape.

On the third day the Manchester Regiment, which formed part of the advanced guard, arrived at Macclesfield. Next morning, at an early hour, they proceeded to Manchester. Alarming reports had been spread that the Duke of Cumberland was in hot pursuit with his whole army; but the rumour turned out to be false.

If the officers and men composing the insurgent army expected a reception like that they had previously experienced in Manchester, they were greatly mistaken. No sooner was the town cleared of the invading army, than the Whigs and Presbyterians resumed their influence, and the fickle mob changed with them.

Tumultuous crowds now went about the town shouting "Down with the Pretender! Down with the Jacobites!" Nor did the authorities interfere, but let them have their own way.

In consequence of this license great mischief was done. The mob threatened to pull down Dr. Deacon's house in Fennel-street, broke his windows, and might have proceeded to frightful extremities if they had laid hands upon him.

Two days afterwards a rumour was designedly spread by

OF THE FATAL '45.

the Presbyterians that Marshal Wade had arrived at Rochdale with his army, and would shortly enter Manchester; and this had the effect intended of exciting the mob to further violence. The rumour, however, had no foundation, and the tumult began to subside.

Meantime, the magistrates and many of the important personages who had quitted the town, began to return, thinking the danger was past, and something like order was restored.

The position, however, of the Jacobites was by no means secure, since disturbances might at any time occur, and they were afforded very little protection.

After the lapse of a week, during which reliable intelligence had been received that the Highland army had arrived at Derby without encountering any opposition, and even staunch Whigs had began to think that the intrepid young prince would actually succeed in reaching London, news came that the rebels were retreating without a battle, and were then at Leek on their way back.

At first this news, which appeared improbable, was received with incredulity, but it was speedily confirmed by other messengers.

A consultation was then held by the boroughreeve, constables, and other magistrates, as to the possibility of offering any resistance; but as the militia had been disbanded, and it was doubtful whether Marshal Wade would come to their assistance, the idea was given up.

But after some discussion Dr. Mainwaring and Justice Bradshaw sent the bellman round to give notice that, as the rebels might be speedily expected, all the loyal inhabitants were enjoined to rise and arm themselves with guns, swords, halberts, pickaxes, shovels, or any other weapons, to resist the rebels, and prevent them from entering the town until the arrival of the king's forces.

In consequence of this notice several thousand persons, armed in the manner snggested, assembled in the open fields beyond Market Street Lane, where they were harangued by Dr.

Mainwaring, who urged them to spoil the roads by breaking them up, and throwing trees across them, and promised to send the country folk to their aid.

Having uttered this he left the defence of the town to the inhabitants, and rode off; but he fulfilled his promise, and sent a number of country folk armed with scythes and sickles, but these rough fellows caused such a tumult that another notice had to be given by the bellman commanding the mob to lay down their arms and disperse, and the country folk to return to their domiciles.

These contradictory orders produced considerable dissatisfaction, and were not obeyed.

One party more valiant than the rest marched to Cheadle ford, under the leadership of Mr. Hilton, with the intention of destroying the temporary bridge contrived by the insurgents, but before they could accomplish their task, they were disturbed and ignominiously put to flight by Colonel Townley and the Manchester Regiment.

On arriving at Manchester, Colonel Townley and his men were welcomed by a shower of stones and other missiles from the mob assembled at the top of Market Street Lane. Upon this the colonel called out that if another stone was thrown, and the mob did not quietly disperse, he would fire upon them.

Alarmed by the menacing looks of the soldiers, who were greatly incensed by this treatment on the part of their fellow-townsmen, the mob took to their heels.

During a subsequent disturbance Ensign Syddall was taken prisoner, but was rescued by his comrades.

CHAPTER V.

A FRESH SUBSIDY DEMANDED.

ON the arrival of the prince with the main body of the army, comparative tranquillity was restored. But it was evident that the feeling of the inhabitants was totally changed. There were no joyful demonstrations—no bonfires—no illuminations.

Charles returned to his former residence at the top of Market Street Lane; the Duke of Perth, Lord Tullibardine, Lord George Murray, Lord Pitsligo, and the other Scottish nobles and chiefs repaired to the houses they had previously occupied; and the men billeted themselves in their old quarters. But so unfriendly were the inhabitants to the Manchester Regiment that it was with difficulty that the officers and men could find quarters.

As night drew on, and a tendency to riot was again manifested, the bellman was sent round to warn the inhabitants that not more than two persons would be allowed to walk together in the streets after dark, unless guarded by the prince's troops, and that any attempt at tumult or disturbance would be severely punished.

In addition to this, pickets of men patrolled the streets throughout the night, so that the town was kept tolerably quiet.

On the same evening about eight o'clock a meeting of the principal inhabitants took place at the Bull's Head—a warrant having been sent to the magistrates by the prince's secretary, Mr. Murray, commanding them, on pain of military execution, to raise a subsidy of five thousand pounds from the town by four o'clock on the following day.

"What is to be done?" demanded Mr. Walley. "I fear it will be impossible to raise the large sum required by the appointed time—and if we fail we are to be held responsible with our lives. You must help us, gentlemen."

And he looked round at the assemblage, but no offer was made.

"Surely you won't allow us to be shot?" cried Mr. Fowden.

"This is a mere threat," said old Mr. James Bayley, an eminent merchant of the town. "The prince cannot be in earnest."

"You are mistaken, Mr. Bayley," rejoined Mr. Fowden.

"It is no idle threat. The prince is so highly offended by the reception given him that he has laid this heavy tax upon the town—and he will have it paid."

"The contributions must be levied by force," observed Mr. Walley. "We shall never get the money in any other way."

"Such a course will render you extremely unpopular," observed Mr. Bayley.

"Better be unpopular than be shot, Mr. Bayley," rejoined Mr. Fowden. "Try to place yourselves in our position, gentlemen. Will you help us to pay the money in case we should be driven to extremity?"

But no answer was made to the appeal, and the magistrates were in despair.

At this moment the door opened, and Colonel Townley, attended by Captain Dawson, Captain Deacon, and Ensign Syddall, entered the room.

The magistrates rose in consternation, wondering what was the meaning of the visit.

"Pardon my intrusion, gentlemen," said the colonel, saluting them. "But I think I can help you out of a difficulty. I am aware that five thousand pounds must be raised from the town by to-morrow afternoon. Feeling certain you will never be able to accomplish this task unassisted, I beg to offer you my aid. You shall have a party of men, under the command of these officers, to go round with you, and help you to make the collection."

"We gladly accept your offer, colonel," cried both magistrates eagerly.

"The plan will relieve you from all personal responsibility," said Colonel Townley, "and will secure the contributions."

The magistrates were profuse in their thanks, and it was then arranged that the party should commence their rounds at an early hour next morning

CHAPTER VI.

A FALSE MESSAGE BROUGHT TO HELEN.

HELEN CARNEGIE had not accompanied her lover in the march to Derby, but had been persuaded by Beppy Byrom to remain with her at Manchester. Thinking that an immediate engagement with the Duke of Cumberland was inevitable, the sergeant consented to the arrangement; but he missed his faithful companion sadly. He had become so accustomed to having her by his side that it seemed as if he had lost his right hand. He tried to occupy his thoughts by strict attention to his duty—but it would not do. So miserable did he feel at the separation, that he was half reconciled to the retreat from Derby by the thought that he should soon see her again.

Helen suffered quite as much—perhaps more. Independently of being constantly near her lover, it had been her pride and pleasure to be with the Highland army, and when the troops moved off without her, she felt as if her heart would break; and she would certainly have followed, if she had not been restrained by Beppy. Familiar as she was with all the various incidents of a march, she pictured them to herself with the greatest distinctness, and spoke of all that the sergeant was doing.

"Oh! he win miss me sairly," she cried, "He win want me to cheer him up, when his spirits are low. I ought not to have left him. And what if he shouldna come back!"

"Don't make yourself uneasy, Helen," said Beppy. "He is certain to return. Papa says the prince's army will be forced to retreat."

"Na! na! that win never be!" cried Helen. "The prince win never turn back! The Highlanders may be all kilt, but turn back!—never!"

The rumour, however, at length reached Manchester that

the prince was actually retreating, and Helen's delight at the thought of seeing her lover again quite overcame her vexation at what she looked upon as a disgrace.

But the regiment to which the sergeant belonged, and which was commanded by the Chevalier de Johnstone, did not reach Manchester till late in the day, and Erick having a great deal to do on his arrival, could not present himself to Helen.

She had been in quest of him, but had encountered Captain Lindsay, who addressed her more boldly than ever, and to escape his persecutions she was compelled to return.

As evening came her anxiety increased, and she was in all the agony of expectation, when a message came from her lover.

It was brought by Rollo, who informed her that the sergeant had just arrived with his regiment, and wished to see her immediately.

"Where is he?" asked Helen. "Why does he not come to me, himself?"

"He would come, if he could," replied Rollo; "but he is busy with the men in St. Ann's Square. Come with me and I will take you to him."

Wholly unsuspicious of ill, Helen instantly prepared to accompany the messenger, and they quitted the house together.

The night was dark but clear, and, as they crossed the churchyard, she perceived a tall Highland officer advancing towards her, and guessing who it was, she stopped, and said to Rollo, "What is Captain Lindsay doing here?"

"How should I know?" rejoined the other. "He won't meddle with us. Come on. I'll take care of you."

"I don't feel sure of that," she cried. "I shall go back."

"No, you won't," said Rollo, seizing her arm, and detaining her.

"Ah! you have basely betrayed me," she cried. "But Sergeant Dickson will punish you."

Rollo replied by a coarse laugh, and the next moment Captain Lindsay came up.

"Free me from this man," she cried.

"He is acting by my orders, Helen," said Lindsay. "This time I have taken such precautions that you cannot escape me."

"You cannot mean to carry me off against my will, Captain Lindsay," she cried.   "I winna believe it of ye."

"I hope you will come quietly, Helen," he said, "and not compel me to resort to force. But come you shall."

"Never!" she rejoined. "Ye ken fu' weel that I am Erick Dickson's affianced wife. 'Twad be an infamy if ye were to tae me frae him."

"I care not," replied Lindsay. "I am determined to make you mine. Fleet horses and trusty men are waiting outside the churchyard to bear you off. In half-an-hour you will be far from Manchester, and out of Erick's reach."

"If ye hae the heart o' a man, Rollo, ye will not aid in this wicked deed," cried Helen.

But Rollo shook his head, and she made another appeal to Captain Lindsay.

"Let me gae for pity's sake," she cried. "I wad kneel to you, if I could."

"No, no, Helen," he rejoined. "I don't mean to part with you. But we waste time. Bring her along."

Finding all entreaties unavailing, and that she could not extricate herself from Rollo, who was a very powerful man, the unfortunate girl uttered a loud shriek; but her cries were instantly stifled by Captain Lindsay, who took off his scarf, and threw it over her head.

But her cry had reached other ears than they expected. As they were hurrying her towards the spot where the horses were waiting for them, a well-known voice was heard, exclaiming:

"Haud there, ye waur than rievers. When I saw the

horses outside the kirkyard, and noticed that one on 'em had a pillion, I suspected something wrang; but when I heard the cry, I felt sure. Set her down, ye villains!" cried Sergeant Dickson, rushing towards them.

"Heed him not, Rollo," said Captain Lindsay. "Place her on the pillion and ride off with her. Leave me to deal with the noisy fool."

And, as he spoke, he drew his sword, planted himself in Dickson's way, while Rollo moved off with his burden.

"Ye had better not hinder me, captain," cried the half-maddened sergeant, drawing a pistol. "Bid that dastardly ruffian set her down at once, or I'll send a bullet through your head."

"You dare not," said Lindsay, contemptuously.

"I will not see her stolen from me," cried the sergeant, furiously. "Set her down, I say."

But finding his cries disregarded, he fired, and Captain Lindsay fell dead at his feet.

On hearing the report of the pistol, Rollo looked round, and seeing what had happened, instantly set down Helen and fled. Extricating herself from the scarf, Helen rushed towards the spot where the unfortunate officer was lying. Her lover was kneeling beside the body.

"Wae's me, Helen!" he exclaimed. "Wae's me, I hae kilt the captain."

"Ye canna be blamed for his death, Erick," she rejoined. "He brought his punishment on himsel."

"I shall die for it, nevertheless, lassie," he rejoined.

"Die! you die, Erick, for savin' me frae dishonour!" she cried.

"Ay, ay, lass. He was my superior officer, and by the rules of war I shall die. No escape for me."

"Oh! if you think sae, Erick, let us flee before ye can be taken," she cried. "Come wi' me."

"Na! na!" he rejoined, gently resisting her. "I maun answer for what I hae done. Leave me, lassie; gae back to the young leddy. Tell her what has happened, and she will take care of you."

"Na, Erick, I winna leave you," she rejoined. "If ye are to dee, I'se e'en dee wi' ye. Och!" she exclaimed, "here they come to tak ye! Get up, lad, and flee!"

As a file of soldiers could be seen approaching, the sergeant rose to his feet, but did not attempt to fly.

Immediately afterwards the soldiers came up. With them were two or three men bearing torches, and as these were held down, the unfortunate officer could be seen lying on his back, with his skull shattered by the bullet.

The sergeant averted his gaze from the ghastly spectacle.

The soldiers belonged to the Manchester Regiment, and at their head was Captain Dawson.

"How did this sad event occur, sergeant?" demanded Jemmy, after he had examined the body.

"Captain Lindsay fell by my hand," replied Dickson. "I surrender myself your prisoner, and am ready to answer for the deed."

"You must have done it in self-defence," said Jemmy. "I know you too well to suppose you could have committed such a crime without some strong motive."

"The deed was done in my rescue," cried Helen. "Captain Lindsay was carrying me off when he was shot."

"I trust that will save him from the consequences of the act," replied Jemmy, sadly. "My duty is to deliver him to the provost-marshal."

"That is all that I could desire," said the sergeant. "I ask no greater favour from you."

"Oh! let me gae wi' him—let me gae wi' him," cried Helen, distractedly. "I am the sad cause of it a'."

"Ye canna gang wi' me, lassie, unless you compose yersel," said the sergeant, somewhat sternly.

"Dinna fear me—dinna fear me—I winna greet mair," she cried, controlling her emotion by a powerful effort.

"May she walk by my side to the guard-room, Captain Dawson?" asked the sergeant.

"She may," replied the other, adding to the men, "conduct the prisoner to the guard-room near the prince's quarters."

The sergeant was then deprived of his arms, and the pistol with which he had fired the fatal shot was picked up, and preserved as evidence against him.

As Erick and Helen were marched off in the midst of the guard, another file of men entered the churchyard, took up the body of the unfortunate Captain Lindsay, and conveyed it to the quarters of the commanding officer.

CHAPTER VII.

A COURT-MARTIAL.

DELIVERED over to the custody of the provost, the unfortunate Sergeant Dickson was placed in the guard-room near the prince's head-quarters, and a sentinel was stationed at the door. Helen was allowed to remain with him. The greatest sympathy was felt for the sergeant, for he was a universal favourite.

Full of anxiety, Captain Dawson sought an interview with the prince, who, though engaged on business, immediately received him.

Charles looked very grave.

"I am greatly distressed by what has happened," he said. "There is not a man in my whole army for whom I have a greater regard than Erick Dickson, but I fear his sentence will be death. However, I will do what I can for him. A court-martial shall be held immediately, and I have sent for Lord George Murray to preside over it, and we must wait the result of the investigation. As yet I cannot interfere."

As the prince had ordered that the examination should

take place without delay, a court-martial was held in a room on the ground floor of the mansion occupied by his royal highness. Lord George Murray presided, and with him were Lord Elcho, Lord Pitsligo, Colonel Townley, and the Chevalier de Johnstone; Captain Legh, Captain Deacon, Captain Dawson, and several other officers were likewise present.

The president occupied a raised chair at the head of the table, round which the others were seated. The room was only imperfectly lighted.

After a short deliberation, the prisoner was brought in by two soldiers, who stood on either side of him.

Bowing respectfully to the court, he drew himself up to his full height, and maintained a firm deportment throughout his examination.

"Sergeant Dickson," said Lord George Murray, in a stern and solemn voice, "you are charged with the dreadful crime of murder—aggravated in your instance, because your hand has been raised against your superior officer. If you have aught to state in mitigation of your offence, the court will listen to you."

"My lord," replied Dickson, firmly, "I confess myself guilty of the crime with which I am charged. I did shoot Captain Lindsay, but perhaps the provocation I received, which roused me beyond all endurance, may be held as some extenuation of the offence. Nothing, I am well aware, can justify the act. My lord, I could not see the girl I love carried off before my eyes, and not demand her release. Captain Lindsay refused—mocked me—and I shot him. That is all I have to say."

Brief as was this address, it produced a most powerful effect. After a short deliberation by the court, Lord George thus addressed the prisoner:

"Sergeant Dickson, since you acknowledge your guilt, it is not necessary to pursue the examination, but before pronouncing sentence, the court desires to interrogate Helen Carnegie."

"She is without, my lord," replied the sergeant.

On the order of Lord George, Helen was then introduced, and as she was well known to the president, and to every member of the council, the greatest sympathy was manifested for her.

She was very pale, and did not venture to look at the sergeant, lest her composure should be shaken, but made a simple reverence to the president and the council.

"Sergeant Dickson has confessed his guilt, Helen," observed Lord George. "But we desire to have some information from your lips. How came you to meet Captain Lindsay in the churchyard?"

"I did na meet him, my lord," she replied, with indignation. "It was a base and dishonourable trick on his part. Little did I ken that he was lyin' in wait for me. Rollo Forbes brought me word that Erick wished me to come to him, and when I went forth into the kirkyard, Captain Lindsay seized me, and wad have carried me aff. He has long persecuted me wi' his addresses, but I ha' gien him nae encouragement, and wad ha' shunned him if I could. A scarf was thrown over my head by the captain to stifle my cries, and had not Erick came to my rescue I should ha' been carried off. Captain Lindsay deserved his fate, and so all men will feel who prize their sweethearts. Erick was bound to defend me."

"His first duty was to observe the rules of war," remarked Lord George sternly. "We are willing to believe your story, Helen, but we have no proof that you did not voluntarily meet Captain Lindsay."

"That fawse villain, Rollo, has fled, but there is a young leddy without, my lord—Miss Byrom—who will testify to the truth of my statement, if you will hear her."

"Let her come in," said the president.

Beppy Byrom was then introduced.

She was accompanied by her father, who remained near her during her brief examination.

Though looking very pale, Beppy was perfectly self-possessed, and quite confirmed Helen's statement that she had been lured from the house by a supposed message from the sergeant; adding emphatically:

"I am sure she would never have gone forth to meet Captain Lindsay, for I know she detested him."

"Ay, that I did!" exclaimed Helen, unable to control her feelings, and wholly unconscious that she was guilty of disrespect.

Lord George then ordered the court to be cleared, and Beppy and Dr. Byrom went out, but Helen, scarcely comprehending the order, did not move, till her arm was touched by the officer.

She then cast an agonised look at Erick, and would have flung herself into his arms if she had not been prevented.

As she went out, she turned to the judges and said:

"Be merciful to him, I pray you, my lords."

The court then deliberated for a short time, during which Lord George was earnestly addressed in a low tone both by Colonel Townley and the Chevalier de Johnstone, but his countenance remained very grave.

At last, amid profound silence, he addressed the prisoner in the following terms: "Sergeant Dickson, the court has taken into consideration your excellent character, and the strong provocation that impelled you to commit this desperate act, and which certainly mitigates the offence; and such is our pity for you, that, were it in our power, we would pardon your offence, or at all events would visit it with a slight punishment; but we have no option—leniency on our part would be culpable. You have murdered an officer, and must die. Sentence of death is therefore passed upon you by the court."

"I expected this, my lord," observed the sergeant firmly, "and am prepared to meet my fate. But I would not die as a murderer."

"The crime you have committed is murder," said Lord George; "and I can hold out no hope whatever of pardon.

You are too good a soldier not to know that if your life were spared it would be an ill example to the army, besides being a violation of the law."

An awful pause ensued.

The profound silence was then broken by the prisoner, who said, in a low, firm voice:

"All the grace I will ask from your lordship and the court is, that execution of the sentence you have passed upon me, the justice of which I do not deny, may not be delayed."

"We willingly grant your request," replied Lord George. "The execution shall take place at an early hour in the morning."

"I humbly thank your lordship," said Dickson. "But I would further pray that my affianced wife, who has been unwittingly the cause of this disaster, be permitted to bear me company during the few hours I have left; and that she also be permitted to attend my execution."

"To the former part of the request there can be no objection," said Lord George. "Helen shall remain with you during the night, but she can scarcely desire to be present at your execution."

"She will never leave me to the last," said the sergeant.

"Be it as you will," replied Lord George.

The sergeant was then removed by the guard, and given in charge of the provost, and the court broke up.

CHAPTER VIII.

HELEN PLEADS IN VAIN.

IMMEDIATELY after the breaking up of the court, Lord George Murray and the other members of the council waited upon the prince to acquaint him with their decision.

Though greatly pained, he thought they were right, and after some discussion they retired and left him alone.

But the prince was so much troubled, that though excessively fatigued he could not retire to rest, but continued to pace his chamber till past midnight, when Captain Dawson entered and informed him that Miss Byrom earnestly craved an audience of him.

"She is not alone," added Jemmy. "Helen Carnegie is with her."

Charles hesitated for a short time, and said, "I would have avoided this, if possible. But let them come in."

Beppy was then ushered in by Jemmy, and made a profound obeisance to the prince.

Behind her stood Helen, who seemed quite overwhelmed with grief.

"I trust your highness will pardon me," said Beppy. "I have consented to accompany this poor heart-broken girl, and I am sure you will listen to her, and if possible grant her prayer."

"I will readily listen to what she has to say," replied the prince, in a compassionate tone; "but I can hold out little hope."

"Oh, do not say so, most gracious prince!" cried Helen, springing forward, and catching his hand, while he averted his face. "For the love of Heaven have pity upon him! His death win be my death, for I canna survive him. Ye havena a mair leal subject nor a better sodger than Erick Dickson. Willingly wad he shed his heart's bluid for ye! Were he to dee, claymore in hand, for you, I should not lament him—but to dee the death o' a red-handed murtherer, is not fit for a brave man like Erick."

"I feel the force of all you say, Helen," replied Charles, sadly. "Erick is brave and loyal, and has served me well."

"Then show him mercy, sweet prince," she rejoined. "He is no murtherer—not he! Pit the case to yersel, prince.

Wad ye hae seen the mistress o' yer heart carried off, and not hae slain the base villain who took her? I ken not."

" 'Tis hard to tell what I might do, Helen," observed Charles. "But the rules of war cannot be broken. A court-martial has been held, and has pronounced its sentence. I must not reverse it."

"But you are above the court-martial, prince," she cried, "You can change its decree. If any one is guilty—'tis I! Had I not come wi' Erick this wad never have happened. He has committed no other fawt."

"On the contrary, he has always done his duty—done it well," said the prince. "Both Colonel Johnstone and Colonel Townley have testified strongly in his favour. But I required no testimony, for I well know what he has done."

"And yet ye winna pardon him?" she cried, reproachfully.

"I cannot, Helen—I cannot," replied Charles. "My heart bleeds for you, but I must be firm."

"Think not you will set an ill example by showing mercy in this instance, prince," she said. "Erick's worth and valour are known. Sae beloved is he, that were there time, hundreds of his comrades wad beg his life. If he be put to death for nae fawt, men win think he has been cruelly dealt with."

"You go too far, Helen," said the prince, compassionately, "but I do not blame your zeal."

"Pardon me, sweet prince—pardon me if I have said mair than I ought. My heart overflows, and I must gie vent to my feelings, or it will break! Oh, that I were able to touch your heart, prince!"

"You do touch it, Helen. Never did I feel greater difficulty in acting firmly than I do at this moment."

"Then yield to your feelings, prince—yield to them, I implore you," she cried, passionately. "Oh, madam!" she added to Beppy, "join your prayers to mine, and perchance his highness may listen to us!"

Thus urged, Beppy knelt by Helen's side, and said, in an earnest voice:

"I would plead earnestly with you, prince, to spare Erick. By putting him to death you will deprive yourself of an excellent soldier, whose place you can ill supply."

"Very true," murmured Charles. "Very true."

"Then listen to the promptings of your own heart, which counsels you to spare him," she continued.

For a moment it seemed as if Charles was about to yield, but he remained firm, and raising her from her kneeling posture, said:

"This interview must not be prolonged."

Helen, however, would not rise, but clung to his knees, exclaiming, distractedly:

"Ye winna kill him! ye winna kill him!"

Jemmy removed her gently, and with Beppy's aid she was taken from the room.

CHAPTER IX.

TOGETHER TO THE LAST.

For a few minutes after her removal from the cabinet, Helen was in a state of distraction, but at length she listened to Beppy's consolations and grew calmer.

She then besought Captain Dawson to take her to the guard-chamber, where Erick was confined. Before going thither she bade adieu to Beppy. It was a sad parting, and drew tears from those who witnessed it.

"Fare ye weel, dear young leddy!" she said. "May every blessing leet upon your bonnie head, and on that ov yer dear, gude feyther! Most like I shan never see you again on this airth, but I hope you win sometimes think o' the puir Scottish lassie that lood ye weel!"

"Heaven strengthen you and support you, Helen!" cried Beppy, kissing her. "I trust we shall meet again."

"Dinna think it," replied the other, sadly. "I hope and trust we may meet again in a better world."

Beppy could make no reply—her heart was too full.

Embracing the poor girl affectionately, she hurried to her father, who was waiting for her, and hastily quitted the house.

Helen was then conducted to the guard-room in which the sergeant was confined.

Erick was seated on a wooden stool near a small table, on which a light was placed, and was reading the Bible. He rose on her entrance, and looked inquiringly at her.

"Na hope, Erick," she said, mournfully.

"I had nane, lassie," he replied.

They passed several hours of the night in calm converse, talking of the past, and of the happy hours they had spent together; but at last Helen yielded to fatigue, and when the guard entered the chamber he found her asleep with her head resting on Erick's shoulder.

The man retired gently without disturbing her.

Meanwhile, the warrant, signed by Lord George Gordon, appointing the execution to take place at seven o'clock in the morning, had been delivered to the Chevalier de Johnstone, as commander of the corps to which the unfortunate sergeant belonged, and all the necessary preparations had been made.

There was some difficulty in arranging the execution party, for the sergeant was so much beloved that none of his comrades would undertake the dreadful task, alleging that their aim would not be steady. No Highlander, indeed, could be found to shoot him.

Recourse was then had to the Manchester Regiment, and from this corps a dozen men were selected.

The place of execution was fixed in an open field at the back of Market Street Lane, and at no great distance from the prince's residence.

The Rev. Mr. Coppock, chaplain of the regiment, volunteered to attend the prisoner.

Helen slept on peacefully till near six o'clock, when a noise, caused by the entrance of Colonel Johnstone and Mr. Coppock, aroused her, and she started up.

"Oh! I have had such a pleasant dream, Erick," she said. "I thought we were in the Highlands together. But I woke, and find mysel here," she added, with a shudder.

"Well, you will soon be in the Highlands again, dear lassie," he said.

She looked at him wistfully, but made no answer.

"Are you prepared, sergeant?" asked Colonel Johnstone, after bidding him good morrow.

"I am, sir," replied Dickson.

"'Tis well," said the colonel. "In half an hour you will set forth. Employ the interval in prayer."

Colonel Johnstone then retired, and the chaplain began to perform the sacred rites, in which both Erick and Helen took part.

Just as Mr. Coppock had finished, the sound of martial footsteps was heard outside, and immediately afterwards the door was opened and the provost entered the chamber, attended by a couple of men. Behind them came Colonel Johnstone.

"Bind him," said the provost to his aids.

"Must this be?" cried Dickson.

"'Tis part of the regulation," rejoined the provost.

"It need not be observed on the present occasion," said Colonel Johnstone. "I will answer for the prisoner's quiet deportment."

"You need fear nothing from me, sir," said Dickson.

"I will take your word," rejoined the provost. "Let his arms remain free," he added to the men.

The order to march being given, the door was thrown open, and all passed out.

Outside was a detachment from the corps to which Sergeant Dickson had belonged. With them was the execution party, consisting of a dozen picked men from the Manchester Regiment, commanded by Ensign Syddall, who looked very sad. The detachment of Highlanders likewise looked very sorrowful. With them were a piper and a drummer. The pipes were draped in black, and the drum muffled. Though the morning was dull and dark, a good many persons were looking on, apparently much impressed by the scene.

Having placed himself at the head of the detachment, Colonel Johnstone gave the word to march, and the men moved slowly on. The muffled drum was beaten, and the pipes uttered a low wailing sound very doleful to hear.

Then came Erick, with Helen by his side, and attended by the chaplain.

The sergeant's deportment was resolute, and he held his head erect. He was in full Highland costume, and wore his bonnet and scarf.

All the spectators were struck by his tall fine figure, and grieved that such a splendid man should be put to death.

But Helen exited the greatest sympathy. Though her features were excessively pale, they had lost none of their beauty. The occasional quivering of her lip was the only external sign of emotion, her step being light and firm. Her eyes were constantly fixed upon her lover.

Prayers were read by the chaplain as they marched along.

The execution party brought up the rear of the melancholy procession. As it moved slowly through a side street towards the field, the number of spectators increased, but the greatest decorum was observed.

At length the place of execution was reached. It was the spot where the attempt had been made to capture the prince; and on that dull and dismal morning had a very gloomy appearance, quite in harmony with the tragical event about to take place.

On reaching the centre of the field, the detachment of Highlanders formed a semicircle, and a general halt took place

—the prisoner and those with him standing in the midst, and the execution party remaining at the back.

Some short prayers were then recited by Mr. Coppock, in which both the sergeant and Helen joined very earnestly.

These prayers over, the sergeant took leave of Helen, and strained her to his breast.

At this moment, her firmness seemed to desert her, and her head fell upon his shoulder. Colonel Johnstone stepped forward, and took her gently away.

The provost then ordered a handkerchief to be bound over the sergeant's eyes, but at the prisoner's earnest request this formality was omitted.

The fatal moment had now arrived. The detachment of Highlanders drew back, and Erick knelt down.

The execution party made ready, and moved up within six or seven yards of the kneeling man.

"Fire!" exclaimed Syddall, and the fatal discharge took place—doubly fatal as it turned out.

At the very instant when the word was given by Syddall, Helen rushed up to her lover, and kneeling by his side, died with him.

Her faithful breast was pierced by the same shower of bullets that stopped the beating of his valiant heart.

CHAPTER X.

MR. JAMES BAYLEY.

In spite of the exertions of the magistrates, only a very small sum could be obtained from the inhabitants of the town, upon which another meeting took place at the Bull's Head, and a deputation was formed to wait upon the prince.

Accordingly, a large body of gentlemen proceeded to the prince's head-quarters, and some half-dozen of them, including the two magistrates and Mr. James Bayley, were ushered into the council-chamber, where they found Charles and his secretary.

Mr. Fowden, who acted as spokesman, represented to the prince the utter impossibility of raising the money, and besought that the payment might be excused

Charles, however, answered sternly:

"Your fellow-townsmen have behaved so badly that they deserve no consideration from me. The subsidy must be paid."

"I do not see how it can be accomplished," said Mr. Fowden.

"If it is not paid by one o'clock, you will incur the penalty," rejoined Mr. Murray. "Meantime, stringent measures must be adopted. I am aware, Mr. Bayley, that you are one of the wealthiest merchants of the town, and I shall therefore detain you as a hostage for the payment. If the money is not forthcoming at the appointed time, we shall carry you along with us."

"Surely your royal highness will not countenance this severity," said Mr. Bayley, appealing to the prince. "I have not slept out of my own house for the last two years, and am quite unable to travel. If I am forced off in this manner I shall have a dangerous illness."

"I cannot part with you, Mr. Bayley," said the prince. "But I will put you to as little personal inconvenience as possible. You shall have my carriage."

"I humbly thank your royal highness for your consideration, but I still hope I may be excused on the score of my age and infirmities."

"You cannot expect it, Mr. Bayley," interposed Mr. Murray. "Your case is not so bad as that of the two magistrates, who will certainly be shot if the money is not forthcoming."

"We have done our best to raise it, but we find it quite impossible," said Mr. Fowden. "The amount is too large.

I do not think there is five thousand pounds in the whole town."

"I am sure there is not," added Mr. Walley, with a groan.

"Since you give me this positive assurance, gentlemen," said Charles, "I consent to reduce the amount to half. But I will make no further concession. Meantime, Mr. Bayley must remain a prisoner."

"I pray your royal highness to listen to me," said the old gentleman. "By detaining me you will defeat your object. If I am kept here I can do nothing, but if you will allow me to go free I may be able to borrow the money."

Apparently convinced by this reasoning, Charles spoke to his secretary, who said:

"Mr. Bayley, if you will give the prince your word of honour that you will bring him the sum of two thousand five hundred pounds in two hours, or return and surrender yourself a prisoner, his royal highness is willing to set you at liberty."

"I agree to the conditions," replied the old gentleman.

With a profound obeisance to the prince, he then withdrew with the magistrates.

Accompanied by the rest of the deputation, who had waited outside in the hall, Mr. Bayley returned to the Bull's Head, where a conference was held.

After some discussion, Mr. Bayley thus addressed the assemblage: "You see, gentlemen, the very serious position in which I am placed—and our worthy magistrates are still worse off. The money must be raised—that is certain. Let us regard it as a business transaction. You shall lend me the sum required. I and my friend Mr. Dickenson will give you our promissory notes at three months for the amount."

The proposition was immediately agreed to. The meeting broke up, and in less than an hour the money was brought to Mr. Bayley. Promissory notes were given in exchange, and the sum required was taken to Mr. Murray by the two magistrates, who were thus freed from further responsibility.

CHAPTER XI.

THE VISION.

NEARLY a fortnight had passed since Constance's return to Rawcliffe Hall, and during that interval much had happened. Sir Richard had been laid in the family vault. The interment took place at night, and was witnessed only by the household, the last rites being performed by Father Jerome. Mrs. Butler and her daughter were now inmates of the hall, but the old lady seldom left her chamber. Gloom seemed to have settled upon the mansion. The two young damsels never strayed beyond the park, and rarely beyond the garden. As yet, they had received no tidings of the Highland army, except that it had arrived at Derby. They knew nothing of the retreat, and fancied that the prince was on his way to London. The next news they received might be of a glorious victory—or of a signal defeat. Rumours there were of all kinds, but to these they attached no importance.

It was a dark dull December afternoon, and the principal inmates of the hall were assembled in the library. A cheerful fire blazed on the hearth, and lighted up the sombre apartment. Father Jerome was reading near the window. Mrs. Butler was reciting her prayers, and the two girls were conversing together, when the door opened, and an unexpected visitor entered the room. It was Atherton. Uttering a cry of delight, Constance sprang to her feet, and was instantly folded to his breast.

Before he could answer any questions, Monica rushed up to him, and said:

"Oh! relieve my anxiety. Is Jemmy safe?"

"Safe and well," replied Atherton. "He is in Manchester with the regiment, but Colonel Townley would not allow him to accompany me."

"What am I to understand by all this?" cried Constance.

Lancaster — scene of the end for the Manchester Regiment.

"All chance of our gaining London is over," replied Atherton. "The prince has retreated from Derby, and is now returning to Scotland."

"Without a battle?" cried Constance.

"Ay, without a battle," he replied, sadly.

"I can scarcely believe what I hear," cried Monica. "I would rather a sanguinary engagement had taken place than this should have happened."

"The prince was forced to retreat," rejoined Atherton. "The Highland chiefs would proceed no further."

"Will Jemmy retire from the regiment?" cried Monica.

"No, he will proceed with it to Carlisle. I shall go there likewise. I have obtained leave from the prince to pay this hasty visit. I must return in the morning. We may yet have to fight a battle, for it is reported that the Duke of Cumberland is in hot pursuit, and Marshal Wade may cut off our retreat."

"I will not say that all is lost," observed Constance. "But it seems to me that the prince has lost all chance of recovering the throne. His army and his friends will be alike discouraged, and the attempt cannot be renewed."

"Such is my own opinion, I confess," replied Atherton "Nevertheless, I cannot leave him."

He then addressed himself to Mrs. Butler and Father Jerome, who had been looking anxiously towards him, and acquainted them with the cause of his unexpected return. They were both deeply grieved to hear of the prince's retreat.

Tears were shed by all the ladies when they were told of the execution of poor Erick Dickson, and they deplored the fate of the faithful Helen Carnegie. Atherton had a long conversation with Constance, but they could not arrange any plans for the future. At last the hour came for separation for the night, and it was in a very depressed state of mind that he sought his chamber.

It was a large apartment, panelled with oak, and contained a massive oak bedstead with huge twisted columns, and a large canopy. Though a wood fire blazed on the hearth, and cast a glow on the panels, the appearance of the room was exceedingly gloomy.

"'Tis the best bedroom in the house, and I have therefore prepared it for you," observed old Markland, who had conducted him to the room. "You will easily recognise the portrait over the mantelpiece. I have not removed it, as I have not received orders to do so."

Atherton looked up at the picture indicated by the old butler, and could not repress a shudder as he perceived it was a portrait of his uncle, Sir Richard.

However, he made no remark, and shortly afterwards Markland quitted the room.

Seating himself in an easy-chair by the fire, Atherton began to reflect upon the many strange events that had occurred to him, and he almost began to regret that he had ever joined the unlucky expedition.

While indulging these meditations, he fell into a sort of doze, and fancied that a figure slowly approached him.

How the person had entered the room he could not tell, for he had not heard the door open, nor any sound of footsteps. The figure seemed to glide towards him, rather than walk, and, as it drew nearer, he recognised the ghastly and cadaverous countenance.

Transfixed with horror, he could neither stir nor speak. For some time the phantom stood there, with its melancholy gaze fixed upon him.

At last a lugubrious voice, that sounded as if it came from the grave, reached his ear.

"I have come to warn you," said the phantom. "You have neglected my counsel. Be warned now, or you will lose all!"

For a few moments the phantom continued to gaze earnestly at him and then disappeared.

At the same time the strange oppression that had benumbed his faculties left him, and he was able to move.

As he rose from his chair, he found that the fire was almost extinct, and that his taper had burnt low.

On consulting his watch he perceived that it was long past midnight. He could not be quite sure whether he had been dreaming, or had beheld a vision; but he felt the necessity of rest, and hastily disrobing himself, he sought the couch, and slept soundly till morning.

He was awake when old Markland entered his room, but he said nothing to him about the mysterious occurrence of the night.

Determined to abide by his plans, and fearing his resolution might be shaken, he ordered his horses to be got ready in half an hour. He did not see Constance before his departure, but left kind messages for her, and for Mrs. Butler and Monica, by Markland.

The old butler looked very sad, and when Atherton told him he should soon be back again, he did not seem very hopeful.

A fog hung over the moat as he crossed the drawbridge, followed by his groom. On gaining the park, he cast a look back at the old mansion, and fancying he descried Constance at one of the windows, he waved an adieu to her.

As it was not his intention to return to Manchester, but to rejoin the retreating army at Preston, he forded the Mersey at a spot known to Holden, and avoiding Warrington, rode on through a series of lanes to Newton—proceeding thence to Wigan, where he halted for an hour to refresh his horse, and breakfast, after which he continued his course to Preston.

On arriving there he found the town in a state of great confusion. The Highland army was expected, but it was also thought that Marshal Wade would intercept the retreat.

To the latter rumour Atherton attached very little credence, but put up at an inn to await the arrival of the prince.

CHAPTER XII.

THE RETREAT FROM MANCHESTER TO CARLISLE.

On the evening when Atherton visited Rawcliffe Hall, intelligence was received that the Duke of Cumberland was advancing by forced marches to Manchester, and as it was not the prince's intention to give the duke battle, he prepared for an immediate retreat.

Early on the following morning, therefore, the main body of the army, with Charles at its head, quitted the town, and crossed Salford Bridge on the way to Wigan.

Very different was the departure from the arrival. Those who witnessed it did not attempt to conceal their satisfaction, and but few cheers were given to the prince.

At a later hour the Manchester Regiment commenced its march. Its numbers had again been reduced, several desertions having taken place. Some of the officers went on very reluctantly, and one of them, Captain Fletcher, who had refused to proceed further, was dragged off by a party of soldiers.

Shortly after Colonel Townley's departure an express from the Duke of Cumberland was received by the magistrates, enjoining them to seize all stragglers from the rebel army, and detain them until his arrival. The duke also promised to send on a party of dragoons, but as they had not yet come up, and several regiments had not yet quitted the town, the magistrates did not dare to act.

However, as the rear-guard of the army was passing down Smithy Bank to the bridge, a shot was fired from a garret-window, by which a dragoon was killed, upon which the regiment immediately faced about, and the colonel commanding it was so enraged that he gave orders to fire the town.

In an instant all was confusion and dismay. The men, who were quite as infuriated as their leader, were preparing to execute the order, when they were pacified by the capture of the author of the outrage, and summary justice having been inflicted upon him, the regiment quitted Manchester, very much to the relief of the inhabitants.

On that night the prince slept at Wigan; on the following day he marched with his whole forces to Preston, and here Atherton joined him.

Next day, Charles pursued his march to Lancaster, where he remained for a couple of days to recruit his men before entering upon the fells of Westmoreland.

After quitting Lancaster, the army moved on in two divisions, one of which rested at Burton, and the other at Kirkby Lonsdale, but they joined again at Kendal, and then continued their march over Shap Fells. The weather was exceedingly unpropitious, and the fine views from the hills were totally obscured by mist.

The prince's deportment seemed entirely changed. He had quite lost the spirit and ardour that characterised him on the onward march, and he seemed perpetually to regret that he had turned back. He thought he had thrown away his chance, and should never recover it.

One day he unburdened his breast to Captain Legh, for whom he had conceived a great regard, and said:

"I ought to have gone on at all hazards. The army would not have abandoned me—even if their leaders had turned back. By this time I should have been master of London—or nothing."

In vain Atherton tried to cheer him. For a few minutes he roused himself, but speedily relapsed into the same state of dejection.

Heretofore, as we have stated, the prince had marched on foot at the head of one column of the army, but he now left the command of this division to the Duke of Perth, and rode in the rear, attended by the Marquis d'Eguilles, Sir Thomas Sheridan, Secretary Murray, and Captain Legh.

Lord George Gordon commanded the rear-guard, and was

more than a day's march behind the van—great fears being entertained lest the retreating army should be overtaken by the Duke of Cumberland, who was in full pursuit. At length, these apprehensions were realised.

The duke came up with the rear-guard at Clifton, near Penrith, and immediately attacked it, but was most vigorously and successfully repulsed by Lord George; and little doubt can be entertained that if Charles, who was at Penrith, had sent reinforcements, the duke would have been defeated, and perhaps might have been taken prisoner.

Be this as it may, the pursuit was checked, and Charles reached Carlisle without further interruption.

End of the Third Book.

Lord George Murray, Prince Charles' Senior Lieutenant-General.

BOOK IV.

CARLISLE.

CHAPTER I.

COLONEL TOWNLEY APPOINTED COMMANDANT OF THE CARLISLE GARRISON.

On the prince's march south, three companies of Highlanders had been left at Carlisle under the command of Colonel Hamilton, but it was now proposed to strengthen the garrison by the addition of the Manchester Regiment, in case the town should be besieged by the Duke of Cumberland.

To this plan Colonel Townley raised no objection, as his men were disinclined to proceed further, and he doubted whether they could be induced to cross the Border. He was therefore appointed commander of the town garrison, while Colonel Hamilton retained the governorship of the citadel.

The Scottish army did not remain more than a day in Carlisle, and none of the men wished to be left behind.

On the contrary, it was sorely against their inclination that the three companies of the Duke of Perth's regiment remained with Colonel Hamilton.

On the morning of the prince's departure from Carlisle, the Manchester Regiment, now reduced to a hundred and twenty men, was drawn up on the esplanade of the old castle. With it was Colonel Townley, now commandant of the garrison

On the glacis, also, were ranged the three companies of Highlanders who were to be left with Colonel Hamilton.

Already the greater portion of the Scottish army had quitted the town, but Charles remained behind to bid adieu to his devoted adherents. Apparently he was much moved as he thus addressed the officers and men of the Manchester Regiment:

"I am loth to leave you here, but since it is your wish not to cross the Border, I do not urge you to accompany me to Scotland." Then addressing the Highland companies, he added: "Scotsmen, you must remain here for a short time longer. Should the town be besieged, you need have no fear. The castle can hold out for a month, and long before that time I will come to your assistance with a strong force."

This address was received with loud cheers, both by Englishmen and Scots.

Colonel Townley then stepped forward and said:

"Your royal highness may rely upon it that we will hold the place till your return. We will never surrender."

"I will answer for my men," added Colonel Hamilton. The Duke of Cumberland and Marshal Wade shall batter the castle about our ears before we will give it up."

"I am quite satisfied with this assurance," rejoined the prince. Then turning to Captain Legh, he said to him: "Will you remain, or accompany me to Scotland?"

"Since your royal highness allows me the choice, I will remain with the regiment," replied Atherton. "I think I can best serve you here."

Charles looked hard at him, but did not attempt to dissuade him from his purpose.

"I leave you in a perilous post," he said; "but I am well aware of your bravery. I hope we shall soon meet again. Adieu!"

He then mounted his steed, and waving his hand to the two colonels, rode off.

CHAPTER II.

ATHERTON TAKEN PRISONER.

SURROUNDED by walls built in the time of Henry the Eighth, Carlisle, at the period of our history, boasted a fortress that had successfully resisted many an attack made upon it by the Scots.

Situated on an eminence, and partly surrounded by a broad, deep moat, fed by the river Eden, the citadel, strongly garrisoned and well provided with guns and ammunition, would seem to be almost impregnable. At the foot of the western walls flowed the river Caldew, while the castle overlooked the beautiful river Eden.

On the summit of the keep floated the prince's standard, and from this lofty station remarkably fine views could be obtained. On one side could be noted the junction of the Caldew and the Eden that takes place below the castle, and adds to the strength of its position. The course of the Eden could likewise be traced as it flowed through fertile meadows, to pour its waters, augmented by those of the Caldew, into the Solway Frith.

From the same point of observation could likewise be descried the borders of Dumfries, with the Cheviot Hills on the right, while on the other side the view extended to the stern grey hills of Northumberland. Looking south, the eye ranged over a sweeping tract in the direction of Penrith. Of course the keep looked down upon the ancient cathedral which closely adjoined the castle, and upon the town with its old gates and bulwarks.

Though the walls had become dilapidated, and were of no great strength, yet, from its position and from its castle, it would seem that Carlisle was able to stand a lengthened siege; and such was the opinion of Colonel Townley, who considered it tenable against any force that could be brought against it by the Duke of Cumberland.

One important matter, however, could not be overlooked. The inhabitants were hostile, and were only controlled by the garrison. In Carlisle, as in all Border towns, there was an hereditary dislike of the Scots, and this feeling had been heightened by the recent events.

Immediately after the prince's departure, Colonel Townley examined the walls, and caused certain repairs to be made. Guns were mounted by his direction, and chevaux de frise fixed at all the gates and entrances.

A house from which the prince's army had been fired upon was likewise burnt, to intimidate the inhabitants; and notice was given that any violation of the commandant's orders would be severely punished. A sallying party was sent out under the command of Captain Legh to procure forage and provisions, and returned well supplied.

Amongst the most active and efficient of the officers was Tom Syddall, who had now been raised to the post of adjutant, and rendered the colonel great service. As the number of men ran short, Parson Coppock, whose military ardour equalled his religious zeal, abandoned his gown and cassock, and putting on military accoutrements, acted as quarter-master to the regiment.

The greatest zeal and activity were displayed both by the officers and men of the corps, and Colonel Townley seemed almost ubiquitous.

Colonel Hamilton lacked the spirit and energy displayed by the commandant of the town, and was content to remain quietly shut up within the walls of the castle, leaving the more arduous duties to Colonel Townley, who discharged them, as we have shown, most efficiently. Moreover, though he kept the opinion to himself, Colonel Hamilton felt that the garrison would be compelled to capitulate, unless it should be reinforced.

By the end of the third day all possible preparations for

the siege had been made by Colonel Townley, and he now deemed himself secure.

On the following day Captain Legh was sent with a message to the governor, and found the castle in a good state of defence. The court-yard was full of Highland soldiers; a few cannon were planted on the battlements, and sentinels were pacing to and fro on the walls.

Colonel Hamilton was on the esplanade at the time, conversing with Captain Abernethy and some other Scottish officers, and Atherton waited till he was disengaged to deliver his message to him; but before the governor could send a reply, a small party of horse, with an officer at their head, could be seen approaching the city from the Penrith Road.

Evidently they were English dragoons. After reconnoitring for a few moments, Colonel Hamilton gave his glass to Atherton, who thought they must be coming to summon the city to surrender.

"No doubt of it," replied the governor. "I wonder what Colonel Townley's answer will be?"

"A scornful refusal," rejoined Captain Legh, surprised.

"That is all very well now," remarked the governor, shrugging his shoulders; "but we shall have to capitulate in the end."

"Does your excellency really think so?"

"I do," replied Hamilton.

The answer returned by Colonel Townley was such as Atherton had anticipated. He positively refused to surrender the city, and declared he would hold it to the last extremity.

On the following day the Duke of Cumberland appeared before the town with his whole army, and immediately began to invest it on all sides. He continued his siege operations for nearly a week, during which a constant fire was kept up from the walls and from the larger guns of the castle, and frequent sallies were made by the garrison. One of these, headed by Captain Legh, was attended with some little success.

He drove the enemy from their trenches, and nearly captured the Duke of Richmond.

Hitherto, the besieged party had sustained very little damage, and had only lost a few men. The duke had not indeed opened fire upon them, because he had not received some artillery which he expected from Whitehaven.

Colonel Townley, therefore, continued in high spirits, and even Colonel Hamilton acquired greater confidence. One morning, however, they were startled by perceiving a six-gun battery, which had been erected during the night. Colonel Townley did not lose courage even at this sight; but the governor was seriously alarmed.

"We shall be compelled to submit," he said; "and must make the best terms we can."

"Submit! never!" cried Colonel Townley. "We had better die by the sword than fall into the hands of those cursed Hanoverians. The duke will show us no mercy. Oh that we could but get possession of those guns!"

"Give me twenty well-mounted men and a dozen led horses, and I will bring off a couple of the guns," cried Atherton.

"The attempt were madness," cried Colonel Townley.

"Madness or not, I am ready to make it," rejoined Captain Legh.

Half-an-hour afterwards the north gate, which was nearest the battery, was suddenly thrown open, and Captain Legh, mounted on a strong horse, and followed by twenty well-mounted men, half of whom had spare horses furnished with stout pieces of rope, dashed at a headlong pace towards the battery. The attack was so sudden and unexpected that the enemy was quite taken by surprise. Only an officer of artillery and half-a-dozen artillerymen were near the battery at the time, and before they could fly to their guns, Captain Legh and his party were upon them, and drove them off. A desperate effort was made to carry off two of the guns, but it was found impossible to move the heavy carriages.

Lancaster Castle.

The Duke of Cumberland, who was at a short distance with his aide-de-camp, Colonel Conway, planning and directing the operations, witnessed the attack, and instantly ordered Conway with a troop of horse to seize the daring assailants.

But the latter dashed off as hard as they could to the gate, and gained it just in time. All got in safely with the exception of their leader, who was captured by Colonel Conway and led back to the duke.

CHAPTER III.

THE DUKE OF CUMBERLAND.

WILLIAM, Duke of Cumberland, second surviving son of the reigning sovereign, was at this time a handsome young man of twenty-four.

Strongly built, but well proportioned, he had bluff and rather coarse but striking features. Young as he was, the duke had gained considerable military experience. He had fought with his father, George the Second, at the battle of Dettingen, in 1743, and in May, 1745, he engaged Marshal Saxe at Fontenoy, and sustained a most crushing defeat—highly prejudicial to English renown.

Though thus defeated by the superior military skill of Marshal Saxe, the duke displayed so much gallantry and personal courage during the action, that he did not lose his popularity in England, but was very well received on his return; and on the outbreak of the rebellion in the same year, followed by the defeat of General Cope at Preston Pans, the attack on Edinburgh, and the march of the young Chevalier at the head of the Highland army into England, he assumed the command of the royal forces, and prepared to drive the rebels out of the kingdom. But instead of doing this, to the general surprise, he allowed the Scots to continue their advance as far as Derby, and it will always remain doubtful whether, if the prince had marched on to London, his daring attempt would not have been crowned by success. A contemporary historian unquestionably thought so, and emphatically declares: "Had the adventurer proceeded in his career with the expedition which he had hitherto used, he might have made himself master of the metropolis, where he would have been certainly joined by a considerable number of his well-wishers, who waited impatiently for his approach."* But when the prince commenced his retreat the duke immediately started in pursuit, though he made no real efforts to overtake him; and, as we have seen, he was repulsed by Lord George Gordon at Clifton, near Penrith. Again, instead of pursuing the rebels into Scotland, he sat down to besiege Carlisle. The duke was surrounded by his staff when Captain Legh was brought before him by Colonel Conway.

"Who is this rash fellow, who seems anxious to throw away his life?" demanded the duke.

"I thought I knew him, for his features seem strangely familiar to me," replied Colonel Conway. "But I must be mistaken. He gives his name as Atherton Legh, captain of the Manchester Regiment."

"Atherton Legh! ha!" cried the duke. Then fixing a stern look upon the young man, he said:

"You had better have remained faithful to the Government, sir. Now you will die as a traitor and a rebel."

"I am prepared to meet my fate, whatever it may be," replied Atherton, firmly.

"I might order you for instant execution," pursued the duke. "But you shall have a fair trial with the rest of the garrison. It must surrender to-morrow."

"Your royal highness is mistaken—the garrison can hold out for a week."

"'Tis you who are mistaken, Captain Legh," rejoined the

---

* Smollett's History of England, Reign of George the Second.

duke, haughtily. "I have just received a letter from Colonel Hamilton, offering me terms of submission."

"I am indeed surprised to hear it," said Atherton. "Your royal highness may credit me when I affirm that the citadel is in a very good state of defence, has plenty of arms and ammunition, and ought to hold out for a month."

"That may be," rejoined the duke. "But I tell you I have received a letter from the governor, asking for terms. However, I will only accept an unconditional surrender."

"Colonel Townley, the commander of the city garrison, will hold out to the last," said Atherton.

"Colonel Townley is a brave man, and may die sword in hand; but hold the town he cannot. His regiment does not number a hundred men. You see I am well informed, Captain Legh. To-morrow you will see your colonel again."

"I shall be glad to see him again—but not here," replied Atherton.

"Take the prisoner hence," said the duke to Colonel Conway. "Let him be well treated—but carefully watched."

Colonel Conway bowed, and Atherton was removed by the guard.

CHAPTER IV.

SURRENDER OF CARLISLE TO THE DUKE OF CUMBERLAND.

SHORTLY after the incident just related, fire was opened from the battery, but not much damage was done; it being the duke's intention to alarm the garrison, rather than injure the town. A few shots were directed against the castle, and struck the massive walls of the keep. The fire was answered by the besieged—but without any effect.

At this juncture it was with great difficulty that the inhabitants could be kept in check, and, with the small force at his command, it became evident to Colonel Townley that he must surrender.

Calling his officers together, he thus addressed them :

" Our position is most critical. Outside the walls we are completely blockaded, and inside the inhabitants are against us. One means of escape has occurred to me ; but it is so hazardous, that it ought scarcely to be adopted. A sortie might be made by a small party of horse, and these might succeed in cutting their way through the enemy. If a couple of barges could be found, the rest might manage to float down the Eden."

" That plan has occurred to me, colonel," said Captain Dawson. " But it is impracticable, since all the barges and boats have been destroyed. Possibly a few men might escape by swimming down the river—but in no other way."

" No," said Colonel Townley ; " we are so completely environed that escape is impossible, unless we could cut our way through the enemy, and this cannot be done, since there are no horses for the men. I will never abandon my gallant regiment. Since Colonel Hamilton has resolved to surrender, it is impossible for me to hold out longer—though I would a thousand times rather die with arms in my hand than submit to the mercy of the Duke of Cumberland."

Several plans were then proposed, but were rejected, as none seemed feasible ; and at last a muster was made of the regiment, and Colonel Townley's resolution being communicated to the men, was received by them with the greatest sorrow.

Later on in the day, Colonel Townley repaired to the citadel, where he had a conference with the governor, and endeavoured to induce him to change his purpose, but in vain.

On the following morning the besieged town of Carlisle presented a singular spectacle. The inhabitants, who had hitherto been kept in awe by the garrison, assembled in the streets, and did not attempt to hide their exultation ; while the Highlanders in the castle, and the officers and men of the

Manchester Regiment, looked deeply dejected, and stood listlessly at their posts. The cause of all these mingled feelings of ill-concealed satisfaction on one side, and deep dejection on the other, was, that the garrison had declared its intention to surrender by hanging out the white flag. The men still stood to their arms—the engineers and artillerymen remained upon the walls—the gates of the city were still guarded—but not a gun had been fired. All was terrible expectation.

Colonel Hamilton, Captain Abernethy, Colonel Townley, and some of the officers of the Manchester Regiment, were assembled on the esplanade of the castle, when Captain Vere, an officer of the English army, attended by an orderly, rode towards them. As the bearer of a despatch for the governor, he had been allowed to enter the city.

Dismounting, Captain Vere marched up to the governor, and, with a formal salute, delivered a missive to him, saying, "This from his royal highness."

The governor took the letter, and, walking aside with Colonel Townley, read as follows:

"'All the terms his royal highness will or can grant to the rebel garrison of Carlisle are, that they shall not be put to the sword, but be reserved for the king's pleasure.'"

"The king's pleasure!" exclaimed Colonel Townley. "We have nothing but death to expect from the usurper. But go on."

"'If they consent to these conditions, the governor and the principal officers are to deliver themselves up immediately; and the castle, citadel, and all the gates of the town are to be taken possession of forthwith by the king's troops."

"I cannot make up my mind to this," cried Colonel Townley.

"Unfortunately there is no help for it," observed Colonel Hamilton. "But hear what follows: 'All the small arms are to be lodged in the town guard-room, and the rest of the garrison are to retire to the cathedral, where a guard is to be placed over them. No damage is to be done to the artillery, arms, or ammunition.' That is all."

"And enough too," rejoined Colonel Townley. "The conditions are sufficiently hard and humiliating."

"Gentlemen," said the governor, addressing the officers, "'tis proper you should hear the terms offered by the duke."

And he proceeded to read the letter to them.

Murmurs arose when he had done, and a voice—it was that of Adjutant Syddall—called out:

"Reject them!"

"Impossible," exclaimed Hamilton.

Thinking he had been kept waiting long enough, Captain Vere then stepped forward and enquired, "What answer shall I take to his royal highness?"

Colonel Townley and his officers were all eagerness to send a refusal; but the governor cried out, "Tell the duke that his terms are accepted."

"In that case, gentlemen," said Captain Vere, "you will all prepare to deliver yourselves up. His royal highness will at once take possession of the town."

With this, he mounted his horse, and rode off, attended by his orderly.

About an hour afterwards, the gates being thrown open, Brigadier Bligh entered the town with a troop of horse, and rode to the market-place, where, in front of the guard-room, he found Colonel Hamilton, Captain Abernethy, Colonel Townley, and the officers of the Manchester Regiment, a French officer, and half a dozen Irish officers.

They all yielded themselves up as prisoners, and the brigadier desired them to enter the guard-room, and when they had complied with the order, placed a guard at the door.

The Highlanders, the non-commissioned officers and privates of the Manchester Regiment, with a few French and Irish soldiers, who were drawn up in the market-place, then piled their arms, and retired to the cathedral, where a strong guard was set over them.

Crowded with these prisoners, the interior of the sacred building presented a very singular picture. Most of the men looked sullen and angry, and their rage was increased when the sound of martial music proclaimed the entrance of the Duke of Cumberland with his whole army into the town.

Attended by General Hawley, Colonel Conway, Colonel York, and a large staff of officers, the duke was received with acclamations by the townspeople who had come forth to meet him. Riding on to the citadel, he dismounted with his staff, and, entering a large room recently occupied by the governor, ordered the prisoners to be brought before him. After charging them with rebellion and treason, he told them they would be sent under a strong guard to London, there to take their trial.

When he had finished, Colonel Townley stepped forward, and said:

"I claim to be treated as a prisoner of war. For sixteen years I have been in the service of the King of France, and I now hold a commission from his majesty, which I can lay before your royal highness if you will deign to look at it."

"But you have received another commission from the son of the Pretender, and have acted as colonel of the rebel regiment raised by yourself in Manchester," interposed General Hawley. "Your plea is therefore inadmissible."

"I have as much right to the cartel as any French officer taken by his royal highness at the battle of Fontenoy," rejoined Townley.

"As a liege subject of his majesty, you are not justified in serving a prince at war with him," said the Duke of Cumberland, sternly. "I cannot entertain your plea. You will be tried for rebellion and treason with the rest of the prisoners."

Seeing it would be useless to urge anything further, Colonel Townley stepped back.

The only person allowed the cartel was the French officer.

The prisoners were then removed, and ordered to be kept in strict confinement in the castle until they could be conveyed to London.

Some deserters from the king's army were then brought before the duke, who ordered them to be hanged, and the sentence was forthwith carried out on a piece of ground at the back of the castle.

The prisoners passed the night in strict confinement in the castle, their gloom being heightened by the sound of the rejoicings that took place in the town at the Duke of Cumberland's success.

On the following morning, at an early hour, three large waggons, each having a team of strong horses, were drawn up near the gates of the castle. These were destined to convey the prisoners to London. The foremost waggon was assigned to Colonel Townley, Captain Dawson, Captain Deacon, and Captain Legh. The rest of the officers of the Manchester Regiment were similarly bestowed. A strong mounted guard accompanied the conveyances, having orders to shoot any prisoner who might attempt to escape.

As the waggons moved slowly through the streets towards the south gate, groans and execrations arose from the spectators, and missiles were hurled at the prisoners, who no doubt would have fared ill if they had not been protected.

The Duke of Cumberland remained for two days longer at Carlisle, when having received a despatch from the king enjoining his immediate return, as an invasion from France was apprehended, he posted back to London, taking Colonel Conway with him, and leaving the command of the army to General Hawley, who started in pursuit of Prince Charles.

End of the Fourth Book.

BOOK V.

JEMMY DAWSON.

CHAPTER I.

THE ESCAPE AT WIGAN.

THE prisoners were treated very considerately on their journey to London. Whenever the waggons stopped at an inn, their occupants were allowed to alight and order what they pleased, and as they had plenty of money, they were served with the best the house could afford. At night they sometimes slept in the waggons, sometimes at an inn, if sufficient accommodation could be found. In the latter case, of course, a guard was placed at the doors.

Passed in this way, the journey might not have been disagreeable, if it had not been for the indignities to which they were occasionally exposed. None of the officers felt any great uneasiness as to their fate. Despite what the Duke of Cumberland had said to Colonel Townley, they were led to expect that they would be treated as prisoners of war, and regularly exchanged.

Entertaining this conviction, they managed to keep up their spirits, and some of them led a very jovial life.

A great change, however, had taken place in Colonel Townley's deportment. He had become extremely reserved, and associated only with Captain Deacon, Captain Dawson, and Atherton. The two latter would have been far more cheerful if they had obtained any tidings of those to whom they were tenderly attached.

On the third day after leaving Carlisle, the prisoners arrived at Lancaster, and on the following day they were taken to Preston. Here the feeling of the inhabitants was so strong against them that they had to be protected by the guard.

At Wigan, where the next halt was made for the night, Atherton remarked that John Holgate, the host of the Bear's Paw, the inn at which they stopped, looked very hard at him. He thought he knew the man's face, and subsequently remembered him as a tradesman in Manchester.

In the course of the evening Holgate found an opportunity of speaking to him privately, and told him not to go to bed, but to leave his window slightly open—as something might happen. Having given him these directions, Holgate hastily left him.

On entering his room, which was at the back of the house, Atherton found it looked into the inn-yard, where the waggons were drawn up, and as some men were going in and out of the stables with lanterns, he perceived that several of the troopers were preparing to take their night's rest in the waggons.

Immediately beneath the window, which was at some height from the ground, a sentinel was posted.

Having made the observations, Atherton withdrew, leaving the window slightly open, as he had been enjoined, and put out the light.

In about an hour all became quiet in the yard—the troopers had got into the waggons, and no doubt were fast asleep, but he could hear the measured tread of the sentinel as he paced to and fro.

Another hour elapsed, and the sentinel being still at his post, Atherton began to fear that Holgate might fail in his design. But his hopes revived when the footsteps could no longer be heard, and softly approaching the window he looked out.

The sentinel was gone. But in his place stood another person, whom Atherton had no doubt was the friendly landlord.

Having intimated his presence by a slight signal, Holgate retreated, and Atherton instantly prepared to join him. Emerging from the window as noiselessly as he could, he let himself drop to the ground, and achieved the feat so cleverly, that he was only heard by Holgate, who immediately took him to the back of the yard, where they clambered over a low wall, and gained a narrow lane, along which they hastened.

"I think you are now safe," said Holgate. "At any rate, you will be so when we reach our destination. I have brought you this way because it would have been impossible to elude the vigilance of the sentinel placed in front of the house. I have given the man who was stationed in the yard a pot of ale, and he has retired to the stable to drink it."

"You have proved yourself a good friend to me, Holgate," said Atherton; "but I fear you are running great risk on my account."

"I don't mind that," replied the other. "The moment I saw you, I determined to liberate you. I dare say you've forgotten the circumstance, but I haven't. You saved me from being drowned in the Irwell—now we're quits. I'm going to take you to the old Manor House in Bishopsgate Street. It belongs to Captain Hulton, who is in the king's army, but he is away, and my aunt, Mrs. Scholes, who is his housekeeper, has charge of the house. She is a staunch Jacobite. I have seen her and told her all about you. You may trust her perfectly."

Proceeding with the utmost caution, they soon came to Bishopsgate Street, in which the old Manor House was situated.

Taking his companion to the back of the premises, Holgate tapped at a door, which was immediately opened by a very respectable-looking middle-aged woman, who curtsied to Atherton as she admitted him. Holgate did not enter the house, but with a hasty "good-night," departed, and the door was closed and bolted.

Mrs. Scholes then took Atherton to the kitchen, and explained that she meant to put him in the "secret room" in case the house should be searched.

"You will be indifferently lodged, sir," she said; "but you will be safe, and that's the chief thing."

Atherton entirely concurred with her, and without wasting any further time in talk, she led him up a back staircase to a bedroom, from which there was a secret entrance through a closet, to a small inner chamber. The latter was destined for Atherton, and scantily furnished as it was, he was very well content with it, and slept soundly in the little couch prepared for him.

Next morning, when the prisoners were mustered, the greatest consternation was caused by the discovery that Captain Legh was missing. It was quite clear that he had got out of the window, and it was equally clear that the sentinel must have neglected his duty, or the prisoner could not have escaped; but no suspicion attached to the landlord.

Of course the departure of the waggons was delayed, and strict search was made for the fugitive throughout the town. A proclamation was likewise issued, announcing that any one harbouring him would be liable to severe penalties. But the notice had no effect.

In consequence of some information received by the officer in command of the escort that two persons had been seen to enter the Manor House in Bishopsgate Street late at night, the house was strictly searched, but the secret chamber was not discovered, nor was anything found to indicate that the fugitive was concealed there.

CHAPTER II.

THE MEETING AT WARRINGTON.

At Warrington, where the visitors were conveyed next day, a meeting took place between Jemmy and Monica, who had come over from Rawcliffe Hall to see her unfortunate lover. She was accompanied by Father Jerome.

Jemmy was alone in a little parlour of the inn at which the waggons had stopped, when Monica was admitted by the guard, who immediately withdrew, and left them together.

Springing forward, Jemmy clasped her to his heart.

So overpowered were they both, that for some minutes they could not give utterance to their feelings, but gazed at each other through eyes streaming with tears.

"Alas! alas!" cried Monica, at length. "Is it come to this? Do I find my dearest Jemmy a prisoner?"

"A prisoner of war," he replied, in as cheerful a tone as he could assume. "I am sure to be exchanged. We shall be separated for a time, but shall meet again in another country. You imagine we shall all be put to death, but believe me the Elector of Hanover has no such intention. He dare not execute us."

"Hush! Jemmy—not so loud. I have been wretched ever since the retreat from Derby took place, for I foresaw what it would come to. I have never ceased to reproach myself with being the cause of your destruction."

"You have nothing to reproach yourself with, dearest girl," he rejoined, tenderly. "'Tis a pity the prince did not march to London. 'Tis a still greater pity the regiment was left at Carlisle."

"Yes, you have been sacrificed, Jemmy—cruelly sacrificed. I shall never think otherwise."

"Such imputations, I am aware, are laid to the prince's charge, but he doesn't deserve them—indeed he doesn't. He is the soul of honour. No one believed the Duke of Cumberland would stop to besiege the town; and those best informed thought it could hold out for a month. However, fortune has declared against us. But I won't allow myself to be cast down." Then lowering his tone, he added, "You know that Atherton has escaped?"

"Yes, I know it," she rejoined. "And so does Constance. Oh, that you had been with him, Jemmy!"

"I shall find means to follow—never doubt it," he rejoined. "But it won't do to make the attempt just yet, for we shall be much more strictly watched than before. But I have a plan, which I mean to put in practice when an opportunity offers, and I hope it will succeed."

"Can I aid you, Jemmy?" she asked, anxiously.

"No," he replied. "But don't be surprised if you see me some night at Rawcliffe Hall."

"Now, indeed, you give me fresh spirits," she cried. "Heaven grant I may see you soon! But there may be danger in your coming to Rawcliffe, and you mustn't run any needless risk on my account."

"The first use I shall make of my liberty will be to fly to you, dearest girl. Of that you may be quite sure. But we are talking only of ourselves. You have scarcely mentioned Constance or your mother. How are they both?"

"They have been full of anxiety, as you may easily imagine. But Constance has somewhat revived since she heard of Atherton's escape, and the tidings I shall be able to give her of you will make her feel more easy. As to my mother, whatever she may suffer—and I am sure she suffers much—she is perfectly resigned. Father Jerome is without. Will you see him?"

"No. I will devote each moment to you. Ah! we are interrupted!" he exclaimed, as the guard came in to say that the time allowed them had expired.

Again they were locked in each other's arms, and when they were forced to separate, it seemed as if their hearts were torn asunder. Even the guard was moved by their distress.

Nevertheless, Monica returned to Rawcliffe Hall in far better spirits than she had quitted it in the morning. She had now some hopes that her lover would escape.

Shortly after her departure Jemmy was obliged to take his place in the waggon, and for some time felt very wretched; but at length he consoled himself by thinking that his separation from the object of his affections would not be long.

The waggons proceeded so slowly on their journey to London, that before they reached Dunstable news was received of the defeat of General Hawley, at Falkirk, by the prince. These tidings caused great alarm throughout the country, as the opinion generally prevailed that after the siege of Carlisle the rebellion had been completely suppressed.

Though the prisoners rejoiced at the prince's success, they felt that their own peril was considerably increased by the event, and that in all probability the severest measures would now be adopted against them.

Hitherto, such strict watch had been kept that Jemmy Dawson had found no means of executing his plan of escape.

CHAPTER III.

ATHERTON TAKES REFUGE AT RAWCLIFFE HALL.

On the third day after Atherton's escape at Wigan, as Constance and Monica, who had been tempted forth by the fineness of the weather, were walking in the park, a young man, in a plain country dress that gave him the appearance of a farmer, made his way towards them.

From the first moment when they beheld this personage

their suspicions were excited, but as he drew nearer they perceived it was Atherton. Constance would have hurried forward to meet him, but feeling the necessity of caution she restrained herself. Presently, he came up, and thinking he might be noticed by some observer, he adopted a very respectful and distant manner, consistent with the character he had assumed, and took off his hat while addressing them.

"Of course you have heard of my escape," he said. "I did not attempt to communicate with you, for I had no one whom I could trust to convey a message, and I did not dare to write lest my letter should fall into wrong hands. For two days I was concealed in the old Manor House at Wigan, and most carefully attended to by the housekeeper, who provided for all my wants. I had some difficulty in getting away, for the house was watched, but on the second night I ventured out, and soon got clear of the town. Before I left, Mrs. Scholes procured me this disguise, without which I should infallibly have been captured, for my uniform must have betrayed me. Even thus attired, I have had more than one narrow escape. If I can only get into the house unobserved I shall be perfectly safe."

"You must wait till night and all shall be ready for you," rejoined Constance. "As soon as it grows dark Markland shall come out into the park."

"He will find me near this spot," replied Atherton.

"But what will you do in the interim?" asked Constance, anxiously.

"Give yourself no concern about me," he rejoined. "You may be sure I will not expose myself to any needless risk. Adieu!"

With a rustic bow he then moved off, and the two damsels returned to the hall.

Constance's first business was to summon Markland and tell him what had occurred.

The old butler did not manifest much surprise at the intelligence, for when he had first heard of Atherton's escape he felt certain the young gentleman would seek refuge at the hall, and he had already made some quiet preparations for his concealment. He therefore expressed the utmost readiness to carry out his young mistress's instructions, and declared that he could easily manage matters so that none of the servants should be aware that Captain Legh was hidden in the house.

"Even if he should remain here for a month," he said, "with common caution I will engage he shall not be discovered."

"I am very glad to hear you speak so confidently, Markland," she rejoined; "for I feared it would be impossible to conceal him for more than a day or two."

Having made all needful arrangements, Markland stole out quietly as soon as it became dark, and found Atherton at the spot indicated.

"You are so well disguised, sir," he said, "that if I hadn't been prepared I should certainly not have known you. But don't let us waste time in talking here. I must get you into the house."

The night being very dark their approach to the hall could not be perceived. On reaching the drawbridge Markland told his companion to slip past while he went into the gate-house to speak to the porter, and by observing these instructions, Atherton gained the court-yard unperceived.

The butler then gave orders that the drawbridge should be raised, and while the porter was thus employed, he opened the postern and admitted Captain Legh into the house. Having first satisfied himself that no one was in the way, Markland then led the young man along a passage to his own room on the ground floor.

All danger was now over. The small room into which Atherton had been ushered looked exceedingly snug and comfortable. Thick curtains drawn over the narrow window facing the moat prevented any inquisitive eye from peering into the chamber. A bright fire burnt on the hearth, and near it stood a table on which a cold pasty was placed, with a bottle of claret.

"I have prepared a little supper for you, sir," said Markland. "Pray sit down to it. I'll take care you shan't be disturbed. You will please to excuse me. I have some other matters to attend to."

He then went out, taking the precaution to lock the door, and Atherton partook of the first quiet meal he had enjoyed for some time.

Old Markland did not return for nearly three hours, and when he unlocked the door, he found Atherton fast asleep in the chair. Great havoc had been made with the pasty, and the flask of claret was nearly emptied.

"I have got a bed ready for you, sir," he said. "It isn't quite so comfortable as I could wish, but you will make allowances."

"No need of apologies, Markland. I could sleep very well in this chair."

"That's just what I mean to do myself, sir," replied the butler, laughing.

With this, he took Captain Legh up a back staircase to a disused suite of apartments, in one of which a bed had been prepared, while a wood fire blazing on the hearth gave a cheerful air to the otherwise gloomy-looking room.

"I have had this room got ready as if for myself, sir," observed Markland; "but as I have just told you, I mean to sleep in a chair below stairs. I wish you a good-night, sir. I'll come to you in the morning."

So saying, he quitted the room, and Atherton shortly afterwards sought his couch, and slept very soundly.

Next morning, the old butler visited him before he had begun to dress, and opening the drawers of a wardrobe that stood in the room, took out two or three handsome suits of clothes—somewhat old-fashioned, inasmuch as they belonged to the period of George the First, but still attire that could be worn.

"These habiliments belonged to your father, Sir Oswald," said Markland; "and as you are about his size, I am sure they will fit you."

"But are they not out of fashion, Markland?" cried Atherton. "People will stare at me if I appear in a costume of five-and-twenty years ago."

"Well, perhaps they might," rejoined the butler; "but there can be no objection to this dark riding-dress."

"No, that will do very well," said Atherton, in an approving tone, after he had examined it.

"You will find plenty of linen in this drawer—laced shirts, solitaires, cravats, silk stockings," continued the butler; "and in that cupboard there are three or four pairs of jack-boots, with as many cocked-hats."

"Bravo!" exclaimed Atherton. "You have quite set me up, Markland. But now leave me for a short time, that I may try the effect of this riding-dress."

The butler then withdrew, but returned in about half an hour with a pot of chocolate and some slices of toast on a tray.

By this time Atherton was fully attired, and everything fitted him—even to the boots, which he had got out of the cupboard.

"Why, I declare, you are the very image of your father!" exclaimed Markland, as he gazed at him in astonishment. "If I had not known who you are, I should have thought Sir Oswald had come to life again. If any of the old servants should see you, you will certainly be taken for a ghost."

"That's exactly what I should desire," replied Atherton; "and should it be necessary, I shall endeavour to keep up the character. However, I don't mean to qualify myself for the part by eating nothing, so pour me out a cup of chocolate."

The butler obeyed, and Atherton sat down and made a very good breakfast.

Before he had quite finished his repast, the butler left him, and did not reappear.

CHAPTER IV.

AN ENEMY IN THE HOUSE.

Not having anything better to do, Atherton began to wander about the deserted suite of apartments, with which his own chamber communicated by a side door.

As the windows were closed, the rooms looked very dark, and he could see but little, and what he did see, impressed him with a melancholy feeling; but the furthest room in the suite looked lighter and more cheerful than the others, simply because the shutters had been opened.

It was a parlour, but most of the furniture had been removed, and only a few chairs and a table were left.

Atherton sat down, and was ruminating upon his position, when a door behind was softly opened—so very softly that he heard no sound.

But he felt a gentle touch on his shoulder, and, looking up, beheld Constance standing beside him.

When he met her in the park with Monica, he had not noticed any material alteration in her appearance; but now that he gazed into her face, he was very much struck by the change which a week or two had wrought in her looks.

Dressed in deep mourning, she looked much thinner than heretofore, and the roses had entirely flown from her cheeks; but the extreme paleness of her complexion heightened the lustre of her magnificent black eyes, and contrasted forcibly with her dark locks, while the traces of sadness lent fresh interest to her features.

Not without anxiety did Atherton gaze at her, and at last he said:

"You have been ill, Constance?"

"Not very ill," she replied, with a faint smile. "I am better—and shall soon be quite well. My illness has been rather mental than bodily. I have never quite recovered from the terrible shock which I had to undergo—and, besides, I have been very uneasy about you. Now that you are safe I shall soon recover my health and spirits. At one time I feared I should never behold you again, and then I began to droop."

"I thought you possessed great firmness, Constance," he remarked.

"So I fancied, but I found myself unequal to the trial," she rejoined. "I had no one to cheer me. Monica's distress was even greater than my own, and her mother did not offer us much consolation, for she seemed convinced that both you and Jemmy were doomed to die as traitors."

"Well, your apprehensions are now at an end, so far as I am concerned," said Atherton; "and I see no cause for uneasiness in regard to Jemmy, for he is certain to escape in one way or other. I hope to meet him a month hence in Paris. But I shall not leave England till I learn he is free, as if he fails to escape, I must try to accomplish his deliverance."

"Do not run any further risk," she cried.

"I have promised to help him, and I must keep my word," he rejoined.

"I ought not to attempt to dissuade you, for I love Jemmy dearly, but I love you still better, and I therefore implore you for my sake—if not for your own—not to expose yourself to further danger. I will now tell you frankly that I could not go through such another week as I have just passed."

"But you must now feel that your apprehensions were groundless; and if I should be placed in any fresh danger you must take courage from the past."

"Perhaps you will say that I am grown very timorous, and I can scarcely account for my misgivings—but I will not conceal them. I don't think you are quite safe in this house."

"Why not? Old Markland is devoted to me, I am quite

sure, and no one else among the household is aware of my arrival."

"But I am sadly afraid they may discover you."

"You are indeed timorous. Even if I should be discovered, I don't think any of them would be base enough to betray me."

"I have another ground for uneasiness, more serious than this, but I scarcely like to allude to it, because I may be doing an injustice to the person who causes my alarm. I fear you have an enemy in the house."

Atherton looked at her inquiringly, and then said:

"I can only have one enemy—Father Jerome."

She made no answer, but he perceived from her looks that he had guessed aright.

"'Tis unlucky he is established in the house. Why did you bring him here?"

"I could not help it. And he has been most useful to me. But I know he does not like you; and I also know that his nature is malicious and vindictive. I hope he may not find out that you are concealed in the house. I have cautioned Markland, and Monica does not require to be cautioned. Ah! what was that?" she added, listening anxiously. "I thought I heard a noise in the adjoining chamber."

"It may be Markland," said Atherton. "But I will go and see."

With this, he stepped quickly into the next room, the door of which stood ajar.

As we have mentioned, the shutters were closed, and the room was dark, but still, if any listener had been there, he must have been detected. The room, however, seemed quite empty.

Not satisfied with this inspection, Atherton went on through the whole suite of apartments, and with a like result.

"You must have been mistaken," he said on his return to Constance. "I could find no eaves-dropper."

"I am glad to hear it, for I feared that a certain person

might be there. But I must now leave you. I hope you will not find your confinement intolerably wearisome. You will be able to get out at night—but during the daytime you must not quit these rooms."

"Come frequently to see me, and the time will pass pleasantly enough," he rejoined.

"I must not come too often or my visits will excite suspicion," she replied. "But I will send you some books by Markland."

"There is a private communication between this part of the house and the library. May I not venture to make use of it?"

"Not without great caution," she rejoined. "Father Jerome is constantly in the library. But I will try to get him away in the evening, and Markland shall bring you word when you can descend with safety."

"Surely some plan might be devised by which Father Jerome could be got rid of for a time?" said Atherton.

"I have thought the matter over, but no such plan occurs to me," replied Constance. "He rarely quits the house, and were I to propose to him to take a journey, or pay a visit, he would immediately suspect I had an object in doing so. But even if he were willing to go, my Aunt Butler I am sure would object."

"Is she not aware that I am in the house?"

"No, Monica and I thought it better not to trust her. She could not keep the secret from Father Jerome."

"Then since the evil cannot be remedied it must be endured," said Atherton.

"That is the right way to view it," rejoined Constance. "Not till the moment of your departure must Father Jerome learn that you have taken refuge here. And now, adieu!"

CHAPTER V.

A POINT OF FAITH.

Left alone, Atherton endeavoured to reconcile himself to his imprisonment, but with very indifferent success.

How he longed to join the party downstairs—to go forth into the garden or the park—to do anything, in short, rather than remain shut up in those gloomy rooms! But stay there he must!—so he amused himself as well as he could by looking into the cupboards with which the rooms abounded.

In the course of his examination he found some books, and with these he contrived to beguile the time till old Markland made his appearance.

The old butler brought with him a well-filled basket, from which he produced the materials of a very good cold dinner, including a flask of wine; and a cloth being spread upon a small table in the room we have described as less gloomy than the other apartments, the young man sat down to the repast.

"I have had some difficulty in bringing you these provisions, sir," observed Markland. "Father Jerome has been playing the spy upon me all the morning—hovering about my room, so that I couldn't stir without running against him. Whether he heard anything last night I can't say, but I'm sure he suspects you are hidden in the house."

"What if he does suspect, Markland?" observed Atherton. "Do you think he would betray me? If you believe so, you must have a very bad opinion of him."

"I can tell you one thing, sir; he was far from pleased when he heard of your escape, and wished it had been Captain Dawson instead. I told him I thought you might seek refuge here, and he said he hoped not; adding, 'If you were foolish enough to do so you would certainly be discovered.' I repeated these observations to Miss Rawcliffe, and she agreed with me that they argued an ill-feeling towards you."

"What can I have done to offend him?" exclaimed Atherton.

"I don't know, sir, except that you are heir to the property. But give yourself no uneasiness. I will take care he shan't harm you. Don't on any account leave these rooms till you see me again."

"Has Father Jerome access to this part of the house, Markland?"

"No; I keep the door of the gallery constantly locked; and he is not aware of the secret entrance to the library."

"Are you sure of that?"

"Quite sure, sir. I never heard him allude to it."

"He is frequently in the library, I understand?"

"Yes, he sits there for hours; but he generally keeps in his own room in the evening, and you might then come down with safety. Have you everything you require at present?"

"Everything. You have taken excellent care of me, Markland."

"I am sorry I can't do better. I'll return by-and-by to take away the things."

With this he departed, and Atherton soon made an end of his meal.

Time seemed to pass very slowly, but at length evening arrived, and the butler reappeared.

"You will find Miss Rawcliffe in the library," he said, "and need fear no interruption, for Father Jerome is with Mrs. Butler. I shall be on the watch, and will give timely notice should any danger arise."

Instantly shaking off the gloom that had oppressed him, Atherton set off. The butler accompanied him to the head of the private staircase, but went no further. Though all was buried in darkness, the young man easily found his way to the secret door, and cautiously stepped into the library.

Lights placed upon the table showed him that Constance was in the room, and so noiselessly had he entered, that she was not aware of his presence till he moved towards her.

She then rose from the sofa to meet him, and was clasped to his breast. Need we detail their converse? It was like all lovers' talk—deeply interesting to the parties concerned, but of little interest to any one else. However, we must refer to one part of it. They had been speaking of their prospects of future happiness, when he might be able to procure a pardon from the Government and return to Rawcliffe—or she might join him in France.

"But why should our union be delayed?" he cried. "Why should we not be united before my departure?"

"'Tis too soon after my unhappy father's death," she replied. "I could not show such disrespect to his memory."

"But the marriage would be strictly private, and consequently there could be no indecorum. You can remain here for awhile, and then rejoin me. I shall be better able to endure the separation when I feel certain you are mine."

"I am yours already—linked to you as indissolubly as if our hands had been joined at the altar. But the ceremony cannot be performed at present. Our faiths are different. Without a dispensation from a bishop of the Church of Rome, which could not be obtained here, no Romish priest would unite us. But were Father Jerome willing to disobey the canons of the Church, I should have scruples."

"You never alluded to such scruples before."

"I knew not of the prohibition. I dare not break the rules of the Church I belong to."

"But you say that a license can be procured," he cried eagerly.

"Not here," she rejoined; "and this would be a sufficient reason for the delay, if none other existed. Let us look upon this as a trial to which we must submit, and patiently wait for happier days, when all difficulties may be removed."

"You do not love me as much as I thought you did, Constance," he said, in a reproachful tone. "'Tis plain you are under the influence of this malicious and designing priest."

"Do not disquiet yourself," she rejoined, calmly. "Father

Jerome has no undue influence over me, and could never change my sentiments towards you. I admit that he is not favourably disposed towards our union, and would prevent it if he could, but he is powerless."

"I shall be miserable if I leave him with you, Constance. He ought to be driven from the house."

"I cannot do that," she rejoined. "But depend upon it he shall never prejudice me against you."

Little more passed between them, for Constance did not dare to prolong the interview.

CHAPTER VI.

A LETTER FROM BEPPY BYROM.

ANOTHER day of imprisonment—for such Atherton deemed it Markland brought him his meals as before, and strove to cheer him, for the young man looked very dull and dispirited.

"I can't remain here much longer, Markland," he said. "Something in the atmosphere of these deserted rooms strangely oppresses me. I seem to be surrounded by beings of another world, who, though invisible to mortal eye, make their presence felt. I know this is mere imagination, and I am ashamed of myself for indulging such idle fancies, but I cannot help it. Tell me, Markland," he added, "are these rooms supposed to be haunted?"

"Since you ask me the question, sir, I must answer it truthfully. They are. It was reported long ago that apparitions had been seen in them; and since nobody liked to occupy the rooms, they were shut up. But you needn't be frightened, sir. The ghosts will do you no harm."

"I am not frightened, Markland. But I confess I prefer the society of the living to that of the dead. Last night— whether I was sleeping or waking at the time I can't exactly tell—but I thought Sir Richard appeared to me; and this is the second time I have seen him, for he warned me before I went to Carlisle. And now he has warned me again of some approaching danger. The spirit—if spirit it was—had a grieved and angry look, and seemed to reproach me with neglect."

The latter was deeply interested in what was told him, and, after a moment's reflection, said:

"This is very strange. Have you disregarded Sir Richard's dying injunctions? Bethink you, sir!"

"I would not abandon the expedition as he counselled me, and I went on to Carlisle—but since my return I cannot charge myself with any neglect. Ah! one thing occurs to me. I ought to see that certain documents which he left me are safe."

"Where did you place them, sir, may I ask?" said the butler.

"In the ebony cabinet in the library. I have the key."

"Then, no doubt, they are perfectly safe, sir. But it may be well to satisfy yourself on the point when you go down to the library."

"I will do so. Shall I find Miss Rawcliffe there this evening?"

"You will, sir, at the same hour as last night. She bade me tell you so."

Shortly afterwards, the butler took his departure, and Atherton was again left to himself for several hours.

When evening came, Markland had not reappeared; but doubtless something had detained him, and concluding all was right, Atherton descended the private staircase, and passed through the secret door into the library.

Constance was there and alone. Lights were placed upon the table beside which she was seated. She was reading a letter at the moment, and seemed deeply interested in its contents; but on hearing his footsteps, she rose to welcome him.

"This letter relates entirely to you," she said.

"And judging from your looks it does not bring good news," he remarked.

"It does not," she rejoined. "It is from Beppy Byrom, and was brought by a special messenger from Manchester. She informs me that a warrant for your arrest has just been received by the authorities of the town, who are enjoined to offer a reward for your capture. Strict search will, consequently, be made for you, she says; and as Rawcliffe Hall may be visited, she sends this notice. She also states that it will be impossible to escape to France from any English port, as an embargo is now laid on all vessels. The letter thus concludes: 'If you have any communication with Captain Legh, pray tell him, if he should be driven to extremity, he will find an asylum in my father's house.'"

"Have you returned any answer to this kind letter?" inquired Atherton.

"No—it would not have been prudent to detain the messenger. During his brief stay, Markland took care he should not have any conversation with the servants. Father Jerome was curious to ascertain the nature of his errand, and learnt that he came from Manchester—but nothing more. I know not what you may resolve upon; but if you decide on flight, you will need funds. In this pocket-book are bank-notes to a considerable amount. Nay, do not hesitate to take it," she added, "you are under no obligation to me. The money is your own."

Thus urged, Atherton took the pocket-book, and said:

"Before I decide upon the steps I ought to take in this dangerous emergency, let me mention a matter to you that has weighed upon my mind. In yonder cabinet are certain papers which I desire to confide to your care. They contain proofs that I am the righful heir to this property—the most important of the documents being a statement drawn up by your father, and signed by him, immediately before his death. Now listen to me, Constance. Should I fall into the hands of the enemy—should I die the death of a traitor—it is my wish that those documents should never be produced."

Constance could not repress an exclamation.

"All will be over then," he proceeded, calmly. "And why should a dark story, which can only bring dishonour on our family, be revealed? Let the secret be buried in my grave. If I am remembered at all, let it be as Atherton Legh, and not as Oswald Rawcliffe."

"Your wishes shall be fulfilled," she replied, deeply moved. "But I trust the dire necessity may never arise."

"We must prepare for the worst," he said. "Here is the key. See that the papers are safe."

She unlocked the cabinet, and opened all the drawers. They were empty.

"The papers are gone," she cried.

"Impossible!" exclaimed Atherton, springing towards her.

'Twas perfectly true, nevertheless. Further investigation showed that the documents must have been abstracted.

"There is but one person who can have taken them," said Atherton. "To that person the importance of the papers would be known—nor would he hesitate to deprive me of the proofs of my birth."

"I think you wrong him by these suspicions," said Constance—though her looks showed that she herself shared them. "What motive could he have for such an infamous act?"

"I cannot penetrate his motive, unless it is that he seeks to prevent my claim to the title and property. But malignant as he is, I could scarcely have imagined he would proceed to such a length as this."

"Granting you are right in your surmise, how can Father Jerome have discovered the existence of the papers? You placed them in the cabinet yourself I presume, and the key has been in your own possession ever since."

"True. But from him a lock would be no safeguard. If he knew the papers were there, their removal would be easy.

But he will not destroy them, because their possession will give him the power he covets, and no doubt he persuades himself he will be able to obtain his own price for them. But I will force him to give them up."

At this juncture the door was opened, and Monica, entering hastily, called out to Atherton:

"Away at once, or you will be discovered. Father Jerome is coming hither. He has just left my mother's room."

But the young man did not move.

"I have something to say to him."

"Do not say it now!" implored Constance.

"No better opportunity could offer," rejoined Atherton. "I will tax him with his villainy."

"What does all this mean?" cried Monica, astonished and alarmed.

But before any explanation could be given, the door again opened, and Father Jerome stood before them.

CHAPTER VII.

ATHERTON QUESTIONS THE PRIEST.

THE priest did not manifest any surprise on beholding Atherton, but saluting him formally, said:

"I did not expect to find you here, sir, or I should not have intruded. But I will retire."

"Stay!" cried Atherton. "I have a few questions to put to you. First let me ask if you knew I was in the house?"

"I fancied so," replied the priest—"though no one has told me you were here. I suppose it was thought best not to trust me," he added, glancing at Constance.

"It was my wish that you should be kept in ignorance of the matter," observed Atherton.

"I am to understand, then, that you doubt me, sir,"

observed the priest. "I am sorry for it. You do me a great injustice. I am most anxious to serve you. Had I been consulted I should have deemed it my duty to represent to you the great risk you would run in taking refuge here—but I would have aided in your concealment, as I will do now; and my services may be called in question sooner, perhaps, than you imagine, for the house is likely to be searched."

"How know you that?" demanded Atherton.

"There has been a messenger here from Manchester——"

"I thought you did not see him, father?" interrupted Constance.

"I saw him and conversed with him," rejoined the priest; "and I learnt that a warrant is out for the arrest of Captain Atherton Legh, and a large reward offered for his apprehension. At the same time I learnt that this house would be strictly searched. Whether you will remain here, or fly, is for your own consideration."

"I shall remain here at all hazards," replied Atherton, fixing a keen look upon him.

"I think you have decided rightly, sir," observed the priest. "Should they come, I will do my best to baffle the officers."

"I will take good care you shall not betray me," said Atherton.

"Betray you, sir!" exclaimed the priest, indignantly. "I have no such intention."

"You shall not have the opportunity," was the rejoinder.

At a sign from Atherton, Constance and Monica withdrew to the further end of the room.

"Now, sir, you will guess what is coming," said Atherton, addressing the priest in a stern tone. "I desire you will instantly restore the papers you have taken from yonder cabinet."

"What papers?" asked Father Jerome.

"Nay, never feign surprise. You know well what I mean.

I want Sir Richard Rawcliffe's confession, and the other documents accompanying it."

"Has any person but yourself seen Sir Richard's written confession?"

"No one."

"Then if it is lost you cannot prove that such a document ever existed."

"It is not lost," said Atherton. "You know where to find it, and find it you shall."

"Calm yourself, or you will alarm the ladies. I have not got the papers you require, but you ought to have taken better care of them, since without them you will be unable to establish your claim to the Rawcliffe estates and title."

"No more of this trifling," said Atherton. "I am not in the humour for it. I must have the papers without further delay."

"I know nothing about them," said the priest, doggedly. "You tell me there were such documents, and I am willing to believe you, but sceptical persons may doubt whether they ever existed."

"Will you produce them?"

"How can I, since I have them not."

"Their destruction would be an execrable act."

"It would—but it is not likely they will be destroyed. On the contrary, I should think they will be carefully preserved."

Very significantly uttered, these words left Atherton in no doubt as to their import.

While he was meditating a reply, Markland hurriedly entered the room—alarm depicted in his countenance.

Startled by his looks, Constance and Monica immediately came forward.

"You must instantly return to your hiding-place, sir," said the butler to Atherton. "The officers are here, and mean to search the house. Fortunately, the drawbridge is raised, and I would not allow it to be lowered till I had warned you."

"Are you sure they are the officers?" exclaimed Constance.

"Quite sure. I have seen them and spoken with them. They have a warrant."

"Then it will be impossible to refuse them admittance."

"Impossible," cried the butler.

While this conversation took place, Atherton had opened the secret door in the bookcase, but he now came back, and said to the priest:

"You must bear me company, father. I shall feel safer if I have you with me."

"But I may be of use in misleading the officers," said Father Jerome.

"Markland will take care of them. He can be trusted. Come along!"

And seizing the priest's arm, he dragged him through the secret door.

As soon as this was accomplished, Markland rushed out of the room, and hurried to the porter's lodge.

CHAPTER VIII.

THE SEARCH.

No sooner was the drawbridge lowered than several persons on horseback rode into the court-yard.

By this time, some of the servants had come forth with lights, so that the unwelcome visitors could be distinguished. The party consisted of half a dozen mounted constables, at the head of whom was Mr. Fowden, the Manchester magistrate. Ordering two of the officers to station themselves near the drawbridge, and enjoining the others to keep strict watch over the house, Mr. Fowden dismounted, and addressing Markland, who was standing near, desired to be conducted to Miss Rawcliffe.

"Inform her that I am Mr. Fowden, one of the Manchester magistrates," he said. "I will explain my errand myself."

"Pray step this way, sir," rejoined Markland, bowing respectfully.

Ushering the magistrate into the entrance hall, Markland helped to disencumber him of his heavy cloak, which he laid with the magistrate's cocked-hat and whip upon a side-table, and then led him to the library—announcing him, as he had been desired, to Constance, who with her cousin received him in a very stately manner, and requested him to be seated.

"I am sorry to intrude upon you at this hour, Miss Rawcliffe," said Mr. Fowden; "but I have no option, as you will understand, when I explain my errand. I hold a warrant for the arrest of Captain Atherton Legh, late of the Manchester Regiment, who has been guilty of levying war against our sovereign lord the king; and having received information that he is concealed here, I must require that he may be immediately delivered up to me. In the event of your refusal to comply with my order, I shall be compelled to search the house, while you will render yourself liable to a heavy penalty, and perhaps imprisonment, for harbouring him after this notice."

"You are at liberty to search the house, Mr. Fowden," replied Constance, with as much firmness as she could command; "and if you find Captain Legh I must bear the penalties with which you threaten me."

"'Tis a disagreeable duty that I have to perform, I can assure you, Miss Rawcliffe," said Mr. Fowden. "I knew Captain Legh before he joined the rebellion, and I regret that by his folly—for I will call it by no harsher name—he should have cut short his career. I also knew Captain Dawson very well, and am equally sorry for him—poor misguided youth! he is certain to suffer for his rash and criminal act."

Here a sob burst from Monica, and drew the magistrate's attention to her.

"I was not aware of your presence, Miss Butler," he said, "or I would not have hurt your feelings by the remark. I know you are engaged to poor Jemmy Dawson. I sincerely hope that clemency may be shown him—and all those who have acted from a mistaken sense of loyalty. I will frankly confess that I myself was much captivated by the manner of the young Chevalier when I saw him as he passed through Manchester. But you will think I am a Jacobite, if I talk thus—whereas, I am a staunch Whig. I must again express my regret at the steps I am obliged to take, Miss Rawcliffe," he continued, addressing Constance; "and if I seem to discredit your assurance that Captain Legh is not concealed here, it is because it is at variance with information I have received, and which I have reason to believe must be correct. As a Catholic, you have a priest resident in the house—Father Jerome. Pray send for him!"

Scarcely able to hide her embarrassment, Constance rang the bell, and when Markland answered the summons, she told him Mr. Fowden desired to see Father Jerome.

"His reverence has gone to Newton, and won't return to-night," replied the butler.

The magistrate looked very hard at him, but Markland bore the scrutiny well.

"I think you could find him if you chose," remarked Mr. Fowden.

"I must go to Newton, then, to do it, sir. I'll take you to his room, if you please."

"Nay, I don't doubt what you tell me, but 'tis strange he should have gone out. However, I must make a perquisition of the house."

"Markland will attend you, Mr. Fowden, and show you into the rooms," said Constance," who had become far less uneasy since her conversation with the good-natured magistrate. "Before you commence your investigations, perhaps you will satisfy yourself that no one is concealed in this room. There is a screen—pray look behind it!"

"I will take your word, Miss Rawcliffe, that no one is here," replied the magistrate, bowing.

"I won't bid you good-night, Mr. Fowden," said Constance, "because I hope when you have completed your search you will take supper with us."

The magistrate again bowed and quitted the room.

Attended by Markland, bearing a light, Mr. Fowden then began his survey, but it soon became evident to the butler that he did not mean the search to be very strict. Ascending the great oak staircase, he looked into the different rooms in the corridor, as they passed them. On being told that one of these rooms belonged to Miss Rawcliffe, the magistrate declined to enter it, and so in the case of another, which he learnt was occupied by Monica. In the adjoining chamber they found Mrs. Butler kneeling before a crucifix, and Mr. Fowden immediately retired without disturbing her.

CHAPTER IX.

WHO WAS FOUND IN THE DISMANTLED ROOMS.

AFTER opening the doors of several other rooms, and casting a hasty glance inside, the magistrate said:

"I understand there is a portion of the house which for some time has been shut up. Take me to it."

Markland obeyed rather reluctantly, and when he came to a door at the end of the corridor, communicating, as he said, with the dismantled apartments, it took him some time to unlock it.

"I ought to tell you, sir," he said, assuming a very mysterious manner, calculated to impress his hearer, "that these rooms are said to be haunted, and none of the servants like to enter them, even in the daytime. I don't share their superstitious fears, but I certainly have heard strange noises——"

"There! what was that?" exclaimed Mr. Fowden. "I thought I saw a dark figure glide past, but I could not detect the sound of footsteps."

"Turn back, if you're at all afraid, sir," suggested Markland.

"I'm not afraid of ghosts," rejoined the magistrate; "and as to human beings I don't fear them, because I have pistols in my pockets. Go on."

Markland said nothing more, but opened the first door on the left, and led his companion into a room which was almost destitute of furniture, and had a most melancholy air; but it did not look so dreary as the next room they entered. Here the atmosphere was so damp that the butler was seized with a fit of coughing which lasted for more than a minute, and Mr. Fowden declared there must be echoes in the rooms, for he had certainly heard sounds at a distance.

"No doubt there are echoes, sir," said the butler.

"But these must be peculiar to the place," observed the magistrate; "for they sounded uncommonly like footsteps. Give me the light."

And taking the candle from the butler, and drawing a pistol from his pocket, he marched quickly into the next room. No one was there, but as he hastened on he caught sight of a retreating figure, and called out:

"Stand! or I fire."

Heedless of the injunction, the person made a rapid exit through the side door, but was prevented from fastening it by the magistrate, who followed him so quickly that he had no time to hide himself, and stood revealed to his pursuer.

"What do I see?" exclaimed Mr. Fowden, in astonishment, "Father Jerome here! Why I was told you were in Newton."

"His reverence ought to be there," said Markland, who had now come up.

"I must have an explanation of your strange conduct, sir," said the magistrate.

"His reverence had better be careful what he says," observed Markland.

"Answer one question, and answer it truly, as you value

your own safety," pursued Mr. Fowden. "Are you alone in these rooms?"

The priest looked greatly embarrassed. Markland made a gesture to him behind the magistrate's back.

"Are you alone here, I repeat?" demanded Mr. Fowden.

"I have no one with me now, sir, if that is what you would learn," replied the priest.

"Then you have had a companion. Where is he? He cannot have left the house. The drawbridge is guarded."

"He is not in this part of the house," replied the priest. "I will give you further explanation anon," he added, in a lower tone. "All I need now say is, that I am here on compulsion."

Mr. Fowden forbore to interrogate him further, and after examining the room, which was that wherein Atherton had passed the two previous nights as related, and discovering nothing to reward his scrutiny, he expressed his intention of going down-stairs.

"I don't think I shall make any capture here," he remarked.

"I am sure you won't," replied the priest.

Very much to Markland's relief, the magistrate then quitted the disused rooms, and taking Father Jerome with him, descended to the hall.

After a little private conversation with the priest, he made a fresh investigation of the lower apartments, but with no better success than heretofore, and he was by no means sorry when Miss Rawcliffe sent a message to him begging his company at supper. The servant who brought the message likewise informed him that the constables in the court-yard had been well supplied with ale.

"I hope they haven't drunk too much," said the magistrate. "Don't let them have any more, and tell them I shall come out presently."

CHAPTER X.

A SUCCESSFUL STRATAGEM.

ACCOMPANIED by the priest, he then proceeded to the dining-room, where he found Constance and Monica. A very nice supper had been prepared, and he did ample justice to the good things set before him. Markland, who had been absent for a short time, appeared with a bottle of old madeira, and a look passed between him and the young ladies, which did not escape the quick eyes of the priest.

The magistrate could not fail to be struck by the splendid wine brought him, and the butler took care to replenish his glass whenever it chanced to be empty.

Altogether the supper passed off more agreeably than could have been expected under such circumstances, for the young ladies had recovered their spirits, and the only person who seemed ill at ease was Father Jerome.

Towards the close of the repast, Mr. Fowden said:

"I fear I shall be obliged to trespass a little further on your hospitality, Miss Rawcliffe. I hope I shall not put you to inconvenience if I take up my quarters here to-night. I care not how you lodge me—put me in a haunted room if you think proper."

"You are quite welcome to remain here as long as you please, Mr. Fowden," said Constance—"the rather that I feel certain you will make no discovery. Markland will find you a chamber, where I hope you may rest comfortably."

"I will order a room to be got ready at once for his honour," said Markland.

"In the locked-up corridor?" observed the magistrate, with a laugh.

"No, not there, sir," said the butler.

"With your permission, Miss Rawcliffe, my men must also be quartered in the house," said Mr. Fowden.

"You hear, Markland," observed Constance.

"I will give directions accordingly," replied the butler.

And he quitted the room.

"I shall be blamed for neglect of duty if I do not make a thorough search," said the magistrate. "But I fancy the bird has flown," he added, with a glance at the priest.

Father Jerome made no reply, but Constance remarked, with apparent indifference:

"No one can have left the house without crossing the drawbridge, and that has been guarded. You will be able to state that you took all necessary precautions to prevent an escape."

"Yes, I shall be able to state that—and something besides," replied the magistrate, again glancing at the priest.

Just then, a noise was heard like the trampling of horses. Mr. Fowden uttered an exclamation of surprise, and a smile passed over the countenances of the two young ladies.

"I should have thought the men were crossing the drawbridge if I had not felt quite sure they would not depart without me," said Mr. Fowden.

"They have crossed the drawbridge—that's quite certain," observed the priest.

At this moment Markland entered the room.

"What have you been about?" cried the magistrate, angrily. "Have you dared to send my men away?"

"No, sir," replied the butler, vainly endeavouring to maintain a grave countenance; "but it seems that a trick has been played upon them."

"A trick!" exclaimed the magistrate.

"Yes, and it has proved highly successful. Some one has taken your honour's hat and cloak from the hall, and thus disguised, has ridden off with the men, who didn't find out their mistake in the darkness."

The two girls could not control their laughter.

"This may appear a good joke to you, sir," cried the magistrate, who was highly incensed, addressing the butler;

"but you'll pay dearly for it, I can promise you. You have aided and abetted the escape of a rebel and a traitor, and will be transported, if not hanged."

"I have aided no escape, sir," replied the butler. "All I know is, that some one wrapped in a cloak, whom I took to be you, came out of the house, sprang on a horse, and bidding the men follow him, rode off."

"He has prevented pursuit by taking my horse," cried Mr. Fowden; "and the worst of it is he is so much better mounted than the men that he can ride away from them at any moment. No chance now of his capture. Well, I shall be laughed at as an egregious dupe, but I must own I have been very cleverly outwitted.

"You are too kind-hearted, I am sure, Mr. Fowden," said Constance, "not to be better pleased that things have turned out thus, than if you had carried back a prisoner. And pray don't trouble yourself about the loss of your horse. You shall have the best in the stable. But you won't think of returning to Manchester to-night."

"Well—no," he replied, after a few moments' deliberation. "I am very comfortable here, and don't feel inclined to stir. I shouldn't be surprised if we had some intelligence before morning."

"Very likely," replied Constance; "and I think you have decided wisely to remain. It's a long ride at this time of night."

Mr. Fowden, as we have shown, was very good-tempered, and disposed to take things easily.

He was secretly not sorry that Atherton had eluded him, though he would rather the escape had been managed differently.

However it was quite clear it could not have been accomplished by his connivance. That was something.

Consoled by this reflection, he finished his supper as quietly as if nothing had occurred to interrupt it.

Immediately after supper Constance and her cousin

retired, and left him to enjoy a bottle of claret with the priest.

They were still discussing it when a great bustle in the court-yard announced that the constables had come back.

"Here they are!" cried the magistrate, springing to his feet. "I must go and see what has happened."

And he hurried out of the room, followed by Father Jerome.

By the time they reached the court-yard the constables had dismounted, and were talking to Markland and the gate-porter. Two other men-servants were standing by, bearing torches.

No sooner did Mr. Fowden make his appearance than one of the constables came up.

"Here's a pretty business, sir," said the man in an apologetic tone. "We've been nicely taken in. We thought we had you with us, and never suspected anything wrong till we got out of the park, when the gentleman at our head suddenly dashed off at full speed, and disappeared in the darkness. We were so confounded at first that we didn't know what to do, but the truth soon flashed upon us, and we galloped after him as hard as we could. Though we could see nothing of him, the clatter of his horse's hoofs guided us for a time, but by-and-by this ceased, and we fancied he must have quitted the road and taken to the open. We were quite certain he hadn't forded the Mersey, or we must have heard him."

"No—no—he wouldn't do that, Glossop," remarked the magistrate.

"Well, we rode on till we got to a lane," pursued the constable, "and two of our party went down it, while the rest kept to the high road. About a mile further we encountered a waggon, and questioned the driver, but no one had passed him; so we turned back, and were soon afterwards joined by our mates, who had been equally unsuccessful. Feeling now quite nonplussed, we deemed it best to return to the hall—and here we are, ready to attend to your honour's orders."

"'Twould be useless to attempt further pursuit to-night, Glossop," rejoined the magistrate. "Captain Legh has got off by a very clever stratagem, and will take good care you don't come near him. By this time, he's far enough off, you may depend upon it."

"Exactly my opinion, sir," observed Glossop. "We've lost him for the present, that's quite certain."

"Well, we'll consider what is best to be done in the morning," said Mr. Fowden. "Meantime you can take up your quarters here for the night. Stable your horses, and then go to bed."

"Not without supper, your honour," pleaded Glossop. "We're desperately hungry."

"Why you're never satisfied," cried the magistrate. "But perhaps Mr. Markland will find something for you."

Leaving the constables to shift for themselves, which he knew they were very well able to do, Mr. Fowden then returned to the dining-room, and finished the bottle of claret with the priest. Though his plans had been frustrated, and he had lost both his horse and his expected prisoner, he could not help laughing very heartily at the occurence of the evening.

Later on, he was conducted to a comfortable bed-chamber by the butler.

CHAPTER XI.

ATHERTON MEETS WITH DR. DEACON AT ROSTHERN.

HAVING distanced his pursuers as related, Atherton speeded across the country till he reached Bucklow Hill, where a solitary roadside inn was then to be found, and thinking he should be safe there, he resolved to stop at the house for the night.

Accordingly, he roused up the host and soon procured accommodation for himself and his steed.

The chamber in which he was lodged was small, with a low ceiling, encumbered by a large rafter, but it was scrupulously clean and tidy, and the bed-linen was white as snow, and smelt of lavender.

Next morning, he was up betimes, and his first business was to hire a man to take back Mr. Fowden's horse. The ostler readily undertook the job, and set out for Manchester, charged with a letter of explanation, while Atherton, having breakfasted and paid his score, proceeded on foot along the road to Knutsford.

Before leaving the inn he informed the landlord that he was going to Northwich, and thence to Chester; but, in reality, he had no fixed plan, and meant to be guided by circumstances. If the risk had not been so great, he would gladly have availed himself of Dr. Byrom's offer, conveyed by Beppy to Constance, of a temporary asylum in the doctor's house at Manchester—but he did not dare to venture thither.

After revolving several plans, all of which were fraught with difficulties and dangers, he came to the conclusion that it would be best to proceed to London, where he would be safer than elsewhere, and might possibly find an opportunity of embarking for Flanders or Holland. Moreover, he might be able to render some assistance to his unfortunate friends. But, as we have said, he had no decided plans; and it is quite certain that nothing but the apprehension of further treachery on the part of Father Jerome prevented him from secretly returning to Rawcliffe Hall.

He walked on briskly for about a mile, and then struck into a path on the left, which he thought would lead him through the fields to Tatton Park, but it brought him to a height from which he obtained a charming view of Rosthern Mere—the whole expanse of this lovely lake being spread out before him. On the summit of a high bank, at the southern extremity of the mere, stood the ancient church, embosomed in trees, and near it were the few scattered farm-houses and cottages that constituted the village.

The morning being very bright and clear, the prospect was seen to the greatest advantage, and, after contemplating it for a few minutes, he descended the woody slopes, and on reaching the valley shaped his course along the margin of the lake towards the village, which was not very far distant.

As he proceeded fresh beauties were disclosed, and he more than once stopped to gaze at them. Presently he drew near a delightful spot, where a babbling brook, issuing from the mere, crossed the road, and disappeared amid an adjoining grove. Leaning against the rail of a little wooden bridge, and listening to the murmuring brooklet, stood an elderly personage. His features were stamped with melancholy, and his general appearance seemed much changed, but Atherton at once recognised Dr. Deacon.

Surprised at seeing him there, the young man hastened on, and as he advanced the doctor raised his head and looked at him.

After a moment's scrutiny, he exclaimed:

"Do my eyes deceive me, or is it Atherton Legh?" And when the other replied in the affirmative, he said: "What are you doing here? Are you aware that a reward has been offered for your apprehension? You are running into danger."

"I have just had a very narrow escape of arrest," replied Atherton; "and am in search of a place of concealment. If I could be safe anywhere, I should think it must be in this secluded village."

"I will give you temporary shelter," said the doctor. "I have been so persecuted in Manchester since the prince's retreat, and the surrender of Carlisle, that I have been compelled to retire to this quiet place. Come with me to my cottage—but I cannot answer for your safety."

"I would willingly accept the offer if I did not fear I should endanger you," replied Atherton.

"Let not that consideration deter you," said Dr. Deacon.

"It matters little what happens to me now that I have lost my sons."

"You need not despair about them, sir," rejoined Atherton. "They will be allowed the cartel."

"No—no—no," cried the doctor. "They will be put to death. I ought to be resigned to their cruel fate, since they have done their duty, but I have not the fortitude I deemed I had."

And he groaned aloud.

"Better and braver young men never lived," said Atherton, in accents of deep commiseration. "And if they must die, they will perish in a noble cause. But I still hope they may be spared."

"They would not ask or accept a pardon from the usurper," said Dr. Deacon. "No, they are doomed—unless they can escape as you have done."

"Have you heard of your second son, Robert, whom we were obliged to leave at Kendal, owing to an attack of fever?" inquired Atherton.

"Yes—he is better. He will do well if he has not a relapse," replied the doctor. "He wrote to me, begging me not to go to him, or I should have set off to Kendal at once. But do not let us stand talking here. My cottage is close by."

So saying, he led Atherton to a pretty little tenement, situated near the lake. A garden ran down to the water's edge, where was a landing-place with wooden steps, beside which a boat was moored.

The cottage, which was more roomy and convenient than it looked, belonged to an old couple named Brereton, who were devoted to Dr. Deacon; and he had strong claims to their gratitude, as he had cured Dame Brereton of a disorder, pronounced fatal by other medical men.

On entering the cottage, the doctor deemed it necessary to caution Mrs. Brereton in regard to Atherton, and then ushered his guest into a small parlour, the windows of which commanded a lovely view of the lake. Had the doctor been free from anxiety he must have been happy in such a tranquil abode. But he was well-nigh heart-broken, and ever dwelling upon the sad position of his sons.

A simple breakfast, consisting of a bowl of milk and a brown loaf, awaited him, and he invited Atherton to partake of the rustic fare, offering him some cold meat and new-laid eggs in addition, but the young man declined, having already breakfasted.

Very little satisfied the doctor, and having quickly finished his meal, he resumed his conversation with Atherton.

"I know not what your opinion may be," he said; "but I think the grand error committed by the prince was in avoiding an engagement. He ought to have attacked the Duke of Cumberland at Lichfield. A battle would have been decisive, and if the prince had been victorious his ultimate success must have been assured. But the retreat without an engagement was fatal to the cause. The Scottish chiefs, I know, refused to march further than Derby, but if they had been forced to fight, their conduct would have been totally different. Even if the prince had been worsted—had he fallen—he would have left a glorious name behind him! Had my own brave sons died sword in hand, I should have been reconciled to their loss, but to think that they have been compelled to retreat ingloriously, without striking a blow, because their leaders lost heart, enrages me, and sharpens my affliction. Then I consider that the Manchester Regiment has been wantonly sacrificed. It ought never to have been left at Carlisle. That the prince thought the place tenable, and meant to reinforce the scanty garrison, I nothing doubt—but he lacked the means. Surrender was therefore unavoidable. I shall always think that the regiment has been sacrificed—but I blame Colonel Townley, and not the prince."

"Disastrous as the result has been, I must take up Colonel Townley's defence," said Atherton. "He felt certain he could hold out till he was relieved by the prince, and all the officers shared his opinion—none being more confident than your gallant son Theodore."

"Alas!" exclaimed the doctor, bitterly. "Of what avail is bravery against such engines of destruction as were brought to bear against the town by the Duke of Cumberland. But could not a desperate sortie have been made? Could you not have cut your way through the enemy? Death would have been preferable to such terms of surrender as were exacted by the duke."

"Such an attempt as you describe was made, sir," replied Atherton, "but it failed; I, myself, was engaged in it, and was captured."

"True, I now remember. Forgive me. Grief has made me oblivious. But I must not allow my own private sorrows to engross me to the neglect of others. Can I assist you in any way?"

Atherton then informed him of his design to proceed to London, and the doctor approved of the plan, though he thought the journey would be attended by considerable risk.

"Still, if you get to London you will be comparatively secure, and may perhaps be able to negotiate a pardon. Dr. Byrom has promised to come over to me to-day, and may perhaps bring his daughter with him. He has considerable influence with several persons of importance in London, and may be able to serve you. We shall hear what he says."

"But why think of me?" cried Atherton. "Why do you not urge him to use his influence in behalf of your sons?"

"He requires no urging," replied Dr. Deacon. "But I have told you that I will not ask a pardon for them—nor would they accept it if clogged with certain conditions."

Atherton said no more, for he felt that the doctor was immovable.

Shortly afterwards Dr. Deacon arose and begged Atherton to excuse him, as he usually devoted an hour in each day to a religious work on which he was engaged. Before leaving the room, he placed a book on the table near Atherton, and on opening it the young man found it was a prayer-book published some years previously by the doctor, entitled, "*A Complete Collection of Devotions, both public and private, taken from the Apostolic Constitution, Liturgies, and Common Prayers of the Catholic Church.*"

Atherton was familiar with the volume, as he had occasionally attended Dr. Deacon's church, but being now in a serious frame of mind, some of the prayers to which he turned and recited aloud produced a deeper effect upon him than heretofore.

When Dr. Deacon returned and found him thus occupied he expressed great satisfaction, and joined him in his devotions.

Before concluding, the doctor dropped on his knees, and offered up an earnest supplication for the restoration to health of his son Robert, and for the deliverance of his two other sons.

CHAPTER XII.

A SAD COMMUNICATION IS MADE TO DR. DEACON.

HALF an hour later Dr. Byrom and his daughter arrived. They came on horseback—one steed sufficing for both—Beppy being seated behind her father on a pillion, as was then the pleasant custom.

Dr. Byrom put up his horse at the little village inn, and then walked with his daughter to the cottage. Dr. Deacon met them at the door, and while greeting them kindly, informed them in a whisper whom they would find within.

Both were rejoiced to see Atherton, and congratulated him on his escape from arrest.

"I saw Mr. Fowden this morning at Manchester," said Dr. Byrom. "He had just returned from Rawcliffe Hall. I laughed very heartily when he told me how cleverly you had tricked him; but I really believe he had no desire to arrest you, and was glad when you got off. The horse you appropriated for the nonce was brought back from Bucklow Hill, and is now in its owner's possession, but I think you carried your scruples to the extreme, as you have given him a clue to the route you have taken, and the constables have been sent on both to Northwich and Macclesfield."

"I don't think they will look for me here," observed Atherton.

"No, Mr. Fowden's notion is that you will make for London, and I should have thought so too, had you not sent back the horse; but now you had better keep quiet for a few days."

"Why not come to us?" cried Beppy. "You will be in the very midst of your enemies, it is true, but no search will be made for you. No one would think you could be there."

"But some one would be sure to discover me. No; I am infinitely obliged, but I could not do it—I should only involve Dr. Byrom in trouble."

"Don't heed my risk," said Dr. Byrom. "I will give you shelter, if you require it."

"I'm quite sure we could conceal you," cried Beppy; "and only think how exciting it would be if the boroughreeve should call, and you had to be shut up in a closet! Or, better still, if you were carefully disguised, you might be presented to him without fear of detection. As to Mr. Fowden, I shouldn't mind him, even if he came on purpose to search for you. I'm sure I could contrive some little plot that would effectually delude him. 'Twould only be like a game at hide-and-seek."

"But if I lost the game, the penalty would be rather serious," replied Atherton. "I have no doubt of your cleverness, Miss Byrom; but I must not expose myself to needless risk."

While this conversation was going on, Dr. Byrom

observed to his old friend, "I have something to say to you in private. Can we go into another room?"

Struck by the gravity of his manner, Dr. Deacon took him into an adjoining apartment.

"I am afraid you have some bad news for me," he remarked.

"I have," replied Dr. Byrom, still more gravely. "Your son Robert——"

"What of him?" interrupted Dr. Deacon. "Has he had a relapse of the fever? If so, I must go to him at once."

"'Twill not be necessary, my good friend," replied Dr. Byrom, mournfully. "He does not require your attendance."

Dr. Deacon looked at him fixedly for a moment, and reading the truth in his countenance, murmured, "He is gone!"

"Yes, he has escaped the malice of his enemies," said Dr. Byrom.

"Heaven's will be done!" ejaculated Dr. Deacon, with a look of profound resignation. "Truly I have need of fortitude to bear the weight of affliction laid upon me. Robert!—my dear, brave son!—gone!—gone!"

"Be comforted, my good friend," said Dr. Byrom, in accents of profound sympathy. "His troubles are over."

"True," replied the other. "But the blow has well-nigh stunned me. Give me a chair, I pray you."

As Dr. Byrom complied, he remarked:

"I ought to have broken this sad news to you with greater care—and, indeed, I hesitated to mention it."

"You have acted most kindly—most judiciously—like the friend you have ever shown yourself," rejoined Dr. Deacon. "All is for the best, I doubt not. But when I think of my dear boy Robert, my heart is like to burst. He was so kind, so gallant, so loyal, so true."

"He has been removed from a world of misery," said Dr. Byrom. "Reflection, I am sure, will reconcile you to his fate, sad as it now may seem."

"I have misjudged myself," said Dr. Deacon. "When I sent forth my three sons on this expedition, I thought I was prepared for any eventuality, but I now find I was wrong. One I have already lost—the other two will follow quickly."

CHAPTER XIII.

A JOURNEY TO LONDON PROPOSED.

"You will be much grieved to hear that poor Robert Deacon is dead," observed Beppy, when she was left alone with Atherton. "Papa had just received the sad intelligence before we left Manchester, and he is now about to communicate it to the doctor. I pity Dr. Deacon from my heart, for I fear the loss of his sons will kill him. But I have other news for you, which papa has not had time to relate. Jemmy Dawson has made an attempt to escape; but has failed. At Dunstable he contrived to elude the guard, and got out upon the downs, but his flight being discovered, he was pursued and captured. He is now lodged in Newgate. Papa has just received a letter from him. It was confided to a Manchester friend who visited him in prison. The same gentleman brought another letter for Monica, which papa undertook to send to her privately—for the post is no longer safe—all suspected letters being opened and examined. Poor Jemmy seems very despondent. Papa is going to London shortly, and no doubt will see him."

"If Dr. Byrom goes to London, would he take charge of Monica and Constance, think you?" cried Atherton.

"I am sure he would," she replied. "But here he comes," she continued, as Dr. Byrom entered the room. "I will put the question to him. Papa," she went on, "I have been talking matters over to Captain Legh, and have mentioned to him that you are likely to go to London before long. Should you do so, he hopes you will take charge of Monica and Miss Rawcliffe."

"They will require an escort," added Atherton; "and there is no one whom they would prefer to you—especially under present circumstances."

Thus appealed to, Dr. Byrom very readily assented, and inquired when the young ladies would be disposed to undertake the journey.

"No arrangement has been made as yet," said Atherton; "but I am sure when Monica receives the letter from Jemmy Dawson, which I understand you are about to forward to her, she will be all anxiety to be near him; and I am equally sure that Constance will desire to accompany her."

"I will ascertain their wishes without delay," said Dr. Byrom. "Before returning to Manchester, I will ride over to Rawcliffe Hall, and deliver poor Jemmy's letter in person. I shall then hear what Miss Butler says. My visit will answer a double purpose, for I shall be able to give them some intelligence of you, and convey any message you may desire to send them."

"I cannot thank you sufficiently for your kindness, sir," said Atherton. "Pray tell Constance that I shall make my way to London in such manner as may best consist with safety, and I hope she will feel no uneasiness on my account. I sincerely trust she will go to London, as in that case I shall see her again before I embark for Flanders."

"I will deliver your message," replied Dr. Byrom, "and I hope we shall all meet in London. Immediately on my arrival there I shall endeavour to procure a pardon for you. Do not raise your expectations too high, for I may not be able to accomplish my purpose. But you may rely upon it I will do my best."

Atherton could scarcely find words to express his thanks.

"Say no more," cried the doctor, grasping his hand warmly. "I shall be amply rewarded if I am successful."

"You have not said anything about it, papa," interposed

Beppy. "But I hope you mean to take me with you to London. I must form one of the party."

"You would only be in the way," observed the doctor.

"Nothing of the sort. I should be of the greatest use, as you will find. You are the best and most good-natured papa in the world, and never refuse your daughter anything," she added, in a coaxing tone, which the doctor could not resist.

"I ought not to consent, but I suppose I must," he said.

"Yes, yes—it's quite settled," cried Beppy, with a glance of satisfaction at Atherton.

"Where are we to meet in London?" inquired the young man. "Possibly I may not see you again till I arrive there."

"You will hear of me at the St. James's Hotel, in Jermyn Street," replied the doctor. "And now I think we ought to start," he added to his daughter, "since we have to go to Rawcliffe Hall."

"But you have not taken leave of Dr. Deacon," cried Beppy.

"I shall not interrupt the prayers he is offering up for his son," replied her father. "Bid him adieu for us," he added to Atherton. "And now farewell, my dear young friend! Heaven guard you from all perils! May we meet again safely in London!"

Atherton attended his friends to the garden gate, but went no further. He watched them till they disappeared, and then returned sadly to the cottage.

CHAPTER XIV.

JEMMY DAWSON'S LETTER.

THE unexpected arrival of Dr. Byrom and Beppy at Rawcliffe Hall caused considerable perturbation to Constance and her cousin; but this was relieved as soon as the doctor explained that he brought good news of Atherton.

Before entering into any particulars, however, he delivered Jemmy Dawson's letter to Monica, telling her in what manner he had received it. Murmuring a few grateful words, she withdrew to her own room, and we shall follow her thither, leaving the others to talk over matters with which the reader is already acquainted.

The letter filled several sheets of paper, and had evidently been written at intervals.

Thus it ran.

St. Albans.

For a short time I have been free, and fondly persuaded myself I should soon behold you again. Alas! no such bliss was reserved for me. My fate is ever perverse. I had not long regained my liberty, when I was captured and taken back, and I am now so strictly watched that I shall have no second chance of escape.

Enraged at my attempt at flight, the officer in command of the guard threatened to fetter me, like a common felon, but as yet I have been spared that indignity.

You will easily imagine the state of grief and despair into which I was plunged by my ill success. I had buoyed myself up with false hopes. I felt quite sure that in a few days I should again clasp you to my heart. Deprived by a cruel fate of such unspeakable happiness, can you wonder at my distraction? While thus frenzied, had I possessed a weapon, I should certainly have put an end to my wretched existence. But I am somewhat calmer now, though still deeply depressed.

Oh! dearest Monica—the one being whom I love best!—I cannot longer endure this enforced separation from you. Never till now did I know how necessary you are to my existence. Pity me! pity me! I am sore afflicted.

Your presence would restore the serenity of mind I once enjoyed, and which I have now utterly lost. Come to me, and shed a gleam of happiness over the residue of my life.

In a few days I shall be lodged in a prison, but I shall not heed my confinement if you will visit me daily.

Should the worst fate befall me—as I have sad presentiments that it will—I shall be prepared to meet it, if you are with me at the last. Without you to strengthen me, my courage may fail. I need you, dearest Monica—need you more than ever. Come to me, I implore you!

I am ashamed of what I have written, but you will not despise me for my weakness. 'Tis not imprisonment I dread, but the torture of prolonged separation from you. Did I not love you so passionately I should be as careless as my companions in misfortune. They have little sympathy for me, for they cannot understand my grief. They would laugh at me if I told them I was ever thinking of you. Most of them live jovially enough, and appear entirely unconcerned as to the future. Whether they are really as indifferent as they seem, I much doubt. But they drink hard to drown care. The two Deacons, however, keep aloof from the rest. Colonel Townley, also, is greatly changed. He does not look downcast, but he has become exceedingly serious, and passes his time in long discourses with Father Saunderson, his priest and confessor, who is allowed to attend him. He often talks to me of you and Constance, and hopes that Atherton has been able to embark for France. We have heard nothing of the latter, of course; and in his case no news is good news.

The inhabitants of the different towns and villages through which we have passed on our way to the metropolis have displayed great animosity towards us, chiefly owing to the mischievous placards which have been everywhere spread about by the Government. In these placards the most monstrous charges are brought against us. It is gravely asserted that if we had defeated the Duke of Cumberland we meant to spit him alive and roast him. The bishops were to be burnt at the stake like Ridley and Latimer, and all the Protestant clergy massacred. That such absurd statements should have obtained credence seems impossible; but it is certain they have produced the effect designed, and that the minds of the common folk have been violently inflamed, as we have learnt to our cost, and as we may experience to a still greater extent when we reach London.

Newgate.

You will tremble, dearest Monica, when you learn that I am now immured in that dismal dungeon, the very name of which inspires terror; and yet the prison is not so formidable as it has been represented.

I have a small cell on the master's side, as it is termed, and though the walls are of stone, the little window grated, and the door barred, I have no right to complain. I am far from harshly treated—indeed, every comfort I choose to pay for is allowed me. Nor am I locked up in my cell, except at night.

A great stone hall is our place of resort during the day. There my brother officers assemble, and there we are served —not with prison fare, as you may imagine—but with as good provisions and as good wine as we could obtain at a tavern. For breakfast we have tea, coffee, or chocolate, according to choice—roast beef or mutton for dinner—claret or canary to wash it down—and some of my companions regale themselves after supper with a bowl of punch. Smoking, also, is allowed, and indeed several of the prisoners have pipes in their mouths all day long. From the stone hall a passage communicates with a tap-room, where different beverages are sold. Here the common malefactors repair, but happily they are prevented from coming further. From what I have just stated you will infer that we are not in that part of the gaol appropriated to felons—though we are stigmatised as the worst of criminals; but with a certain leniency, for which we ought to feel grateful, we have been placed among the debtors.

Colonel Townley, Captain Moss, and Captain Holker,

OF THE FATAL '45.   345

have each a commodious room. Tom Deacon and his brother Charles have the next cell to mine—but poor Adjutant Syddall is lodged in an infamous hole, owing to lack of money. All the officials, high and low, within the prison, seem anxious to lessen the rigour of our confinement as much as they can—especially, since most of us are able to live like gentlemen, and fee them handsomely.

For a prison, Newgate is comfortable enough, and, as far as my own experience goes, its ill reputation seems undeserved. No doubt the wards devoted to common felons are horrible, and I should die if I were shut up with the dreadful miscreants of whom I have caught a glimpse—but fortunately they are kept completely apart from us. We can hear their voices, and that is enough.

That I am melancholy in my prison does not proceed from any hardship I have to undergo—or from solitude, for I have too much society—but I pine and languish because I am separated from her I love.

Think not, if you come, in response to my entreaties, that you will be prevented from visiting me. You will be admitted without difficulty, and no prying eye will disturb us.

And now, since I have spoken of the good treatment we have experienced in prison, I must describe the indignities to which we were subjected on our way hither.

I have already mentioned that every effort has been made by the Government to inflame the minds of the populace against us. On our arrival at Islington, we learnt to our dismay that tumultuous crowds were collected in the streets through which we should have to pass; and to afford them a gratifying spectacle, it was arranged that we should be led to prison in mock triumph.

Accordingly, the waggons in which we were placed were uncovered, so that we had no protection from the numerous missiles hurled at us as we were borne slowly along through the howling multitude, and I verily believe we should have been torn in pieces if the mob could have got at us. Rebels and traitors were the mildest terms applied to us.

On the foremost waggon the rent and discoloured standard of our regiment was displayed, and a wretched creature, dressed up for the occasion as a bagpiper, sat behind the horses, playing a coronach. But he was soon silenced, for a well-aimed brickbat knocked him from his seat.

But though the crowd hooted us, pelted us, and shook their sticks at us, we met with some compassion from the female spectators. Many ladies were stationed at the windows, and their looks betokened pity and sympathy.

Our progress through the streets was slow, owing to the vast crowd, and frequent hindrances occurred, but at the entrance to Newgate Street we were brought to a complete standstill, and had to endure all the terrible ribaldry of the mob, mingled with yells and groans, and followed up by showers of missiles, such as are hurled at poor wretches in the pillory, till the thoroughfare could be cleared.

At this juncture, a chance of escape was offered to Colonel Townley. Half a dozen sturdy fellows, who looked like professional pugilists, forced their way to the waggon, and one of the stoutest of the party called to him to jump out and trust to them. The colonel thanked them, but refused, and they were immediately afterwards thrust back by the guard.

Had the chance been mine I would have availed myself of it unhesitatingly. But Colonel Townley feels certain of obtaining the cartel, and would therefore run no risk.

Another tremendous scene occurred at the gates of the prison, and we were glad to find refuge in its walls. Here, at least, we were free from the insults of the rabble, and though we were all in a sorry plight, none of us, except poor Tom Syddall, had sustained any personal injury. Nor was he much hurt.

Our deplorable condition seemed to recommend us to the governor, and he showed us much kindness. Through his attention we were soon enabled to put on fresh habiliments, and make a decent appearance.

Thus I have discovered, as you see, that there may be worse places than Newgate. My confinement may be irksome, but I could bear it were I certain as to the future; but I am not so sanguine as my companions, and dare not indulge hopes that may never be realised.

Not a single person has visited me till to-day, when a Manchester gentleman, with whom I am acquainted, has come to see me in prison—and he offers to take charge of a letter, and will cause it to be safely delivered to you. He is a friend of Dr. Byrom. A private hand is better than the post, for they tell me all our letters are opened and read, and in some cases not even forwarded.

I therefore add these few hasty lines to what I have already written. I am less wretched than I have been, but am still greatly dejected, and by no mental effort can I conquer the melancholy that oppresses me.

Come to me, then, dearest Monica! By all the love you bear me, I implore you come!

"I see how wretched thou art without me, dearest Jemmy," exclaimed Monica, as she finished the letter; "and I should be the cruellest of my sex if I did not instantly obey thy summons. Comfort thee, my beloved! comfort thee! I fly to thee at once!"

CHAPTER XV.

THE PARTING BETWEEN MONICA AND HER MOTHER.

BY this time, Dr. Byrom had not only delivered Atherton's message to Constance, but explained his own intentions, and she had at once decided upon accompanying him to London.

When Monica, therefore, appeared and announced her design, she learnt that her wishes had been anticipated. After some little discussion it was settled—at Monica's urgent entreaty—that they should start on the following day. Constance and Monica were to post in the family coach to Macclesfield, where they would be joined by Dr. Byrom and his daughter; and from this point they were all to travel to town together in the same roomy conveyance. The plan gave general satisfaction, and was particularly agreeable to Beppy.

All being settled, the party repaired to the dining-room, where luncheon had been set out for the visitors. Scarcely had they sat down, when Father Jerome made his appearance, and though the ordinary courtesies were exchanged between him and Dr. Byrom, it was evident there was mutual distrust.

As they rose from table, the doctor took Constance aside, and said to her in a low tone:

"What do you mean to do in regard to Father Jerome? Will you leave him here?"

"I must," she replied. "He is necessary to my Aunt Butler. During my absence I shall commit the entire control of the house to my father's faithful old servant, Markland, on whom I can entirely rely."

"You could not do better," remarked Dr. Byrom, approvingly. And he added, with a certain significance, "I was about to give you a caution, but I find it is not needed."

Shortly afterwards the doctor and Beppy took their departure, and proceeded to Manchester.

Constance and Monica spent the rest of the day in making preparations for the journey. As may be supposed, Constance had many directions to give to old Markland, who seemed much gratified by the trust reposed in him, and promised the utmost attention to his young mistress's injunctions.

Clearly Father Jerome felt himself aggrieved that the old butler was preferred to him, for he intimated that he should have been very happy to undertake the management of the house, if Miss Rawcliffe desired it; but she declared she would not give him the trouble.

"I should not deem it a trouble," he said. "Is Markland to have all the keys?"

"Yes, your reverence," interposed the butler. "Since I am made responsible for everything, it is necessary that I should have the keys. Miss Rawcliffe can depend on me."

"That I can, Markland," she rejoined. "I have had abundant proofs of your trustiness. My return is uncertain. I may be away for two or three months—perhaps for a longer period. During my absence you have full power to act for me; but in any emergency you will of course consult Father Jerome."

"I shall always be ready to advise him, and I trust he will be guided by my counsel," said the priest.

"I will act for the best," observed Markland. "Nothing shall go wrong if I can help it. But you must please excuse me, miss. I have much to do, and not too much time to do it in. I must get the old coach put in order for the journey. As you know, it has not been out for this many a day."

"Daughter," said the priest, as soon as Markland was gone, "you place too much confidence in that man. I hope you may not be deceived in him. He ought not to have access to the strong room. Better leave the key of that room with me."

"I would not hurt his feelings by withholding that key from him," replied Constance. "But I have no fear of Markland. He is honesty itself."

Later on in the day, Constance had some further conversation in private with the old butler, and, notwithstanding Father Jerome's disparaging observations, she showed no diminution in her confidence in him; but gave him particular instructions as to how he was to act under certain circumstances, and concluded by desiring him on no account to allow the priest to enter the strong room.

"He has no business there, Markland," she observed, significantly.

"And I will take good care he doesn't get in," rejoined the old butler. "I think I shall prove a match for Father Jerome, with all his cunning. But oh! my dear young lady," ne added, "how it would gladden my heart if you should be able to bring back Sir Conway with you. Oh! if I should see him restored to his own, and made happy with her he loves best, I shall die content!"

"Well, Markland, Dr. Byrom holds out a hope of pardon. Should I have any good news to communicate, you shall be among the first to hear it."

"Thank you! thank you, miss!" he cried, hastening out of the room to hide his emotion.

The parting between Monica and her mother took place in the invalid lady's room. No one was present at the time, for Constance had just bade adieu to her aunt. As Monica knelt on a footstool beside her mother, the latter gazed long and earnestly into her face, as if regarding her for the last time.

"We shall never meet again in this world, my dear child," she said. "I shall be gone before you return. But do not heed me. You cannot disobey the summons you have received. Go!—attend your affianced husband in his prison. Lighten his captivity. Solace him—pray with him—and should his judges condemn him, prepare him to meet his fate!"

"I will—I will," cried Monica. "But do not utterly dishearten me."

"I would not pain you, my dear child," said her mother, in accents of deepest sympathy. "But the words rise unbidden to my lips, and I must give utterance to them. Your case has been my case. Agony, such as I once endured, you will have to endure. But your trial will not be prolonged like mine. I had a terrible dream last night. I cannot recount it to you, but it has left a profound impression on my mind. I fear what I beheld may come to pass."

"What was it?" exclaimed Monica, shuddering. "Let me know the worst. I can bear it."

"No—I have said too much already. And now embrace me, dearest child. We shall not be long separated."

Monica flung her arms round her mother's neck, and kissed her again and again—sobbing a tender farewell.

She then moved slowly towards the door, but on reaching it, she rushed back, and once more embraced her.

Thus they parted. Mrs. Butler's presentiments were justified. They never met again.

CHAPTER XVI.

THE JOURNEY.

THE old family coach, with four horses attached to it, was drawn up in the court-yard. The luggage was packed. The servants were assembled in the hall to bid their young mistress good-bye, when Constance and Monica came downstairs fully attired for the journey.

They were followed by Miss Rawcliffe's pretty maid, Lettice, who, with the man-servant, Gregory, had been chosen to accompany them to London. Lettice carried a great bundle of cloaks, and looked full of delight, forming a strong contrast to the young ladies. Monica, indeed, was dissolved in tears, and hurried on to bury herself in the furthest corner of the carriage.

Constance, though wearing a sad expression, was far more composed, and replied kindly to the valedictions of the household. She also bade adieu to Father Jerome, who attended her to the door, and gave her his benediction. To Markland she had a few words to say, and she then stepped into the carriage, followed by Lettice. After putting up the steps, and fastening the door, Gregory mounted to the box.

All being now ready, Markland bowed respectfully, and ordered the postillions to drive on. Next moment the large coach rolled over the drawbridge, and the old butler and the gate-keeper watched it as it took its way through the park. The drive was not very cheerful, but before they reached Macclesfield, Constance had recovered her spirits.

At the Old Angel they found Dr. Byrom and his daughter, who had posted from Manchester, waiting for them. The doctor's trunks were quickly transferred to the carriage, while he and Beppy took their seats inside. No inconvenience whatever was caused by this addition to the party, for the coach was capacious enough to hold half-a-dozen persons comfortably. That night they stopped at Ashbourne, and next day proceeded to Leicester.

It is not our intention to describe the journey to London, unmarked as it was by any incident worthy of note, but we must mention that, owing to the unfailing good humour of Dr. Byrom and his daughter, the three days spent on the road passed away very pleasantly.

No more agreeable companion could be found than the doctor, and if Beppy did not possess the remarkable conversational powers of her father, she was extremely lively and entertaining. She made every effort to cheer Monica, and to a certain extent succeeded.

"Dr. Byrom had far less difficulty in dissipating Constance's gloom, and leading her to take a brighter view of the future. So confident did he seem that a pardon could be obtained for Atherton, that her uneasiness on that score, if not removed, was materially lightened.

With the exception of Dr. Byrom, not one of the travellers had previously visited London, and when they first caught sight of the vast city from Highgate Hill, and noted its numerous towers and spires, with the dome of St. Paul's rising in the midst of them, they were struck with admiration.

They were still gazing at the prospect, and Dr. Byrom was pointing out the Tower and other celebrated structures, when the clatter of hoofs reached their ears, and in another minute a well-mounted horseman presented himself at the carriage window. At first the young ladies thought it was a highwayman, and even Dr. Byrom shared the opinion, but a second glance showed them that the formidable equestrian was no other than Atherton Legh.

"My sudden appearance seems to alarm you," he cried smiling, as he bowed to the party. "I have been nearer to you than you imagined, and could at any time have overtaken you had I thought proper. But before you enter yonder mighty city I should like to know where I shall find you."

"We shall put up at the St. James's Hotel in Jermyn Street," replied Dr. Byrom, "but you had better not come there at first. I will give you a place of rendezvous. Be in the Mall in St. James's Park to-morrow afternoon, about four o'clock, and look out for me."

"I will not fail," replied Atherton. Again bowing round and glancing tenderly at Constance, he galloped off.

Gregory, the man-servant on the box, and the postillions, had seen his approach with dismay, being under the same impression as the gentlefolks inside, and fully expected the carriage would be stopped. Gregory, however, speedily recognised the young gentleman, and called to the postillions that it was all right.

Brief as it was, the unexpected rencounter was highly satisfactory to Constance, as it relieved her mind of any anxiety she had felt as to Atherton's safety.

Within half an hour after this little incident, which furnished them with abundant materials for conversation, they reached the outskirts of London, and were soon making their way through a variety of streets towards the west end of the town.

Prepared as they were for something extraordinary, our

young country ladies were fairly bewildered by all they beheld. Oxford Street they thought wonderful, but it was quite eclipsed by Hanover Square, Bond Street, and Piccadilly.

At length they reached Jermyn-street, where they found very charming apartments at the St. James's Hotel.

End of the Fifth Book.

The Duke of Cumberland, son of George II.

BOOK VI.

KENNINGTON COMMON.

CHAPTER I.

MONICA VISITS JEMMY IN NEWGATE.

On the morning after the arrival of the party in town, Monica being all anxiety to see her lover, Dr. Byrom accompanied her in a hackney-coach to the prison in which poor Jemmy was confined. During the drive she supported herself tolerably well, but on reaching Newgate she well-nigh fainted.

The necessary arrangements for her admittance to the prisoner having been made by the doctor, he assisted her out of the coach.

On entering the lodge she was obliged to remove her hood. A gaoler then conducted them along a passage that skirted the refection-hall, after which they ascended a short stone staircase which brought them to a gallery containing several chambers.

Unlocking the door of one of these cells the gaoler disclosed Jemmy. He was seated at a small table reading, and on raising his head, and beholding Monica, he sprang to his feet, and with a cry of delight clasped her to his breast.

So tender was their meeting that even the hardened gaoler was touched by it.

For a minute or two Jemmy did not notice Dr. Byrom,

but on becoming sensible of his presence he wrung his hand, and thanked him in heartfelt tones for bringing his mistress to him. The doctor then told Monica that he would wait for her in the hall below, and quitted the cell.

"And so this is your prison-chamber, dearest Jemmy!" said Monica, glancing round it. "'Tis just the room I pictured from your description."

"I thought it dismal at first," he rejoined; "but I have become quite content with it. I shall feel no longer miserable since you are come. You must never leave me more."

"I never will," she replied.

They then lapsed into silence. Words seemed unnecessary to express their thoughts, and it was quite happiness enough to them to be together.

Leaving them we shall follow Dr. Byrom to the hall ward, where he found several prisoners assembled. Amongst them were Theodore Deacon and Tom Syddall. Taking the former aside he acquainted him with the death of his brother Robert, of which the young man had not heard. Though deeply affected by the intelligence, Captain Deacon bore it firmly.

Shortly afterwards Colonel Townley entered the hall, and on seeing Dr. Byrom immediately came up to him, and shook hands with him very cordially.

"We meet again under rather melancholy circumstances, my dear doctor," he said. "But I am extremely glad to see you. Fortune has played me false, but I hope she has nothing worse in store for me. The Government must deliver me up. They cannot deny that I hold a commission from the King of France, and that I have been fifteen years in the French service. Still I know the hazard I run," he added, shrugging his shoulders. "But come with me to my room. I want to say a word to you in private."

With this, he led the doctor to a cell situated near the hall. It was somewhat larger than the chamber allotted to Captain Dawson, and better furnished.

"Pray take a seat," said the colonel, doing the honours of his room. "I want to learn something about Atherton Legh."

"He is safe and in London," replied Dr. Byrom. "I expect to see him to-day. I hope to procure him a pardon, and I will tell you how. You are aware that his mother was Miss Conway. She was sister to Colonel Conway, who is now aide-de-camp to the Duke of Cumberland, and a great favourite of his royal highness. If Colonel Conway will intercede for his nephew with the duke, no doubt he will be successful."

"I should think so," replied Townley. "But is Colonel Conway aware of his nephew's existence?"

"No," replied Dr. Byrom. "If he has heard of him at all, it must be as Captain Legh. He may have seen him at Carlisle."

"Yes, when the young man was captured during a sally," said Townley; "but he knew nothing of the relationship. However, unless the Colonel should be deeply offended with his nephew for joining the prince, he can obtain his pardon, that is certain. Was there any intercourse between Sir Richard Rawcliffe and the Conway family?"

"Not since the death of Sir Oswald's widow. They did not like him—and no wonder. But all this is favourable to our young friend. They will be glad to recognise him as Sir Conway."

"I don't doubt it," replied Townley. "I hope he may regain Rawcliffe Hall, and marry his fair cousin."

They then began to discuss political matters, and were talking together in a low tone when the gaoler entered the cell, and informed Dr. Byrom that the young lady he had brought to the prison was waiting for him. The doctor then took leave of his friend, promising to visit him again very shortly, and accompanied the gaoler to the lodge, where he found Monica. A coach was then called and took them to Jermyn Street.

CHAPTER II.

COLONEL CONWAY.

They found Constance and Beppy prepared for a walk. Beppy had taken particular pains with her toilette, and being rather gaily attired, formed a contrast to Constance, who was still in deep mourning. They tried to persuade Monica to accompany them, but she declined, so they went out with Dr. Byrom, and walked down St. James's Street to the Park. The day was fine, and they were quite enchanted with the novelty and brilliancy of the scene. Both young ladies looked so well that they attracted considerable attention among the gaily-attired company. After walking about for some time they perceived Atherton, who immediately joined them. He was plainly but handsomely dressed, and looked exceedingly well.

"I have arranged matters for you," said Dr. Byrom. "A room is secured for you at the St. James's Hotel. You must pass as my son Edward. That will remove all suspicion."

"I shall be quite content to do so," replied the young man.

They then continued their walk, and had quitted the crowded part of the Mall, when an officer in full uniform, and followed by an orderly, was seen riding slowly down the avenue in the direction of the Horse Guards. He was a fine handsome man in the prime of life, and of very distinguished appearance. Atherton immediately recognised him as Colonel Conway, and, acting upon a sudden impulse, stepped forward to address him.

Colonel Conway reined in his steed, and returned the young man's salute.

"I forget your name," said the colonel. "But unless my eyes deceive me, I have seen you before."

"You saw me at Carlisle, colonel."

"Why, then, you were in Colonel Townley's Manchester Regiment—you are the rebel officer whom I myself captured. How is it that you act in this foolhardy manner? I shall be compelled to order your immediate arrest!"

"Not so, colonel. I am perfectly safe with you."

"How, sir!" cried Colonel Conway, sharply. "Dare you presume?"

"You will not arrest your sister's son," replied Atherton.

"Did I hear aright?" exclaimed the colonel, scanning him narrowly.

"Yes, I am your nephew, the son of Sir Oswald Rawcliffe," replied the young man.

Colonel Conway uttered an exclamation of surprise.

"I don't doubt what you say," he cried. "You certainly bear a remarkable resemblance to your father. Am I to conclude you are the missing heir?"

"Even so," replied Atherton. "I have sufficient proofs to support my claim whenever I choose to make it. But it is a long story, and cannot be told now. Dr. Byrom of Manchester will vouch for the truth of the statement."

And at a sign from the young man the doctor stepped forward.

"I did not expect to be called up at this moment, colonel," said the doctor. "But you may rest satisfied that this young gentleman is your nephew. He is the lost Sir Conway Rawcliffe."

"But you did not serve under that name at Carlisle?" cried the colonel, eagerly. "If I remember right, you were known as Atherton Legh?"

"Exactly," replied the young man. "I have not yet assumed my rightful name and title."

"I am glad of it," cried the colonel. "By heaven! I am fairly perplexed how to act."

"You will not act precipitately, colonel," said Dr. Byrom "It was my intention to communicate with you on your nephew's behalf this very day."

"I wish I had not seen him," cried the colonel. "Why did he put himself in my way?"

"I had no such design, sir, I assure you," said Atherton.

"Will you allow us to wait on you, colonel?" asked Dr. Byrom.

"Wait on me! No! unless you want the young man to be arrested. Where are you staying?" he added to Atherton.

"You will find me at the St. James's Hotel at any hour you may please to appoint, colonel."

"I am staying there, colonel," said Dr. Byrom; "and so is Miss Rawcliffe—the late Sir Richard Rawcliffe's daughter."

Colonel Conway reflected for a moment. Then addressing Atherton, he said:

"On consideration, I will see you. Be with me at Cumberland House to-morrow morning at ten o'clock."

"I will be there," was the reply.

"Mind, I make no promises, but I will see what can be done. I should wish you to accompany the young man, Dr. Byrom."

The doctor bowed.

"You say Miss Rawcliffe is staying at the St. James's Hotel?"

"She is staying there with my daughter and myself, colonel. They are both yonder. May I present you to them?"

"Not now," replied the colonel. "Bring them with you to Cumberland House to-morrow. They may be of use." Then turning to Atherton, he added, "I shall expect you."

With a military salute, he then rode off towards the Horse Guards, followed by his orderly, leaving both his nephew and the doctor full of hope, which was shared by Constance and Beppy when they learnt what had occurred.

CHAPTER III.

CUMBERLAND HOUSE.

Next morning, at the hour appointed, Constance and Beppy, accompanied by Dr. Byrom and Atherton, repaired to Cumberland House in Arlington Street. Sentinels were stationed at the gates, and in the court half-a-dozen officers were standing, who glanced at the party as they passed by. In the spacious vestibule stood a stout hall-porter and a couple of tall and consequential-looking footmen in royal liveries. One of the latter seemed to expect them, for, bowing deferentially, he conducted them into a handsome apartment looking towards the Park.

Here they remained for a few minutes, when a side door opened and an usher in plain attire came in, and addressing the two young ladies, begged them to follow him.

After consulting Dr. Byrom by a look they complied, and the usher led them into an adjoining apartment, which appeared to be a cabinet, and where they found a tall, well-proportioned man in military undress, whom they took to be Colonel Conway, though they thought he looked younger than they expected to find him.

This personage received them rather haughtily and distantly, and in a manner far from calculated to set them at their ease. He did not even beg them to be seated, but addressing Constance, said:

"Miss Rawcliffe, I presume?"

Constance answered in the affirmative, and presented Beppy, to whom the supposed colonel bowed.

"I have heard of your father," he said. "A clever man, but a Jacobite." Then turning to Constance, he remarked, " efore you say anything to me understand that every word will each the ears of the Duke of Cumberland. Now what have you to allege in behalf of your cousin? On what grounds does he merit clemency?"

"I am bound to intercede for him, sir," she replied; "since it was by my persuasion that he was induced to join the insurrection."

"You avow yourself a Jacobite, then?" said the colonel, gruffly. "But no wonder. Your father, Sir Richard, belonged to the disaffected party, and you naturally share his opinions."

"I have changed my opinions since then," said Constance; "but I was undoubtedly the cause of this rash young man joining the insurgent army. Pray use the influence you possess over the duke to obtain him a pardon."

"What am I to say to the duke?"

"Say to his royal highness that my cousin deeply regrets the rash step he has taken, and is sensible of the crime he has committed in rising in rebellion against the king. He is at large, as you know, but is ready to give himself up, and submit to his majesty's mercy."

"If grace be extended to him I am certain he will serve the king faithfully," said Beppy.

"I will tell you one thing, Miss Rawcliffe, and you too, Miss Byrom; the Duke of Cumberland feels that a severe example ought to be made of the officers of the Manchester Regiment. They are double-dyed rebels and traitors."

"But we trust his royal highness will make an exception in this case," said Beppy. "We would plead his youth and inexperience, and the influence brought to bear upon him."

"But all this might be urged in behalf of the other officers—notably in the case of Captain James Dawson."

"True," said Beppy. "But as I understand, they are not willing to submit themselves, whereas Sir Conway Rawcliffe has come to throw himself upon the king's mercy."

"But how can we be certain he will not take up arms again?"

"Such a thing would be impossible," cried Constance, earnestly. "I will answer for him with my life."

"And so will I," cried Beppy, with equal fervour.

"Once more I implore you to intercede for him with the duke," cried Constance. "Do not allow him to be sacrificed."

"Sacrificed! His life is justly forfeited. When he took this step he knew perfectly well what the consequences would be if he failed."

"I cannot deny it," replied Constance. "But he now bitterly repents."

"Surely, sir, you will answer for him," cried Beppy.

"I answer for him!" exclaimed the supposed colonel.

"Yes, for your nephew," said Beppy. "Had you been with him he would never have taken this false step."

"Well, I will hear what he has to say. But I must first make a memorandum."

He then sat down at a table on which writing materials were placed, and traced a few lines on a sheet of paper, attaching a seal to what he had written. This done he struck a small silver bell, and, in answer to the summons, the usher immediately appeared. Having received his instructions, which were delivered in a low tone, the usher bowed profoundly, and quitted the cabinet.

Scarcely was he gone when an officer entered—a fine commanding-looking person, but several years older than the other.

On the entrance of this individual a strange suspicion crossed the minds of both the young ladies. But they were left in no doubt when the new-comer said:

"I trust Miss Rawcliffe has prevailed?"

"I must talk with your nephew, Colonel Conway, before I can say more."

"Colonel Conway!" exclaimed Constance. "Have I been all this time in the presence of——"

"You have been conversing with the Duke of Cumberland," supplied Colonel Conway.

"Oh, I implore your royal highness to forgive me!" exclaimed Constance. "Had I known——"

"I shall die with shame!" cried Beppy.

At this moment Dr. Byrom and Atherton were ushered into the cabinet.

On beholding the Duke of Cumberland, whom both the new-comers recognised, they knew not what to think, but each made a profound obeisance.

"This is my nephew, Sir Conway Rawcliffe, your royal highness," said the colonel.

"Hitherto, I have only known him as Captain Legh, the rebel," observed the duke, rather sternly.

"Rebel no longer," said Colonel Conway. "He has come to deliver himself up to your royal highness, and to solicit your gracious forgiveness for his misdeeds."

"Does he acknowledge his errors?" demanded the duke.

"He heartily and sincerely abjures them. If a pardon be extended to him, your august sire will ever find him a loyal subject."

"Is this so?" demanded the duke.

"It is," replied the young man, bending lowly before the duke. "I here vow allegiance to the king, your father."

"Well, Sir Conway," replied the duke, "since you are sensible of your errors, I will promise you a pardon from his majesty. But you will understand that a point has been strained in your favour, and that you owe your life partly to the intercession of your uncle, whose great services I desire to reward, and partly to the solicitations of these your friends. It has been said of me, I know, that I am of a savage and inflexible disposition; but I should be savage, indeed, if I could resist such prayers as have been addressed to me—especially by your fair cousin," he added, glancing at Constance.

"Those who have termed your royal highness savage have done you a great injustice," she said.

"I must bear the remarks of my enemies," pursued the duke, "satisfied that I act for the best. Here is your protection," he continued, giving Sir Conway the document he had just drawn up and signed. "You will receive your pardon hereafter."

"I thank your royal highness from the bottom of my heart," said Sir Conway. "You will have no reason to regret your clemency."

"Serve the king as well as you have served his enemies, and I shall be content," said the duke. "'Tis lucky for you that your estates will not be forfeited. But I hope your fair cousin may still continue mistress of Rawcliffe."

"I would never deprive her of the property," said Sir Conway.

"Nay, you must share it with her. And take heed, my dear young lady, if you are united to Sir Conway, as I hope you may be, that you do not shake his loyalty. You must forswear all your Jacobite principles."

"They are forsworn already," she said.

"May I venture to put in a word?" observed Dr. Byrom. "Such faith had I in your royal highness's clemency, and in your known friendship for Colonel Conway, that I urged his nephew to take this step which has had so happy a result."

"You then are the author of the plot?" cried the duke.

"Perhaps I was at the bottom of it all," cried Beppy. "I don't like to lose my share of the credit. I had the most perfect confidence in your royal highness's good-nature."

"'Tis the first time I have been complimented on my good-nature," observed the duke, smiling—"especially by a Jacobite, as I believe you are, Miss Byrom."

"After what has just occurred I could not possibly remain a Jacobite," she said. "I shall trumpet forth your royal highness's magnanimity to all."

"And so shall I," said her father.

"When next I see Sir Conway Rawcliffe," said the duke, "I trust it will be at St. James's Palace, and I also hope he will bring Lady Rawcliffe to town with him. Meantime, I advise him to retire to his country seat till this storm has blown over. It may possibly fall on some heads."

"I shall not fail to profit by your royal highness's advice," replied Sir Conway, bowing deeply.

Profound obeisances were then made by all the party, and they were about to depart, when the duke said in a low tone to Constance:

"I depend upon you to maintain your cousin in his present disposition. Go back to Rawcliffe Hall."

"Alas!" she rejoined, "I would obey your royal highness, but I cannot leave just now. My cousin, Miss Butler, is betrothed to Captain Dawson, of the Manchester Regiment. I must remain with her."

"Better not," rejoined the duke, in an altered tone. "But as you will. 'Twill be vain to plead to me again. I can do nothing more."

Colonel Conway here interposed, and, taking her hand, led her towards the door.

"Say not a word more," he whispered; "or you will undo all the good that has been done."

The party then quitted Cumberland House, and returned to the St. James's Hotel.

Needless to say, they all felt happy—the happiest of all being Sir Conway.

The Duke of Cumberland's injunctions were strictly obeyed. Next day, the family coach was on its way back, containing the whole party, with the exception of poor Monica, who would not return, but was left behind with Lettice.

Three days afterwards the Duke of Cumberland, attended by Colonel Conway, proceeded to Scotland, where the decisive battle of Culloden was fought.

CHAPTER IV.

THE TRIAL OF THE MANCHESTER REBELS.

An interval of some months being allowed to elapse, we come to a very melancholy period of our story.

The unfortunate prisoners, who had languished during the whole time in Newgate, were ordered to prepare for their trial, which was intended to take place in the Court House at St. Margaret's Hill, Southwark, before Lord Chief Justice Lee, Lord Chief Justice Willes, Justice Wright, Justice Dennison, Justice Foster, Baron Reynolds, Baron Clive, and other commissioners specially appointed for the purpose.

Previously to the trial the prisoners were ordered to be removed to the new goal at Southwark.

'Twas a sad blow both to Monica and her unfortunate lover. So much kindness and consideration had been shown to Jemmy during his long confinement in Newgate by all the officials, that he was quite grieved to leave the prison.

Familiar with every little object in his cell, he was unwilling to exchange it for another prison-chamber. In this narrow room he and Monica had passed several hours of each day. Their converse had been chiefly of another world, for Jemmy had given up all hopes of a pardon, or an exchange, and they had prayed fervently together, or with the ordinary. Monica, as we know, was a Papist, but Jemmy still adhered to the Protestant faith. Before her departure from London, Constance had taken leave of him; but Sir Conway could not consistently visit the prison after the pardon he had received from the Duke of Cumberland. Dr. Byrom and his daughter had likewise visited him before they left town.

About a week after Constance's return to Rawcliffe Hall, Mrs. Butler died, and the sad tidings were communicated with as much care as possible to Monica. Prepared for the event, the poor girl bore it with pious resignation.

"My mother was right," she said. "She foresaw that we should never meet again."

At length the hour for departure came, and Jemmy was forced to quit his cell. As he stepped forth, his heart died within him.

In the lodge he took leave of the goaler who had attended him, and of the other officials, and they all expressed an earnest hope that he might be exchanged. All had been interested in the tender attachment between him and Monica, which had formed a little romance in the prison.

The removal took place at night. Jemmy was permitted to take a hackney-coach, and, as a special favour, Monica was allowed to accompany him—a guard being placed on the box.

To prevent any attempt at escape he was fettered, and this grieved him sorely, for he had not been placed in irons during his confinement in Newgate.

On London Bridge, a stoppage occurred, during which the coaches were examined.

On their arrival at the prison at Southwark, the lovers were separated. Immured in a fresh cell, Jemmy felt completely wretched, and Monica, more dead than alive, was driven back to Jermyn-street.

Next day, however, she was allowed to see her lover, but only for a few minutes, and under greater restrictions than had been enforced in Newgate. Jemmy, however, had in some degree recovered his spirits, and strove to reassure her.

Three days afterwards the trials commenced. They took place, as appointed, at the Court House, in St. Margaret's Hill.

Colonel Townley was first arraigned, and maintained an undaunted demeanour. When he appeared in the dock a murmur ran through the crowded court, which was immediately checked. The counsel for the king were the Attorney-General, Sir John Strange, the Solicitor-General, Sir Richard Lloyd, and the Honourable Mr. York—those for the prisoner were Mr. Serjeant Wynne and Mr. Clayton. The prisoner was charged with procuring arms, ammunition, and other instruments, and composing a regiment for the service of the Pretender to wage war against his most sacred majesty; with marching through and invading several parts of the kingdom, and unlawfully seizing his majesty's treasure in many places for the service of his villainous cause, and taking away the horses and other goods of his majesty's peaceful subjects. The prisoner was furthermore charged, in open defiance of his majesty's undoubted right and title to the crown of these realms, with frequently causing the Pretender's son to be proclaimed in a public and solemn manner as regent, and himself marching at the head of a pretended regiment, which he called the Manchester Regiment.

To this indictment the prisoner pleaded not guilty.

The chief witness against the prisoner was Ensign Maddox, an officer of the regiment, who had consented to turn evidence for the Crown. Maddox declared that he had marched out with the prisoner as an ensign, but never had any commission, though he carried the colours; that the prisoner gave command as colonel of the Manchester Regiment; and that he ordered the regiment to be drawn up in the churchyard in Manchester, where the Pretender's son reviewed them, and that he marched at the head of the regiment to Derby. That the prisoner marched as colonel of the Manchester Regiment in their retreat from Derby to Carlisle; that he was made by the Pretender's son commandant of Carlisle, and that he took on him the command of the whole rebel forces left there; that he had heard the prisoner have some words with Colonel Hamilton, who was governor of the citadel, for surrendering the place, and not holding out to the last; and that he had particularly seen the prisoner encourage the rebel officers and soldiers to make sallies out on the king's forces.

After Maddox's cross examination evidence was produced that Colonel Townley was many years in the French service under a commission from the French king; and since he was taken at Carlisle had been constantly supplied with money from France. Other witnesses were called to invalidate the evidence of Maddox by showing that he was unworthy of credit.

But the court ruled that no man who is a liege subject of his majesty can justify taking up arms, and acting in the service of a prince who is actually at war with his majesty.

After the prisoner's evidence had been gone through, the Solicitor-General declared, "That he felt certain the jury would consider that the overt acts of high treason charged against the prisoner in compassing and imagining the death of the king, and in levying war against his majesty's person and government, had been sufficiently proved."

While the jury withdrew to consider their verdict, Colonel Townley looked more indifferent than any other person in court. On their return, in about ten minutes, the clerk of arraigns said:

"How say you, gentlemen, are you agreed on your verdict? Do you find Francis Townley guilty of the high treason whereof he stands indicted, or not guilty?"

"Guilty," replied the foreman.

Sentence of death was then pronounced upon him by Lord Chief Justice Lee, and during that awful moment he did not betray the slightest discomposure.

He was then delivered to the care of Mr. Jones, keeper of the county gaol of Surrey.

Captain Dawson's trial next took place. His youth and good looks excited general sympathy.

The indictment was similar to that of Colonel Townley—the treason being alleged to be committed at the same time. The Attorney-General set forth that the prisoner, contrary to his allegiance, accepted a commission in the Manchester Regiment raised by Colonel Townley for the service of the Pretender, and acted as captain; that he marched to Derby in a hostile manner; that he retreated with the rebel army from Derby to Manchester, and thence to Clifton Moor, where in a skirmish he headed his men against the Duke of Cumberland's troops; and that he had surrendered at the same time as Colonel Townley and the other officers.

Evidence to the above effect was given by Maddox and other witnesses.

No defence was made by the prisoner, and the jury, without going out of court, brought him in guilty.

As their verdict was delivered, a convulsive sob was heard, and attention being directed to the spot whence the sound proceeded, it was found that a young lady had fainted. As she was carried out the prisoner's eyes anxiously followed her, and it was soon known that she was his betrothed.

The rest of the rebel officers were subsequently tried and found guilty, and sentence of death was passed upon them all.

The order for the execution was couched in the following terms:

"Let the several prisoners herein named return to the goal of the county of Surrey whence they came. Thence they must be drawn to the place of execution, on Kennington Common, and when brought there must be hanged by the neck—but not till they are dead, for they must be cut down alive. Then their hearts must be taken out and burnt before their faces. Their heads must be severed from their bodies, and their bodies divided into quarters, and these must be at the king's disposal."

CHAPTER V.

THE NIGHT BEFORE THE EXECUTIONS.

ON the night preceding the day appointed for carrying out the terrible sentence, poor Jemmy and his betrothed were allowed by Mr. Jones, the keeper of the prison, to pass an hour together.

While clasping her lover's fettered hands, Monica looked tenderly into his face, and said:

"I shall not long survive you, Jemmy."

"Banish these thoughts," he rejoined. "You are young, and I hope may have many years of happiness. Be constant to my memory, that is all I ask. If disembodied spirits can watch over the living I will watch over you."

With a sad smile he then added: "For a few minutes let us live in the past. Let me look back to the time when I first beheld you, and when your beauty made an impression on me that has never been effaced. Let me recall those happy hours when smiles only lighted up that lovely countenance, and no tear was ever shed. Oh! those were blissful days!"

"Let me also recall the past, dearest Jemmy," she cried. "How well do I recollect our first meeting! I thought I had seen no one like you, and I think so still. I could not be insensible to the devotion of a youth so gallant, and my heart was quickly yours. Alas! alas! I took advantage of your love to induce you to join this fatal expedition."

"Do not reproach yourself, dearest Monica. 'Twas my destiny. I am a true adherent of the Stuarts. Had I ten thousand lives I would give them all to King James and my country! I shall die with those sentiments on my lips."

As he spoke his pale cheek flushed, and his eye kindled with its former fire. She gazed at him with admiration.

But after a few moments a change came over his countenance, and with a look of ill-concealed anguish, he said:

"We must part to-night, dearest Monica. 'Tis better you should not come to me to-morrow."

"Nay, dearest Jemmy, I will attend you to the last."

"Impossible! it cannot be. My execution will be accompanied by barbarities worthy of savages, and not of civilised beings. You must not—shall not witness such a frightful spectacle."

"If the sight kills me I will be present."

"Since you are resolved, I will say no more. At least, you will see how firmly I can die."

Just then Mr. Jones came in to remind them that it was time to part, and with a tender embrace, Jemmy consigned her to his care.

On learning that she meant to attend the execution, Mr. Jones endeavoured to dissuade her, but she continued unshaken in her purpose.

CHAPTER VI.

THE FATAL DAY.

NEXT morning all those condemned to die breakfasted together in a large room on the ground floor of the prison. Their fetters had been previously removed.

There was no bravado, no undue levity in their manner or discourse, but they looked surprisingly cheerful, in spite of the near approach of death under the most dreadful form.

All had passed the greater part of the night in prayer. And as they hoped they had settled their account on high, there was nothing to disturb their serenity.

"Our time draws very near," observed Syddall to Captain Dawson, who sat next him. "But for my part I feel as hearty as ever I did in my life. Indeed, I think we all look remarkably well considering our position."

"Death does not terrify me in the least," said Jemmy. "Its bitterness is past with me. May Heaven have mercy on us all!"

"We die in a good cause," observed Captain Deacon. "I heartily forgive all my enemies—even the chief of them, the Elector of Hanover and the Duke of Cumberland. It has been falsely said that I was induced by my revered father to take up arms for the prince. The assertion I shall contradict in the manifesto I have prepared. For the rest I care not what my enemies say of me."

"The Duke of Cumberland has not kept faith with us," exclaimed Captain Fletcher. "When we surrendered at Carlisle, he declared that the garrison should not be put to the sword, but reserved for his father's pleasure—the Elector's pleasure being that we should be hung, drawn, and quartered. Gracious Heaven! deliver all Englishmen from this Hanoverian clemency!"

"My sole regret is that we ever surrendered," cried Colonel Townley. "Would we all had died sword in hand! However, since we are brought to this pass, we must meet our fate like brave men. As we have been allowed wine with our last repast, let us drink to King James the Third!"

Every glass was raised in response, after which they all rose from the table.

Several friends of the prisoners were now permitted to enter the room. Among them were Mr. Saunderson, Colonel Townley's confessor, and Captain Deacon's youngest brother, Charles.

Charles Deacon had been reprieved; but, while embracing his brother for the last time, he expressed deep regret that he could not share his fate.

Poor Monica was there—dressed in deep mourning. She and her lover were somewhat removed from the rest; but they were so engrossed by each other, that they seemed to be quite alone.

Their parting attracted the attention of Tom Syddall, and moved him to tears—though he had shed none for his own misfortunes.

"How did you pass the night, dearest Jemmy?" inquired Monica.

"Chiefly in prayer," he replied. "But towards morn I fell asleep, and dreamed that you and I were children, and playing together in the fields. It was a pleasant dream, and I was sorry when I awoke."

"I, too, had a pleasant dream, dearest Jemmy," s. rejoined. "I thought I saw my mother. She had a seraphic aspect, and seemed to smile upon me. That smile has comforted me greatly. Ha! what sound is that?"

"'Tis the guard assembling in the court-yard," he replied. "We must part. Do not give way."

"Fear me not," she cried, throwing her arms around his neck.

At this juncture, the sheriffs entered the room, attended by the keeper of the prison. The sheriffs wore black gowns, and were without their chains.

While the sheriffs were exchanging a few words with Colonel Townley and the other prisoners, Mr. Jones conducted Monica to the mourning-coach which was waiting for her at the gates of the prison.

Meanwhile, a guard of grenadiers had been drawn up in the court-yard, and the ignominious conveyances, destined to take the prisoners to the place of execution, had been got ready.

By-and-by, the unfortunate men were brought down, and in the presence of the sheriffs and the keeper of the prison were bound to the hurdles with cords.

This done, the dismal procession set forth.

At the head of the train marched a party of grenadiers. Then followed the sheriffs in their carriages, with their tipstaves walking beside them.

Those about to suffer came next. On the foremost hurdle were stretched Colonel Townley, Captain Deacon, and Jemmy Dawson. The remaining prisoners were bound in like manner. Another party of grenadiers followed.

Next came several hearses, containing coffins, destined for the mangled bodies of the victims.

After the hearses followed a number of mourning-coaches, drawn by horses decked with trappings of woe. In the foremost of these coaches sat Monica, with her attendant, Lettice

In this order the gloomy procession shaped its cours

slowly towards the place of execution. The streets were crowded with spectators anxious to obtain a sight of the unfortunate men who were dragged in this ignominious manner along the rough pavement. But no groans were uttered—no missiles thrown. On the contrary, much commiseration was manifested by the crowd, especially when the mourning-coaches were seen, and great curiosity was exhibited to obtain a sight of their occupants. For Monica, whose story had become known, unwonted sympathy was displayed.

At length, the train drew near Kennington Common, where a large assemblage was collected to witness the dreadful scene. Hitherto, the crowd had been noisy, but it now became suddenly quiet. In the centre of the common, which of late years has been enclosed, and laid out as a park, a lofty gibbet was reared. Near it was placed a huge block, and close to the latter was a great pile of faggots. On the block were laid an executioner's knife and one or two other butcherly instruments.

At the foot of the fatal tree stood the executioner—a villainous-looking catiff—with two assistants quite as repulsive in appearance as himself. The two latter wore leather vests, and their arms were bared to the shoulder.

On the arrival of the train at the place of execution, the sheriffs alighted, and the grenadiers formed a large circle round the gibbet. The prisoners were then released from the hurdles, but their limbs were so stiffened by the bonds that they could scarcely move.

At the same time the faggots were lighted, and a flame quickly arose, giving a yet more terrible character to the scene.

Some little time was allowed the prisoners for preparation, and such of them as had papers and manifestoes delivered them to the sheriffs, by whom they were handed to the tipstaves to be distributed among the crowd.

At this juncture a fair pale face was seen at the window of the foremost mourning coach, and a hand was waved to one of the prisoners, who returned the farewell salute. This was the lovers' last adieu.

The dreadful business then began.

Colonel Townley was first called upon to mount the ladder. His arms were bound by the executioner, but he was not blindfolded. His deportment was firm—his countenance being lighted up by a scornful smile. After being suspended for a couple of minutes, he was cut down, and laid, still breathing, upon the block, when the terrible sentence was carried out—his heart being flung into the flames and consumed, and his head severed from the body and placed with the quarters in the coffin, which had been brought round to receive the mangled remains.

Colonel Townley's head, we may mention, with that of poor Jemmy Dawson, was afterwards set on Temple Bar.

Many of the spectators of this tragic scene were greatly affected—but those about to suffer a like fate witnessed it with stern and stoical indifference.

Amid a deep and awful hush, broken by an occasional sob, Jemmy Dawson stepped quickly up the ladder, as if anxious to meet his doom; and when his light graceful figure and handsome countenance could be distinguished by the crowd, a murmur of compassion arose.

Again the fair face—now death-like in hue—was seen at the window of the mourning coach, and Jemmy's dying gaze was fixed upon it.

As his lifeless body was cut down and placed upon the block to be mutilated, and the executioner flung his faithful heart, which happily had ceased beating, into the flames, a cry was heard, and those nearest the mourning coach we have alluded to pressed towards it, and beheld the inanimate form of a beautiful girl lying in the arms of an attendant.

All was over.

The story spread from lip to lip among the deeply-sympathising crowd, and many a tear was shed, and many a prayer breathed that lovers so fond and true might be united above.

Before allowing the curtain to drop on this ghastly spectacle, which lasted upwards of an hour, we feel bound to state that all the sufferers died bravely. Not one quailed. With his last breath, and in a loud voice, Captain Deacon called out " God save King James the Third ! "

When the halter was placed round poor Tom Syddall's neck, the executioner remarked that he trembled.

" Tremble ! " exclaimed Tom, indignantly. " I recoil from thy hateful touch—that is all."

And to prove that his courage was unshaken, he took a pinch of snuff.

The heads of these two brave men were sent to Manchester, and fixed upon spikes on the top of the Exchange.

When he heard that this had been done, Dr. Deacon came forth, and gazed steadfastly at the relics, but without manifesting any sign of grief.

To the bystanders, who were astounded at his seeming unconcern, he said:

" Why should I mourn for my son? He has died the death of a martyr."

He then took off his hat, and bowing reverently to the two heads, departed.

But he never came near the Exchange without repeating the ceremony, and many other inhabitants of the town followed his example.

CHAPTER VII.

FIVE YEARS LATER.

ONCE more, and at a somewhat later date, we shall revisit Rawcliffe Hall.

It still wears an antique aspect, but has a far more cheerful look than of yore. Internally many alterations have been made, which may be safely described as improvements. All the disused apartments have been thrown open, and re-furnished. That part of the mansion in which the tragic event we have recounted took place has been pulled down and rebuilt, and the secret entry to the library no longer exists. Everything gloomy and ghostly has disappeared.

Father Jerome no longer darkens the place with his presence, but before his departure he was compelled to give up all the documents he had abstracted. A large establishment is kept up, at the head of which is worthy old Markland.

Sir Conway Rawcliffe has long been in possession of the estates and title. Moreover, he is wedded to the loveliest woman in Cheshire, and their union has been blessed by a son. It is pleasant to see the young baronet in his own house. He has become quite a country gentleman—is fond of all country sports, hunts, shoots, and occupies himself with planting trees in his park, and generally improving his property. So enamoured is he of a country life, so happy at Rawcliffe, that his wife cannot induce him to take a house in town for the spring. His uncle, Colonel Conway, wished him to join the army, but he declined. He avoids all dangerous politics, and is well affected towards the Government.

Lady Rawcliffe is likewise fond of the country, though she would willingly spend a few months in town, now and then, as we have intimated. She looks lovelier than ever. Five years have improved her. Her figure is fuller, bloom has returned to her cheeks, and the melancholy that hung upon her brow has wholly disappeared. Need we say that her husband adores her, and deems himself—and with good reason—the happiest and luckiest of men?

They often talk of Monica and Jemmy Dawson. Time has assuaged their grief, but Constance never thinks of the ill-fated lovers without a sigh. Poor Monica sleeps peacefully beside her mother in the family vault.

Sir Conway and Lady Rawcliffe frequently pass a day at Manchester with the Byroms. The closest friendship subsists between them and that amiable family. Wonderful to relate, Beppy is still unmarried. That she continues single is clearly her own fault, for she has had plenty of offers, not merely from young churchmen, but from persons of wealth and good position. But she would have none of them. Possibly, she may have had some disappointment, but if so it has not soured her singularly sweet temper, or affected her spirits, for she is just as lively and bewitching as ever. She is a frequent visitor at Rawcliffe Hall.

Dr. Deacon is much changed, but if he mourns for his sons it is in private. After a long imprisonment, his youngest son Charles has been sent into exile.

A word in reference to the unfortunate Parson Coppock. He was imprisoned in Carlisle Castle with the other non-commissioned officers of the Manchester Regiment, and brought to the scaffold.

For many months after the suppression of the rebellion the magistrates of Manchester held constant meetings at a room in the little street, most appropriately called Dangerous Corner, to compel all suspected persons to take oaths to the Government, and abjure Popery and the Pretender.

Denounced by some of his brother magistrates, and charged by them with aiding and abetting the cause of the rebels, Mr. Fowden, the constable, was tried for high treason at Lancaster, but honourably acquitted.

On his return the worthy gentleman was met by a large party of friends on horseback, and triumphantly escorted to his own house.

After being exposed for some time on the Exchange, the heads of poor Theodore Deacon and Tom Syddall were carried away one night—perhaps by the contrivance of the doctor—and secretly buried.

Though disheartened by recent events, the Jacobites still continued in force in Manchester. They greatly rejoiced at the escape of the young Chevalier to France, after his wanderings in the Highlands, and the more hopeful of the party predicted that another invasion would soon be made, and frequently discussed it at the meetings of their club at the Bull's Head.

At length, a general amnesty was proclaimed, and several noted Jacobites, compromised by the part they had taken in the rebellion, reappeared in the town.

Amongst them was the Rev. Mr. Clayton, who was reinstated as chaplain of the collegiate church.

Long afterwards, whenever allusion was made at a Jacobite meeting to the eventful year of our story, it was designated the "fatal 'Forty-Five."

A sad period no doubt. Yet some ancient chroniclers of the town, who have long disappeared from the scene, but to whom we listened delightedly in boyhood, were wont to speak of the prince's visit to Manchester as occurring in the Good Old Times.

The Good Old Times!—all times are good when old!

Ensign T. Syddall

Dr. Deacon

SUBSCRIBERS

The publisher's and the B.B.C. (G.M.R.) wish to thank the following worthy people for their kindness and place their names, or names they have requested on record before our distinguished reader.

AFFLECK, David, a gentleman of the booktrade, Herts.
ANGLESEY, Natalie, Stephen and Christian, Jean & Walter, Stephen, George, Margaret, Scott, and Iain McAlpine.
ARMITT, Alex and Pauline, Dale and Dean, Bedford Road, Firswood.

BLOMLEY, Victor and Wendy, Lulworth Road, Middleton, Pearl Wedding 1962-1992.
BROOKER, Mrs, Sheila Brooker, Kennedy Street Coppice, Oldham.

CATHOLIC TRUTH SOCIETY, a good bookshop, South King Street, Manchester M2.

DAVIDSON, Margaret & Andrew, and daughters Laura & Claire, Didsbury, Manchester.

FELLONE, Sisina Fellone & Peter Scott, (Phoenix Books), Duckworth Road, Prestwich.

GAIR, Marge & Ken, Southgate, London.
GALLOP, Marjie, Ken & Angela, Suncroft Close, Woolston, Warrington.
GIBB, Tony, Anne, and Robert, Gibb's Bookshop, Charlotte Street, Manchester.

HICKMAN, Richard John, Ramsbottom, Lancs.
HOLDEN, Austin John (23.1.67) and Howard (6.3.70), Threshfield Close, Bury.
HOLT, Waveney, S.C. (Miss), Barlow Moor Road, West Didsbury, Manchester.
HOUSTON, Elizabeth Joan Houston, Broadway, New Moston. Her grandsons — Matthew, Daniel & Adam.
HOWARTH, Lisa M., 21st Birthday, 24.6.92, Linkway, Gatley, Cheshire.
HULME, David & Ann, son Andrew & daughter Claire, Stockport Cheshire.
HUME, Jean & John; Susan, Graham, Philip & Catherine; Victoria, Julie, Diane & Sarah.
HURSTHOUSE, Catherine Victoria & Wilson, John Robert James, Werneth Low, Cheshire.
HUMPHREY, Phil & Kath, Heywood, Lancashire.

JUDGE, Bernard, Royton North Labour Party.

LOWTON, John Olwyna Lowton; a dedication from Bill, Garath & Lesley; Highfield, Wigan.

MANCHESTER FREE PRESS, Paragon Mill, Jersey St., Manchester M4 6FP.
MARSDEN, Dave, Pat & Family; The Post Office & Newsagents, Greatstone Road, Stretford, M32 8GS.
MATTOCKS, Henry; and old Hydronian now living in America.
MORLEY, Frank & Marilyn Jean, daughters Nicola Jayne and Victoria Louise, Barnsley, Yorkshire.
MORRIS, Joshua & Georgina, Oxford Road, Gee Cross.
MORRIS, Faye Christina, & Twinkle; Barclay Crescent, Gee Cross, Hyde, Cheshire.

SHACKLETON, David Jack, son of Suzy & David, Church Lane, Rainow, Macclesfield.
STANHOPE-BROWN, James, Local Historian, Stretford.

THOMAS, Norm, Ali and little Gareth Thomas; somewhere in Bickerstaff.
TRINITY HIGH SCHOOL, Greenheys, Manchester. Michael Evans, all staff and pupils.

WALSH, Donald & Dorothy, Wolvercote, Oxford.
WALSH, John & Bon, Leyden, Swindon, Wiltshire.
WEST, Steven & Marion, 'Woomin's' Books, Salford 5.
WILLIAMS, Dorribell and Dennis; Egerton Road North, Manchester 16.
WILTON, Andrew J., The best looking book rep., Nethergreen, Sheffield.
WRIGHT, Chloe Rebecca, Chris & Jeff, Spire Walk, Beswick, Manchester.

In Memoriam

BOURNE, Joan, Bedford Road, Firswood, Manchester.

PORTER, Pat, School Brow, Billinge, Wigan; from husband, family & friends.

RAVLEN, Horace; from wife Ida, Mosley Common, Worsley.

SUTTON, Eric Reeves (1922-88) from all the family, Okehampton Cres., Sale, Cheshire.

Manchester has a good supply of bookshops supplying well the needs of the new book readers. But I would like to thank the gentlemen of the second-hand bookshops, who have helped in the search for books worthy of going back into print, and the illustrations to enhance and liven the books up.

May I specially thank:

ALAN SEDDON	Browser's Books, Prestwich
BRIAN BARLOW	Beech Road Bookshop, Chorltonville
BOB DOBSON	Stanning Rise, Blackpool
CHRIS LAWTON	Abacus Books, Altrincham
DAVID WINTERS	The Bookhouse, Preston
GEORGE KELSALL	The Bookshop, Littleborough
HARRY SWEENEY	Heaton's Bookshop, Stockport
JOHN GLENNARD	Fennel Books, Corn Exchange, Manchester
TONY GIBB	Gibbs Books, Charlotte St., Manchester |//
and the many others	

FAREWELL MANCHESTER
WORDS BY NUGENT MONCK

TUNE, FELTON'S GAVOT   ARRANGED BY RICHARD HALL

Fare-well Manchester, tho' my heart for you still beats,
  Ne'er again will I swag-ger down your streets.
I must seek the foe everywhere that I go
  Nor a friend be-side me as in Man-chester.

Fare-well Manchester, bon-nie Char-lie's calling me,
  I must haste a-way for my King to be....
I fall in war none be sore for my death
  I'll be true with my last breath to Man-chester.

Sung by the Manchester Regiment